Praise for Alexis Hall and His Novels

"*How to Blow It with a Billionaire* is zany fun, sexy, and heartbreaking."

—Harlequin Junkie

"Sexy, funny, clever, smart."
—All About Romance on *How to Blow It with a Billionaire*

"Simply the best writer I've come across in years."
—*New York Times* bestselling author Laura Kinsale

"Fans of Hall's amazing debut, *Glitterland*, and the breadth of the author's work since will demand this latest."
—*Library Journal* on *How to Bang a Billionaire*

"5 Stars! Top Pick! Fantastic. Funny and full of feelz."
—Night Owl Reviews on *How to Bang a Billionaire*

"Desert Isle Keeper. *How to Bang a Billionaire* is an entertaining read from beginning to the HFN ending, with the Prologue and the end scenes in Scotland pure undiluted Alexis Hall. Yes, of course, I shall be buying books two and three when they are released. Enjoy."
—All About Romance on *How to Bang a Billionaire*

HOW TO BELONG
WITH A BILLIONAIRE

ALSO BY ALEXIS HALL

How to Bang a Billionaire
How to Blow It with a Billionaire

HOW TO BELONG WITH A BILLIONAIRE

ALEXIS HALL

FOREVER
YOURS

New York   Boston

Forever Yours

Hachette Book Group

1290 Avenue of the Americas, New York, NY 10104

read-forever.com

twitter.com/readforeverpub

First published as an ebook and as a print on demand: September 2019

Forever Yours is an imprint of Grand Central Publishing. The Forever Yours name and logo are trademarks of Hachette Book Group, Inc.

The publisher is not responsible for websites (or their content) that are not owned by the publisher.

The Hachette Speakers Bureau provides a wide range of authors for speaking events. To find out more, go to www.hachettespeakersbureau.com or call (866) 376-6591.

ISBNs: 978-1-4555-7140-6 (ebook), 978-1-4555-7138-3 (print on demand)

If thou remember'st not the slightest folly
That ever love did make thee run into,
Thou hast not loved.
    —William Shakespeare, *As You Like It*

PROLOGUE

In the room where Lancaster Steyne trained me, he kept a bonsai tree. He taught me how to tend it—how to offer care without mercy—and I am not insensible of the irony. I wonder if he still has it, though me, of course, he gave to Caspian. Who, in turn, gave me to counsellors, therapists, psychoanalysts. And finally, he gave me a job.

I would have done anything for him. Tended to his every desire. Surrendered my body for his use. Taken pain for his pleasure, both being equally meaningless to me. The truth is, I still would. So I serve, in the capacities he allows. In the ways his conscience will permit. And I let him pay me for it because he needs to. Because he also needs to believe I am not Lancaster's creature. So he can believe it of himself. Even this, I will do for Caspian. I will lie for him.

The differences between us run deep. I have lost what little sense I ever possessed of who I was before Lancaster found me, and I have no interest in who I could have been without him. There is some part of me that misses still the serenity of those days: dark rooms and light and the comfort of routine. My world was a simpler place with him at its centre. Not necessarily a kinder one, but none of my experiences have taught me to expect kindness, and I certainly value simplicity.

"I will make you perfect," he used to tell me as I knelt at his feet. And I welcomed his making. Until then, I had been nothing. I had been dank places and money changing hands, the course of my life as inevitable as the path of the veins down my forearm. But Caspian is not like me. He has never been as low or as lost. He has always had choices. Whereas I am shaped, either by nature or because of Lancaster, to find solace in constraint, in service, in the abnegation of the self, he suffers. He struggles. Of course, Lancaster has never expected of Caspian what is now an instinct in me. But he was not made to subordinate his will to that of another. He is not to be tamed. Or if he is, neither Lancaster Steyne nor Nathaniel Priest has the heart for it.

And I, what can I do but watch? As I have always watched. My care for him is in everything I do—in his diary, meticulously kept, the reports I prepare, the meetings I schedule and minute, the tasks I perform without question or hesitation—but it is not my care he needs. I have no resentment for that. It is never reciprocation I have sought, only use and, from that, purpose. Though it is far from anything Lancaster intended for me, Caspian has given me both. His generosity leaves me abashed and his gentleness has never been necessary. And this summer I saw him happy for the first time.

It didn't last. And now—also for the first time—I begin to question. Not to him. Never to him. But my hands sometimes shake beneath my desk. Mistakes creep into my work, a double booking, a forgotten duty, not many. But I have never made mistakes before. All Caspian says is that I must be more careful next time, though I can barely bring myself to meet his eyes. The pain is too stark in him.

I have no interest in power. It is a messy thing, unlike the quiet order of submission. But I don't know how to serve a man when his actions are hurtful to himself. I don't know how to obey when my mind is already in open mutiny. I don't know how to help him. Silence is betrayal of his happiness. Action is betrayal of his trust. And it is all a betrayal of me. Or perhaps of Lancaster. He was supposed to make me perfect. Yet here I am in turmoil. And what disturbs me most is that I can see what Caspian cannot. Which is simply this:

Arden St. Ives changed us both.

CHAPTER 1

Stop me if you've heard this one before.

Boy meets billionaire. Billionaire offers boy short-term prearranged sex contract. Boy runs away from billionaire. Billionaire comes after boy. Boy and billionaire get back together. Billionaire sends boy to America on account of boy's best friend having been in horrendous car accident. Boy comes home again. Billionaire freaks out because of abusive history he never fucking told boy about. Boy blows it with billionaire.

Boy gets on with life.

And you know something? Boy's life wasn't too bad.

I'd moved in with Caspian's sister, Ellery—into what I'd thought was going to be a converted warehouse for Spratt's Patent pet foods but turned out to be just a warehouse she blatantly had no intention of converting into anything. Looking back, I wasn't sure why I'd expected otherwise. But I had the loft, and we mostly had electricity and running water, so it was actually semi romantic in a *writing poetry and fucking Kerouac* kind of way. Well, except when I stumbled home drunk and collided with a girder, and Ellery had to take me to A&E. But that was one time.

As for Ellery, she came and went at all hours, shamelessly ate my food, and sometimes crawled into my bed to sleep curled up next to me. It was like having a cat, if the cat also took a lot of drugs and threw wild parties. Not that I think Ellery meant to throw wild parties—they just happened around her, especially now that her band, Murder Ballad, was taking off, or at any rate accruing a devoted cult following. I had no idea *how*, because they didn't seem to advertise their gigs or hold them at, y'know, venues (the last one had been in a derelict church), but somehow, the word got out.

Because apparently songs about child murder, sororicide, and accidentally cheating on your husband with the devil performed in abandoned buildings were less nichey than the elevator pitch suggested. Or maybe it was just Ellery. She was electric on stage. As far as I knew, she arranged most of the music herself and she was in every swoop of the soprano, every cry of the violin, every beat of the drums: savage and mournful and free.

I was still at *Milieu*, though it would have been pretty damning if I hadn't been. An ouchie in the heart region made time drag itself along like a dying cowboy in a western, but it had been a mere handful of months since Caspian had left me. The longest autumn of my life. The coldest winter.

Or else that was nonmetaphorical cold because the heating had gone off again. I pushed my sleep mask onto my forehead and poked my nose out from under the quilt Mum had made. Immediately regretted it and vanished back under my pile of blankets. This was a major disadvantage of being a proper grown-up: You had to get out of bed. Not that I *had* a bed. I couldn't afford a bed. I had a mattress on the ground. But it was probably really good for my back. And at least I wasn't living on Coco Pops in a hovel by myself, which was all I could have managed on my salary without Ellery.

I would have done it, though. Because deep down I knew that no matter how sharp and real and inescapable my pain felt right now, it would fade. My life was more than Caspian Hart. Weird as it seemed, he'd shown me that.

Shown me how to fly, then pushed me through a window.

Some days, I was fucking pissed about it. Others I was just sad. But occasionally, I'd wake up in the rose and silver haze of a London dawn. Sit there on my mattress, wrapped in the quilt that still smelled of home, watching the light gleaming on the mist that coiled off the canal and…feel the shape of something like okayness at the tips of my fingers.

This morning, however, okayness was definitely not within touching distance. In fact, I was all for sticking my head under the pillow and pretending I didn't exist.

Except then I'd be late for work.

I got out of bed and, whimpering softly, peeled off the two pairs of socks I was wearing. The floor was hideously cold against my bare feet, but it was better than slipping on twisty little stairs that led to the main level and ending up in A&E again.

The bathroom was basically a long corridor that had been partitioned off, with a shower over a drain at the far end. Ellery, with the air of someone defiantly uninterested in interior decor, described it as Shawshank chic. And truth be told, it was a bit of a shock to the system after the pristine marble palace that was One Hyde Park. But I adapted, reminding myself I'd washed in way worse places when I was a student.

Morning ablutions complete, I spent some time picking out clothes and making my hair super cute. Life as a junior editor wasn't actually that glamorous—mainly I made tea, wrote boring copy, proofed other people's more interesting copy, and did what was called "gathering assets," which boiled down to Googling shit—but you still had to turn it out. You had to look like the sort of person who worked at a high society lifestyle magazine. Not posh, exactly, but as if you knew what you were doing fashion-wise.

Thankfully, I'd emerged from the womb serving manic pixie dream queer. I went for some skinny leg, windows check trousers, a chunky cable knit jumper, also courtesy of Mum, and my very pointiest shoes. Then hurried downstairs to see if Ellery had eaten all the Coco Pops.

Which, apparently, she had. Or rather was just about to, as she tipped the last of the packet directly into her mouth. She was wearing an oversized T-shirt, which simply said BASTARDS, and some stripy thigh-highs, and was curled in the corner of the vast L-shaped sofa that was our only item of furniture. I mean, unless you counted the table I'd made out of wine crates. And the taxidermy walrus that…actually, I still had no idea about the walrus. Ellery said he was called Broderick.

The rest of the band, who didn't actually live with us but might as well have, were scattered about in various states of consciousness. The drummer—Osian Ap Glyn—was face-down in the middle of the floor in a tumble of red hair. For a moment, I thought he might be legitimately dead, but then he twitched and I heaved a sigh of relief. Innisfree, who did keyboard and soulful vocals, and was essentially the anti-Ellery, was sitting in the lotus position with her face turned ecstatically towards the sunrise. And Dave, the guitarist, was, as ever, just *there*, looking as if he'd blundered into Ellery's life by mistake and couldn't think of a way to politely excuse himself.

"Innis made you a packed lunch," said Ellery as I edged carefully round Osian.

"Oh wow." My heart sank. "She shouldn't have."

Innis turned briefly in my direction, like a more serene version of that scene in *The Exorcist*. "It's my pleasure, Ardy. Healthy body, healthy soul. And compassion in every bite."

"There's a quinoa salad," Ellery told me sadistically. "With kale and avocado."

"Yum."

"And dried beetroot crisps."

"Whoopee."

Innis smiled, showing her perfect, shining teeth. "And, as a special treat, some of my hand-made protein balls."

"Thank you." I squirmed miserably.

"Don't forget your tea."

I was so very doomed. "You made tea too?"

"Nettle and fennel."

"Ardy's favourite," exclaimed Ellery, very much earning the betrayed look I cast in her direction.

I gave her the middle finger, picked up the eco-friendly

silicon storage container Innis had left me, along with the bamboo-fibre travel cup, and made for the door. Closing it firmly on both Ellery's laughter and Innis reminding me to buy a coat.

Because, as it happened, I had a coat. A really fabulous one. But it had been a gift from Caspian. And while I was sure one day it would be a welcome reminder of a man I'd once loved, right now it just hurt too fucking much to wear it.

Besides, I grew up in Scotland. Southerners knew nothing about cold.

CHAPTER 2

I hurried along the canal and then up the steps that took me to street level so I could cross the bridge. And right there, slumped against the railing so inconveniently that I nearly tripped over his feet, was Billy Boyle, Ellery's stalker-paparazzo. I'd only met him a couple of times before, and on each occasion I'd afterwards found myself the subject of some nasty column inches, mostly speculating about which of the Harts I was banging. I didn't like him, is what I'm saying.

He used his teeth to pull a Lucky Strike from the packet he was holding, and lit it with a flick of his lighter. "All right, Ardy?"

"No comment."

"You know nobody really says 'No comment,' don't you? Only Tory MPs when they've been sending pictures of their willies to fourteen-year-old girls."

"Thanks for the tip."

I did my best to evade him, but there wasn't much I could

do short of running into traffic, so he fell into step beside me. His cigarette smelled different—nastier—to whatever Caspian smoked. But still. It was familiar enough to make my heart ache afresh.

"You back with Ellie, then?" he asked.

There was no way I could answer that question without it implying something I didn't want to imply. Which was probably the whole point. "No comment."

"Good choice, mate." Boyle grinned wolfishly. "She's by far the best of them. Can't beat sticking your dick in crazy."

Urgh. He made my skin crawl. "You're disgusting."

"Just telling it like it is." He shrugged. "But what a family, eh?"

I walked a little faster. There were people around and cars on the road, so I had no reason to feel threatened. Which I didn't really—just fucked with and prodded at and imposed upon. And I wasn't sure what I could do about it in any case. Since I was pretty sure being icky wasn't breaking any laws.

"The dad was a Boy Scout. The mum's a snooty bitch. And the brother…well, you'd know more about that than me, wouldn't you, Ardy baby? But the stories you hear."

He was just trying to get a reaction. So I gritted my teeth and refused to give him one.

"That's the rich, though. Think they can do anything."

I kept my head down. Kept walking.

"You should consider telling yours." Boyle cast his cigarette butt carelessly into the gutter. "Story, I mean."

Startled, I stopped a moment. "Wait. What?"

Another of his scavenger's grins. "Thought that'd get your attention."

"Not in a positive way."

"Don't be like that. I'm trying to help you."

"No," I said firmly, "you're not. You're trying to exploit me."

Normally, I cut through Tower Hamlets Cemetery Park on my way to the station—which probably sounds a bit morbid, but it was actually a lovely place, full of grass and stone and quiet, especially in the morning—but the prospect of Billy Boyle chasing me through a graveyard, or lurking there on future occasions, was absolutely horrendous. I turned onto Bow Common Lane instead, stifling a sigh when Boyle turned with me.

"Could you go away," I said, figuring it was worth a shot. "Please?"

But the man was as relentless as a piece of chewing gum stuck to the sole of my shoe. "I'd get you one hell of a deal, Ardy. And it'd be classy. Sunday magazine classy. You should think about it."

"Okay. I'll think about it."

"Chance to tell your side of things. Completely sympathetic to your point of view. And of course, I'd make sure nothing too complicated got in the way of that."

Wait. *Complicated?* I gave him an incredulous look. "Are you threatening me?"

"I wouldn't say that. I'd say"—he stroked his chin thoughtfully—"I'm acknowledging the infinite subtleties of human nature. I mean, you haven't exactly been a saint, have you, mate? And a story like this—if we play our cards right—could be worth a couple of mil at least. Imagine that. You'd never have to work again."

"No thanks."

"Aw, come on, Ardy." Boyle sounded genuinely bewildered—even a little hurt. "Why not?"

"Um, how about because I'm not a total shithead?"

There was a brief pause. And I thought he was going to give up, but no. He kept talking. "Do it for Ellie then."

"Right. Because she'd really appreciate me making her brother the subject of public speculation."

"Bit of payback for all the shit he's put her through."

That made me laugh—in a mean, sceptical sort of way. "You can't really expect me to believe you're doing this for Ellery and not the money."

"Like I said"—he shrugged—"the infinite subtleties of human nature."

I just rolled my eyes.

Boyle reached into an interior pocket of his brown leather jacket and pulled out a scrap of paper with something scribbled on it. "Take my number, at least."

"Fine." I didn't actually want his number—or anything to do with him—but it was clearly the only way I was going to get rid of him.

"Don't wait too long, yeah? You always want to be ahead of a story, not behind it."

He was probably just digging. Trying to freak me out. Unfortunately it was borderline working. "What story? There's no story."

"Thought you were supposed to be a journalist." He flashed his yellowing, pointy-toothed smile at me. "You should know by now, there's *always* a story."

"Well...well...there isn't."

"Whatever you say. See you around, Ardy baby."

He gave me a mocking, two-fingered salute and sauntered off. Finally, fucking finally, leaving me alone. And not feeling great, in all honesty. As well as running late.

I made a dash for the station and made it just in time, leaping between the Tube doors the second before they closed, and then wriggling and squishing my way through a forest of armpits until I was able to wedge myself into a nook at the back of the carriage.

It wasn't a long journey—only about fifteen minutes, if there were no delays—but I felt ridiculous looking back on the time I'd spent at One Hyde Park, believing I lived in London. That wasn't London. *This* was London. Long, dark tunnels, strangers diligently not looking at each other, and the scent of soot and sweat.

Maybe I was a complete weirdo, but I liked it more.

It was real to me in the way that Caspian's cold, beautiful, sealed-off world could never be.

Although, I will admit, I missed being able to call him the moment something went wrong. Not because I wanted him to fix all my problems for me, but because having him on my side—knowing he cared about me and wanted the best for me—was its own magic. Like Queen Susan's horn, he let me find my way through life, sheltered by the promise that help was always close by.

Though I hoped all I had to do with Boyle was ignore him. Count on my own irrelevance and the fact that Caspian was already well guarded from nonsense like this. I'd pretty much resolved on a course of resolute nonaction as I elbowed my way off the Tube, but then I remembered that I still had Finesilver's business card in my wallet. He was the Harts' lawyer, and from what I'd been told, he specialised in reputation management. Frankly, he was terrifying in this smiling, silk and steel kind of way. But he'd been nice enough to me on the one (also Boyle-related) occasion we'd met. And since this involved Caspian indirectly, maybe he'd be able to give me some advice.

I still had a few minutes before I needed to be in the office, so I nipped past the now-familiar statue of William Pitt the Younger and sat down on one of the benches in Hanover Square. I'd texted Caspian from here when I first got the job at—

Goddamn it.

Why was he everywhere? No wonder I loved the Tube so much. Some days, it felt like it was the only place he wasn't. As if my memories of him had wrapped themselves up in the whole fucking city. And my love was a dog off its lead. Wandering by the roadside, getting ragged and thin, sniffing every street corner for just a trace of Caspian, trying to find its way home.

With shaky fingers, I dug out Finesilver's card and dialled the number. Of course, he was too important to pick up his own phone, so I ended up having to introduce myself to an assistant and explain, not very coherently, who I was and what I wanted. Then, already convinced that this had been a terrible idea, I waited on hold for an uncomfortably long time. And finally:

"Mr. St. Ives." Finesilver sounded very, very different on the phone. Sharper, colder, and a hell of a lot meaner. "How can I help?"

"Um, you remember that reporter guy? Boyle?"

"I'm aware."

I flexed my fingers, horribly aware I was sweating over my phone. "Well, he's been hanging around again. He wants me to sell my story."

"I see. And I presume this call means you're amenable to a counteroffer."

"What? No—"

"You're not amenable?" He cleared his throat. "Mr. St. Ives, I understand that you may be carrying some resentment towards my client, but any attempt to hurt him will cause far more damage to your reputation than it ever could to his."

This was giving me serious déjà vu. Not only was it the second nebulous threat I'd received today, but it wasn't even the first time I'd been accused of trying to spill Caspian's secrets to the press. And it was unbelievably depressing to discover that you could apparently get used to it.

"I'd never do anything to hurt Caspian," I said.

"And your circumspection will be generously recompensed, pending the proper legal assurances."

"Legal assurances?"

"Just a few standard and nonintrusive nondisclosure agreements."

The conversation was getting away from me—thundering off like an out-of-control train down unintended tracks. "You don't understand. I don't want money and I'm not signing an NDA, but it doesn't matter because I will never, *ever* go to the papers."

A very slight pause. "Then why are you calling me?"

"Because…because…Boyle? I thought you needed to know this stuff."

A longer pause. "Arden"—Finesilver's voice softened—"I cannot help Miss Hart unless she allows me to do so, and you are no longer under Mr. Hart's protection."

"But—"

"You may, however, be certain that I will continue to safeguard my client's interests. And I recommend that you continue to ensure that yours align with his."

"I already told you," I muttered, "I won't go to the papers."

"Forgive me, but my profession does not reward the assumption that people will keep their word. Which is to say, if you find your morals wavering, you shouldn't hesitate to contact me, and I will shore them up with material benefit."

Boyle, with his sly glances and nasty insinuations, had made me feel pretty fucking dirty. But this was *way* worse. "Right. Okay."

"Was there anything else you wanted, Mr. St. Ives?"

I should probably have escaped with what remained of my dignity, but bitterness got the better of me. "No, thanks. You've more than satisfied my need to feel cheap and blackmaily."

"That was not my intention."

"Then I guess it's just a bonus." Finesilver started to say something else, and I cut him off. "But for the record, I only phoned because I wanted to get rid of Boyle."

"I'm afraid I'm in no position to advise you."

"Yeah, you've made that very clear."

He sighed. "Start on the website for the Independent Press Standards Organisation. Clause three of the Code of Practice. Goodbye, Mr. St. Ives."

With a click, he was gone. And I was left in a park, in

silence. This was turning into an incredibly shitty morning and it wasn't even nine o'clock yet.

God, I wished I hadn't called Finesilver. Not only because he'd treated me like shit—which, admittedly, was his job— but because it had reminded me how far away Caspian was. I mean, I knew he was. I'd long since stopped harbouring secret hopes he'd come for me again, the way he had once-upon-a-time as I sat on a swing in Kinlochbervie. But the gulf between us had grown so impossibly vast that I wasn't a person to him anymore. I was a problem to be contained.

A mistake he'd made once.

And that hurt most of all.

CHAPTER 3

I pulled myself together, put on my happy face, and bounced into the office. Said my hellos. Did a tea round. Then got sucked into a really intense conversation with Tabitha England-Plume (the features director) about her mum's artisanal marmalade. It was made from fruit grown in the orangery of their stately home and named—in acknowledgement of the fact that Tabs came from legit aristocracy—Lady Marmalade.

Finally, though, I made it to what had become my workspace. As was the *Milieu* way, it was clutter free except for a copy of *Debrett's*, which I'm glad to say I'd never looked at. Not even when I was incredibly bored. That was the weird thing about living your dreams: Sometimes the living part was just kind of routine.

I logged into my email and got stuck in. And then began circling the issue of actual work. There was this piece on microbags I was supposed to be writing copy for. Except I couldn't think of anything witty or interesting to say about them. *These are very expensive and unfit for purpose.* Hmm, wait. Maybe there was something about a lack of adequate storage being a status symbol. Too small for convenience. Too rich to care.

Hurrah. I was a genius.

Or, at least, adequate at my job.

"Smiling, poppet?" drawled a voice. "Thinking of me?"

I glanced up to find George Chase, photographer and self-identified rake, leaning in the doorway, watching me with her usual air of faint amusement. And in high-waisted, wide-leg satin trousers, a white shirt, and purple jacket thing with black velvet lapels that was practically a frock-coat, looking so fabulous it hurt.

"Teeny-tiny handbags actually."

She laughed. "You need to get out more."

"Tell me about it."

"Oh, I can do far better than that."

"Can you?"

"Always." She twitched a wicked eyebrow at me. "Get your coat. We're going on an adventure."

A major component of my job was doing what people needed me to do—whether that was grabbing someone lunch, or finding a prop for the cover shoot, or compiling a top list of llamas who looked like the Duke of Edinburgh—and I'd played assistant to George a couple of times now. Much to the chagrin of some of the associate editors, since "gay for George" was pretty much an office meme. Not that anybody was mean to me about it—*Milieu* wasn't that kind of place. Although I can't say I was completely delighted when I discovered there was a sweepstake for when I'd sleep with her. I was semi-tempted to bet on myself for *never*. Except George was ridiculously hot and never was a long time to wait for a pay-out.

* * *

A few minutes later, I was sitting next to George in her classic Jaguar roadster as she drove slightly too recklessly for my comfort through the London traffic.

"Where exactly is this adventure?" I asked.

"It's a shoot for next year's *List*."

I gave her a severe look. "I'm starting to feel this excursion has been oversold to me."

"Don't count on it, poppet." There was something in her tone I couldn't quite read—a touch of regret, maybe? "I'm taking the pictures, you're doing the interview."

"Okay. Sure."

It was actually a pretty straightforward assignment. Ninety of Britain's hundred most eligible people required only a couple of sentences, usually about how good they looked in a top hat or what dukedom they'd inherit, and a photo dug up from the *Milieu* archives. But numbers one through ten got their own little feature. And the questions were standard, so as long as I didn't call someone "my lord" instead of "Your Grace" or break a Ming vase on my way out, I'd be unlikely to fuck things up. Except wait. Those were probably exactly the kinds of things I'd do. Oh no.

George drummed her fingers lightly against the steering wheel. "Look, I'm sorry to spring this on you. But it's Caspian Hart."

There was nothing in my head but silence, like when a grenade goes off in a movie, and then everything explodes. Except without the explosion. Just the moment before stretching forever. "Ah."

"He's gone from seven to three."

"Yeah. Well. I guess not being with someone would help with that."

"You don't have to do this. I'll tell Mara to back off."

Mara Fairfax was the editor-in-chief. She'd hired me, and was always friendly when our paths crossed, but given she was the most important person at *Milieu*, and I was the opposite of that, I wasn't sure there was all that much off for her to back. "This was her idea?"

"Obviously, Arden."

"And she knows I used to, um, sort of date Caspian?"

"Do you really think," said George with an affection so comfortable, so unabashed, I wondered if she'd even noticed it was there, "Mara got where she is today without the will to exploit every opportunity revealed to her?"

An ache in my shoulders made me realise I wasn't just tense. I was *braced*. For an emotional reaction that just wasn't coming. "But…but…wouldn't I be just about the worst person in the world to send? There's no way he'd want to speak to me."

"He probably wouldn't *want* to, no." She shrugged. "But giving people what they want rarely yields interesting results."

"And this would be interesting?"

"Well, it couldn't be more boring than his usual interviews. Have you read any?"

I shook my head. I'd seen a couple, here and there, but I'd never managed to actually get through one. Too much business talk.

"He gives so little of himself away. My gas bill has more humanity."

For some reason, this made me smile; it was so like Caspian. "He's different when you know him."

George's expression grew wry. "You've just made Mara's point for her. Thankfully, my priorities are different."

"I thought your priorities were sex and art."

"And not traumatising poppets unnecessarily."

I wasn't sure whether I felt patronised or protected. Maybe both. "I have to ask: What would necessarily traumatising me entail?"

"That's for me to know, and you to find out."

"I can never tell," I grumbled, "if you're threatening me or flirting with me."

She shot me an alley-cat grin. "Fun, isn't it?"

"That's for me to know, and you to find out."

"You little minx."

We'd reached the financial district. Not my favourite bit of London, I had to admit. It was almost as if the centuries had been smoothed away with the buildings themselves, leaving nothing but glass, like blinded eyes, reflecting the steel-grey nothing of the sky. Or alternatively: It reminded me of Caspian, so all I was seeing was my own emptied-out heart.

George pulled over in the Barad-dûr–esque shadow of Hart & Associates. "So what's it to be?"

"I…I don't know."

"Nobody'll think less of you, either way."

I peered up at Caspian's place of business. His twenty-first-century fortress, coldly gleaming. "*I* might."

"There's no shame in love or pain."

"Well"—I pushed open the car door and scrambled onto the pavement—"I'm sick of both."

And I marched in like I fucking owned the place.

The effect of which was slightly diminished by the fact nobody really noticed or cared, and I had to stand in the lobby like a lemon while George got her camera bag out of the boot.

But then we were in the lift, being whooshed up to Caspian's floor in that tiny glass bead. And it was impossible not to remember the last time I'd done this. I'd been furious then, but so full of hope.

No hope today.

Just the determination to look Caspian in the eye, and feel whatever I felt, and know I'd keep living after.

George nudged her shoulder gently against mine. "If you need to run away screaming, just pull your ear or something, and I'll cover for you."

"I won't need to."

"What can I say?" She smirked at me. "I'm a fan of safe words."

And so she managed to make me laugh as the doors opened, admitting us into the vestibule outside Caspian's office.

It hadn't changed. Which was to say, it was still as intimidating as hell. Glass and marble and blah blah blah. And Bellerose, at his desk, looking like a terribly severe angel.

"Hi." I waved in a *check me out not being totally destroyed* kind of way.

His head snapped up. And, wow, he was looking rough: dark circles under his eyes, cracked lips, acne rashes across the tops of his cheeks. "Arden. I—"

"We're here from *Milieu*. We've got an appointment."

"Yes, I know. It's just…" He scraped a lank lock of hair away from his brow. "Actually, it's fine. Go right in."

I should probably have been squirrelling my emotional energy away for, well, myself. But for all his chilly ways, Bellerose had been oddly kind to me.

"Are you okay?" I asked.

He frowned, reverting to his more typical mode of Impatient with Arden. "Of course I am."

"Are…are you sure?"

For a moment, he stared at me, his expression almost pleading. But all he said was, "Mr. Hart's in his office."

And so I had no choice but to let it go.

Press forward.

Caspian's door loomed. I took a deep breath, pushed it open, and stepped boldly over the threshold.

Or, at least. That was the plan.

What actually happened was that I contrived to trip over, well, nothing. I tried to catch myself but to absolutely no avail. And one startled yelp later I was facedown, arse up, on the ground.

"Arden?" Oh God. That was Caspian. I hadn't spoken to him for months and yet his voice—so familiar with its upper-class vowels and its secret promise of warmth—pulled at me like an unfulfilled geas.

Footsteps.

Then someone reaching for me. And I let myself be helped before I realised it wasn't Caspian.

You see, I knew his hands. Knew their strength, their elegance, and their restless vulnerability. They'd touched every part of me. Claimed me, in both pleasure and pain.

But these were a stranger's hands. And a stranger's touch. And it was almost impossible to imagine that such cool, perfectly manicured fingers—the fourth circled by a milgrain platinum band—could ever falter or flinch or reveal too much.

I made it back to my feet. Looked up.

And died in Nathaniel's honey-golden gaze.

"Are you all right," he asked, with the easy solicitude of the victorious. "Did you hurt yourself?"

I opened my mouth and waited for words to happen. They didn't.

George stepped forward, her body briefly blocking mine. "Your assistant said you were free. We're here about the interview."

"Darling"—Nathaniel cast a look of amused exasperation in Caspian's direction—"I thought you cancelled that?"

He frowned. "So did I."

"Well," said George, "you didn't. And I'm a very busy woman, so can we get on with it?"

Holy shit. This was basically the bit in a Mafia movie where all the characters started pointing guns at each other and yelling. I mean, apart from the guns and the yelling. We were too British for that.

But some pretty frosty looks were happening, let me tell you.

Nathaniel aimed his at George. "Do you talk to your all subjects like this?"

"Only the very special ones."

"I must apologise." It was odd to hear Caspian being conciliatory but, I guess, someone had to be. "The thing is, I…that is…I'm afraid I'm no longer an appropriate topic for this particular article."

"What do you mean?" Oh. That was me. In the world's smallest voice.

He'd been standing behind his desk, crisscrossed by silver-edged shadows. But now he stepped forward, his hand coming up self-consciously so he could adjust his tie when it didn't need adjusting. And there it was: a dull gleam on his fourth finger. A ring to match Nathaniel's.

"I'm…we're…"

"Engaged," I said.

"Bellerose should have told you. I mean, your magazine."

My world was a platinum circle. It was manacles on my wrists. A vise around my heart. "Congratulations."

"Thank you, Arden." Nathaniel, soft-footed, came to stand beside Caspian. Took his arm. "A shame about your wasted trip."

They already looked like a magazine cover. Caspian, exquisite in dark blue pinstripes, and Nathaniel, tastefully casual. A perfect match, equal in beauty, poise, and sophistication.

And so wrong in every other way.

Oh, Caspian. I was completely fucking furious with him. And desolate all over again. How hurt did you have to be, how terrified of who you were, and what you wanted, to do something like this? Not just to himself.

But to me. And, not that I was super full of shits to give, to Nathaniel.

"We'll get out of your way." George gave my shoulder something between a pat and a shake. "You must have a lot to do."

Except I was stuck. Staring helplessly at Caspian.

Waiting for him, somehow, in a handful of seconds, with nothing but silence between us, to trust, to understand, to change. And at the same time knowing it was utterly beyond him. I'd lost Caspian before we'd even met. To Lancaster Steyne. The man whose cruelty would possess him for the rest of his days.

And Nathaniel was more fucked up than any of us if he didn't see it too.

"How about a different interview," I heard myself say. "The two of you together."

Caspian gave a convulsive start. "No."

The smile I produced felt like an alien's impression of one. "It'd make a wonderful story."

"Absolutely not."

"Let's not be so hasty, my prince." Nathaniel pressed in closer and whispered something in Caspian's ear. And then, "I think it could be rather romantic."

I shrugged. "Well, have a think about it. I'll leave my details with Bellerose if you want to set it up."

Then I wheeled round.

And on barely functioning legs, ran like a motherfucker.

CHAPTER 4

We went to the Starbucks round the corner, where I sat and ugly-cried into a raspberry and white chocolate muffin. Caspian would have had a perfect, probably monogrammed silk handkerchief to give me. George pushed a stack of paper napkins across the table. But then, she'd never broken my heart a bunch of times and topped it off by engaging herself to a man I knew was the last person in the world who could make her happy. Which put her way ahead of the game in the Taking Care of Arden stakes.

In any case, I eventually ran out of tears. Also gulps and hiccoughs and wails and snot. And then George brought me a big glass of water and said, "Do you want to have sex?"

"Um." I blinked my sticky eyes. "What?"

She shrugged. "Well, I'm really bad at reassuring people and really good at fucking them. But I'm open to either."

"I…I think I'll try the reassurance?"

"Ah."

My entire face felt like Violet Beauregarde after she ate the prototype Wonka gum. "What's wrong?"

"I was rather hoping you wouldn't say that." She reached out to pat my hand. "There, there. He's not worth it, girl-friend."

So apparently I hadn't run out of tears.

She regarded me in some dismay. "Oh God. I'm sorry, poppet. I did warn you I'm terrible at this."

"What does *worth* have to do with anything?" I said with great personal dignity.

Okay. That's a lie.

"What does worth have to do with anything?" I wailed wetly. "You don't love people because they're deserving. You love them b-because you love them."

She folded her fingers around mine. "I know."

"He's only doing this because he's been hurt so *so* badly. And he won't let me help."

"You know people can only really help themselves."

"Y-yes. But…he's hurting me too."

"And that is truly unforgivable."

I glanced up and burst out, "I would forgive him. I would forgive him *anything*. And I know that's pathetic and door-matty and weak."

"It sounds the very opposite of those things."

"I wouldn't if I thought he was trying to be cruel to me. In some ways I…I kind of wish he was. Then I could hate him. Instead of…" I put a hand to my chest, which was ridiculously melodramatic, but I was half convinced my poor, ragged little heart was going to bleed right out of me. "Feeling like this."

George was quiet for a moment or two. Then, "The bad will fade in time. And you'll never forget the good."

"How do you know?"

"Because, poppet"—she gave me one of her wryest looks—"I've been there, done that."

"Really? When?"

"A long time ago in a galaxy far, far away."

As rebuffs went, it was pretty gentle. But unfortunately, it just reminded me of Caspian, and I started sniffling helplessly again.

"At least," she went on, "New York in the eighties, which amounts to the same thing. She was my first in, oh, very many things. The other half of my soul."

"I didn't mean to pry."

She shrugged. "It's not exactly a secret."

"What happened?"

"She's irredeemably straight. And now my best friend."

"Wow, I…" I wasn't sure what to say. "Is that okay?"

"As five very wise young ladies once implied, zig-a-zig-ah is transitory. But friendship never ends."

About ten seconds ago I'd been about to die of sorrow. Now I gave a surprised, watery giggle.

George's expression grew a little wistful. "We became, in the end, an impossible choice to each other. But I, at least, have no regrets."

"Does she?"

"As far as I know, she's never regretted anything her entire life."

We fell silent. I picked over the ruins of my muffin, shocked to find myself aching but approaching human. And sufficiently recovered to be embarrassed at having cried my eyes out in Starbucks. Really loudly. In front of George. "Sorry for…being like this."

"No need to apologise. I've always got time for a pretty boy in tears."

I managed a messed-up smile. "I'm such an idiot."

She tilted her head slightly. "How so?"

"Just, y'know, falling apart because of Caspian. *Again.*"

"If it's any consolation, you were magnificent in his office."

"I was?"

"*Mmmhmm.*" She gave a velvety chuckle. "Getting an interview out of him. Mara's going to be so proud of you."

Okay, that *was* fairly consoling. "Yay."

"You've got good instincts. Keep this up, and you'll go far."

For some reason, a brief intermission of feeling less than awful made me tear up again.

"Don't you dare," George growled. "Or I really will insist on fucking you."

Separating one of the napkins from the pile, I blew my nose, suddenly very conscious about how red and damp it was. "I'm not exactly at my best right now."

"And I'm still into you. Isn't that flattering?"

It was…kinda. Maybe. Definitely. "But I'm in love with Caspian."

That only made her laugh. "Why do you think I'm offering? I'm too old for romantic entanglements. Especially with presumptuous little poppets."

"I didn't—"

"Yes you did, and it's adorable."

I cringed in my chair, half tempted to slither out of it and hide under the table for the rest of my life. "Well, what about me? I'm all vulnerable."

"In some ways, perhaps, but not in others. You're in no danger of falling for me, and rebound sex has much to recommend it in terms of pure, unfettered carnality."

"I can't just…not go back to work."

"After the morning you've had, I think it's the least you're owed."

"Oh, right. I'll just tell that to Mara, shall I?"

"All she'll care about is the interview." George leaned back, propping an ankle on the opposite knee, a pose that made her look even more rakish than usual. "So the only thing that matters is this: What do you want? I can take you back to the office, or home if you'd rather. Or you can come back to my place, where you can drink hot chocolate in a fluffy blanket, and cry about your ex some more. Or…"

"Or?"

"We can have the kind of sex you'll remember for the rest of your life."

"I find people who boast about their prowess really hot."

But she only grinned. "That's not a boast, poppet. It's an *amuse bouche*."

From the way an answering smile kept tugging at my lips, my *bouche* seemed pretty amused. I finished my muffin, trying to corral my feelings and make a sensible decision. I mean, I was only human. Of course I wanted to sleep with George. But I couldn't figure out whether I wanted to sleep with her for the right reasons (because she was hot and it would be awesome) or the wrong ones (because I was hurt and she wanted me). Or, even, if the wrong reasons were actually all that wrong. If it was okay to bang someone for love or pleasure, it was okay to bang them for comfort, wasn't it?

I hadn't been with anyone since breaking up with Caspian. I'd been too sad…I mean focused on my career. Okay, sad. And right now, the possibility that I could get laid, and that it could be fun and easy and harmless, was unbelievably tempting. After all, we were both adults. Consenting. Going into it with our eyes open. Dammit, I deserved this. I needed it. I was going to do it. But if my time with Caspian had taught me anything (and honestly, he'd taught me a lot, most of it good), I was done with…denial and uncertainty and shame. I'd seen firsthand what that could do to someone.

"Okay," I said. "Yes. I want to. But there's something I have to tell you first."

One of George's eyebrows twitched curiously. "Oh?"

"The thing is. You should know." I took a deep, only slightly shaky breath. "I'm pretty kinky."

"Well, then you're in trouble," she murmured. "Because you see, poppet, I'm *very* kinky. Shall we go?"

* * *

Ten minutes later, Mara was in the loop, I wasn't fired, and we were in George's car heading east. Because it turned out she didn't live in London.

"I'm feeling a bit kidnapped," I grumbled.

She flicked a glance my way. "And does it turn you on?"

"Maybe."

"I'll drive you back in the morning, safe and sound. Though most likely a little bit worse for wear."

It took me a second or two to realise the slick, twisty feeling in my stomach was anticipation. God. All these months, I'd been telling myself I was okay. Except I blatantly wasn't. I'd just been numb. A half person, drifting through my days. I'd thought seeing Caspian—seeing that ring on his finger, Nathaniel's hand, possessive on his arm—had broken me. When actually the pain was a door opening, and now I could feel again.

Given George's plans for me, I texted Ellery to let her know I wouldn't be home that night, and got back:

so?

Which, y'know, was...very her. And fine. Because I knew it didn't mean she didn't care—just that she didn't signal caring the way most people did. But it made me miss rooming with Nik at Oxford. He would have sent me some suggestive emojis and said something nice like *have fun, I'll miss you*, or possibly, *don't do anything I wouldn't do*. So I could have replied that I *always* do things he wouldn't do.

Tucking my phone back into my pocket, I turned and gazed out of the window, letting the nondescript southern English countryside—grey and brown and tufty green—distract my eyes. Mainly, I was trying very hard not to think about the various journeys I'd taken with Caspian. The time he'd come to get me from Kinlochbervie, and how unexpectedly intimate it had been, sharing a car with him. Or riding with him in one of his endless black billionairemobiles when I'd got back from America. He'd kissed me so desperately then. Held me so tightly. Like he'd never let me go.

Except he had. He totally had.

George tapped my knee lightly. "Pretty kinky, you say?"

"Um. I guess?"

"What are you into?"

"Into?" I tried to sound casual. But ended up squeaking instead.

"*Kinky* is a broad category, poppet. Tell me something you like."

Oh God. It was sort of terrifying to be asked so directly. And a little bit thrilling. With a side order of excruciating. All sprinkled with a generous serving of, *What the fuck do I say?*

"The amount of time it's taking you to answer makes me think you're completely depraved. But don't worry." George let the words hang for a moment. "I'm here for it."

"I'm not depraved. I'm embarrassed."

"Then think of this as foreplay."

"Um. Um." Shit. I'd oversold my own kinkiness in a moment of kamikaze bravado. I mean, how kinky could I be if I couldn't even admit what I wanted? "Spanking. I like spanking. Being spanked, I mean. I like being spanked."

George gave a low rumble of what I assumed was pleasure. "Mmm, me too. Spanking, that is. Being spanked somewhat less so. Is that impact play in general, or just spanking?"

"I…I don't know. I've only ever been spanked."

"Now that is truly a tragedy. What in the world was Caspian doing with you?"

"Stop." The word exploded out of me. "Safe word. Red. Red. Whatever. I'm touching my ear."

"Of course. Do you need me to pull over?"

I sucked in a few frantic breaths and pressed my hands together to stop their sudden shaking. I'd gone from okay to not-okay so fast I'd shocked myself. "N-no. I don't think so. S-sorry."

"Please don't apologise. What did I do?"

"You…" My heart was still racing. And I was actually having trouble figuring out what the problem was for myself. Let alone trying to articulate it to George.

"Take your time. I can turn round. Or we can stop."

"If," I said slowly, the thought squeezing out of my brain like a water droplet from the end of a broken tap, "we're going to do this…you can't make it about Caspian. Because you don't know him. And it's not fair."

"You're right, Arden. It was a glib and thoughtless remark, and I'm sincerely sorry for it. Your relationship with Caspian is none of my business."

It was an odd moment. Firstly, because she hardly ever used my actual name, and secondly, because I wasn't used to her being serious. And now both those things were happening at once. I swallowed. "Okay then."

"As long as you're sure."

"I think I am."

We drove along in silence for a while. And gradually I could breathe again.

"You know," murmured George, "the blanket and hot chocolate option is always on the table."

"But I want the kinky sex."

She laughed. "Then tell me something else you like."

Of course, this was its own piece of pain. Remembering

all the things I'd done with Caspian. How much I'd loved it when he'd pinned me, exposed me, made me beg and squirm and ache. "I like being restrained."

"Well, isn't this my lucky day."

"And I like feeling…I don't know how to explain."

"Well, why don't you try?" The way she said it, commanding, but somehow playful too, sent a happy shiver down my spine.

"Slutty? And embarrassed kind of? A bit. But not, um, *degraded* or anything."

"Anything else you don't like?"

"Yes, I don't like…I don't want…I don't want to be passive. I mean, I know it doesn't make sense because I want all this other stuff that means I'm not in control, so probably I don't know what I'm talking about. But I hate it when…I just. I don't know. I need to be involved. God, I'm being a weirdo, aren't I?"

"We're all weirdos, poppet."

"What I really love is when I can"—a blush charged out of nowhere and tomatoed me—"serve someone's desire. Through surrender and suffering and…stuff."

The corner of George's mouth curled into one of her unreadable half smiles. "It makes you feel powerful."

"Yes. Now I've said it aloud, it doesn't seem very submissive."

"Submission is many things. It can be whatever you want it to be."

An odd sound made its way out of my mouth, eventually resolving into a shaky giggle. "It's nice talking about this. In a strange sort of way."

"Making people articulate their predilections is rather a kink of mine."

"Are you going to articulate any of your own?"

"I thought I just did." I gave her what I hoped was a rebuking look. But it was probably more of a pout. And eventually she went on, "I believe sex, like art, has the capacity to strip people to their essential selves. And I enjoy that. Very much."

"You're not being very illuminating."

"On the contrary, I just told you exactly what I intend to do to you. Is *red* your safe word of choice?"

"It's a classic for a reason."

"Then *red* it is."

I opened my mouth. Then closed it again. Suddenly all I could think about was standing in front of Caspian, telling him I wanted my safe word to be *Mace Windu* when really I just wanted him to believe how safe I felt with him.

"Or not?" George asked into the silence.

"Can I have—" Actually, it wasn't a Samuel L. Jackson moment. It would have reminded me of Caspian in a bad way. Made him, and all the ways we'd failed to understand each other, too present. "How about *Poe*?"

"Works for me."

It worked for me too. Probably in the future I'd want something else, but for now this was what I needed: a memory of Caspian, at his happiest, watching *The Force Awakens* with me, protecting me from hurts I couldn't bear.

I glanced at George. "What about you? Anything you don't like or I shouldn't do?"

"Well, ideally one would be too old for dysphoria but apparently one isn't." Her fingers tapped restlessly against the wheel. "Which is to say, when it comes to my dick, you may touch it, suck it, and beg for it to your heart's content. But it's never going inside you."

"Touch it, suck it, beg for it. Got it. Um…"

"Yes?" she purred.

"What about my dick?"

"I don't know, poppet. What about it?"

"Well. How about…I mean…could it maybe go in you?"

There was a pause. Then laughter. "I'll think about it. If you're *very* good."

CHAPTER 5

George lived in a house—yes, a house, not a hypermodern apartment or a nineteenth-century mansion—in a tiny hamlet near the Swale. It was pretty and white-painted and not at all like anything I would have imagined for her until I stepped inside and saw how the light, silver-spun from the marina, moved through the space like it was alive. She'd done the lateral living thing familiar from Caspian's many, many properties, but I'd always found it on the edge of oppressive before. Intimidation by square footage. Here there was just a clean, bright openness, full of colourful rugs, nooks I wanted to explore, and furniture I actually wanted to sit on. She had books and paintings. Flowers on the kitchen table. Mugs on the drying rack. Fashion magazines piled up in corners. Such beautiful, everyday things.

"Oh wow." I moved over to the French windows. "This is lovely."

George seemed startled by my enthusiasm. "I'm glad you like it."

"Remember, I live in a dog biscuit factory with a feral person. I honestly can't remember the last time I was somewhere that looked like home."

Her eyes swept over me. There was something a little sharp about George's attention—not unpleasant, when you got used to it, but it was always there. The cool edge of a letter opener prising you dextrously apart until all your secrets came spilling out. "Mind if I get my camera?"

"I guess? But why?"

It was never far from her hand. And I'd helped out on enough shoots that the snaps and clicks and whirs of George in action were almost soothing. "Because I'm interested in how you look."

"I'm pretty sure I look ordinary."

"Nobody's ordinary."

I managed to stand still, or at least still-ish, for about five seconds, before asking, "Can I see?"

She nodded and stepped closer so I could peer at the LCD screen. And there I was—not quite in shadow, a delicately dappled boy, half-turned towards some private horizon. My heart squeezed in strange recognition of my own sadness. And then…then I just felt nebulously pissed off.

Because I was so fucking sick of being sad.

There was a soft clack as George put down her camera. She wasn't as tall as Caspian, but she still had a couple of inches on me, which meant I had to look up when she slid a finger under my chin and turned my face to hers. I'd forgotten how vulnerable-making it could be, that teetering expectation of a touch, and I almost flinched, wanting to whoomp myself closed like an anemone. With Caspian, I'd held nothing back. And in return, he'd taught me to be afraid.

The breath shuddered out of me. "I…I don't know what to do."

"You're going to ask me to kiss you."

"Am I? Why?"

"Because you need to. And"—her eyes flared with sudden heat—"I want to hear you."

Fuck, what a mess. I didn't know it was even possible to be miserable and angry, and hating someone and missing them, and kind of into someone else, and scared of that, and what it might mean, all at the same time. But apparently it was. And I was nailing it.

"Oh God," I gasped out. "Kiss me. Fucking kiss me. Please."

And she did, and it was nothing like Caspian, and I didn't die. Of course it hurt, the not being Caspian, I mean. Because, honestly, there was part of me that still believed he was it for me. That I could have lived the rest of my life with no other kisses but his. Except he wasn't and I wouldn't. And George's mouth on mine offered a new surety—a future that could exist for me without Caspian.

She pulled away too soon. "Time to see my studio?"

"Um…okay."

I followed her upstairs on slightly wobbly legs. The space, which took up the entirety of the third floor, was about fifty percent what I was expecting—whitewashed walls, and polished boards, and the paraphernalia of the photographer's art—and fifty percent a whole lot kinkier. I made a heroic effort to look interested in one of those big satin umbrella things, but my gaze kept pinging back to the bondage table on the other side of the room. At least, I assumed it was a bondage table, or else dinner got really unruly around here.

"What can I say?" murmured George. "I like to combine my pleasures."

I made a sound. It was not a dignified sound.

She laughed, crossed to a red velvet-covered chaise that was probably—or maybe not—a prop, and dropped down onto it. The whole scene was so very *Tipping the Velvet* it almost made me wish I had a camera of my own. "Why don't you have a look round?"

It probably said something about the life I'd been leading recently that this wasn't the first time someone had invited me into their dungeon. Well, I say invited. I'd practically forced my way into Caspian's. At the time I'd been pretty excited because I'd wanted to play with all the kinky toys but then he'd had some kind of post-traumatic-stress-related breakdown. And now, whenever I remembered the place, I ended up thinking about Caspian instead. All the pain he'd tried so hard to keep from me. Obviously I wasn't delusional enough to think I could fix it or even make it better but…I could have loved him. And even that he couldn't give himself.

Also: He was engaged to Nathaniel. Engaged. Engaged to fucking Nathaniel. It wasn't a complicated concept. Why couldn't I get it through my stupid head? Except my stupid head wasn't the problem. It was my stupid heart which wouldn't let him go. No matter how comprehensively he was done with me.

"On second thought…" It was only when George spoke that I realised I'd been standing around in a sorrowful daze. Dammit me. "Come here."

As I'd quickly discovered when Caspian got all high-handed with me, I didn't do so well with orders in my daily life. But in a bedroomy-dungeony context? And when the alternative was drifting about like the Ancient Fucking Mariner in a sea of my own memories? Yes please. I trotted gratefully back to the chaise.

"Strip."

"Um. What?"

"You know"—she flashed a grin at me—"remove your clothes so I can subject you to my female gaze. You're pretty, poppet. I want to see you naked."

I swallowed. "What…what happens after I'm naked?"

"All sorts of depraved things."

Well. Guess I was sold. I began pulling at my garments.

"But Arden?"

There was an edge to the way she said my name. It made me pause, half in and half out of my jumper, and peer out through the head hole like an animal from its burrow. "Yes?"

"You know how to stop this. Next time, I tell you to do something, I'd advise you to do it."

"Or what?" I heard myself say. And the worst of it was, I didn't quite know why I was asking. Not to push her exactly. But I think I needed to know, in the same way you'd reach for the wall with your hands when you were trying to find your way in a dark room.

Then came a rough tug and rush of air and I emerged into daylight to find George standing over me. She dropped my jumper to the floor with a soft flump. "Depends on my mood. But I might be inclined to punish you."

"Oh." I swallowed. But in meeting her eyes, found only warmth. "It's been…kind of a while. Sorry."

And with Caspian, it had been instinct. Knowing what he needed perhaps better than he did.

She reached out and twisted the sparkly unicorn horn barbell through my left nipple until I went up on my toes with a squeaky little gasp. "Is that what you're looking for? To be punished?"

"Maybe. I don't know." Weird shivers were racing up my arms. Nothing to do with the temperature. And then I heard myself blurt out, "Am I broken?"

"Broken? Why?"

"I…I used to be really good at casual sex."

This earned me an eyebrow twitch. "I'm glad to hear it. And look forward to reaping the benefits."

"That's not what I"—I twined my hands together—"this isn't how it's supposed to be."

"How is it supposed to be?"

"Easy."

She was quiet for a horrible forever.

"For both of us," I added quickly. "You shouldn't have to deal with my…my…whatever is wrong with me."

"Well," she drawled. "I've never been particularly interested in easy. But I think you need to tell me what you want. As honestly as you can."

I stared at my feet…which were no help. Damn you, feet. "I'm not sure."

"Try again."

God, she could sound stern when she wanted to. And it was super hot.

Closing my eyes, I let the words come before my brain could stop them. Before I even knew myself what they were. "I want to…feel something that isn't about him. I want to have something that isn't his."

Another silence. I risked a peep from beneath my lashes, and found George grinning like a shark. "I can give you that."

"And w-what would I be giving you?"

"The knowledge that you want this from me."

I was used to George's laughter. Her bossiness. The way she teased and flirted. But these glimpses of sincerity were doing funny things to me. Making me feel special.

"I do." It came out in a rush of longing. And all at once, the world got a whole lot simpler. Because I recognised what George was looking for. It was what I'd tried to give to Caspian. What I'd needed to give. The impossible tangle of strength and vulnerability that was submission.

Dropping to my knees felt like fucking homecoming.

"Please," I said.

And George made a rough sound of satisfaction, her fingers light in my hair and against my face. "What a gift you are. So very sweet." Her lips curled into the wickedest smile I'd ever seen. "I am going to *ruin* you, poppet."

It took her about ten minutes.

She chained me to the table thing—actual chains that clipped to the cuffs she put on my wrists, and thighs, and ankles. I'd never been so thoroughly tied up before. Apart from some unexpected bow tie shenanigans at Ellery's birthday, Caspian had always preferred to control me with his hands and body. And I was *fine* with that. But I couldn't help responding to the novelty, my skin prickling with curiosity as

George positioned me the way she wanted—facedown, arse up, legs shamelessly wide—and bound me tight. It was more impersonal than clasped wrists and the heat of someone else on top of me, but fuck, it was intense in a whole different way. When Caspian held me down, I'd always known I was a word away from freedom, but metal couldn't hear me, couldn't feel me. I needed George. And that extra layer of dependence made my stomach flip and my heart quicken. It was sexy and scary and everything I liked.

Then came the blindfold and the heat of George's breath against my ear as she whispered, "Now you'll feel what I want you to feel."

My answer was a whimper and an involuntary wriggle that made the chains rattle. Normally I wouldn't have liked not being able to see, but it was a fear-of-missing-out-type deal—especially with Caspian, who I'd always thought was being stingy with me, rather than just painfully self-conscious for reasons that only now made sense.

Sigh. Regrets. I had a few. I got why he hadn't told me. But why the fuck hadn't he told me? Instead of leaving me floundering, hurting, trying desperately to understand him. Except then I remembered how much he'd given me too. The trust it must have taken to put himself in my hands and let me coax his pleasure through his fear.

My lashes scraped against the fabric over my eyes. Apparently I was crying again. Oh joy. What a bundle of sexy fun I'd turned out to be. But I was also starting to appreciate the darkness. Partly because, the way I was currently arranged, all I was losing was a sideways view of a bare wall. But also because it felt safe.

It was quiet behind my blindfold, the edges of everything inside me *softened* somehow, and everything else magnified until my world was mostly physical. The pressure of the cuffs against my skin. The heat of the leather beneath me. The arch of my spine and the curl of my fingers. The helpless twitching of my toes. Tiny sensations but indisputably there, like stepping-stones leading me back to…me.

"Forgive me a cliché," murmured George, "but you look good enough to eat."

Needless to say, I was well up for being eaten. I just hadn't realised how *literally* she meant it until I felt the too-intimate ripple of her breath against my…well, y'know, my arsehole.

"Oh…oh Jesus. F-f-fuck."

Her only answer was a wicked laugh. And something that involved her mouth, like, on me. Right on me. Enveloping me in this wet heat and…God…suction. There was *suction*. And it was a good job I was chained down, because otherwise I would have hit the fucking ceiling. It was like my sphincter was Monaco and every nerve in my body suddenly wanted to take a luxury vacation.

I'd done this before. Okay, I'd done it once. Because the other guy had really wanted to. Except we'd both been epically wankered, so the only thing I'd really got from the experience was a hazy memory of it not being all that it was cracked up to be. And the first words out of his mouth the next morning had been "*Uhhhhh*, what the fuck kind of kebab did I eat last night," which hadn't made me feel, y'know, great.

But anyway, the belated moral of that story was: "Maybe

don't combine sexual experimentation with being off your face." Because, it turned out, this *was* everything it was cracked up to be. And a bag of chips. I couldn't have told you precisely what she was doing back there—only that it was magic. The tug of her mouth and the prod of her tongue and these long, decadent licks that turned the path from my arse to my balls into a tramline of shuddery bliss.

The thing was, I just wasn't prepared for the pleasure. On any level. Physically, I was making the most outrageous fuss about it—thrashing and bucking in my bonds, and wailing with every fresh touch, as the sweat slid down my back—and emotionally was even worse. It was like I didn't know how to process nice things anymore. Which made no sense because I'd always been a total fan of them before. But I guess feeling them now would have been letting go of Caspian.

Fuuuuuck. I thought I'd *done* that. What with the being dumped and him being engaged and everything. Except I'd always taken pain for him. Even, apparently, when he didn't need me to.

I heard myself sobbing in a sort of heartbroken but also turned on beyond all reason kind of way. George curved a palm soothingly over my upturned cheeks. Which wasn't much of a respite, but truthfully, I didn't really want one. If nothing else, I could recognise a gift when it was offered. And this was its own special torment—a Sisyphean arousal that made it impossible for me to escape my body. It kept me helpless and frantic and wrecked. And took away everything else.

No regrets. No grief. No Caspian.

A pause.

"N-no. Please." I had no idea what I was even begging for. Only that I couldn't stop myself.

George gave a soft chuckle. And then came something new: the cool slap of leather tails against my sweaty, quivering arse. It wasn't a hard blow, but the contrast was instantly the most amazing thing I'd ever felt. I melted against the table, moaning and bouncing my hips in a shameless entreaty for more.

And I got it. A rain of strikes that fell, at first, fast and light. Followed by slower, stronger ones that thudded into me, leaving rich, warm aches behind them. It hurt. But it was the good kind of hurt. The best kind of hurt. The flying kind. And sometimes, one of the tips would flick against my kiss-swollen hole with a sizzle like water hitting hot oil. Making me wail with the pure fucking joy of it.

Time became the gaps between blows. My heart beat for the moment of their landing. Until everything stopped. Well, everything except the pain, which was layered into me so deep and thick it kept right on burning. I was dimly aware someone was crying.

Oh. It was me.

"You're so very pretty, poppet," whispered George, "when you're breaking."

One of her hands closed around my cock. And two strokes later I was coming everywhere. I hadn't even realised I was close until it was happening. As if even my orgasm didn't quite belong to me. My suffering transmuted into ecstasy and released, bright-feathered, like a bird from a cage.

A few clinks and tugs and there was enough slack in the chains for me to sink gently onto my face, basically a puddle.

A minute or so later, George pulled herself onto the table beside me, peeled me up, and helped me to lie with my head in her lap.

"What about you?" I asked, or rather slurred, groping for her erection with all the poise of a kitten chasing a piece of string.

She caught my wrist and pushed it back down against the leather. "Sex is more than ejaculation."

I shivered happily at that. Honestly, I still thought I'd got the better bargain, but I wasn't in any state to debate the point. The room was warm. And so was George. Her leg under my cheek and the hand she was resting on my shoulder. Everything was wonderfully quiet. It settled over me. Pressed into me. My mouth tasted of tears. My eyes were heavy and sticky under the blindfold. But I was okay, drifting through a soft, grey haze, hurting, exhausted, and satisfied.

CHAPTER 6

When next I stirred, I was unchained, and the blindfold was gone, and the studio was silver washed with starlight. I jumped off George's lap with a yelp.

"Oh God. Sorry."

"For what?"

I clutched at the blanket that had been draped over my shoulders. "For totally passing out on you."

"I take it as a compliment, poppet."

"I, uh, I feel like an idiot."

"Well, you shouldn't." She drew me in and kissed the corner of my mouth. "You're terribly sweet and terribly sexy. And I've barely scraped the surface of what I want to do to you."

My cock liked the sound of that and made its opinion known without consulting the rest of me. "W-what do you have in mind?"

I caught the gleam of her smile through the shadows. "A lady must have her secrets."

"You're such a tease."

"And you're only just beginning to figure that out?"

I gave her a pert look. "You know, there's plenty I'd like to do to you as well."

"So you've said. Perhaps we should continue this conversation in the bedroom?"

"I'm game." I jumped down from the table and winced as my arse remembered what it had gone through. And then winced again as I got a sudden whiff of myself. "Although I'm also kind of gross."

"I don't mind. Truthfully, I rather enjoy that"—George gave me a smirk that made me blush—"*ridden hard, put up wet* smell. But you're more than welcome to use the bathroom, if you'd rather?"

"I'd rather."

George's bathroom was charmingly normal—neither a marble palace better suited to a Roman emperor nor the concrete corridor I shared with Ellery. Wow, my sense of perspective was all over the place. I wasn't sure if we were in a washing-sexily-together type space, but she just handed me a clean towel, told me to take my time, and left. Which I was actually sort of glad about. I mean, I wouldn't have objected if she'd wanted to get soapy with me, but as the door clicked closed behind her, I realised the solitude was welcome. I had a lot to process.

Since we didn't have one at the warehouse, I treated myself to a bath, although I had to lie in it really carefully because my bum wasn't a huge fan of hot water right then. As I rested on my elbows amongst the bubbles, I found I was still a little floaty. Not in a bad way, exactly. But there was a lightness inside me that sometimes seemed perilously close to emptiness.

So. Caspian and Nathaniel. Should I have seen that coming? I really didn't think I'd been expecting anything from him. Okay, maybe a little bit, at first. He'd come to get me back before, after all. But as the months had trudged past, I'd come to terms with the fact there weren't going to be any car chases to the airport. No kissing in the rain. No boy dancing down the bleachers singing "Can't Take My Eyes off You." Except maybe some hidden part of me had still been clinging on.

It kind of got me thinking about Pandora's box. Like, the version I vaguely remembered from when we did Greek myths in primary school is that Hope was the thing the gods put in there to protect us from all the other shit. But I was seriously starting to wonder if it hadn't just been their final fuck-you to humanity. I mean, look at me, kidding myself I was being totally mature and moving on. While just a tiny sliver of that sly bastard hope had been dicking with my head this whole time. Which, I guess, meant I was free now? At least I assumed that was the faintly untethered feeling as I sploshed about. Or maybe it was just having come my brains out.

God, I owed George some serious orgasms for this afternoon. Probably jumping into bed—well, onto a table—with the nearest interested person two seconds after learning about Caspian's engagement wasn't the healthiest reaction. But fuck healthy. I was allowed to have nice things. Or fun not-nice things if I wanted them. I'd been braced for guilt, once the happy sex glow dissipated, but…well…maybe it had missed its bus or something. Because it was way late. And part of me, of course, felt guilty for not feeling guilty. But most of me was dead set against it.

We were over. I didn't owe Caspian anything. And I liked George and she was into me, and Caspian was probably doing plenty of boring vanilla bonking with Nathan—

I was so not ready for that thought. It was *horrible*, like my brain was throwing up.

No no no no no no.

I stuck my head under the water, giving myself two options: Stop thinking about it or drown. It worked, because the images finally went away and I sat up, gasping, with a bitter taste somehow in my whole body.

This bath was rapidly losing its charm.

Scrambling out, I began drying off and then remembered I'd left all my clothes in the studio. Sigh. I wasn't exactly opposed to scampering about in the buff or with a towel slung across my hips like Poldark in *And Then There Were None*— except without all the abs and a V-cut you could use to irrigate the Nile Valley. But I'd just been very, *very* naked and so I wasn't in the hugest rush for more exposure. At least, not straightaway.

Then I spotted the dressing gown hanging from a hook on the back of the door. It was big and fluffy, and I sure as hell deserved some big and fluffy. Also it had a hood, which, as far as I was concerned, was just the right amount of extra when it came to sleepwear. I pulled it on and, doing my best impression of a Jawa, went to find George.

She was in the kitchen, faffing with the kettle, and sporting a dressing gown of her own. Nobody should have been able to look hot in paisley, but she was pulling it off. I think it helped she was wearing it over black silk pyjama bottoms—the sexiest kind of pyjama bottoms—and a dark green bra edged in black lace.

"Well," she said as I sidled in, "don't you look adorable?"

I gave her a defiant look from beneath the shadow of my hood. "Yes. Yes I do."

"Tea? Some other hospitality? Aloe vera?"

I'd been on the edge of self-conscious, but this made me laugh. "I'm okay."

"Are you sure? I could rub it lasciviously into you if you wanted." She drifted over and gave my arse a yelp-inducing squeeze.

"I can't tell if you're trying to hurt me or comfort me."

"Oh, poppet. *Both.*"

I went up on tiptoes and, proud of my own bravado, kissed her smirking mouth. "Thank you. Tea for now?"

"Of course."

I sat down (carefully) at the kitchen table and George pulled open a cupboard to reveal not the dizzying array of artisanal loose-leaf blends I'd been expecting but a battered box of Yorkshire teabags and a jumble of mismatched mugs that made me abruptly homesick.

And then my stomach rumbled.

"Sorry." I huddled further into the warmth of my dressing gown. "I forgot lunch, what with the emotional trauma and everything."

"No apologies. I should have fed you. I don't usually have overnight guests, so I'm out of practice."

"You don't?"

She cast me a look of mingled exasperation and fondness. "Yes, yes, you're a very special mushroom. Now, I'm sure I must have something around here somewhere."

"Um, what do you normally eat?" I asked.

"Lemon juice and broken hearts." There followed a series of clashes and clatters as she began opening doors seemingly at random and peering at whatever lay within. "Actually, I usually stay in London, where I eat out or order in. I've never quite got the hang of domesticity."

That figured. I couldn't have imagined George cooking. But then, I'm not sure it would have occurred to me to imagine us in our jammies in her kitchen either. Though more fool me for that, because it was actually really nice. And George was still very George—sardonic and sexy and far kinder than she'd want anyone to know—it was just the new setting shaping my perceptions. Like when you hold a prism to the light and let it turn through all its colours.

"You should see the places I've been living," I said. "They're where domesticity goes to die. Trust me, you have nothing to worry about."

That earned me one of her low chuckles. "I like certain aspects, but not others. If you need a bookshelf building or some cushions buying or a lawn mowing, I'm one hundred percent your huckleberry. If you want fresh milk in the fridge, not a chance. Probably this is God's way of telling me to get married." She paused, putting a thoughtful finger to her lips. "Or a housekeeper."

"Well…you *could* get married?"

"In order to have my kitchen cared for? Arden, I'm not Don Draper."

"No, I mean. If you there was someone you liked."

"Dear me." She turned, with a merciless grin. "A little rimming and you're anybody's."

I went red. All the red. Forever. "Ohmigod, not me. But theoretically."

"Theoretically I could play Maria in the next revival of *The Sound of Music*. It doesn't follow I'd be any good at it."

"Why don't you think you'd be good at being married?"

"My preferences revolve around encouraging others, not forsaking them."

"But with the right person, you could not forsake others together?"

"Why the sudden interest in my marital status?" She paused, leaning her hips against one of the counters. "Do you have five unwed daughters you haven't told me about?"

I heaved a sigh. "And the family estate is entailed as well."

"Seriously, though, where's this coming from?"

"I don't know." I suddenly found I couldn't quite look at her and became very interested in the cuff of my dressing gown. "I was just remembering what you said in Starbucks."

"I said a lot of things in Starbucks." Her voice had gone a little cool.

"You told me you…you were in love with someone. But that doesn't mean you have to be alone."

"At the risk of sounding unnecessarily Garbo about it, I *want* to be alone." She made a derisive sound at the back of her throat. "Do you really think I've spent the last twenty-something years eating my heart out for Mara Fairfax?"

I choked on air. "*Mara?*"

"Well, obviously."

Announcing Arden St. Ives: winner of the prestigious, much-coveted Most Oblivious Doink Award. Now I gave the matter half a second's thought, it all made perfect sense. The way they talked and looked at each other. The trust between them that seemed like second nature. To say nothing of the fact that Mara was six different kinds of scary to pretty much everyone who wasn't George. I opened my mouth, realised I had no idea what I was going to say, and panic blurted out an "I'm sorry."

George's too-mocking brows dipped into the slightest suggestion of a frown. "What for? Even if Mara wasn't straight and I wasn't a woman, I wouldn't be with her. She wants the house in the country, the two-point-four children, the stable full of horses. And she has it. I could never give those to her and I would never take them away."

A weird noise was coming out of my face. I briefly thought I had the hiccoughs. And then discovered I was crying. Again.

Boo.

"Ah." A whisper of silk and George was at my side, her fingers moving gently through my hair. "This wasn't about me at all, was it? Love isn't a bus during the rush hour. You don't have to let people off in order to fit more on. Probably you'll always love Caspian a little bit. But that doesn't mean you won't love someone else."

I blinked up at her through soggy lashes. "But what if I don't?"

"Poppet"—her tone sharpened—"you're in your early twenties, having emerged from your first significant relationship. It's a little early to conclude you're going to die alone."

"Half-eaten by Alsatians." From her quizzical expression, apparently the reference hadn't landed. I sniffed and wiped my eyes. "This is rubbish. I can't seem to stop being pathetic."

"Yes," she drawled. "I'm quite disappointed. I'd been operating under the assumption that fucking me would immediately cure you of all negative emotions."

God. I had to pull myself together, at least a little bit. George had been nothing but patient with me and I was probably about as fun as a wet sock in a duvet. I mustered what I hoped was a flirty smile. "Maybe it's something that requires an extended course of treatment?"

"I'm game. But first"—she pressed a kiss to the top of my head and swooshed back over to the kettle—"you'll be delighted to hear that I found some food. There's caviar and a Pot Noodle."

Various questions ebbed and flowed in my head. "What flavour Pot Noodle?"

"Chinese chow mein. And the caviar is Royal Oscietra, purchased from W.G. White."

"I'll take the Pot Noodle. I only eat caviar if it's beluga."

Laughing, she retrieved a familiar blue-labelled plastic pot from the back of a cupboard, tore off the top, and poured hot water inside. Then set it on the table, along with a small tin of caviar, and two cups of tea.

"There's no milk," she said. "Well, there's something in the milk carton. But I wouldn't recommend allowing it inside your body."

"And no cutlery?" I pointed at the plastic spoon she was wielding.

She arched a brow at me. "Haven't you read your *Debrett's*

yet? Metal is supposed to oxidise the caviar and damage the flavour. Nonsense if you ask me, because the stuff comes in metal tins. But mythologies are far more interesting than truths, don't you think?"

"That's not a question. It's a poorly disguised epigram."

"This is, though: You've never had caviar before, have you?"

"No, for two reasons. Firstly, because I'm a normal person. And secondly"—I eyed the glistening bobbles dubiously— "because it squicks me out."

"Want some?"

"Are you trying to muscle in on my Pot Noodle?"

"I'm *trying* to do you a favour. You know Mara will fire you if she discovers you haven't had caviar." My eyes went wide and George burst out laughing. "God, you're easy. I'm kidding."

I put a hand to my racing heart. "Don't do that to me. I spend all my time convinced I'm about to be dumped as it is."

"Why?"

"Because…" Actually, why did I feel like that? When I'd first got the job at *Milieu*, I'd been convinced I was perfect for it. And it wasn't that I'd changed my mind, exactly, but something wasn't the same. I guess it had just been so much easier to believe in myself and all that malarkey when Caspian had thought I was the bee's knees. Not that I should have been hanging my self-esteem off him in the first place. "I don't know. I mean, I'm not sure what I'm bringing any- more."

"Buck up, poppet. Imposter syndrome isn't cute."

"Y'know"—I poked at the Pot Noodle to see if the peas were still rock solid—"it's funny you mention that. I used to think I had imposter syndrome but then I realised I was only pretending."

George made a sound, halfway between a laugh and a groan, and rapped me lightly on the knuckles. "Mara wouldn't have hired you if she didn't think she could use you. I love her to hell and back, but she's too ambitious to be kind."

"Well, maybe she made a mistake. My last piece was a list of the ten poshest sex toys for the website, which frankly, a teenager with access to Google could have written."

"What," asked George, tilting her head, "*are* the ten poshest sex toys?"

"Oh, I can't remember. Golden butt plugs, diamond-encrusted vibrators, platinum cock rings in the shape of cobras, the usual stuff. I found this spanker that cost, like, three thousand dollars."

"For that price, I'd expect it to come with a spankee."

"I know, right?" I sighed. "The thing is, I love *Milieu*. But I got this job when I was with Caspian and everything felt like this crazy dream. And now he's gone, I keep wondering what's still real."

"You are. So get off your arse and pitch."

"Pitch?" I squeaked. "Pitch what?"

"Something a teenager with access to Google couldn't write. Something only you could. That's what Mara's looking for." George's free hand made a gesture that could have meant anything from "problem solved" to "I'm bored of your insecurities" and was probably a little bit of both. "Now, are you going to try this caviar? It's getting warm."

The shiny fish eggs looked no more appealing than they had five minutes ago. "Why would I want to?"

"Arden." Her expression grew quite severe suddenly. "Why *wouldn't* you? Very few adventures begin with a no."

She was right, of course. And what was the worst that could happen? I would have to swallow a mouthful of salty goo. Been there, done that.

"Okay," I said. "Let's do this."

"Close your eyes."

I subjected her to my best put-upon look before obeying.

"You're cute," she drawled, "when you're doing what you're told."

I opened my mouth to protest, on principle, that I was cute all the damn time, but then I felt the nudge of the spoon against my lips, and the next thing I knew, I had a gob full of fish eggs.

It wasn't nearly as awful as I'd feared. Far less salty and far less, well, *eggy*. If anything, it was like popping candy without the candy: little bursts of flavour that crackled on my tongue and vanished, leaving behind the memory of the sea. I mean, I wouldn't be reaching for a tin of caviar the next time I got the munchies, but at the very least I'd increased my fancy party eligibility.

"Well?" asked George.

I shrugged. "S'okay."

"Eat your damn Pot Noodle." But she was laughing as she said it.

CHAPTER 7

In the end, we shared both the Pot Noodle and the caviar. Of course, they didn't go at all, but that was part of the fun. And afterwards, she took my hand and led me upstairs again. There wasn't anything particularly unusual about George's bedroom, except maybe that it was slightly nicer than average (if by average, you meant "mine," which was mainly socks and my futon mattress), but I'd forgotten how intimate someone else's living spaces could be. Caspian's apartments—including his own—had always been about display: wealth, power, beauty, and all that blah blah blah. But George's home was just…George. Right down to the pile of velvet jackets flung over a chair back.

Her bed had a touch of the fairy tale about it—all silver leaf and swan-neck posts, with pale grey sheets and dusty purple covers. I'd always imagined that—at the point of being able to afford something nice to sleep in—I'd want one of those ornately carved jobbies, so I could be tied to it in a variety of interesting ways. But honestly, this was super romantic. It looked like the sort of bed Louis XIV's gay brother would get sucked off in.

George went to lounge, and me being me, I made a bee-line for the bookcase. Apparently, my post-Caspian fascination for people who had personal belongings wasn't going away anytime soon. But also, you could learn so much about someone from their bookshelves, and I'm nosy as fuck. In my experience there were two kinds of people in the world: people who kept books for show and people who kept them for love, and George was definitely in the second category. There wasn't much order to her books, but they all looked read, and read often.

She seemed to like mysteries, especially classic English ones about dead aristocrats in country houses. But I also recognised the names of a bunch of philosopher-type people I'd diligently avoided while at Oxford, like Walter Benjamin and Susan Sontag. Then came lots of scary art books, which all had titles along the lines of *The Principles of Art History*, *Painting and Experience in Fifteenth-Century Italy*, and *Body, Memory and Architecture*. And after those, biographies and autobiographies of photographers, a scant handful of which I'd vaguely heard of. Well. It was official: I was a cultureless lout.

"If you move the biography of Diane Arbus to a forty-five-degree angle," drawled George, "you'll open the secret passage to my satanic ritual chamber."

I spun round, blushing. "Sorry, I was just looking."

"See anything you like?"

"I don't"—I scuffed sheepishly—"actually know much about art."

"There's someone you might recognise on the top shelf."

I had to go up on my tiptoes. But then I gasped. "Oh, they're your books. Can I look?"

"Certainly not. My retiring disposition could never allow it."

Laughing, I reached up and tugged one down. George was best known for her fashion photography and the occasional Royal Wedding, but she also did these portrait collections. Photographs of a single subject that…well, I only knew what Tabs had told me, which was that the exhibitions were always one-night-only, and what I'd discovered for myself after hours of Googling, which was that the books were nearly impossible to get.

Right now I was holding *Sylvia*: She was a wisp of a woman and eighty if she was a day. Though mostly she was covered in bees. Or surrounded by them, anyway, and looking way happier about it than I would have expected from someone covered in bees. It was kind of amazing, actually— the way the images captured both her stillness and the ceaseless motion around her. I put my fingers to one of the pages, half expecting to feel the stickiness of honey. The hesitant warmth of an English spring. Maybe if I closed my eyes, I'd smell meadow flowers.

"You are wonderful," I whispered.

George huffed out a pleased sound. "I've been doing this for over thirty years. One would hope to be quite accomplished."

"That's a bit modest for someone who once told me her talents were sex and art."

"My talents *are* sex and art. But I leave taking their measure to others."

"Well, I think you rock at both."

"Thank you, poppet." She tucked a hand behind her head, the other wandering blatantly to her erection—which, framed as it was in black silk, was quite a sight. "But do feel free to keep praising me. I'm rather enjoying myself."

I replaced *Sylvia* and picked up *Jules*, a study of cool androgyny, as exquisitely remote as a classical study. Then *Luis*. Who was, um, naked. Unless you counted the tattoos. Before reaching curiously for the very first book on the shelf. Probably, I should have checked the name before opening it, but I didn't. And so I got to see my boss naked. She was probably about twenty in the photograph—which had a stylised, grainy quality like an old black-and-white glamour shot—and reclining on a bearskin. I was pretty sure those sorts of pictures were meant to be a juxtaposition of vulnerability and savagery, but honestly, the way Mara was staring down the camera, if it came to a fight between her and the bear, I'd have picked her every time.

Annnnnnyway.

I stuffed *Mara* back where I'd found her and retreated to the bed. George grinned at me lazily, still stroking.

"I really love your work," I told her. And then, before I even quite knew what I was going to say next, I blurted out, "What's it like?"

"What's what like? My work?"

"No. Like…always, knowing who you are and what you want to be."

She paused, propping herself up on an elbow. "Arden, nobody really knows what they want to be. It's just that for some people—by pure chance—the thing it turns out they actually want to be happens to have the same name as the thing they thought they wanted to be."

"Um. You've lost me."

"The first time I picked up a camera, I felt this tremendous sense of completion. Like I'd found some lost jigsaw piece of my soul. And that made me want to *be* a photographer, but I didn't really know what being a photographer meant or what it was like. And now I've been a photographer for most of my life, and I've loved every minute of it, but it has almost nothing to do with that feeling I had when I was a child."

"But," I protested, "what if your jigsaw is all over the floor and you've lost the box?"

"It doesn't matter. I'm sure plenty of people pick up a camera and feel exactly the way I felt, but then discover that they don't actually enjoy taking pictures for a living. And some people probably stumble into it blindly and never look back. It's not the rush that's real. It's the follow-through. Find out what something *is* and then you'll find out if you love it."

Now there was a statement with broad applicability if ever I heard one. I sighed.

"Stop worrying, poppet. Your face will get stuck like that."

I plonked my chin into my hand. "I've always thought it'd be kind of cool to write for *Milieu*."

"It will never be anything like you thought it would. But that's okay. And it's also okay if you decide it's not what you want."

"But if it's not," I absolutely did not whine, "what do I do then?"

Her brows lifted in mock exasperation, but her voice was

still surprisingly gentle. "Haven't you listened to a damn word I said? Do you want another flogging?"

"No, I mean, yes, I mean I was listening." I drew a deep breath. "I keep trying. Until I find what I love."

As soon as I spoke, I realised I'd heard those words before. How the fuck had I forgotten them? I guess all my mental energy had been focused on surviving. Which was probably fair enough. It was hard to be a carpe-seizing go-getter when your skin felt like a bag full of broken pieces. But my time with a billionaire who believed in me should have taught me better than this. *I* was better than this. So what if Nathaniel had taken Caspian? He didn't get to take me.

"Are you all right?" George asked. "Your nose is all wrinkled up."

"Yeah, I'm good. Just wondering why you're always so nice to me."

She subjected me to her most sardonic look. "Because I want to fuck you. Obviously."

"Works for me." Riding a rush of confidence that was at least sixty percent determination, I knelt up and pulled off my Jedi dressing gown. "Though it's probably about time I was nice to you back."

Her eyes gleamed, gold-sheened by the softer light. "Works for me."

I leaned down and kissed her. First on the mouth and then along her jaw and down her throat, catching against my lips the vibration of her contented sigh. It was actually a little disorientating to have such freedom. I'd never minded that Caspian preferred me helpless and at his mercy. As a matter of fact, I'd loved it. But I'd also been desperate to touch him, believing—like an insecure, oblivious idiot—the fact he wouldn't let me was about me, instead of about him. Looking back, I understood exactly how much of himself he'd given me, when, at the time, I'd seen nothing but barriers. It made me sad in a way: all his unrecognised trust. Sometimes it even kept me up at night, thinking of everything I would have done differently if only I'd known. What did it matter what we got up to in bed? It was him I wanted. His passion, his laughter, his cruelty, his kindness. And his hurt, because that was part of him as well.

I was hesitant with her at first, but grew less so as it turned out my getting-people-off skill set hadn't irredeemably declined. As for George, she came to pleasure like an old friend, neither at war with it as Caspian was, nor submitting to it like me. I almost envied her in a way—I'd been trying to show myself a good time since I first figured out my penis liked me moving my hand up and down it, but George had an ease in her body that you probably only got from a lot more living than I'd managed so far. Mind you, if I looked like her, I'd probably be easy too.

Don't get me wrong, I was fine in cute-at-best kind of way and my arse was at least moderately epic. And while she wasn't a perfect physical specimen like Caspian, George had this rangy sexiness to her, all long, lean limbs and subtle curves. Also I was always up for getting my hands on boobs and George's were *lovely*. The silken weight of them pressed against my palms. The rough-smooth texture of her nipples as they tightened against my tongue. She was pretty sensitive there too, her fingers curling in my hair to keep my attention where she wanted it—a hint of control that turned me on even more.

I didn't worship George the way I would Caspian, but it was still…service, I guess? She could have used me, or bossed me around, and I would probably have enjoyed it just as much, but she didn't. Just accepted my attentions as her due with the indulgence of a decadent empress. Which I, of course, found wildly hot. And made me feel submissive in a whole new way. A supplicant to someone else's desires.

Thank God I'd got off earlier. I was already hot and bothered at the point of kneeling between her thighs, pushing into her, but the hard, lube-slick clench of her body would have finished me off. And I still had to grit my teeth a moment because it had been a while for me this way round and I'd half forgotten how intense it could be. The strength and intimacy of that interior heat.

Her hand came up and closed around my throat. Gently, but yikes. "Don't you dare, poppet."

"I…I…" I sucked in a rough breath. "You feel amazing."

"Yes, I know. But if you even think of coming before I do—"

"I'm not. I won't. I promise."

She slid her thumb caressingly over my pulse, which didn't exactly help with the whole controlling myself deal. "Good boy."

I knew it was a total cliché of me to like being called that. But I did. It was the teeniest bit demeaning, except in a…nice way? Like a full-body toe curl.

Grinning, I nestled my hips against hers. "I'm better than good."

"That, my dear, remains to be seen."

Okay, so, look. I don't want to boast. But I was actually

pretty fucking amazing. I mean, I thought my balls were going to explode for most of it, but they didn't, and in a twisted sort of way, I almost enjoyed it. I mean, not the ball-exploding specifically. Just the gentle, and increasingly ungentle, ache of self-denial. And knowing I was pleasing George.

Because, for the record, I was. I *so* was.

And she was gorgeous like that, her eyes heavy-lidded with bliss and the sardonic twist of her mouth softened in passion. Oh my God, and the *sounds* she made. These deep purring groans, like a tiger in the sun. We ran through the ol' reliables—missionary, and variations, from behind, with us both kneeling, and then George braced on her forearms, missionary again because I was nothing if not ambitious when it came to putting my dick in people—and finally on our sides, while I kissed the sweat from her shoulder and she worked her cock with long, deft strokes. It was vindication and mercy both when she came, and almost enough to send me over too. I clung on nobly, though, and once I'd eased out of her, she flopped onto her back and regarded me with an air of sated amusement.

I, err, I whined.

Her lips twitched. "Something you want, poppet?"

Since my mouth was dry, and my tongue about six sizes too big for it, I gave an emphatic nod.

"Then you'd better ask nicely, hadn't you?"

Fuck. Squirmy-making. But I was also about to lose my mind. "Can," I mumbled, "can I come. Please?"

"Is that really the best you can manage?" George dabbed her fingers into the shiny puddles she'd left across her stomach and chest. Then slipped them between my lips. Which did absolutely nothing for my self-control. She tasted tangy-sweet, and of everything I couldn't have.

I'd always been taught not to talk with my mouth full. But this was an emergency. "*Please.* I need to. I—"

She stroked my tongue, turning my words into a needy gabble.

"I was good," I managed, part plea, part protest.

That made her smile, with a degree of affection I would have appreciated more if not for the whole about-to-die-of-lack-of-orgasm thing. "You were. You were *very* good."

I gazed at her with my biggest eyes.

"Well, all right. But give me a good show."

My hand had jumped to my cock like it was on a string, but now I hesitated. "A...a...what?"

"I like watching."

"You're such a pervert," I wailed, need and denial and the good sort of embarrassment all knotted up inside me.

"I'm not asking for *Les Misérables* at the West End."

"Right now, *Breath* would be pushing it."

She laughed, but without the usual trace of mockery. "Oh, stop dithering and come. You know you deserve to."

I think it hit me about halfway through the sentence: one of those ripped-out-of-you orgasms that give you no time for dignity. Just this razor-edge of ecstasy where it doesn't matter what goofy face you're pulling or what stupid sounds you're making. I heard a wild howl that must have been me. Felt the tightness of my helplessly arching spine. But everything else was drowned in the darkness and brightness of pleasure.

"H-how was it?" I asked, when I'd got my breath back.

"Four stars. Four and a half if I'm feeling generous."

"I'll take it."

I flopped down next to George, awkward in a different way to when I'd been begging and moaning and coming in her face. I mean, not literally in her face—that wasn't something you did without direct invitation—but at the very least near her face. Anyway, maybe I was just being weird. I'd shared a bed, both sexually and otherwise, with loads of people at university, and Caspian had found it difficult to sleep with me at all. So I shouldn't have been conscious of his absence. Of the fact me and George smelled different to me and Caspian. I shouldn't have felt lonely.

Except, y'know, I did.

Rolling onto my side, I gazed at George. Possibly a bit too intently, because one of her eyes popped open. "What are you searching for, poppet? The Amber Room?"

"No, I was just..."

"Just what?"

Fuck. George was great, and I knew she wouldn't particularly care, but for my own damn sake, I couldn't keep whining to her about my stupid emotions and my stupid ex-boyfriend. "I was just wondering why photography."

"Is this an interview?"

"I'm curious. Don't I get to be curious?"

"Always. But I suspect you're indulging me."

"Isn't that what people do when they like each other?" I sidled a little closer across the covers. "And you've indulged me plenty."

She gave me a sharp look. "Does your none-too-subtle

Battle of the Somme approach to bedspace mean you want to be snuggled?"

"Would…would that be okay?"

"Of course." Flinging out an arm, she made a nook for me against her side and I gratefully wriggled into it. We were both still pretty sticky, but it didn't matter—the warmth and welcome were what I really wanted. "Just be aware that I'm rolling away later. I can't have you lolling on top of me all night. A lady needs her sleeping space."

I kissed the nearest available piece of skin, which turned out to be the crease of her shoulder. "This is perfect. Will you talk to me about photography now?"

She was quiet for so long I didn't think she was going to, but then she said, "I suppose, being an English graduate, you're familiar with Roland Barthes?"

"Yep, yep. I got familiar with avoiding him for three years."

"Perhaps you'll become better friends when it's not required. His last book, *Camera Lucida*, was written after the death of his mother—he was, of course, terribly French and terribly homosexual, so they were close."

"If you'd been my tutor at Oxford," I told her, "I'd have got a first."

"If I'd been your tutor at Oxford, I'd have been fired for fucking you against the fourteenth-century oak panelling."

"Not true. You don't get fired for fucking people at Oxford. They just tell you that you probably shouldn't."

That made her grin. "Good to know."

"So what's the deal with *Camera Lucida*?"

"It's a very strange piece of writing: a famous work on the

subject of photography that is, in many ways, barely about the subject of photography."

I blinked. "And that made you want to be a photographer?"

"Towards the end of book, Barthes is looking through pictures, trying to find what he calls 'the air'—the truth or the spirit—of his mother within these collected images of her. Eventually he finds what he's looking for in a photograph of her in a winter garden, taken in 1898. And he weeps."

"Oh wow. Maybe I shouldn't have pretended I had a stomach bug when we did the post-structuralists."

"It moved me." George gave a clumsy shrug, given she was lying down and I was plastered against her. "It still does. The vulnerability in that work. And in that moment, when critical objectivity—when the discipline he himself helped shape—gave way to the subjectivity of pure emotion. I would love to make someone feel like that. Even if only for a moment."

I opened my mouth, then closed it again, slightly overwhelmed. A huffed breath from George could have just been, well, a huffed breath. Or a sign she'd revealed more than she'd entirely intended—a state of affairs I was far too familiar with, albeit usually from the other direction.

"So," I said slowly, "what you're basically saying is: You want to fuck people in the heart."

She let loose a great bark of laughter. "Yes. Yes. That's it exactly. I want to fuck people in the heart."

Then I was being unceremoniously tumbled out of her arms, pinned down, and kissed hard and rough and just the way I liked it. I emerged, a few minutes later, breathless, with stinging lips, and watering eyes, and found George staring at me with unabashed ferocity.

"I'd like to photograph you, Arden."

I made an uncertain giggle-hiccough-type noise. "Haven't you already?"

"For a book."

"A book? One of *your* books? Me?"

"Yes, you. Yes, one of my books."

"You mean like"—I glanced over towards her bookshelf—"there'd be an *Arden*?"

"There's already an Arden. But yes."

My mind was a haze of *omigodomigodomigod*. "Are you serious?"

"I never joke about art."

"But I'm…I'm not art."

She bit the edge of my jaw, not exactly gently, and I was too dazed to even yelp. "Don't say stupid things, poppet."

"Sorry. It's just—actually, I don't know what it's just." *Breathe. Do some breathing.* "What do you…I mean, how does it work?"

"I spend time with someone. And I take pictures."

"But isn't us spending time together, y'know, sex?"

"Yes. I was rather hoping you'd noticed."

It was at that moment that I apparently chose to remember *Luis*. In all his very intimate glory. "Does that mean they'd, um, be sexy pictures?"

"They could be. As long as you weren't uncomfortable."

"Uncomfortable?" I repeated. "Why would I be? The Internet is already covered in photos of me looking goofy as fuck."

"It can feel quite different, though—to move from private subject to public object."

I shrugged. "Maybe. But honestly, it's the idea that you think I'm good enough that I'm having trouble getting my head round."

"If you can't find faith in you—which you should have, by the way—at least have faith in me."

"Oh my God, I do," I cried. "What I'm trying to say here is…if you think I could be, y'know, not terrible, I am in. I am *so* in."

A smile, softer than any I'd seen on her face before, tugged her lips. "Then it's settled."

I nodded.

"You know"—she nudged my legs open with hers and pressed our hips together—"I was about to say something sensible about how late it was getting and sleep being generally considered beneficial, but I'm rather too horny to care. Think you can get hard again?"

"I can try."

And for the record, I succeeded. *Admirably.*

CHAPTER 8

Τrue to her word, George dropped me off at *Milieu* the next morning. Of course, I was wearing the same clothes and moving rather gingerly, which led to Tabs greeting me with: "Oh, you dirty stop-out."

So I shot her my best and sassiest look. "*Very* dirty."

And then limped sassily to my desk. I could already tell sitting down and me were not going to be friends today, but I booted up my computer and got stuck into polishing up a feature about the best diamonds to wear with leather. Mainly because I didn't want to deal with the fact I'd accidentally volunteered for or been tasked with a piece on beard gadgets.

I was on my third Diet Coke (which I had hidden in my top drawer because it probably counted as clutter) when my phone rang. This usually meant the caller had dialled my number by accident while trying to get someone more important.

"Arden St. Ives."

"Hello," came a voice I sort of recognised but couldn't place, "this is Nathaniel."

Oh.

My.

Fucking.

God.

"Nathaniel who?" Okay, so that was cheap. But the bastard had called me Aidan at least twice.

He made this soft sound, like a laugh with extra condescension—as if to say, *I am aware you're being incredibly and potentially self-destructively petty right now, but being the better person, I shall rise above it.* Then he actually said, "Nathaniel Priest."

"Sorry. Yes. Of course."

The office had gone night-before-Christmas still around me. When something significant was happening at *Milieu*, everyone just kind of sensed it. Probably you only got such finely honed gossip antennae from years of exposure. At least, I hoped that was the case, because I was seriously not there yet. I'd even managed to miss Donna Karan's chocolate Labrador getting briefly but dramatically stuck in the revolving door because I'd been scoffing a cheese sandwich.

"So," I asked, "can I help you?"

There was a moment of silence across the line. Shit—I could see the dark shadow behind the far wall, which meant Mara was lurking.

Then, "Caspian and I have discussed it. And we would like to do the interview."

"Oh. Wow." No matter how hard I tried, I couldn't get *anything* into my tone. Not a single flicker of human-ness. It was like I'd been replaced by Alexa. "That's so terrific."

"Excellent. I'll have our assistants coordinate our schedules and send you some dates."

The rest of the call, brief though it was, went by in a blur of logistics and email addresses. It was all totally civil, but by the time I put the phone down, my palms were sweaty and my face felt as red as my arse had been last night.

"That better be the interview George promised me," said Mara, swooping in.

The first time I met *Milieu*'s editor-in-chief, I'd been expecting Miranda Priestly because, frankly, who wouldn't. But Mara was very much opposite of that. She was lively and vigorous—even warm when she chose to be—with a passion for horses and the English countryside. Which was helpful because her husband apparently owned a lot of both. And while there was definitely a glamour to her, the vibe was much more *matriarch in a Jilly Cooper novel* than bulletproof fashionista.

I nodded. Tried to think of something unbothered and audacious to say. Came up empty. Settled on "Yes."

"Good." She began prowling thoughtfully between the cubbies and I hastily closed my drawer on my Diet Coke. "You know, I'm thinking we should run with this. Go full rainbow for February."

Tabs's head came up. "Oh?"

"Why not? Diversity's on trend right now."

"Is it?" I asked, in a smaller voice than I'd have hoped. "Or is it more of a thing that some people just kind of, like, are?"

"Not the cover line we'll be going with." Mara's attention—always erratic—landed on me momentarily, flicked away again, and then returned. "The Hart-Whatshisname piece: Let's try a romance angle with it. *Pretty Woman* if one of them wasn't a hooker. Cinderella except with more dicks."

I shifted a bit on my chair. "I can try, but we're still talking about two privileged white guys getting hitched here. It's not exactly Evelina and Lord Orville, is it?"

"Caspian Hart's a bajillionaire," put in Tabs. "That's almost as good as a nonracist royal or a semi-attractive earl. And he's marrying the sort of person anyone could be. What a story."

If I could have climbed into my desk alongside my Diet Coke, I would have. And never come out again.

"That reminds me." Mara turned on Tabs. "Find me a gay duke. Let's do a feature on him as well."

Tabs fiddled with an earring, frowning slightly. "I'm not sure there are any."

That was met by an impatient snort. Mara tended to get horsey-er when crossed.

"Wait, what about Lord Mountbatten?"

"The younger son of a marquess? Get a grip, Tabitha. You know nobody will care unless it's a duke."

"Poshest historical gays?" I suggested. "Then we'd be able to include actual kings."

Mara gave a sharp nod. "Yes. Good. Get someone on that."

The conversation moved rapidly, as did most Mara-centric conversation, but I tuned it out. After all, I had a job to do. A horrible job I had brought upon myself through a frankly incoherent combination of bravado and personal masochism. But in those first moments of seeing Caspian again, I would have done almost anything to pretend I wasn't utterly destroyed. All the power he had over me, I'd given him willingly enough, believing love would make me invincible, but God, it hurt. Sometimes it hurt so fucking much.

Anyway. The interview had been a bluff, and a pretty transparent one at that. A way to get out of the room with some semblance of pride. I couldn't imagine Caspian actively wanting to take me up on it. So that left me wondering: Why had Nathaniel? What was he trying to prove? And to whom? Because if this was aimed at me, I'd already got the message. Loud and fucking clear.

Although my feelings on the subject were actually more mixed than they probably should have been. I mean, it was a bit of a Lady Catherine de Bourgh–type situation, wasn't it? You didn't go around telling people they had no right to marry Mr. Darcy unless there was the teeniest tiniest possibility Mr. Darcy wanted to marry them. By the same token, Nathaniel wouldn't need to make big *I'm with Caspian* gestures if he truly believed he was. And wasn't that a whiskey sour of an emotional cocktail? Being smug and hopeful and bitter and sad all at the same time. Which so wasn't me. I was a strawberry daiquiri boy, through and through.

The worst of it was, I didn't actually want Nathaniel to be insecure or uncertain—even if it meant I was completely out of the picture. I'd spent quite a lot of my relationship with Caspian that way and it hadn't been a whole lot of fun. I guess I'd just assumed Nathaniel would have been basking in victory, but maybe it didn't look like victory to him. Maybe it looked like he was second choice. That Caspian had only come back because what he'd tried to have with me hadn't worked out.

Urrrrrrgh. Having to think about Nathaniel like he was a real person was literally the worst. And now I was pretty much mandated to do it for work. I could probably have claimed personal issues—because I did, actually, have personal issues—and passed the interview to someone else. But this was a big deal. Not career defining, perhaps. But most likely career delaying if I walked away. So fuck it. And fuck Caspian. I chose me.

Did it make it more or less creepy to be Googling your ex-boyfriend's ex-boyfriend-turned-present-fiancé when it was your job? Well, it didn't matter either way. I was doing it. Research and shit. I was mildly proud of the fact I'd never e-stalked Nathaniel before—I thought it demonstrated, if not actual sanity, at least some degree of self-preservation. And in the end, the results surprised me. Well, I say surprised. It didn't turn out he was secretly a stripper or a superhero or already married or anything. He just wasn't quite what I'd been expecting.

I'd always taken it for granted he was like Caspian: born to wealth and power. But he'd grown up in Manchester. Gone to university in Leeds. His father had his own accounting firm. The sort of place that proclaimed, *Forty years of experience working with entrepreneurs based in Manchester and the surrounding areas*, as if that was something special. His mother taught in an inner-city school. The Internet being what it is, I even managed to look up their house on Streetview. It was a three-bedroom, redbrick semi with a pointy roof and a bog-standard hatchback parked in the drive.

My mind was honestly blown. Nathaniel was just so polished that I couldn't imagine him ever having lived such an ordinary a life. Walked to school under grey skies and the shadows of old factories. Slept in a bedroom that probably always felt too small. Carried the burden of his parents' pride with him all the way to his mid-tier university. It had never occurred to me that he might have worked for anything. That success hadn't just been brushed over him like gold leaf by a benevolent universe. That he had, in fact, *earned* his place in the world. His identity. His chance at happiness. Same as me.

Or, y'know, probably more so. Because if you got past the whole *having to run away from my abusive father when I was barely old enough to remember* situation, the most traumatising experience of my life was the first person I'd fallen properly in love with deciding to marry someone else. In any case, creepin' on Nathaniel, and having slightly uncomfortable realisations about myself, kept me pretty busy until home time. I can't say it was the best day in the office I'd ever had.

Ellery was there when I got back to the warehouse. She was sitting on the sofa, with her feet pulled up, painting what looked like angry pig faces onto her toenails.

"Hi, honey," I trilled, "I'm home."

She glanced up briefly. "Dinner's on the table."

"Seriously?"

"No. But there's Coke in the fridge."

"The kind you put in your mouth or up your nose?"

"Maybe"—she thought about it—"both?"

Ever the optimist, I checked. And it turned out there was only the undrinkable variety. Sigh.

Neither quenched nor on drugs, I slumped down next to Ellery. "Caspian and Nathaniel are engaged."

There followed a very long silence. "I suppose you're going to want a hug or some shit like that?"

"Yes please."

A deep, pained sigh. Then, with great deliberation, she put down her brush and held out her arms. I bounced into them and cuddled for all I was worth. Which, on the cuddle front, amounted to a lot. Believe me.

She made a sound like a cat bringing up a furball. "Your hair's in my mouth."

I squeezed harder.

"Ow. Arden."

Probably best to let go. I did and Ellery withdrew to a corner, all aggressive knees and elbows.

"Fuck," she said, after a moment or two. "That shit's fucked up."

"Hugging?"

"Caspian."

"I thought you didn't care about him."

Her head snapped up, eyes flashing—the blue fractals in their depths most reminiscent of her brother when she was annoyed. "I don't. He can be miserable forever and I hope he is. But I hate the way he always drags other people down with him."

Ouch. Caspian and Ellery's relationship wasn't so much a car crash as a pileup on the M1. I'd accidentally got caught up in it once before and the situation had become so unspeakably horrendous that it had left me questioning whether I could actually be with Caspian. It was the first time, outside of a sexual context, I'd seen him be cruel for the sake of it. And to Ellery, whom I loved. The worst of it was, I was sure he loved her too, and the way he treated her was his twisted idea of looking after her.

Talk about some Greek tragedy–level irony: Caspian had cast my heart away like a peach stone, and I'd never seen him so clearly or understood him so well. It left me full of hollow places—this useless knowledge, like my useless love. Probably that was why I said something, even though it wasn't my business to.

"You do know that…that what happened with Lancaster Steyne wasn't Caspian's fault, right?"

Ellery curled her lip scornfully. "Yeah, I figured that out."

"It's just sometimes it almost seems as if you blame him? Maybe?"

"Well, I don't. Adults shouldn't fuck kids. And"—she hesitated, only for a second, which was extra startling because Ellery never hesitated—"I could have spoken up."

More than once it had crossed my mind that if cats could talk, they'd talk like Ellery. She walked this impossible line between guarded and vulnerable, and woe betide anyone who couldn't keep up. I kind of *mostly* kept up, and, for whatever reason, she liked me enough that when I didn't, she chose not to claw my face off. But I wasn't ready for this.

"Oh my God," I blurted out. "That's so not on you."

She just shrugged. And suddenly, I was breaking up with Caspian all over again—helpless against his suffering and his terrible certainties. Thinking about it usually made me want to cry, as if I could somehow fix the universe by feeding it all the tears he couldn't shed for himself. Today, though, I was really fucking angry. This huge rusty spike of rage for Lancaster Steyne, the man who had gouged this wound so deeply and into so many people. I hadn't been able to do anything for Caspian, but I would fight the same fight for Ellery. A thousand times if I had to.

I nudged her very lightly, just enough to earn a listless glance. "Listen to me. Please. You aren't the person who fucked up here and neither is Caspian. The person who fucked up is Lancaster Steyne. Who"—my voice lost some of its steadiness—"seems to be the only damn person who *isn't* taking responsibility for it."

Honestly, it messed with my mind. I'd met the man very briefly at Ellery's birthday. Thought he was attractive, almost *because* there was something slightly intimidating about him. And yes, I did hate myself a little bit for that in retrospect. Occasionally, I'd remember his eyes on me like rust flecks on my soul. But what I just couldn't…*process* was how normal he seemed. How untouched by shame. When everyone and everything around him was fucking poisoned.

Ellery tucked her knees under her chin and wrapped her arms around them. "You don't get it."

"I get an eight-year-old shouldn't—"

"For fuck's sake," she snapped. "I know that. It's not the *should*, it's the *could*. Like a fucking car alarm two streets over in my head all the time, knowing it could have easily gone differently."

"But doesn't that apply to everything? I mean, it probably wouldn't have happened at all if your father hadn't died."

The warehouse was old and echoey, so the word *died* took a really long time to go away. I listened to it bouncing off the crossbeams—*di-di-di-died-died-died*—with my hands over my mouth, horrified by what I'd said.

Then Ellery gave a snort of laughter. "Your face."

"I'm sorry. I'm so sorry."

"S'okay. People dying sucks, but it's normal. People fucking your underage brother, not so much."

"I know. And I'm sorry about that too."

That just got another shrug. But then, very quietly, "It was just like everything was being taken away from me. Dad. Then his best friend. Then Caspian."

I wasn't sure I ought to be allowed words anymore. So I made what I hoped was an understanding noise.

"I just"—she waved a dismissive hand, but what she was dismissing, I wasn't sure—"really needed him to be my big brother right then. But I guess it turned out okay in the end."

"Um. How?"

She flashed me a rather feral grin. "I figured out early that needing people is bullshit."

"I'm not *super* sure that's the moral of the story here."

"Well, it works for me."

I really wanted to make a big speech about the power of love and how it didn't have to be weakness to open yourself to others. But I'd believed all that stuff and now I was relationship roadkill. So probably I should have been listening to Ellery, not the other way round.

"Look," I said instead, "for what it's worth, I don't think Caspian ever meant to make you feel like that."

"But he did, so what does it matter?"

"I think it's more that, after what happened with Lancaster, he's sort of convinced himself he…doesn't deserve to have a sister?" Like maybe he'd convinced himself he didn't deserve to have me?

There was a long silence. Ellery's face was turned away, her expression almost entirely concealed beneath the fall of her hair. When she finally spoke, it was in little more than a whisper. "You still don't get it."

"Get what?"

"That it's not"—her voice rose, then broke—"for him to decide."

Before I could answer—though God knows what I would have said—she leapt off the sofa and grabbed her violin case from the table. "I'm going out. You coming?"

"Ellery, I—"

"Yes or no."

"Of course I am."

Her only response was an odd twist of a smile. Well, that and calling us a taxi. And ten minutes later we were off.

CHAPTER 9

Ellery was almost completely silent as we travelled and I knew better than to ask where we were going, so it was very much a *sit back and enjoy the ride*–type deal. Anyway, it wasn't as if I'd had major evening plans. Not unless you counted masturbating and crying over Caspian—activities, let me make it very clear, I intended to pursue sequentially, not concurrently. But I was at least seventy percent certain Ellery wouldn't abandon me in some derelict corner of London. I mean, she hadn't so far.

We followed the curve of the river, through which mellow evening light had woven ribbons of silver and gold, heading west, then south, with London getting leafier and the houses getting fancier the farther we went. When we finally disembarked, it was on one of those time-frozen streets, a wide green common to the left, a march of sprawling Victorian homes on the right, all red brick, ornate windows, and balustrades that looked like they'd been iced on.

Ellery strode off without a second glance, leading me a

short way down the road and then abruptly off it, down a narrow footpath and onto the common. As we pushed our way through some bushes, I found myself wondering—as I often did on my Ellery-related adventures—if I was going to be murdered or arrested or both. Concerns that were not entirely relieved when I suddenly found myself in a graveyard.

A really profoundly derelict graveyard, a maze of shattered stonework, half-drowned in trees and bracken, and watched over by headless angels. So absolute was the desolation, it was hard to believe we were only a few steps away from tennis courts and picnic benches, dog walkers and families and technophobic queers trying to discreetly cruise each other.

"Where are we?" I asked, my voice sinking into the silence as my feet sank into the undergrowth.

"Barnes Old Cemetery." She shot me a speculative look. "It's meant to be haunted."

"Then the joke's on Barnes Old Cemetery because I don't believe in ghosts."

"Maybe they believe in you, Arden."

I shivered, though mostly because it was chilly in the shade. The leaf cover was so thick it gave the light a heavy, greenish tint. Even the wintery sun dapple had a tarnished quality, speckling the stonework with circles the colour of old coins. "What are we doing here?"

"I like it." She sat down on the steps of a monument, its crumbling cross casting misshapen shadows over her face.

"You would," I muttered, rolling my eyes.

"It's where the legend of Spring-heeled Jack began."

"You mean the guy who jumped on people? It's not exactly up there with the Texas Chainsaw Massacre, is it?"

At that moment, something touched my shoulder. Which I handled with great poise by screaming the place down until I realised it had only been a leaf.

When I'd chilled the fuck out, and Ellery had finished laughing at me, she asked, "Do you want to hear a song about a man who murdered his wife?"

"What? Now? Isn't it disrespectful or something?"

She gave me a look. "To dead people? Who are dead?"

I guess she had a point. "To their families?"

"Oh, come on. Does it look like anyone gives a fuck about what happens here?"

"But"—I shuffled awkwardly, the movement turning over several layers of leaf gunge and sending the scent of decay rushing up my nose—"that doesn't mean we shouldn't either."

Ellery was already dragging her violin out of its case. "Who says I don't. Are you listening or fucking off?"

"I'm listening. But why are these things always about men who murder their wives?"

"That's not true. Sometimes they're about men who murder their wives *and* their children."

I looked around for somewhere to sit but it was dead people or bust. So I leaned against a tree instead.

"Okay so," said Ellery, "out of respect for your feelings, this is about a man who murders his wife, but he does it with his wife's sister because they're banging."

"His wife is banging her own sister? They lezed up hardcore in Victorian times."

"No, he's banging the sister. Hence the murder."

"Oh." My face fell. "That's way less interesting."

An Ellery shrug. "I'm not really into dating, but I hear it's good to have interests in common."

"Yeah, but ice-skating or playing board games. Not killing people."

"But what if"—she gave me a flat stare—"you don't like ice-skating or playing board games?"

"Stop being a creeper and play your damn music."

She ducked her head to hide her expression, but I'm pretty sure she was smiling. "You have to help with the chorus. You know I'm not into singing."

This was a trap. This was totally a trap. "What's the chorus?"

"'Oh, what thousands are approaching / Our unhappy fate to see / Elias Lucas, Mary Reeder / Die in Cambridge on a tree.'"

I opened my mouth, then closed it again. And then said, "I'm not even going to ask about the verses."

Putting the violin to her shoulder, Ellery launched into what could only be called a horrifically jolly air, the sharp, bright notes piercing the stillness of the cemetery in the eeriest possible way. The song, as I could have guessed and in fact did guess, was grim AF—but points to a random street balladeer for rhyming *wife and me* with *adultery*. When the band performed, Innisfree did most of the singing, apart from the occasional duet with Dave. She had one of those crystalline sopranos that could make damn near anything sound sweet. Ellery's contralto, on the other hand, rough from lack of use, brought exactly zero sweetness. Just its rare and fragile heart.

It was the only song she sang that night. After that, she mainly idled, playing snatches of things I wasn't anywhere near cultured enough to recognise, although she told me some of it—the most painfully frenetic—was Bartók worrying about fascism. And at some point the rest of the band turned up, Dave with his guitar flung across his back. I couldn't imagine Ellery ever bothering to tell anyone where she was, or where she was going, so God knows how they'd found us. But I guess highly developed Ellery-tracking skills would be a requirement if you wanted to work with her. She looked neither surprised nor displeased to see them all. Which was basically the equivalent of glad.

"Cup of tea, Ardy?" Innisfree was waving an eco-friendly bamboo thermos at me and I suddenly realised that I hadn't eaten since lunchtime and I had no idea how long had gone by while I'd been graveyarding it up with Ellery.

"God. Yes. Please." She passed me the lid and, blowing off the steam, I took a heedless gulp of the liquid within. Regretted it instantly but, sadly, had been raised with good manners when it came to spitting or swallowing. "Uhm. Uh. That's an interesting flavour. What, um, is it? Actually?"

"Milk thistle and dandelion."

"Oh. Uh. Wow. Yes, you can really taste the…um. Those things."

"I know, right?" She smiled radiantly at me. "They're both so good for the liver. And assist with the production of bile."

I gazed disconsolately into the murky depths of my milk thistle and dandelion tea. "I believe you."

Newcomers were starting to drift into the graveyard, finding places to sit or stand or sprawl amongst the thorns and fallen monuments. And in a little while, perhaps at Ellery's instigation, the band began to play. I'd seen them before, several times actually, on account of me being an amazing, supportive friend, but not like this. Without the drums or the keyboard, the music had a raw, stripped-back quality— the sort of intimacy that Ellery usually went out of her way to resist.

I found myself thinking about her birthday party performance. She'd been this piece of wildness then, in her red dress, with her bare feet, and her bow flying across the strings. Tonight, there was just Ellery and the music that spilled from beneath her fingers. And when the last of the light faded, her fans took out their phones so that the darkness around her danced with electric fireflies.

CHAPTER 10

The week or so leading up to my interview with Caspian and Nathaniel was awful. Turned out, dreading something while simultaneously being desperate to get it over with was kind of a headfuck. But having spent three years at Oxford doing pretty much anything to avoid having to get a degree, I was a grand high master of distracting myself. And having a…a…whatever George was to me…lover…person-with-benefits…*paramour* (gosh, that sounded sexy) helped immensely too. I'd slept around plenty and even had a couple of boyfriends before Caspian, but I'd never actually been with someone I was banging regularly in an emotionally uncomplicated way.

Of course, the weirdest thing about it was that what I had with George now was probably exactly what Caspian had tried to set up with me at the beginning. What had he called it again? Sex on a short-term prearranged basis? It was so strange, remembering stuff like that. The scene was still vivid in my mind—the view of the Martyrs Memorial from the Randolph windows, the precise blue of Caspian's eyes on that grey-golden morning, the restless tapping of his foot as he delivered his mildly indecent proposal—and yet felt so long ago. At the time, it had been confusing and actually a little bit humiliating, but thinking about it now filled me with a strange, sad tenderness. If nothing else, that lost boy and equally lost man were going to have an amazing summer together.

Of course, they'd have wasted less of it if they hadn't agreed to such a fundamentally stupid plan in the first place. What was right for me and George could never have been right for me and Caspian. When it came to him, I had way too many emotions, complicated or otherwise. And as much as he'd struggled to admit it, so did he.

Of course, I had emotions for George too. I mean, let's face it, I had emotions about bin liners. But these were nice, safe emotions—liking her, fancying her, knowing I could trust her. On top of which I was getting the kinky education of my dreams. One I would gladly have forgone to have stayed with Caspian, but as consolation prizes went, it was pretty damn consoling.

The night before the interview I mostly spent whining at Nik over Skype, failing to sleep, and fretting about failing to sleep, before dropping off at about five thirty only to have weird but oddly plausible dreams about the interview and then wake unrefreshed and slightly unsure what was real and what wasn't. Except for the fact my phone had run out of battery during the night and therefore my alarm hadn't gone off, so it very rapidly became apparent that what was real was that I was fucking late.

Argh! Just...*arghhhhhhh!* My whole strategy for surviving the day had revolved around being fabulous. Now even showering had gone out the window. And my hair, which had apparently decided to manifest my inner turmoil, just wouldn't calm down. Even the clothes I'd painstakingly laid out last night suddenly looked wrong. But how could they ever look right? There was no dress code for interviewing your ex-boyfriend and the man he was engaged to about their engagement.

Fuck, fuck, oh fucking fuck.

I'd been out of bed for less than three minutes and everything was already disastrous. Also, I'd fallen into a dither-loop, which meant the more aware I was of wasting time, the less capable of action I became. Just standing there blankly in the middle of my bedroom in my tiniest rainbow pants—the one part of my outfit that, barring extreme disaster or good fortune, nobody was actually going to see. In the end I pulled on a pair of unnecessarily tight jeans and a shirt through which I knew you could—in the right light—see the faintest outline of my nipple rings, and threw my old plum velvet jacket on over the top. Yes, it wasn't the most mature decision I could have made, and definitely wouldn't have passed muster with *Debrett's* ("Gentlemen are generally encouraged *not* to display their assets like a right Tarty McTartface"), and probably Caspian wouldn't notice or care, but I don't know, it made me feel more in control of the situation. Even though I wasn't remotely in control of anything.

An hour or so later, sweaty and Tube-battered and still borked in the brain department over what was about to happen, I was sprinting across the marble atrium of Hart &

Associates—a state of affairs that was practically, at this point in my life, a habit. Except when I tumbled out of the lift at Caspian's floor, there was no immaculate and cool-eyed Bellerose to ignite my every match-spark of inadequacy into a forest fire of insecurity. Not something I ever thought I'd miss. And yet there was something deeply, profoundly wrong about seeing a stranger at his desk: one of those elegant middle-aged women who have coiffures instead of haircuts.

Having managed to get less of my breath back than I might have hoped on the ascent, I made a wheezy sound.

"Arden St. Ives?" She had powerful eyebrows and clearly wasn't afraid to use them, lofting them into enquiring domes. "From *Milieu*?"

"Yes. Sorry I'm late. Circle line was carnage."

She was way too professional to acknowledge this transparent lie. "They're waiting for you in the conference room."

"Thank you." I found myself weaving from foot to foot like a small child who has forgotten to use the bathroom. "Should I just, like, go in?"

Bellerose would have said something cutting that would have, in some perverse way, made me feel better. The newcomer just gave me a meaningless smile. "Whenever you're ready, Mr. St. Ives."

Welp. I guess this was it. And it didn't help that the last time I'd been in the conference room, I'd gate-crashed a meeting of Important People TM in order to confront Caspian with my feelings. Of course, it had ended with an arse-twitcher of a kiss against the floor-to-ceiling windows of Caspian's office. But that probably wasn't on the cards today—or ever again—unless Caspian and Nathaniel had way less conservative ideas about matrimony than I'd imagined.

Taking a deep breath, I made my way *extremely carefully* to the conference room. Frankly, I'd already pratfallen enough around both of them. And as God was my witness, I would pratfall no more. I was going to conduct myself like a motherfucking professional.

Except the door wouldn't open. I pressed harder. Then nudged it with my shoulder, probably looking like a really bad mime—Arden trapped in a glass box—to the people inside.

Not-Bellerose cleared her throat. "Next one along."

Fuck me. I finally saw the metal edge that differentiated the door from the windows and seemed to have been designed with the express purpose of being as obscure as possible. Seriously, what was the point of that? Who had thought it was a good idea? Because, if you asked me, that was some hard-core Bernard Tschumi space-violating-bodies shit.

Annoyed, embarrassed, and nonconsensually architecturally defiled, I finally got inside. Caspian, of course, was at his most icy and expressionless. Nathaniel just looked politely bemused.

"The door"—I flapped my hand at it—"looks like the windows. Or the windows look like the door. Either way, you should know it's pretty nonideal in terms of accessibility."

There was a long silence.

"Where's Bellerose?" I asked.

There was another long silence.

Nathaniel, somehow, got even more polite and even more bemused. "Is that part of the interview?"

"No." I stared at Caspian, right into the diamond laser of his gaze. "I just want to know."

"I'm not sure," he said finally, "why it is your business how I conduct mine."

"What happened? Is he okay? Are you?"

"Why would we not be?"

Apparently making a fool of myself in Caspian Hart's conference room was not a one-off for me. "Because he loves you. And he would never have left you voluntarily."

Nathaniel made a gently disbelieving sound. "I think you might have misinterpreted my fiancé's relationship with his executive assistant."

"Oh God, no." I gave a nervous wriggle—wondering if this was how magazines got sued for slander. "I didn't mean they were shagging. I just…I don't know what I meant… nothing bad."

Nathaniel looked like he was about to reply, but then Caspian put a hand on his arm, which, frankly, I did not enjoy. "Even so," he said, "Nathaniel is right. Bellerose was my employee. I have never treated him otherwise, nor would I, nor should he have expected such a thing."

"What did he do?" The glassy emptiness of the conference room seemed to swallow my voice. Swallow me.

"That is not your concern." Caspian had never been such a stranger to me. Even when he'd been nothing more than a voice on the phone. "And you have no reason to think it is."

Oh God, I was going to cry. Please no. Not that. Not now. "I know. But, Caspian, he cared about you. You…you shouldn't…I mean, nobody should…throw that away."

"Perhaps," put in Nathaniel softly, "you should start your

interview. Since you seem so interested in the people who care for Caspian."

Right. The interview. The fucking interview. Caspian seemed on the verge of saying something else—ideally, *This is a terrible idea, why don't we stop*—but he didn't. So I had no choice, really, except to sit down uninvited and plonk my phone on the table.

CHAPTER 11

I'll be recording this," I announced, "to make sure I don't forget anything."

Nothing from Caspian, but a slight nod from Nathaniel.

There was a bottle of excruciatingly posh mineral water in the middle of the conference table, except I would literally have had to crawl across the glass to get it. That left me, dry-mouthed and sick to my stomach, peering at it longingly.

I pushed the corners of my lips into a distorted coat hanger of a smile. "Congratulations on your engagement. How did it happen? Who asked whom?"

"I asked Nathaniel," offered Caspian, finally. "I'm afraid it wasn't as romantic as these things should probably be."

Nathaniel cast him a glowy smile that made me want to kill myself. "It was romantic enough for me, my prince. You see"—he glanced at me again—"we have a long and somewhat complicated history together. But don't they say the course of true love never runs smooth?"

Yeah, they did say that. Shame they didn't also say, when

you're being interviewed for a magazine, don't talk in fucking clichés. God. This was awful and I was *being* awful too. I could barely look at either of them, and the bitter little voice inside me that was providing running commentary on the whole thing was making it difficult to do the actual job I was here to do.

Most basic rule of interviewing: fucking *listen*.

Which meant I had two choices. Give up and run away and spend the rest of my life—or at least the next few years—proofing other people's more exciting stories. Or channel Tim Gunn and make it work. And there was no way I was letting down Tim Gunn. Even in my imagination.

"Did your complicated history," I asked, "mean you were surprised when Caspian asked you to marry him?"

"Hmm." Nathaniel frowned thoughtfully. "Yes and no? We'd broken up a few years ago, but Caspian has always had my friendship. And deep down I think I knew it wasn't over between us."

I turned to Caspian with what I hoped was a super bland look. "Did you feel the same way?"

"It's…" Caspian paused a moment too long. "It's complicated."

"Complicated seems to be coming up a lot."

I hadn't meant to sound arch but I guess I must have, because Caspian instantly frosted over. "That's because adult relationships tend to be, Arden. Passion can be a compelling distraction, but what you want is less important than what is good for you."

Watching Caspian piss off both his ex and current partner simultaneously shouldn't have been endearing. But you had to admit, it took some skill. I mean, I wasn't mad keen on being characterised as the romantic equivalent of a McFlurry, but then, I don't think Nathaniel could have been enjoying his role as love kale either. And maybe I'd just hit my *how much hurt can this one person cause me* limit because, right then, I felt sorry for Nathaniel. Yuck.

"So...uh..." I tried to get his attention, but it just wasn't happening. Instead I volumed up, with about the same poise and naturalness I had, at the age of six, delivered the line "I bring Frankenstein" during the school nativity play. "Tell me about the proposal?"

Nathaniel had been staring at his hands, but now he looked up again. And God knows I hated to admit it, but he was such a pretty man, all gold and chiselled like the sort of classical sculpture owned by especially dodgy popes. "Caspian had been staying with me for a while after some adverse personal circumstances, just as friends. But I think it reminded us both of all the ways we worked. And then he woke me up one night and we had a long talk about our history and our future. At the end of which he told me he couldn't live a life without me in it anymore, and promised to become the man I deserved." Nathaniel paused briefly, the tawny shades of his eyes softening. "Perhaps Caspian's right that it wasn't conventionally romantic, but I'm not really interested in the...the...markers of things. I prefer what's real and comes from the heart."

"Yeah, I get that." It scraped at my soul a bit to agree with Nathaniel. But I did actually agree with him. And I wasn't going to get through this interview at all if I kept responding to him as if he was the villain in my story. Rather than an ordinary person who was the protagonist of his own. "But given you'd broken up before, didn't you have any concerns?"

Nathaniel blinked. Even his fucking lashes were gold. "No. My feelings hadn't changed. But then, I don't believe love does change, only context."

"And how is the context different for you both this time?"

At this, they exchanged the swiftest of looks, but it was still Nathaniel who answered. "Obviously, it's been difficult these last few years, for each of us, in our different ways, but being apart has made us stronger. It's helped us to understand what's important and what's worth fighting for. Looking back, I don't think it was the right time for us before. Now I know it is."

"Not least," I offered, "because you *can* get married. Not so long ago that wouldn't have been possible."

"Indeed."

I tilted my head in what I hoped was a journalist-asking-an-incisive-question way. But truthfully, I just needed a break from Nathaniel telling me all the ways he was better for Caspian than I was. "How do you feel about that?"

"I'm a businessman"—Caspian shrugged—"not a politician."

"Well, yes. But you're a gay businessman."

"My sexual preferences have never been a strong part of my identity."

This left me kind of stymied. I guess in an ideal world nobody's sexuality would *have* to be a strong part of their identity, but my queerness felt integral to me like…my arm or something. I mean, obviously I'd still cope without an arm, but my life would be very different.

"That's because," Nathaniel said softly, "you're rich and

white and upper class enough that it has never mattered."

"Has it mattered to you?" I asked him.

He was silent a moment. Then, "I've never been ashamed or wished I was otherwise and my family have learned to accept me—despite the fact my sexuality is beyond their understanding. But I do remember my father telling me that I would always have to work harder, do more, be better than everyone else around me. Simply because of who I am and who I love."

"Do you think that still holds true?"

"My experiences tend to bear it out. And"—Nathaniel's eyes slid to Caspian—"I don't know how you can insist on an apolitical position when one in five LGBTQ people living in this country have experienced hate crimes, nearly half of LGBTQ students are bullied because of their identity, and in seventy-two countries across the world, same-sex relationships are actually criminalised."

"It's yet another example," murmured Caspian, "of your being an infinitely better man than I am."

The thing is, he was speaking to Nathaniel but he was looking at me. And there it was. Finally. A crack in his prison of ice. I couldn't have told you what I'd been wanting to see—a hint of who I'd fallen in love with or maybe some soft echo of my own sadness. But not the utter desolation of him, like coming back to the place you once called home, and finding it in ruins.

I don't know how long we stared at each other, his eyes as blue and empty as a noonday sky, but he was the first to glance away. And there was something so fucking defeated about it that it caused this volcano of new hurt to open up inside me. I really *really* needed that bastard to stop breaking my heart. I'd thought him being over me was rough. But not being able to comfort him was way worse.

In my head, I was on my knees for him and not in submission, exactly, but because we both needed it. That impossible spinning top of give and take and strength and vulnerability. But obviously, all I could actually do was sit there at the opposite end of a conference table, nodding intelligently, and making the occasional note that I knew I would later find absolutely meaningless.

I shifted my attention to Nathaniel, but he didn't seem inclined to comment further. Which left me holding the ball…or bat…or other kind of sporting-type metaphor I had no idea how to use.

"But," I said to Caspian, "don't you donate a lot of your personal fortune, as well as some proportion of your company's profits, to a range of charitable causes?"

Caspian crossed one leg over the other, his foot moving restlessly. "I don't see why that's relevant."

"It's my interview. I decide what's relevant, Mr. Hart."

His attention snapped back to me with the force of a cane strike—something I now had legit experience of, and had discovered I was not at all into. I honestly hadn't meant to call him that. It had just slipped out. A glob of ectoplasm from the ghost of happier times, when I got to cheek him, and tease him, and turn him on, and he'd not only let me, but maybe even loved me a little bit for it. "I only discuss money in the context of business."

"But this is, like, a matter of public record. It's in your company's annual report. You donated over two billion last year alone."

If he was remotely impressed I'd read, well, downloaded and flicked through Hart & Associates' annual reports (Arden St. Ives: Totes Profesh), he didn't show it. In fact, he just sighed one of his most impatient sighs. "I did, but I couldn't tell you who it went to. I hire people to make these decisions for me."

"Okay. And how do they decide?"

"They do research within a framework I provide for them."

Jesus. This was like pulling teeth. From inside other teeth. Which were in cement. "What's. The. Framework."

"It's complex, but it's mostly a question of efficiency. Emotional appeal and personal experience are extremely ineffective guides for the distribution of resources. My team is tasked with funding projects that produce desirable outcomes, not desirable photo opportunities."

"So," I said slowly, "what you're essentially saying here is that you want to help as many people as possible in the best way you can, rather than choosing causes you feel a personal connection to."

He blinked. "I would never say anything so sentimental. I merely believe that there is a fundamental structural flaw in our approach to large-scale philanthropy. A cause is not inherently worthy of support just because a rich person happens to identify with it."

"So I guess in certain contexts, being apolitical can be just as much an ethical position as…um, not being?"

"For God's sake, Arden." Caspian sounded somewhere between exasperated, amused, and lost. "Why are you so absurdly committed to seeing the good in every situation, irrespective of the futility of the endeavour?"

I shrugged. "What can I say? I'm a billionaire half-full kind of guy."

Caspian raised a hand to cover his mouth, but not before I'd seen his smile. And before I knew it, I was smiling back.

A cough from Nathaniel. He didn't seem too happy right now. I'm not sure I entirely blamed him, but at the same time, someone should have told him you didn't need to cast other people as sinners in order to play the saint.

"We must be close to done here," he said. And then, touching Caspian in a totally unnecessary fashion, "I know how demanding your schedule is, my prince."

I'd been monitoring the clock on my mobile. With this being my actual job and everything, and me not being a hundred percent screwup despite my holiday villa in Screwupville. "We've still got about ten minutes. But speaking of schedules"—I attempted something vaguely conciliatory in Nathaniel's direction, though I'm not sure he bought it—"you've recently been appointed director of the Ainsworth-Singh Foundation. How do you balance your relationship with two such high-powered careers?"

"Actually," came Nathaniel's reply, "it makes it easier because it means you know your partner will always understand that there are times when you have to make work your priority. We both have lives outside the relationship, so neither of us is sitting around in an empty flat all day waiting for the other to come home. I believe the strongest relationships come from a place of equality in all areas."

Well. That wasn't so much a burn as an attempt to salt the fucking earth. "What would you say were the main challenges in your relationship, then?"

Nathaniel's hand had settled lightly on Caspian's knee. "For me, it's when the person you love does things you know are bad for him. When you're with someone, you have a duty to help him be the best version of himself." He got that glowy look again. "Caspian made me very proud when I convinced him to give up smoking again."

"Good for you." I grit my teeth. "How about you, Caspian?"

He'd vanished again. No more secret smiles for me. "Striving to be worthy."

"But is love really about being worthy?"

Nathaniel curled his fingers, stilling the restless motions of Caspian's foot. "I was raised to believe that things that don't take hard work and sacrifice aren't worth having."

"I think"—Caspian hesitated, his voice barely more than a whisper—"I just want to make Nathaniel happy."

Okay. I was done. So *so* done. Turning off the recorder, I stuffed my phone into my pocket and lunged to my feet. "Thank you for your time. This has been..." Out of nowhere I was suddenly giving them a thumbs-up. Even though nobody has given anybody a thumbs-up since 1973. When I was minus twenty-something years old. "This has been *great*."

"I look forward to reading your piece," said Nathaniel, with what seemed to be something close to sincerity. I guess I'd been right—this was more than an Arden-punching exercise to him. He'd really wanted it for some reason: a public statement of their unity.

"Enjoy your, y'know, lives."

I was halfway to the door at a full canter when Nathaniel's voice stopped me. "Arden?"

"Yes?"

"Now that we're done with the business side of things, I was wondering…" He broke off, and there was something oddly vulnerable about it. "Would you like to come to dinner with us?"

I lost control of my shoulder bag. Scrappy pieces of paper, old bus tickets, a tampon Ellery had made me carry for her once, and the remains of a half-eaten packet of sweets spilled across the pristine office floor. "What? Shit. Oh no, my jellybeans. What?"

"Well," Nathaniel went on, making a tremendous effort to ignore the fact I was crawling about on my hands and knees, "I've thought for a while we didn't get off to what you might call the best start. And since you're a friend of Caspian's, I would like to remedy that."

I paused, jellybeans bouncing from between my fingers. The thing is, I did not want to go for dinner with Caspian and Nathaniel. Because, while I could theoretically imagine worse things—being stuck on an alien spaceship and hunted by a Xenomorph, for example—they weren't happening to me there and then, and I could be pretty sure I wouldn't be expected to smile and say thank you afterwards. On top of which, I was not Caspian's fucking friend. I was his ex who was still in love with him.

"Look," I tried. "Like, the thing is—"

Fuck. He'd got me. There was no way I could get out of this. I couldn't claim to be busy because the invitation was too vague ("Unfortunately, Nathaniel, I'm washing my hair literally forever"), and I couldn't just refuse because that would make me look like a total dick in front of Caspian. To him, this probably seemed like his current partner doing the decent thing by his previous, so my options were: Be the bad guy who rejected a peace offering, or tacitly accept Nathaniel's reframing of my role in Caspian's life. Basically I'd been friend-zoned by proxy. If he hadn't been doing it right to my face, I'd have been a little bit impressed.

Suddenly, Caspian was out of his chair and kneeling in front of me. I'd forgotten the grace in him when he wasn't self-conscious. The heedless power. And God, that cologne of his: those sweet, dark notes, all cocoa and sandalwood and the promise of wicked things. Oh help. He was too close and too beautiful and I wanted him too much.

He offered me a slightly fluffy jellybean. "Do come, Arden. It would be good to see you."

"Would it?" That was fucking news to me. "Would it really?"

"Of course it would. As Nathaniel says, we're friends… aren't we?"

Oh, for God's sake. *Et tu, Caspian?* But I didn't quite have the bollocks to say *No actually, I'm your scorned ex-lover and you know it.* The thing is, Nathaniel inviting me to a Yah Boo Sucks Ardy dinner, I could just about get my head round. But why the fuck was Caspian on board with this? He didn't *actually* want to see me, did he? And if he did, he had a fucking funny way of showing it.

Oh, wait. What was I saying? This was Caspian Hart. Not speaking to you for three months, then glaring at you coldly was practically his love language.

"Of course," I said, through gritted teeth. "And dinner would be lovely."

CHAPTER 12

Somehow, I made it out of Caspian's office. But as soon as I was safely on the street, I collapsed into a huddle against the wall of the building, not sure whether I was going to pass out or throw up, my body reacting about as well as it had the time they made us do one of those beep test things in PE. But I got over it, and quite a bit faster than I had the beep test, which had left me so emotionally and physically traumatised Hazel had stormed into school and got it banned. Shame she couldn't do that to Nathaniel, really. Although probably part of being a responsible grown-up and shit meant you couldn't get your mum's girlfriend to handle all your problems for you.

At any rate, I was starting to get funny looks. I was already way out of place in this part of London—probably I was the only person within a square-mile radius who wasn't wearing a suit—but I wasn't helping my case by throwing a massive wobbly. Time to limp back to the office. And at least I could compose myself on the Tube, since, far as I could tell, the whole point of being on the Tube was to ignore the existence of as many as people as possible.

Before I vanished underground, though, I stood in Liverpool Street Station, underneath the great iron ribs of its vaulted ceiling, scrolling through my contacts, looking for Bellerose. He'd given me his number while I'd been dating Caspian, but Caspian had also insisted I use a second phone and I couldn't remember if it had occurred to me to synch my data in the haze of newly dumped heartache. Oh. Apparently I had. But then, there had been a small window of crystal-sharp competence when I'd been moving out of One Hyde Park. Having fucked up so many things with Caspian, and in so many ways, I'd taken a terrible pride in clearing out of his life neatly and efficiently.

He was a big fan of efficiency, was Caspian. And suddenly I was remembering him ruining Carcassonne, and missing him so very much. Missing him and mourning all the could-have-beens that had been trampled underfoot like cherry blossom in spring.

Enough. I called Bellerose.

The phone rang for a really long time. Just rang and rang—not even cutting off or going to voicemail. And I was just about to give up and try again later when he answered, managing to sound both exactly the same as ever, and not at all like himself: "What do you need, Arden?"

My mouth plopped open unhelpfully. Probably I should have, y'know, at least thought about what I was going to say to him. "I…I don't think I need anything. I mean…I was kind of wondering if you were okay?"

"Why wouldn't I be?"

"Well, I saw Caspian today. With Nathaniel, I mean. And you weren't there."

"He didn't fire me, if that's what you're concerned about." An odd note of bitterness touched Bellerose's voice. "I'm *taking some time*. Involuntarily."

What the fuck did that mean? Bellerose was the perfect, um, whatever the hell his job was. And he was devoted to Caspian to a degree that, in any other context, would have been creepy. Actually, maybe it was creepy. But that just made this whole thing weirder. I was pretty sure it was psychologically impossible for Bellerose to do anything that Caspian didn't want. "What I'm concerned about," I said, "is you. I know how you feel about Caspian."

He made a contemptuous sound—a sort of laugh, if laughing had a nasty second cousin nobody liked. "Don't turn this into something sentimental. It's humiliating enough already."

"God, you're so fucking like him." Maybe that was why I wanted to shake both of them. "It's okay to have feelings."

"I am well aware of that, thank you. But I wouldn't expect you to understand mine."

I gave up. I was starting to wonder why I'd tried at all. Why I kept on trying when the only thing it accomplished was making me feel small and crappy and useless. "Have it your way. Sorry to bother you." Yet still something kept me on the phone. "Look, you've got people, right?"

"Excuse me?"

"People who are there for you."

"Oh yes," he said airily. "I'm surrounded by them. Beating them off with sticks."

"Okay now you're just, like, *lying* to me."

Another pause. "I…I'm not really a people person."

"So in other words, Caspian has forced you into exile, you're all alone, and you're not okay."

"Well, somebody got out the feisty side of bed this morning."

"Bellerose…and, for the record it seems really weird to be calling you Bellerose, but I don't quite have the balls to use Justin…you can be as salty as you like, but"—and I actually stamped my foot in the middle of a train station—"I'm trying to be your people here."

More silence. Even deeper than before. "Why?"

"Because you've been there for me."

"I was there for Caspian. You were incidental."

"If you're trying to hurt my feelings, you have chosen an epically bad time. Because that doesn't even make the top ten of shitty things said to me today."

"I'm not trying to hurt your feelings." There was something about Bellerose's too-clean, too-sharp accent that made nearly everything sound faintly sarcastic. But right now, it seemed like he meant what he was saying. "I just don't want you to be under any illusions."

I'd had perilously similar talks with Caspian. Usually with unhappy outcomes. "I'm not. Whether you wanted to or not, whether you would have chosen to or not, you've helped me a lot. And I would like you to know that means something."

I was ninety-nine percent certain he was going to reject me. And thirty-nine percent certain he was going to do it in a totally soul-destroying way. Because, let's face it, soul destroying was the theme of my day.

"Very well," he said. "What do you want to do?"

Good question. Very good question. "Um. We could meet up? Talk or something?"

"Tell me when, tell me where. I have nothing but time."

He offered this up so matter-of-factly that it sounded bleak as fuck. "Tonight? It'll have to be after work. So maybe sixish? The Shaston Arms, just off Carnaby Street?"

"I'll be there."

He'd hung up before I could even say goodbye. Bellerose was also way into efficiency.

And holy shit, we were meeting for drinks. The whole idea suddenly seemed wildly outlandish. I mean, given that all our previous conversations had revolved around whatever crisis I happened to be having at the time, what the fuck was I going to say to him? Well, I guess I'd figure it out. And rely on the fact that Bellerose had told me once he didn't find me completely repulsive. Truly, was that not the bedrock of friendship?

* * *

Once I got back to the office, I fully intended to dive straight into transcribing the conversation from the recording like a proper grown-up journalist but foundered on account of it turning out to be a horrendously shitty job. Every time I heard Caspian, I wanted to cry, and every time I heard Nathaniel, I…also wanted to cry. But in a really angry way. None of which was really conducive to, y'know, professionalism.

"Hello, poppet."

I glanced up to discover George lounging at the end of my desk and looking impossibly hot in a very fitted, bottle-green suit and skyscraper Louboutins. "Go away please," I said virtuously. "I am very busy and important."

"Very busy and important taking all the staples out your stapler and putting them back in again?"

"That's very vital maintenance. Otherwise I could try to staple something and it wouldn't work and the world would end."

One of her eyebrows lifted in this unconvinced way. "How was the interview?"

I was pretty sure keeping track of days when I'd have to do something miserable-making was above and beyond the call of duty for a kinky fuckbuddy. But then, George was kind of above and beyond in most areas. She'd even tactfully excluded me from the photoshoot so I wouldn't have to carry things and be helpful while my ex-boyfriend looked happy and beautiful with his new fiancé. "Sort of a disaster," I admitted. "But not in any way that will stop me writing a bunch of fluff about how lovely it is that rich gays can get married now."

George gave a theatrical sigh. "Sometimes I think same-sex marriage is the worst thing that could have happened to us. It's only been legal for ten minutes and already queer relationships are getting stuffed into all the same anodyne little boxes as straight ones."

"And there was me, dreaming of the day you were going to walk me down the aisle."

"How about"—she smirked at me—"I walk you to lunch?"

Tempting. Except I was a mature, career-minded adult

who wasn't going to run away from his own interview. "I'd love to, but I really do need to get on with this."

"Your stapler will still be here when you get back. And taking some time to clear your head might let you actually do the job you're currently pretending to do."

"What if it just makes it worse? And I spend the rest of my life trying to write this article."

"Then at least you'll have had lunch."

I drooped.

"There, there, Ardy." Reaching out, she chucked me lightly under the chin. "I'm going to take you to my club. Which you're going to like very much because it has panelled walls and a wonderful menu and very long tablecloths."

"Why am I suddenly into tablecloths?"

"I'm implying something lewd. Do try to keep up."

"*Ohhh.* You mean you want me to blow you under the table?"

She laughed. "No, poppet. I mean I will *allow* you to blow me under the table if you're good."

Guess what? I was good.

* * *

Of course, when I got back—probably later than I should have—the recording was still waiting for me, but I felt altogether better about grappling with it. And the wine I'd had at lunch certainly didn't hurt. I stuck in my headphones and got back to Nathaniel and Caspian. I'd expected only hearing their voices would give me a little bit of distance, but it didn't at all. It took me straight back to the conference room but in this "freeze rotate enhance" Blade Runnery way that let me pick up on details I hadn't been in any state to handle at the time. Like the fact they looked so damn good together. Elegant, sophisticated, but not too threatening: the gay couple you'd invite to your dinner party to prove you weren't a homophobe.

In retrospect, it hadn't been the perfect interview. But it wasn't exactly a Frost-Nixon situation. It was mostly just, *Gays can marry now, look how nice and handsome they are.* Depressingly enough, I found it the easiest thing in the world to spin Caspian and Nathaniel into exactly the sort of story Mara was looking for. The ruthless billionaire and the passionate altruist. Just enough queer to be affirming but not so much it was challenging. A relationship that was aspirational and yet still accessible. I honestly couldn't tell if I was rocking my job or destroying my soul. Maybe a little bit of both? And this being *Milieu*, I managed to get at least five hundred words out of Caspian's family, the aristocratic patrons of Nathaniel's charity, and the jeweller behind their bespoke engagement rings.

By end of day, I'd drunk four cans of Diet Coke, spilled one, and eaten all the loose jellybeans I'd been able to dig out of the lining of my bag. But I'd also banged out a solid first draft. And y'know something, despite a faintly queasy feeling that could just as well have been down to the jellybeans-fluff-caffeine combo, I was calling that a win.

CHAPTER 13

I saved the document eighty-five thousand gazillion times, just to be on the safe side, packed myself up, made sure my desk was pristine, and hurried off to meet Bellerose. What with being slap bang in the middle of Mayfair, the get-drunk-after-work options were plentiful but not entirely to my taste—chain pubs that tried to pretend they weren't by making a big deal of their authentic Tudor fittings, and cocktail bars where you had to pay twenty quid for a martini. But make for Soho and you could find places like the Shaston Arms, with hanging baskets and fire-engine-red paintwork and, um, the two doors on account of the legit actual wall running down the middle of the building. It was also so dinky that in the summer and early autumn most of the patrons ended up spilling onto the pavement with their beers. Basically, it was a pub that was quirky beyond the point of practicality. Which, of course, meant I was way into it.

It was early enough that it wasn't yet impossible to squidge in. And having squidged, I found Bellerose already occupying one of the booths—which were my favourite place to sit, because they made me feel like a ne'er-do-well in a Victorian novel.

"Hi." I managed to put my shoulder bag down without spilling anything and slid in opposite.

"Arden."

Bellerose was getting some attention—furtive, English attention but attention nonetheless. Partly, I think, because he looked too attractive to be real. But also because he was knitting.

"Can I get you a drink?" I asked, trying not to stare. It wasn't that my mind was being blown by the sight of a man engaged in a hobby traditionally practiced by grandmas. It was more that we were in a pub and that it was Bellerose. I mean, he'd told me he knitted. But I'd found it impossible to imagine and, consequently, only half believed him.

He shook his head. "No thank you."

"So, like, we're in this place called a pub. And what pubs do is they own a building, and in that building they sell beer and other alcoholic beverages, and in return for buying the beer and other alcoholic beverages they let people stay, for free, in the building that they own. And from the money they make from selling their beer and other alcoholic beverages, the pub gets to keep their building and the people who bought the beer and other alcoholic beverages get to have fun, and everyone lives happily ever after."

At this, Bellerose glanced up, though his needles didn't stop moving. "I'll have water."

"Bellerose—"

"I'm an alcoholic."

"Water it is then. Unless," I added quickly, "you'd rather go somewhere else. Coffee? Juice bar? Bubble tea? I think there's a bubble tea place round the corner. Except I don't really get bubble tea because there's the whole liquid thing but also the bubble element and that makes my throat confused, so I keep thinking I'm going to choke. And once I was so confused I sneezed and that was bad. That was *so* bad."

"I'm fine."

"Okie-dokie."

Trying not to dwell on the fact I'd just said "okie-dokie" in cold blood, I slunk over to the bar and ordered a mineral water for Bellerose and, after dithering for about six years over whether it would come across as patronizing or supportive if I had water too, a bottle of Blandford Fly for me. I'd never been a huge beer drinker, but I'd learned real quick when I discovered how expensive wine and cocktails were in London.

"So"—I made it all the way back to the booth without spilling anything—"what are you knitting?"

"A shawl."

"Is it for you?"

Oh yay. Another Bellerose Look TM. Just what I wanted. "Under what circumstances would I wear a shawl?"

"For your Elinor Dashwood cosplay?" When he didn't respond—not even a smile—I had to go on. "Who is it for?"

"It's not for anyone."

"Then why are you knitting it?"

"Because I like knitting."

I suddenly had this vision of Bellerose living in a house full of unwanted shawls. "Couldn't you make something for you?"

"I like shawls."

"What's so good about shawls?"

He paused for a moment, apparently seriously thinking about it. "The construction is interesting, they're fairly quick to knit, and I find there are many opportunities for colour."

"It's really pretty," I offered. "Like a sunset."

"Thank you."

"Doesn't it make you sad, though? Creating something that won't get used?"

"I've never really thought about it." His hands stilled and I noticed they weren't quite steady, the nails bitten almost to nothing. "Knitting is the thing I do for myself."

Oh God, I was out of my depth already. I'd never really interacted with Bellerose outside of a context that wasn't defined by Caspian, so I had no idea who he was the rest of the time. And the thing was, I was sort of getting the sense he didn't either.

"Look"—I took a huge gulp of beer, and immediately regretted it because the sharp ginger aftertaste gave me hiccoughs—"is it (hic) okay if I ask what happened with (hic) Caspian?"

"There's not much to tell. I asked him if he believed Nathaniel could truly make him happy."

This gave me a bunch of awkfeels because, on the one hand, I was the tiniest bit thrilled Bellerose thought that way—not least because it validated my own relationship with Caspian—but this was supposed to be about him, not about me. "And he (hic) fired you? What the fuck?"

"It's not my place to question him."

"What? Ever? Like (hic) you've never said, would you like

a cup of coffee or can you fit in an extra (hic) meeting on the (hic) twenty-third?"

"Arden, the next time you hiccough, I will give you fifty pounds."

I stared at him wide-eyed and absolutely unable to hiccough. "How…how did you do that?"

"I'm magic."

"You *are*."

To my surprise, he went a little pink. "I have some facility when it comes to solving other people's problems, even when they are profoundly superficial. And as regards Caspian, of course I don't mean I've never literally asked him questions. But he certainly didn't invite my trespass into his personal affairs."

"It wasn't a trespass. You were looking out for him."

"I serve. I don't second-guess."

"For fuck's sake," I said, in my very outsidest voice. "You were his executive assistant, not his slave."

No reply.

And I was only human, so I couldn't quite resist asking, "Did you mean it, though? About Nathaniel?"

"I don't know. I only know that Caspian was different when he was with you. There was a lightness in him I hadn't realised wasn't there before."

"Oh…" I guess I'd been hoping to be further vindicated. But no. This was just depressing.

"I even heard him singing in the office once, when he thought I'd left for the day."

"Caspian can sing?"

"Most assuredly he cannot." Bellerose put his needles on

the table and his hands on top of them, his gaze directed downwards so I couldn't read his expression. "I would have done anything to help him hold on to that peace. But it wasn't in my power."

To my dismay, I caught the gleam of moisture against his cheek. "Hey now." Wanting to comfort him, but not knowing how he'd take a touch, I reached out and patted his knitting gently. "Nobody has that kind of power in someone else's life. While I can't say I've been entirely thrilled with Caspian's decision making over the past however-many months, he's still responsible for his own choices."

"And I," whispered Bellerose, with a depth of sorrow I wasn't remotely prepared for, "am useless to him."

"Believe me, you are the least useless person I've ever met. You are so not useless that if you look up *useless* in the dictionary, it says, 'antonyms: see *Bellerose*.'"

He snuck a glance at me, his eyes hopeless, and shiny with tears. "I was made for Caspian."

"Uh. Made?" Maybe he was actually a robot. It would explain his hyper-competence and eerie perfection—and at this point, I wouldn't put anything past Google.

"It"—he blinked—"it's a long story. It doesn't matter."

"Are you sure? I'm good to hear a long story, if you want to tell it."

"I…not at the moment."

"Okay. But listen." I rested my elbows on the table and shuffled in closer. "Firstly, you said yourself this was temporary or whatever. Caspian won't want you to leave."

"Perhaps, but I must. I don't know how to help him anymore. And without him, I don't—I am nothing."

I was starting to regret the beer because my head was spinning. "Don't say that. *Please* don't say that."

"I'm an addict and a whore." He spoke without rancour—without any particular emotion, actually. "If Mr. Steyne hadn't seen something in me he could use, I would most likely be dead by now."

That name was pretty much guaranteed to ruin my day. And my day hadn't been much to write home about to begin with. Fuck, I should have known Bellerose would have some messed-up connection to Lancaster "BDSM Svengali" Steyne. I mean, he'd given Caspian a bespoke bondage dungeon. Of course he'd also given him someone to put in it. And I had no idea what to say because *Would you like to go into more detail about your emotional trauma with a known abuser?* just seemed kind of…not okay.

"Well," I said finally, and only slightly pathetically, "I'm really glad you're not dead, Bellerose."

"Ilya. My mother called me Ilya."

"And you're sure you want me to use it too?"

"You said you felt uncomfortable with Bellerose."

"I'll deal. It's your name—you get to choose."

"I don't like choices." He picked up his knitting again. "I never have."

This left me faffing helplessly with the label on my Blandford Fly. "What will you do? I mean, if you don't think you can work for Caspian anymore?"

"Mr. Steyne will be expecting me back."

"Do *not*"—I said fiercely—"do that."

Ilya gave a faint smile. "I wasn't intending to."

I de-hackled. "Oh. Okay then. Good."

"What he found in me was always there, and I'm grateful. What he did to Caspian was wrong, and I shall never forgive him."

Apparently I wasn't capable of moderation when it came to Lancaster Steyne. "I've got to tell you, from everything I've heard about the man, if I learned he'd saved a kitten from a fire, I'd be inclined to think it was for his own fucked-up purposes."

"Yes, of course." The click of Ilya's needles seemed disconcertingly merry given the topic of conversation. "But the kitten would still be broadly better off."

"If that kitten was me, I'd take the *burn to the death* option."

"That's because you've never been on fire."

I opened my mouth to argue, but then realised I didn't actually have a counterpoint. Largely because he was right. "I'm sorry," I said instead, "your life has taken you to such shitty places that you needed Lancaster Steyne."

"I have no regrets. Salvation and destruction can be remarkably similar experiences, and I much prefer the way I live now to the way I did before. In any case, you don't need to worry. I will not return to him."

"And he'll let you go?"

"Of course. He has no interest in me whatsoever." Ilya gave the slightest of shrugs. "He only cares about Caspian—to a definition of caring that most would find alien."

My stomach roiled unhappily. "Why the fuck isn't he in prison?"

"Because that's not what happens to people like him."

"I hate everything." I plonked my head down on the table and lay there for a little bit.

Ilya reached out and stroked my hair in a slightly mechanical way. "There, there."

"What...um...what was that?"

"I'm comforting you. I think."

I couldn't help giggling at his uncertainty. "Thank you."

"I'm sorry. It's not really part of my skill set."

"It's okay. And none of this is about me. So"—I pulled myself upright again—"I should really stop whining."

He gazed at me solemnly. "Not on my account."

"I'm good. I promise." I mean, I wasn't good. I was sad and fucked up and angry on behalf of a lot of people. But I wasn't quite selfish enough to expect consolation for it."

"You look tired."

"Long day. I had to interview Caspian and Nathaniel for *Milieu*, though honestly it went about as well as could be expected, considering. I just"—a yawn pounced on me out of nowhere—"gosh, sorry. I just didn't sleep so well last night because I was worrying about it."

"Understandably. And I shouldn't keep you."

Urgh. Why did people say stuff like that? I could never tell if they meant "I would really like to hang out with you longer but I feel self-conscious about taking up your time," "this has been lovely but I have other things to do," or "this has been awful and now I am trying to get to rid of you." Anyway, I was still a little scared of...Bellerose? Ilya? So in case it was Option 3, I nodded. "I'm really glad you agreed to meet me, though."

"Yes, I"—a bemused expression crossed his face—"haven't entirely hated it either."

"I aim to please."

I grinned at him in what I hoped was a winning fashion, but he sort of flinched. "I don't have much interest in my own pleasure and I'd prefer it wasn't a concern for others."

"Sorry." I can't say I was all that okay with the idea, but it was a world of not my call. "I mean, I wouldn't want you to do anything against your comfort on my behalf. But if it helps, you pleased me."

It was the first time I'd really seen him smile. And, God, what a smile it was, as heart-stoppingly perfect as the rest of him. "Thank you."

We left our booth, eased our way through the crowds and out into the street. I wasn't entirely sure how to say goodbye—it didn't seem like we were in hug territory yet—so I just mumbled something incoherent, slung my bag over my shoulder, and took off. The day had properly taken its toll, and I was seriously looking forward to falling face-first onto my mattress, except something made me pause. Glance behind me. And there was Ilya, a lost angel in the fading light, watching me leave.

I went back. "Are you all right?"

He nodded slowly.

"Are you sure?"

Another nod.

Clearly, I could ask a thousand times and not get a different answer. But I could recognise not-okayness when it was standing right in front of me. Weirdly, it made me think of Nik—who for three years of my life had been there for me, in my okayness, and not-okayness, and everything in between. Guess it was time to pay it forward.

"Look," I said, "if you don't want to be alone right now—

which is something I totally get—you can come home with me. Though I should warn you, I live with Ellery and there will be no food, probably no hot water, and also people sitting around singing about dead babies."

His gaze slid away from mine. "I…"

"And I'm going to be shit company."

"I'll be in your way."

"I'll be unconscious. You will not be in my way."

"Then"—he swallowed—"yes. Thank you."

"Just be aware: If I keel over from exhaustion en route, you'll have to give me a piggyback."

I was kidding. Mostly. But of course, Ilya didn't take it that way—and for a second or two, I really thought he was going to sweep me up Disney prince style. It was kind of a relief, in the end, that he didn't. Between Caspian and Nathaniel, and my own confused, hurting little heart, my world felt enough like Silly Putty as it was. Maybe if I…if things…if Ilya…had been just one squeeze of lemon juice different, then letting him carry me home could have been the start of something. And the end. But we weren't and it wasn't. And so we walked back together, with the loss of the man we both loved between us like a shadow.

CHAPTER 14

An hour or so later, I arrived home with Ilya. An event which didn't even merit a slow blink from Ellery.

"Hi, Bellerose," she said. "The bathroom's a state if you want to clean it."

Somewhere between the Tube station and the warehouse, he'd started carrying my stuff. I still wasn't quite sure how it had happened, but one thing had emerged clearly from the experience: My shoulder bag made me look like a womble; Ilya wore it like it was high fashion. Right now, he put it carefully down by the door. "I'd be glad to."

"No way." I made what I hoped was an Ellery-checking gesture. If such gestures even existed. "He's not cleaning the bathroom."

"Why not? It needs doing."

"He's my guest. Guests do not clean bathrooms."

Ellery scowled. "He's my brother's lapdog."

"Actually, he's not. So you're not going to get to Caspian through him."

"Oh. Well, in that case, don't bother."

"What," asked Ilya unhelpfully, "about the bathroom?"

This earned him one of Ellery's long, hard stares. "Who gives a fuck about the bathroom?"

I did. A little bit. But it was winter in the garden of my fucks right now. "I'm not doing this. My face needs food and then all of me needs to be unconscious."

At this, Innisfree, who had been absorbed in the piece of music she was writing with Ellery, looked up. "I can make you something if you like."

I wilted like old broccoli. "Oh God, Inn, please don't think I'm ungrateful. It's the sweetest thing in the world the way you try to take care of me. But what I really want right now is a cheese toastie on, like, bad-for-me white bread full of gluten, with bright yellow cheese that has been squeezed directly out of a cow. And maybe some artificially preserved factory-made Branston Pickle."

There was a long silence. Innisfree's mouth opened and closed a few times. Fuck, I think I'd really upset her.

Eventually she said, "Are you sure you can eat that?"

"I'm going to eat it so hard."

"No, I just mean…"

Ellery had covered her mouth with both hands, and was now actually rocking back and forth as if she was having some kind of seizure. Well, that was in no way worrying.

"I don't understand," Innisfree went on slowly. "Ellery told me you were a lactose-intolerant vegan with coeliac disease."

A wild honking sound emerged from between Ellery's fingers. After a second or two, I realised she was laughing—

and laughing like I'd never heard her laugh before, without a trace of control or self-consciousness.

Innisfree gazed at Ellery with utter incomprehension. "Why did you do that?"

"Because...because..." Ellery's eyeliner was running unchecked down her cheeks, giving her the air of a deranged harlequin. "Because...I knew you'd both be...too nice to say anything."

"For most people," said Innisfree, "that wouldn't be a good reason."

Ellery shrugged. "You know how I feel about most people."

I left them to what would inevitably devolve into gentle bickering and wandered into the kitchen area, where I was relieved to discover half a loaf of bread and some moderately unmolested cheddar in the fridge. Of course, there was no Branston, or even Marmite, because Ellery had a somewhat disturbing capacity for both—and tended to eat them straight from the jar.

Ilya trailed after me, in a far too puppyish fashion for a man who looked like a catwalk model. "Can I help?"

I was going to point out that it was a cheese toastie, not the storming of the Bastille, but he seemed to like being involved in things, no matter how menial. "Sure. You can grate and I'll butter."

It was strange to see him clumsy, especially after the ease and effortlessness of his knitting. I didn't say anything, though. Just stuffed my toastie with too much cheese and covered the bread with too much butter, and flopped the whole thing into a frying pan, Ilya watching me with an intensity the task really didn't deserve.

"There's not going to be a test later," I told him.

"But maybe"—he gave me this forlorn little smile—"someday I will meet someone who would like a cheese toastie."

"Well, this is how my mum makes them. The key is cheddar that tastes just a little bit like socks and lots of butter on the outside."

In a minute or two, I was done. The bread, which had gone a perfect golden-brown in the pan, had lost a little bit of structural integrity, but thankfully all the cheese that had squoodged out the sides had acted as a sealant. It was a perfect specimen of toastiness is what I'm saying. I eased it onto the one clean plate I could find and sawed it diagonally—it *had* to be diagonally—in half. Nudged one side towards Ilya.

"There you go."

He blinked. "For me?"

"Greater love hath no man than this, that a man lay down his toastie for his friends."

"But…"

"I'm kidding. Have a piece. I mean"—let's face it, authority did not come naturally to me—"unless you don't want to. Then, obviously, um, don't."

"Thank you."

Gingerly, he manoeuvred his half off the plate and took a bite. I should probably have warned him that toasties tend to fight back, because within seconds he was embroiled in his very own action thriller: *Attack of the Sixty-Foot Cheese String*. In general, people did not look good with food dangling out of their mouths. But I guess because Ilya was usually so terrifyingly immaculate, I actually found him kind of adorable just then.

"I'm sorry," he said, blushing, and not very successfully trying to return at least some of the cheese to the bread. "That was not very dignified."

"Dignity's overrated." I hopped up onto the edge of the counter to finish my sandwich.

"You're only saying that because you don't have any."

I laughed. "Harsh words considering you're in my house eating my toastie."

"I'm sorry." He hung his head. "I don't cope very well with messy things."

Urgh. Having Bellerose—having *Ilya*—apologise to me was just weird. Maybe I was more masochistic than I thought, but I'd always secretly enjoyed his sharpness. "Then this is really not the supper dish for you."

"I still appreciate your sharing it."

"My mum used to make them. I don't remember all that well because I was so young, but I can remember sneaking downstairs when my dad was sleeping. How we knew the creak in every stair. And how magical it felt, even on bad days, to have cheese toasties at midnight."

Ilya narrowed his eyes. "Were there are a lot of bad days for you when you were growing up?"

"Towards the end, yes. But then we left." I swung my feet idly and peeled a piece of crust away from the bread. "And we took our toasties with us."

"Are they still magical to you?"

They reminded me of Mum. Her strength. "Hell yes they are."

When we were done eating, Ilya wanted to do the washing up, but I wouldn't let him—not least because he would have had to excavate the sink before the task could even be attempted—and then we trooped past Innisfree and Ellery, who were smoking a joint, and up to my loft. Which was looking even more chaotic than usual since, in my morning panic, I had apparently taken out every item of clothing I owned from whatever receptacle that held it, be it suitcase, drawer, laundry basket, or hanging rail, and cast it across the floor.

"Um." I picked up a sock, as if that was going to make any difference at all. "Sorry. You know, you can leave if you want to."

Ilya gave me one of his rare smiles. "You did warn me. And I think I'll survive."

"But you said you didn't like mess."

"My own."

"You're not a mess, Ilya." I dug out my hippo pyjamas and began complicatedly getting into them, trying not to be too naked at any point during the process. I mean, I'd invited him back for company and support. Not to bear witness to my wang. "You're just in a temporary state of reorganisation."

Another faint, fleeting smile. And, oh God help me, he was taking his clothes off, and with much less awkwardness than I had. I tried not to look but, I mean, I'm only human. I looked. Yep, he was perfect. Gold and smooth and exquisite, in that impossibly lean and muscular way that was the current fashion for male bodies. Seriously, I could have used the grooves of his abs as an inkwell. And isn't that quite the image?

"You know you're stunning, right?" I said.

He shrugged. "I'm glad to please."

Tossing T-shirts and jeans and jumpers off the mattress, I de-rumpled my duvet and climbed under it. Ilya joined me a moment or two later, bringing very welcome heat, and the clean scent of his skin.

"And you're sure," he whispered, "this is still all right?"

"It would be a shitty time to decide it wasn't." I retrieved my Rainbow Dash pillow and plumped it up. "Honestly, though, it's good. I enjoy having sleep company."

"Would you like to have sex?"

Okay, so I hadn't seen that coming. "Pardon me?"

He rolled onto his side, all his absurd loveliness suddenly far too close. "I have some facility at it."

"I'm sure that's true, but are you even attracted to me that way?"

"I'm not attracted to anyone that way. But you've had a difficult day and seem to have a very sensuous nature, so I thought you might appreciate a sexual release."

He wasn't wrong. Under other circumstances, I would definitely have been indulging in a consolation wank. However… "That's really nice of you," I said carefully, "except I'm kind of only into sleeping with people who want to sleep with me."

"I didn't say I didn't want to sleep with you."

"And who would also get something out of it."

"I would get something out of it." It was too dark to read his expression, but he sounded sad. Which wasn't exactly a turn-on for me. "I would dearly love to make you feel good, Arden."

"I…uh." Help, I had no idea how to respond.

My initial instinct was that this was a Fibonacci Sequence of a bad idea, an ever-expanding spiral of infinite nope for both of us. But I didn't want to just dismiss him either. I'd learned from George that sex came in many colours—even if Ilya wasn't interested in fucking the way I was, that didn't mean I got to second-guess his choices. Which was the other thing. I had to believe these *were* his choices. That who he was, and what he wanted, existed separately from Lancaster Steyne—something Caspian had never been able to accept for himself. Or even accept from me.

And yet Ilya wasn't Caspian. I didn't know him well enough to understand what would help him and what would hurt him—and while it wasn't on me to make those calls on his behalf, I got to make them for me. I couldn't deny there was a kinky appeal in the idea of being sexually indulged by a gorgeous man solely committed to my pleasure, but given we'd both been semi-recently dumped by Caspian, there was no guarantee the whole business wouldn't devolve into a two-way pity-fuck of woe and desperation.

Which…just. No.

Maybe I'd keep it for a fantasy—the sort of fantasy where I'd be wearing riding boots, and nobody was real or suffering or alone.

"Would you take it the wrong way," I asked, "if I turned you down?"

"What would be taking it the wrong way?"

"Thinking I didn't like you. Or that you weren't insanely attractive and desirable."

"I'm not interested in whether you like me or find me attractive."

"Wow. Thanks."

He turned onto his back again, an arm coming up to deepen the shadows across his face. "I expressed that badly."

"You think?"

"It's simply that I prefer to be useful."

We fell silent. I wasn't sure there was much else to say. But apparently my mouth had other ideas. "You know, there are people out there who'll get who you are and what you're into."

"I was satisfied being Caspian's assistant."

"And you were brilliant at it. But you don't have to, like, sublimate yourself into your job. I mean, obviously you should also get a job at some point. Jobs are good. But you can have more."

I felt him shift a little restlessly beside me. "I'm not sure where this is going."

"You deserve to be with someone who wants all of you."

"Oh." He let out a soft breath. "You're talking about a relationship. I think you're trying to be kind, but love and romance mean very little to me."

"Only because Lancaster Steyne treated you like a toy and Caspian couldn't cope with what you represented, so he rejected everything you offered him."

"On the contrary, my feelings on this matter precede both Caspian and Mr. Steyne. And"—his tone sharpened—"you have profoundly mischaracterised my relationship with Caspian."

"How?" I asked. "You care about him and he's never acknowledged it."

"What does that matter? He let me stay with him anyway. He gave me a job to help me find a sense of purpose. And, I suspect, to ensure I would always be able to provide for myself in future. So that I would never be a whore or…a toy again."

How easy it was, when you were hurt, to lose track of the goodness of people. The truth was, I'd seen Caspian act in anger and fear and pain, but I'd never seen him be selfish. And now I was ashamed. "I'm sorry. I shouldn't have judged your relationship."

"It's all right. I know you mean well." Ilya turned his face into the crook of his elbow—I think he might have been crying again. "But working for Caspian has been invaluable to me. Though professionally speaking, it will not be difficult to f-find another position."

"Well, that's good," I responded way too heartily. The problem was, I really wanted to comfort him, but I had no idea how to go about it. That is, I knew how to be generically consoling but not how to be specifically consoling to Ilya.

He didn't reply and I didn't blame him. "Well, that's good" had been a pretty rubbish thing to say.

I tried again. "If love doesn't mean much to you, do you mind if I ask what does?"

"Hmm?" I must have lost him a little to his grief.

"What does mean something to you? What are you looking for?"

"What I'm looking for…" he repeated, as if he'd never encountered those words in that order before. And then, rather dreamily, "What I'm looking for is to be owned."

"And is there anything I can do for you now that would feel a little bit like that?"

I really didn't think he would answer. It was a wildly intimate thing to ask, and even vulnerable, Ilya was one of the most put-together people I'd ever met, the confidences he permitted himself to share as self-contained as hard-boiled sweets.

"Yes. You could hold me…" His voice caught, then steadied. "You could hold me like you need me."

I was so relieved not to be useless to him that I probably got far too excited. "Oh my God, I can totally do that."

"You shouldn't feel you have to."

"Are you kidding me? This is right in my wheelhouse—even though, now I think about it, I don't actually know what a wheelhouse is, and since I'm not a wheel, then maybe it would be overall a bad thing if I was put in one."

"I think it's to do with the steering of a ship."

"Point is, I'm *super needy*. Roll over."

He rolled over with the kind of instinctive obedience that eluded me even in my subbiest moments, and then I hustled up behind him like I was the biggest spoon in the goddamn universe. I pretty much *glued* us together, shoving my ever-chilly feet between his knees, and pressing my face to the gorgeous silky planes of his back.

Finally, I inveigled an arm over him and used that to pull him in even tighter. "How's this?"

"Surprisingly effective." In that moment, he sounded both more like Bellerose and more like Ilya—an unexpected combination of sharp and soft that reminded me of the horse chestnuts I used to collect in autumn. After all, they too had smooth and secret hearts.

Remembering the way Caspian had touched me sometimes, and how much I'd loved feeling possessed by him, I lifted my head and dragged my teeth lightly against the nape of Ilya's neck. He responded with a deep, blissed-out shudder. And within a matter of minutes, was fast asleep.

It took me a little longer to drop off, mainly because I wasn't used to the position, but the events of the day, general exhaustion, and the luxurious warmth of Ilya slumbering trustfully in my arms did the job in the end. He was gone, of course, when my alarm went off next morning, and his phone just rang and rang when I dialled his number—which I did, a bunch of times. Honestly, it was probably for the best he didn't have voicemail. God knows what I might have said.

In any case, a couple of days later, I came home to find a parcel waiting for me, hand-delivered, and wrapped with terrifying precision. No note, but inside was a long rainbow scarf, knitted from wool so soft it was like having a cloud wrapped round my neck. Ilya still didn't answer when I called him, but somehow I knew he was okay.

CHAPTER 15

Between finishing my article, editing the living fuck out of it, and worrying about Ilya, I was hoping Nathaniel would think better of inviting me to dinner. I mean, I got why he'd done it in the moment—it was a textbook power move. But actually going through with it just seemed pissy. I was essentially out of his life now. He'd won. He had Caspian. I didn't. And so there was no need for us all to get together and pretend we were friends. Maybe he needed the reassurance of it—my love stripped, chained, and forced to wear a mask—but he must have known how much that would hurt me. Of course, he had no reason to care about my feelings. But as much as I wasn't his biggest fan, he'd never struck me as intentionally cruel. Anyway, tl;dr and fml: Nathaniel did not think better of inviting me to dinner.

Said invitation came in the form of an email that was better written and better pitched than any article I'd ever put together, and cc-ed to Caspian, so I couldn't say no. I said yes, and there followed a low-key excruciating exchange in which we had to agree to a date, and Nathaniel had to tell me where he lived, and I had to let him know about any dietary requirements I might have and blah blah blah. Basically, it was kind of like being capitally punished in the seventeenth century, and then having to have a polite chat with the judge about whether you were available to die on Monday and if you were allergic to hemp. And no, I hadn't lost all sense of proportion.

In any case, I did what I usually did when I was having a crisis—which was Skype Nik in Boston, and panic.

"…and now," I finished, throwing myself on the bed so dramatically I nearly kicked the laptop onto the floor, "I have to go to dinner with the bastards. And Nathaniel's going to be smug and perfect and use the right fork, and Caspian's going to be all *nothing nothing nothing nothing* fuck with my head *nothing nothing*. What am I going to *doooo*?"

Nik idled back and forth in his wheelchair as he pondered. "You're going to have to kill yourself. It's the only way."

"Someday you'll say that to me, and I actually will, and then you'll be all sorry and sad and *oops, I shouldn't have been sarcastic*."

"Oh, come on, Ardy. Just tell them no."

"I can't. I've already said yes."

He did this thing that was half sigh, half growl. "You know that's not how consent works."

"Does that apply to dinner parties?"

"It applies to everything. You taught me that, you daffy twit."

I rolled about in helpless dismay. "Why is past me so wise when present me is a hot mess?"

"No, no," said Nik reassuringly, "past you was a hot mess too. It's just you very occasionally say sensible things and it's so shocking I always remember them."

I made pathetic noises.

"Seriously." He folded his arms. "Tell them to fuck off. One broke your heart, the other is clearly a wanker."

"Yes, but if I don't go, they'll know I think that."

"And we care what they think, why?"

"Because...because they'll win if I have emotions."

There was a pause.

"Okay," said Nik. "You know those sensible things you sometimes say? That *wasn't* one of them."

I made more pathetic noises.

Nik also made noises. They sounded frustrated. "I don't understand what I'm supposed to be doing here. Am I supposed to talking you out of this or talking you into it?"

"Neither. I'm going. I just want...y'know."

"*Ahhhh.* Is this a feelings thing?"

I sat up and gazed adoringly at the camera. "You noticed. You've totally grown as a person."

"All right. Your feelings are valid and I support them, even though there are simple things you could do to make yourself feel better and you're refusing to do them."

"Actually, talking to you is the thing I'm doing to make me feel better. And it's working because you're great."

He looked put-upon. "Okay. Talk about your feelings. I'm here."

"No, no." I crossed my legs and cosied up to the laptop. "I'm done now. How are you?"

"Fine."

"How's the physio?"

"Fine."

"Is it, like, y'know. Helping and stuff?"

He gave a sort of half shrug. "I guess. A bit."

"That's good." I gave him a little smile. "I mean, this stuff takes a while, right?"

"Yeah."

"And you're still keeping up with your nerdy MIT crowd who are way less cool than me?"

"Kind of." Another shrug. "They visit and we play games and talk about all the shit they're doing that I'm not."

My eyes widened. "Oh, Nik. You're, like, genius-level smart. A year or so isn't going to make any difference in the long run."

"Maybe. But as Keynes put it, in the long run we're all dead."

"Wow. That's bleak."

"Sorry. It's just coming up to the holidays and they're all flying home and I'm, obviously, y'know, not. And I'd be on my own anyway, what with my parents being dicks and Poppy being a film star, but it feels way worse when you can't walk."

Honestly, I should have thought of this without him having to tell me. I was a shitty friend. "I'll come," I squeaked.

"You're going to come to Boston? On your own. In winter. To be with your friend who can't do anything."

"No, I'm going to come to Boston on my own in winter to be with my friend who is you."

His mouth did something twitchy—like it wanted to smile but wasn't quite ready. "Ardy, you once got lost in a large Tesco's."

"Yeah, but I'm grown up now. And you can't Google Maps a supermarket."

"Look, this is really sweet of you. But you'll probably die. And you know you can't leave your family at Christmas."

"They'll cope."

"*I'll* cope."

"Not the point. I'm coming and you can't stop me." I leapt decisively off the bed. "Now I have to go because I've got to buy a ticket to Boston and shoot myself before dinner tomorrow."

Obviously I didn't shoot myself. Because I did, in fact, have a sense of proportion and I also had no idea how to get a gun in the UK. Then again, I did buy a ticket to Boston, so maybe I could pick up a Glock from a corner shop while I was over there. Y'know, just on the off-chance Nathaniel invited me back.

Anyway, ticketed and ungunned, I left work promptly so as not to be late for the thing I desperately wanted to be late for. I can't say I hadn't fabricated and discarded about sixty-three million potential excuses over the course of the afternoon, but now that going had become unavoidable, I didn't feel quite as bad about it as I'd been expecting. It helped that I was looking extra cute today, in pink jeans and a dark blue shirt, the coat Caspian had bought me (mainly because it was the only one I owned), and Ilya's scarf. And I'd even nipped out at lunchtime and bought a bottle of wine: A+ guesting.

Nathaniel lived in Muswell Hill, which was about half an hour up the Northern Line, but I decided to walk to Warren Street in order to cut down on the Tube changes. My route took me along Regent Street, which was ablaze with Christmas gold, spilling like glitter from the shop fronts and the electric angels who hovered above us on wings of light. The road rumbled with taxis and buses, and I got fairly jostled as I wriggled through the crowds, but I was nevertheless caught by the most unexpected sense of belonging. I'd been in London for over six months, watched the greens of summer in Hyde Park, walked by the river on silver autumn evenings, and turned up the collar of my coat against the December dark. This was my city now. And even though I was a pindrop of a nobody amongst a cacophony of strangers, I didn't feel alone.

Having factored getting lost into my ETA, I made it to Nathaniel's house bang on seven. And then lurked in a bush round the corner for ten minutes because I wanted to make damn sure Caspian would be there before me. The idea of having to make awkward small talk with Nathaniel on my own was, frankly, too horrible to contemplate. It also gave me an opportunity to get the lie of land, in case my nerves gave way and I had to run screaming into the night. The street was leafy and suburban, and lined with those generous Edwardian houses that always seemed a bit smug. Nathaniel's was the end terrace, white-painted and pretty, with mock Tudor gables, a parquet path leading to the door, and a front garden that looked genuinely cared for. There wasn't much to see at the moment, since all the plants were bare, but I was sure some of them were actual motherfucking roses. While I lived in a disused dog biscuit factory. Yay.

Once I was sure it was safe, and not late enough to be actively rude, I extricated myself from my shrubbery and went to knock. There were stained glass flower patterns in the door, and they didn't look even a little bit tacky. After a second or two, Nathaniel answered, bringing with him a swirl of warm air and some truly delicious food smells.

"Arden," he said. "Come on in. I'm afraid Caspian got delayed at work, but he's on his way now."

Shit fuck wankery shit on a stick up your arse with bells on. "Oh. Err. Right."

The hallway was spacious and light and gorgeous and fuck him. Just fuck him.

And he was smiling at me. "Let me take your coat."

"Oh. Err. Right."

Except I was holding the bottle of wine, so this led to me getting my arm stuck, and then my scarf got tangled, and then, about six hours later, when I'd managed to get my outer garments off, I spectacularly failed to give them to Nathaniel and ended up just dropping them on the floor at his feet. I bent to grab everything at about the same time he did, nearly banged heads with him, and finally just fell over in a heap on the polished wooden floorboards. Because of course I did.

"Shoes on or off?" I asked.

"Whatever makes you most comfortable." He began hanging up my coat. "This is a really lovely garment."

"Thank you. It was...uh...kind of a present?"

From Caspian clanged between us like the bells of Notre Dame.

"I brought you some wine." I waved it. "It's probably not very good because it was six ninety-nine, but it's called Green Fish and it has a picture of a green fish on the bottle, so, y'know..."

Having finished draping my scarf artistically over my coat, he took the bottle from my outstretched hand like I'd offered him a live grenade. "Thank you. How very thoughtful. But I should have mentioned in the email we're having lamb."

He *had* mentioned it. Along with the fact the lamb in question would be ethically sourced. "Okay?"

"So," he went on gently, "you would have known to bring red."

I gazed up at him in the throes of an Elizabeth Bennett moment. I know I'm not always as brave or as bold as I'd want to be—on top of possessing the poise of a smooshed grape—but goddamn, I had no time for deliberate attempts to socially shame me. I mean, I am short, skinny, and queer AF: You do not get to pull that shit on people like me. Or to put it another way: My courage always rises with every (well, *some*) attempts to intimidate me.

"Look," I said. "You could have told me we were having roast Martian with cantaloupe and I'd have still got the wrong wine because I know bugger all about the stuff. I brought it because it's the sort of thing you bring to a dinner party. If I knew you better, I'd have tried to find something you'd actually like—flowers or Turkish delight or posh elderflower juice. But I don't, so I couldn't, so you got some crappy wine."

There was a long silence. At this point, being thrown out of the house was looking like a positive outcome. But Nathaniel surprised me.

"I'm sorry, Arden. You're right, of course. And I appreciate the gesture." He helped me to my feet, his eyes steady on mine, their gold sheen luminous and solemn. "The truth is,

I taught myself about wine when I came to London. But it shouldn't be a social mandate, especially if you don't actually enjoy drinking it."

"I don't *mind* it. I just tend to prefer my drinks pink, sweet, and bristling with unnecessary cocktail umbrellas. Y'know, like me."

"I think I have the ingredients on hand to make a cosmopolitan. Though I can't promise a cocktail umbrella."

"Thanks, but I don't want to put you to any trouble." Fuck, we were getting into competitive Good Host and Good Guest territory now. "I'm honestly happy to drink whatever you were intending for us to drink."

"It's no trouble. I'll even have one myself." He gave me a slightly strained smile—which I appreciated a hell of a lot more than an unstrained smile since this was a fucking straining situation. "Unfortunately, I still have some things to take care of in the kitchen. You're welcome to come with me or wait in the living room—I realise in either case I'm treating you badly, but I hadn't anticipated Caspian's absence."

I widened my eyes at him. "What? Caspian Hart? Absent? Say it ain't so."

"Well, I…" Nathaniel's lips twitched uncertainly, as if maybe it had never occurred to him to laugh a little bit at Caspian. "I suppose my entire relationship with Caspian could be characterised as the triumph of hope over experience."

Heh. Mine too. "Dude would take a conference call at his own funeral."

"I'm afraid I really must get back to dinner. The lounge is

just through there"—he waved somewhere off to my right—"and the kitchen down here."

I really wanted Option Lounge. But that would involve essentially admitting I'd rather sit alone in an empty room than spend five minutes in Nathaniel's company. Repressing a sigh, I followed him down the hall. "Is there anything I can do to help?"

"No, it's all ready to go. I just need to keep an eye on the lamb."

"Ah," I said sagely, "but quis lamb custodiet ipsos lamb custodes."

Somehow, Nathaniel's *back* managed to give me a weird look. "I…I have no idea what that means."

Good call, Arden. Because what this evening really needed was a "who watches the watchmen" joke. In Latin. "Don't worry about it. I thought it might be funny, but it just turned out stupid. Story of my life, really."

Needless to say, Nathaniel's kitchen was amazing: spacious and airy and decorated with the sort of subtle sophistication that would probably always be beyond me. The floor was wood, like the hall, the surfaces granite, and the fittings a dusty grey-blue that still managed to work. But what really got me was the way it was so clearly a loved space—the care that had been lavished on the design, with everything to hand and in its proper place, and the American-style breakfast bar that hinted at a wish for company. It was perilously easy to imagine what dating Nathaniel might be like. Sitting at this very breakfast bar in a wash of buttery sunlight, while he…I bet he would make French toast. In his dressing gown, with his hair still tousled, and the taste of cinnamon on his lips.

God. No wonder Caspian wanted to marry him. The best you could hope for from me in the morning was a sloppy bj I'd probably doze back off in the middle of anyway.

"Your house is so nice," I said.

Nathaniel had made a beeline for the cooker, which was big enough it probably qualified as a range, and currently bristling with a terrifying array of pots and pans. But he glanced over his shoulder, blushing faintly. "Thank you. It was a bit of a fixer-upper, to be honest. I could never have afforded it otherwise."

Fan-fucking-tastic. So not only was his house completely ridiculous, but he had made it that way himself. The man was an entire episode of *Queer Eye* all on his own. Actually, he was better than an episode of *Queer Eye* because he seemed legitimately able to cook, and wasn't just going to put cilantro on top of something and call it a meal.

I hoisted myself onto one of the chairs at the breakfast bar. "And the food smells out of this world."

Because it did.

Also, at this rate, I could just keep complimenting Nathaniel on the amazing life he had and we wouldn't have to talk to each other at all.

"Thank you." He threw me a smile, which seemed genuine. And then, in quite a different voice, "Oh, there you are. Hello, sweetness. How's my darling?"

For a brief about-to-throw-up-in-my-mouth moment, I thought Caspian had arrived, but it turned out Nathaniel was talking to a cat which had just come into the kitchen.

Not quite willing to abandon the Admire Everything strategy and conscious that pet owners—much like people with kids—dug it when you made a fuss of their animals, I said, "Oh wow, he's beautiful."

"Isn't she? She's called Lillie, after Lillie Langtry."

"Wasn't she friendly with Oscar Wilde?"

Nathaniel nodded.

"I can see the resemblance." I mean, I couldn't. It was a cat. But what are you gonna do? And I had to admit, she was striking, being long-haired, and silver-coloured, with pale green eyes and an aristocratic better-than-you expression. "What breed is she?"

"I'm not sure—she's a rescue cat."

Of course she was. *Of course.* Nathaniel worked for charity, fixed up his house, cooked with ethically sourced products, and made me want to claw my own skin off with his oblivious commitment to being a good person. His unnaturally lovely cat could only have come from a shelter.

"I think," he was saying, "she probably has some Maine coon blood in her. From the shape of her head and the fluffiness of her tail."

"I can't believe anyone would abandon her in the first place." I'd watched a fair bit of *Pet Rescue* growing up, and catteries tended to be stuffed with sad-looking black-and-white moggies, not lofty feline princesses.

Lillie was twining herself possessively around Nathaniel's ankles, and purring. "Well, she has FIV and people can be ignorant and cruel."

"Eep. Sorry."

"It's a very manageable condition. It just means she can't go outside or interact with other cats very much. But"—and here Nathaniel readopted his cat-voice which, I couldn't deny, was kind of sexy in a messed-up way—"Lillie knows she's my special girl. Who's my special girl? Is it you? Yes it is. But Daddy has to cook now, darling."

Okay. So. Here's hoping I never have to hear Nathaniel refer to himself as Daddy again. While I was still processing, Lillie padded across the floor and leapt up onto the seat next to me, sitting there in the style of one of those ancient Egyptian cat statues, waiting to be worshipped.

"Hi, Lillie," I tried. "What a pretty cat you are."

I went to pet her ears but they snapped down immediately into *hell no* mode. And the next thing I knew, Lillie was a ball of electric fur, glaring at me from the floor, and my hand was covered in scratches.

"Um, Nathaniel?"

"I should probably have warned you. She can be a little nervous around strangers."

"Sorry, but I'm um…bleeding here."

"Oh, Lillie." Nathaniel regarded her with an air of exasperated fondness. "What have you done, you naughty little minx?"

I would have thought it was fairly obvious. Lillie just turned and sauntered off, her tail curled smugly over her back in that *here's my arsehole, sucker* way that cats seemed especially into.

"Do you maybe have a tissue or something?" I asked. "I'm dripping on the floor."

As it turned out, Nathaniel—on account of being a fully functioning grown-up—had a first aid kit. And I had to sit there like a kid who'd fallen over in the playground while he disinfected and bandaged me. As intimacies went, it was pretty banal, but it was still way more intimacy than either of us wanted. Unfortunately, the alternative would have been admitting our preferred level of interaction was *as little as humanly possible*.

Nathaniel's attentions were careful and impersonal as he bent, frowning in concentration, over my gushing cat wounds. But it was still too much, transforming him, very much against my will, from a plaster saint to a flesh-and-blood man. One who touched and felt, and was as real to Caspian as I was.

A different thought occurred to me. "Am I going to get cat AIDS now?"

"No, Arden. You're not going to get cat AIDS." For some reason, it sounded way worse repeated back to me. "FIV is not transferable to humans."

"Good to know."

God, I wanted to go home.

Maybe Nathaniel was thinking along similar lines, because he slid his phone out of his pocket, checked it, and wasn't entirely able to hide a grimace. "Caspian's stuck in traffic."

"Yep yep."

"I think"—Nathaniel finished packing away his gauze and antiseptics—"I'll make those drinks now."

Well, it was that or joint ritual suicide. "Sounds great."

Of course, he just had martini glasses sitting in one of his cupboards. Sigh. And a cocktail shaker, which—while he didn't fling it around or anything—he handled in a manner that suggested he knew what he was doing with it. Sure enough, a minute or so later, he was placing two perfectly made cosmopolitans onto the breakfast bar, each with a slice of lime balanced on the rim.

I was too ground down to tell him it was amazing-wonderful-fabulous, so I just drank the fucking thing, mumbling a half-arsed "Cheers" a second or two before the alcohol hit my mouth. It helped a bit—it tasted good, exactly the right mix of sweet, tart, and fruity, and the vodka was faintly numbing.

Numbing was good. Numbing was my friend.

Nathaniel put down his empty glass with a click. And we sort of stared at each other for a while. I honestly couldn't tell anymore if we were enemies or allies or something in between, like the English and German soldiers playing football in no-man's-land on Christmas Day. Only with less mud and imminent, horrible death. I opened my mouth to say…I don't know…I guess I wanted to be honest? I wasn't made for whatever game we were playing. And I didn't think he was either.

But before I could speak, there came the rattle of a lock and the sound of footsteps in the hall, and my brain went surface-of-Mars desolate apart *from he has a key to Nathaniel's house*, which scored itself into my psyche in letters that could be seen from space. And then Caspian himself walked into the kitchen.

CHAPTER 16

His coat was over his arm, and he was wearing one of his most austere suits: charcoal grey over a blue shirt, with a dark tie, very similar, now I thought about it, to the one he'd worn for the interview. It wasn't my favourite look for him—I missed the sly flamboyance of his pocket squares and silk linings—but it gave him this kind of refined ferocity, all sharp lines and shadows like a thresher shark.

"It seems"—his gaze settled on our empty cocktail glasses—"I've missed quite the party."

"That's what you get for being late," I told him at the same time Nathaniel said, "We had one drink."

God help us, it was going to be a long evening.

Nathaniel slipped away from the breakfast bar and kissed Caspian lightly on the cheek—which I desperately, desperately didn't want to see, but ho hum. "I'm glad you're here. Why don't you take Arden through to the dining room and I'll serve?"

It was, like, literally off the kitchen, so I didn't need an escort. All the same, I waited for Caspian to pass his coat to Nathaniel and then obediently followed him through to another well-proportioned, well-appointed room, this time with a fashionably rustic vibe. Seriously, couldn't Nathaniel own one ugly thing? Just one?

Lillie slunk in and eyed us both with obvious contempt.

"She can be nervous around strangers," explained Caspian.

I have to admit I wasn't feeling super long on social graces right then. "Does she now?" I waved my bloody hand. "I had no idea."

"So"—he cleared his throat—"injuries aside, how are you?"

"Good, thanks. You?"

"Likewise." I gave him a withering look and he had the grace to blush. "That is, I'm quite well. Busy, of course. But well. And what of you?"

"I just told you: I'm good."

There was definitely a panicky glaze in his eyes now. "So you did. But your family? Are all in good health?"

"They were, but then Little Timmy was taken by the sweating sickness. Yes, it's the twenty-first century, so my family are fine. But what the hell is wrong with you? Have you forgotten how to human?" Yikes. I probably shouldn't have drunk that cosmo so quickly.

He dropped into a chair with an unusual lack of elegance. "I'm sorry. It's been a long day."

I plonked my hands on my hips and stared at him in a way I couldn't categorise. "Still want me to be here?"

"Yes." His voice was soft, but terribly sincere. "I've missed you."

"Then"—I also decided being in a chair might be good—

"maybe you should have thought of that before you dumped me."

"Arden."

"What?"

He gave me this impossible look, his eyes as stark as his suit, and I wasn't sure if I wanted to cry or beg or smack him in the nads. "It was the right decision. You have no idea how important your happiness is to me."

"Y'know something? You're right. I don't."

At that moment, Nathaniel came in, balancing dishes, and I realised I didn't know what volume I'd been employing or how much he'd heard. From his serene expression, I was guessing…all of it.

"To start," he said, "halloumi with honey and spiced nuts."

Only Nathaniel could make pieces of cheese look elegant—but they did, artfully balanced against each other, with their almost geometric grill stripes. I mumbled a thank-you.

"Oh"—he set the last plate down in front of Caspian—"and it's nearly eight, my prince. Don't forget."

Caspian glanced over at him. "Hmm?"

With a soft laugh, Nathaniel dropped a thin square of *something* on the table beside Caspian, which, in a moment of legit hysteria, I briefly thought was a condom. Then sanity returned and I saw it was a nicotine patch.

"Of course. Excuse me a moment."

He went to stand but Nathaniel stopped him with a "Here, let me." Caspian didn't object, but he didn't look exactly comfortable either as Nathaniel helped him out of his jacket, undid a cufflink, and rolled up his shirtsleeve. For the record, Nathaniel was far too good at removing other people's cufflinks. As in, practiced good. Which I wasn't—though not for lack of wanting to be.

It was an intimate thing, knowing how to take someone's clothes off, and I'm pretty sure we were all very aware of it. So, yeah, I was miserable. I'd also had kind of a thing for Caspian's arms. Well, I'd had a thing for Caspian in general, but he had such gorgeous arms. I loved the strength of them—to hold me down and hold me close. The tenderness of the secret skin along the underside. The kissable bouquets of bone and sinew at his wrists.

Urrrgh. I suddenly wanted to cry. For fuck's sake, Ardy, get a grip. It's a nicotine patch. They're not dry-humping against the table. Oh God, I bet they *had*, though. If this was my table, I'd want to be fucked over it. Even though it was incredibly rude—and I'd been raised better—I grabbed a fork and stuffed all the halloumi into my very sad mouth.

"This is delicious," I announced, somewhat muffled through the food. "Cheese and honey. Who'd've thought it."

Cheese and honey and *ashes.*

Eventually, Nathaniel finished faffing with Caspian and took a seat. "Sorry about that. Shall we star—oh."

"I was hungry." I blinked defiantly.

"Of course you were." He was giving me an *oh, poor starveling wolf doesn't know any different* look that was not liable to improve my behaviour. "We're all running late."

Caspian poured Nathaniel some wine—it had been perspiring gently in an ice bucket much like the rest of us. "My fault, as ever. Arden?"

"What? No. It's fine. I could have waited."

"Actually I meant, did you want some wine?"

"Hey"—probably I should have kept my mouth shut but I was feeling aggrieved on way too many levels—"you had a go at me for bringing white wine this evening."

Nathaniel gave a polite cough. "I thought we'd come to a truce on that. It's customary for a guest to bring wine to accompany the main course rather than the starter. But as we've established, it was unfair of me to expect you to know that."

Well fuck. Now I looked both uncultured and petty. Scrutinising the place settings, which included a small orchard of glassware, I picked one at random. "Wine me."

With a slight glance towards Nathaniel—searching for who knew what, permission?—Caspian rose, took the glass from my hand, replaced it amongst its fellows, and splashed a frankly meagre measure of liquid into a different one. I thought about protesting but there were few better ways to demonstrate your immaturity than by asserting your right to consume alcohol to excess. Besides, as much as I might like to, getting sloshed was not going to help anybody here. Me, least of all.

"Ta." I took a restrained sip. But Caspian had given me even less wine than I'd thought, so I ended up just knocking it all back.

Sitting down again, Caspian lifted his own glass. "Anyway, to you, Nathan—oh."

They both stared at me.

"I was thirsty? Sorry. I'll just get some water." I leaned across the table to grab the bottle of fancy mineral water Nathaniel had provided, accidentally splotting my elbow into a carved butter flower. "Shit. Sorry." Twisting my arm round revealed a yellow smudge on my jumper. "It's fine. It's fine. I've got this." Thankfully, a napkin did a pretty decent job of mopping up the worst of it. Except—"Fuck, that's the tablecloth. Nathaniel, I'm so sorry. I swear I had a napkin. Where's my napkin? Fuck, it's on the floor. Fuck, I'm sorry."

Caspian had actually covered his face with his hands.

"Should I just leave?" I asked.

Which was when I realised: He was laughing. Quietly. Then not so quietly. In that beautiful, helpless way he did so very rarely. "Arden, my Arden," he said, his voice still full of mirth, and this infinite gentleness, "what has happened to you? Have you forgotten *how to human*?"

"I see what you did there." I tried to scowl at him, but instead I was smiling. "You should be nicer to me. I'm nervous as fuck." Also apparently incapable of making myself look good when Nathaniel was present.

"And you think I'm not?"

I fluttered my lashes at him. "Because of li'l ol' me?"

"I was afraid I would never see you again."

"And now we're all friends," said Nathaniel, way too sharply for the sentiment. "But if you don't mind, I spent rather a lot of time preparing this meal—so do you think perhaps we could eat it before it's entirely ruined?"

Caspian touched a finger to his laugh-damp lashes. "Of course. Nathaniel, thank you so much for cooking for us."

"It was nothing. That is"—he seemed to remember he'd just drawn attention to his efforts—"it was my pleasure."

I scraped the last swirl of honey off the plate. "It was my pleasure, for sure. This was so good."

"I'm glad you enjoyed it." Nathaniel did not sound even the slightest bit glad.

Silence settled as cheese was eaten—eaten, I should stress, by people who weren't me because I'd already impetuously de-haloumied myself. And then Nathaniel brought out the next course, which was pea soup with harissa. I wasn't entirely sure what harissa was, but I got the answer a spoonful later: What it was, was hot as fuck. A rich, deep, flavoursome hot, but Jesus Christ on a moose. Thank God for the artful spiral of sour cream or I might have spontaneously combusted. Although if I had, it would probably only have improved Nathaniel's evening.

"*Soooo.*" I couldn't tell if I was socially uncomfortable or just sweaty, but either way, saying something was becoming necessary. "How's the…um…the giving up smoking going, Caspian?"

The fingers of his left hand curled self-consciously on the tabletop. "Well, I think? At least, I assume it is."

"We can assume that," agreed Nathaniel mildly, "unless you're cheating."

"I'm not."

Nathaniel's lips curled upwards, and while there was definitely warmth in his smile, there was also a bunch of other things I couldn't even begin to interpret. "Would you even tell me if you were?"

"Would you want to know?"

"Yes, I would want to know."

"Then I would tell you."

I made a weird bleating sound, which was meant to be a light *aren't we all having a lovely time* laugh. "But isn't it kind of up to Caspian?"

"Honesty?" asked Nathaniel, with a tilt of his head.

"Smoking."

"I'm not sure to what degree choice is a factor when it comes to addiction."

So, I'd lost this conversation. It had more layers than a goddamn cheesecake—one of the fancy ones from Maison Bertaux—and there was no way Nathaniel's smoking talk wasn't a backhanded dig at all of Caspian's other "harmful habits." And while from my point of view there was clear blue water between consensual kinky sex and something that literally gave you lung cancer, Nathaniel clearly had different opinions. And had framed his way better than I'd framed mine.

"As it happens"—Caspian had conquered his soup without any sign of struggle—"giving up smoking is very much my choice. I prefer not to be controlled by my weaknesses."

"Obviously smoking is bad for you," I began.

At which point Nathaniel murmured, "We agree on that at least."

"*But*," I pushed on, "weakness is a deeply subjective concept."

"I'm sure you know more about that than I do."

Snide!Nathaniel was probably my least favourite Nathaniel. And believe me, there was a lot of competition. "What's that supposed to mean?"

He shrugged. "Only that I was raised to value strength. It is, despite our very different backgrounds, something Caspian and I share."

That…did not add up. Well, it made sense for Nathaniel. For Caspian, though, given what I knew of his family? Not so much. I turned to him. "Is it?"

"The world is a cold place, Arden." Despite my name on his lips, Caspian didn't seem to be speaking to me at all. His attention was fixed on his wineglass, and the refracted light caught in the dregs. "We master it or we are mastered by it."

"From everything you've told me about your dad," I said, as gently as I could, "that doesn't sound like any sort of lesson he'd want you to learn."

At that, Caspian's gaze snapped to mine. "I didn't say he taught it to me."

"Oh, Caspian." I blinked against the prickle of tears. "Please—"

"And I would prefer not to discuss my father at the moment. It isn't an appropriate topic for the dinner table."

"There should always be a place for love."

"But this is death."

"Look," I said. "Clearly, this is a mess. We're all miserable. Nathaniel's not right for you, and you're not right for him. You should be with me."

Okay, that's a lie. I didn't say that. But I really *really* wanted to. And in my head, when I did, Caspian believed me. And then there was kissing. Lots and lots of kissing.

Also an orchestra. And roll credits.

The End in big swirly letters.

What actually happened was Nathaniel muttered something about it being time for the lamb, and took our soup bowls into the kitchen, Lillie—who had extricated herself from a shadow in the corner of the room like a squid from seaweed—padding at his heels.

CHAPTER 17

Probably I should have tried to get the conversation going again but I felt like Cool Hand Luke digging a pit over and over again and couldn't quite find the strength. So Nathaniel's lamb with caramelised figs and pine nuts, in saffron sauce with couscous, arrived to deathly silence. Shame, really, because like everything else he'd made, it was really good—even if each portion came in its own little bowl so it was all a bit *I heard you like crockery, so I put a crockery in your crockery*. I never knew what to do with compartmentalised food—did you cross the barricades with it or respect its hauteur? Personally, I preferred stuff that came in a big pot where everyone got to help themselves. Much less complicated.

"Arden"—Nathaniel, wielding a bottle of wine apparently more appropriate to the meal than Green Fish, yanked me out of my food dilemma—"I'm conscious that since you had to interview us, you must know far more about me than I do about you."

I frowned, not quite sure what he was getting at, but fairly convinced I wouldn't like it. "No more than what you told me plus what an average person can find on the Internet."

"I just think it would be good to restore the balance."

"It's not a competition."

He gave me a smile that was trying very hard not to be exasperated. "What I'm saying is that I'd like to know you better."

"Uh?" A piece of lamb plopped pathetically off my fork and into my couscous.

"There's no need to look horrified. Since Caspian rarely allows people to grow close to him, I'm interested in anyone he calls a friend." Nathaniel turned his luminous, earnest gaze on me. "Tell me about yourself."

What? Oh no. I hope there's a special place in hell reserved for people who say "Tell me about yourself." Maybe not right in Satan's arsehole with the betrayers, but pretty damn near it. Satan's taint? Just behind his balls, where it'd be all sweaty with hellfire. "There's not much to tell."

"There's no need to be modest," said Caspian. "You're a very special and accomplished young man."

When we'd been dating, Caspian's commitment to believing I was awesome had been at once overwhelming and a little bit magical. It had helped me find my way back to myself when I was so lost I hadn't even realised how fucking lost I was. But now? It was a knife cutting me open. Streams of *then why did you dump me* pouring from my veins.

"I'm not being modest." I took a probably inadvisable gulp of wine—and, okay, fine, it did go well with the lamb, the touch of bitterness in the fruit drawing out the sweetness of the meat. "*Tell me about yourself* is a crappy thing to throw at someone because it makes them do all the conversational work while you get to act like you're taking an interest without actually having to be interested."

Nathaniel looked genuinely hurt, thus making me look genuinely like a monster. "I'm sorry you feel that way. It wasn't my intent."

Get on your unicycle, Arden. Start backpedalling. "It's okay. I mean, I overreacted. I'm sorry. I guess I read *Jane Eyre* at an impressionable age."

Another of those *you're a nonsensical weirdo* head tilts from Nathaniel. "I don't follow."

"There's a bit early on when Rochester is being all autocratic lord of the manor and he's, like, *entertain me* to Jane, and she's, like, *fuck you, I'm a person.* But it's this totally amazing moment because she's this disempowered nobody and he's supposed to be her better in every conceivable way."

"I see."

It really didn't seem that he did see, so I pressed on. "Because, like, for Jane, the things we ascribe power to don't matter. Just the inherent equality of hearts and souls and minds."

"You seem very passionate about her."

"Well"—I attempted a smile—"she was very passionate too. Don't get me wrong, the book is batshit crazy and kinda racist, but I guess she's a hero of mine."

"Is that so?"

My grin was fossilizing on my face. "Yep yep. I'd love to be as brave and principled and badass as she is. Unfortunately, in practice, I just end up being a dick at dinner parties."

"It's all right," Nathaniel told me graciously. Fuck's sake, couldn't he meet me halfway on *anything*?

"You weren't a dick." That was Caspian, whose gentleness I really didn't need right now. "Just, as we have discussed, passionate. Which is a trait I've always admired in you."

I closed my eyes in case I lost control and stuck a fork in one. Probably he was only trying to be nice, but I couldn't shake the conviction his one-man Arden Pep Rally was more for his benefit than mine. Like he was trying to prove to Nathaniel he hadn't just been slumming it with me for six months. Which I suspected was just going to make everyone in the room feel shitty. "Thanks," I said, in a totally not-thankful voice. "But we're not together anymore. You don't have to look out for me or take care of me, and my self-esteem is definitely not your problem."

For the first time that evening, Nathaniel looked happy.

Caspian just got frosty. "I apologise."

"I'll get over it."

"Your point is well made. As was your previous."

At this, Nathaniel prickled slightly—if he'd been a cat, I'm sure his ears would have gone back. "I think you're both reading far too much into a simple question, politely meant."

"I'm sure it's equally applicable to me." Caspian's manner softened again. "There must have been many occasions on which I made Arden feel as frustrated as Mr. Rochester did Jane Eyre."

I shrugged. "Reader, she married him, didn't she?" And actually, I'd always found Caspian easy to talk to—even from that very first, bewildering phone call.

"Yes, well." Nathaniel poured himself another glass of wine, splashing a little as he did so. "In that regard, your story and Jane's end rather differently."

"And from your perspective, I'm probably the madwoman in the attic."

"Nonsense." He sighed. "I see no reason why I should be concerned by Caspian's prior associations. It's not as if you have any legal claim on him, and if he wanted to be with you, he would not be with me."

Ouch. But then, if Nathaniel was that fucking unthreatened, he wouldn't feel the need to go on about how threatened he wasn't. I didn't say that, though. On account of being either too nice or too cowardly.

"Nathaniel," said Caspian, very softly. And I couldn't tell if it was reassurance or rebuke or a little bit of both.

"Anyway." Nathaniel dabbed at the red stains on the tablecloth, the closest to flustered I'd ever seen him. "I take it, Arden, from your reliance on literary allusions, you read English at university?"

"Yes, but I'll have you know I'm quite allusively promiscuous."

"And," he asked, "you went to Oxford, like Caspian?"

I stopped trying to be cute, and just nodded.

"How did you find it?"

"Horrible. Basically flunked out. Got a two-two."

"That seems"—he paused, and for once, I didn't think he was trying to get at me—"rather a wasted opportunity."

I finished my last bite of lamb. Shame I was at the Dinner Party of the Damned, because it deserved my appreciation—it was melt-in-the-mouth soft, and touched with a musky sweetness from the saffron. Depressingly delicious. "Yes and no. I spent three years nebulously miserable and confused because Oxford is supposed to be this dream, you know? If nothing else, it taught me to be damn sure your dreams are your own."

"It could never even have been a dream for me." Nathaniel nudged at his couscous. "With my background, it would have been impossible."

"It's not all Russian heiresses and the landed gentry. You'd have done okay."

"I got two B's and a C from an inner-city state school, which was more than anyone expected of me, and better than most of my classmates. Neither I nor anyone I knew aspired to read old books in a city of old stone. We did whatever we thought would help us get jobs so we could support ourselves instead of sponging off our parents or the state."

As much as I hated him taking potshots at me and being good at everything, I hated it even more when he showed me glimpses of who he was. Because that made it hard to keep hating him. "Okay, I get it. I mean, for the record, I'm not a Eton posh boy either, but I know I was lucky in a lot of ways: My school was small, and big on encouraging people to flourish, and my mum used to be a poet and all that. And I get it must suck to have me sitting here whining about how I pissed away something you never had a shot at. If it helps, I spent a really long time feeling rubbish at the thought I'd taken a place from somebody who deserved it more."

"My philosophy is that if you have something you don't think you deserve, you should strive to deserve it."

Welp. Now I hated him again. "Kinda missed the boat on that one."

"I just meant you shouldn't feel bad about what you did

or didn't do at university. Opportunity isn't a moment. It's a path. Anytime you want, you can start being the person you think you should have been."

"Um…I'm think I'm good."

"Oh really?" He blinked. "I believe it's time for pudding."

The fact he said "pudding" was a little bit endearing. Despite his many other manifestly unendearing qualities.

Caspian picked at the edge of his nicotine patch. "So, Arden. How are you?"

"Since the last two times you asked me that question tonight? Still fine, Caspian."

"'Fine' is a rather nonspecific answer."

"Well, I stubbed my toe against the floor when I got out of bed this morning, and I think it's catching in a hole in my sock. Specific enough for you?"

"I just"—he paused, foot jiggling under the table—"I want to know about your life."

"My life is also fine."

"Do you have plans for Christmas?"

"I'm going to Boston to see Nik. He's still in rehab out there—I mean, can't walk rehab. Not drugs rehab." I wrinkled my nose thoughtfully. "Maybe I shouldn't call it rehab."

"I expected you would spend the holiday with your family."

"I wanted to, but Nik doesn't have anyone. So"—wild grin and jazz hands—"he gets me."

Caspian was watching me with an expression I couldn't read. "That's very generous of you. Do you need the jet?"

My mouth fell open.

"I won't be using it, if that's your concern."

"You…you can't just lend me your plane."

"Why not?"

"Because it's too much."

"It's nothing to me," he murmured. "You know that. Let me do this for you, Arden."

"No way. We're not in any sort of place where I would feel comfortable owing you."

He bowed his head. "That…is troubling to me. But I understand."

"Besides"—I did a Scarlett O'Hara head toss—"I paid for that shitty economy ticket on a shitty economy airline out of money I made for myself. At the proper grown-up job I do. So there."

"And how is your work going?"

"Really well, actually." I plonked my elbows on the table and leaned forward, continuing in a stagey whisper. "Believe it or not, I managed to bag an interview with an elusive gay billionaire and his husband-to-be. It's a big deal."

Caspian suddenly couldn't look at me. "I'm glad it was helpful to you. You're living with El—Elean—Ellery, is that correct?"

"Yep. In a disused biscuit factory we share with a stuffed walrus called Broderick. There are a lot of drugs and we party late into the night like the no-fucks-given twenty-somethings we are."

"I hope my sister isn't being a bad influence on you."

"She hasn't broken my heart yet, so I think that puts her well ahead of the family average."

"I'm sorry. But"—and here Caspian's icescape eyes caught mine again—"you will thank me for it one day."

Only the fact that I was in Nathaniel's house stopped me from throwing the furniture at Caspian's head. "You are so *so* wrong."

There was a long silence.

"How is Eleanor?" asked Caspian, apparently deciding to just ignore everything.

"Ellery."

"Yes. How is Ellery?"

"Why don't you ask her?"

"Because she wouldn't tell me."

"Then I'm not going to tell you either." I folded my arms. "You want to know about Ellery, put the work in."

He swallowed. "She would never...that is, she knows what...what I did."

"She knows what Lancaster Steyne did. But he didn't take her brother from her. That was you."

"Arden, please." Caspian pushed away from the table, the legs of his chair rasping against the wooden floor, and surged to his feet. "Must you do this now?"

"No, but..."

He strode across the room to the French windows and stood, caged by their shadows, staring out at what I'm sure was a beautifully kept Nathaniel garden.

"I just think," I told him, "like most things in your life, your relationship with Ellery isn't nearly as irretrievably damaged as you think it is. She's still your sister and she still loves you. That's all still there. It's just hidden. Like the stars in London."

"Stars are dead light."

"Okay then"—my voice exploded out of me at a frankly

socially inappropriate volume—"I chose a bad fucking analogy."

At which point, Nathaniel, gliding in from the kitchen, announced, "Île Flottante with pistachios."

And we had to calm down, sit down, and pretend to give a damn about dessert. I'd seen enough BBC cooking shows to recognise that floating islands demonstrated some hard-core cheffing. But whatever. I smashed those smug meringue bastards with my spoon and drowned them in the crème anglaise.

"Y'know what I don't get?" I heard myself say, when it was too late to shut me up again. "If you're so big on this personal responsibility, be your best self, nobody holds you back but you thing, why do you work for an organisation that gives out free money?"

"Arden." That was Caspian, in much the same tone he'd said "Nathaniel" earlier. Guess that put us 1:1 on diners behaving badly.

"No, it's all right." Nathaniel cast a sweet smile across the table. Evidently he was into Caspian defending his honour. "I'm happy to discuss this, although I'm not sure that's an entirely fair characterisation of my position."

I rolled my eyes. "I'm sorry you feel that way. It wasn't my intent."

"Please don't worry. Misunderstandings happen. But frankly, I'm not sure what you think the contradiction is."

"Ten minutes ago, you were lecturing me on how I had this duty to better myself in order to deserve the opportunities I'd been given. But isn't your entire job all about giving opportunities to people who, by definition, haven't"—I threw sarcasm tongs—"*earned* them?"

Nathaniel gave me a sanctimonious look. "I'm not sure if you have a poorer opinion of me or the causes I support."

"Hey now. I'm not the one going around saying people have to jump through a bunch of hoops just to be worthy of the nice things that happen to them."

"I wasn't talking about people in general, Arden, I was talking about you."

"Wow. You're not even going to pretend this isn't personal."

"You freely admit that you squandered an opportunity that most of us can't even imagine, but you clearly think that this is some kind of charming foible instead of a character defect that you could correct if you wanted to."

"Perhaps," suggested Caspian, "we should change the subject."

"No." I tossed my spoon into my sunken island and stood up. "Let's not change the subject. This is not a change-the-subject situation. Your fiancé insisted I come to dinner, has been a dick to me the whole evening, and has spent dessert trashing my character and my life choices."

Caspian attempted to glare at us both simultaneously, which didn't entirely work. "Arden, be quiet. Nathaniel, apologise."

"I will not," we said in unison.

"For God's sake." He dropped his head into his hands. And then, to Nathaniel, "I told you this was a bad idea."

Nathaniel made a sound like his cat being stood on. "Forgive me for trying to be hospitable to your friends."

"Stop saying that." Oh fuck me. I was yelling. "I'm not his friend. I loved him. I still do. And I'm going home."

Reader, I got the fuck out.

CHAPTER 18

I'd honestly never been so glad to be leaving the country. The run-up to Christmas was fun at work—lots of events, many of them fancy, some of them fabulous—but I couldn't stop thinking about what had gone down at Nathaniel's. Like I was Jack Nicholson, only instead of Chinatown, it was a dinner party. I mean, was what had happened my fault? Given how long I'd spent feeling about myself pretty much the way Nathaniel had said I should, it had been rough having him slap me in the face with it all over again. Not because I believed he was right anymore. But because I shouldn't have to defend my choices to dickhead concern trolls. And what had Caspian meant, at the end, when he said it had been a bad idea to invite me? Hadn't he wanted to see me? Or had he known I'd find a way to fuck everything up?

Also: I'd told him I was still in love with him. In response to which he'd told me precisely fuck all. But what had I been expecting? That Caspian would show up on my doorstep with declarations spilling from between his lips like rose petals? Probably I should have sent him a text to apologise for being the worst dinner guest in history. Except he hadn't apologised to me for having to be a guest at the worst dinner in history. So there were no texts and no apologies, and soon there'd be an ocean between us, and I fucking needed that ocean to be there. Maybe I'd miraculously learn how to transmute physical distance into emotional distance. But even if I didn't, I'd be far away from Caspian, which would hopefully curtail my capacity to make a fool of myself in front of him.

The day of my departure—part of the reason the flight was so cheap was it left England at five in the afternoon and got into Boston at eight o'clock at night, which was a time zone headfuck and a half—I bullied my wheelie case down from the mezzanine and found Ellery slumped on the sofa. This wasn't unusual, but it was unusually early for her, since she normally didn't get out of bed before dark.

"Where are you going?" she asked.

I'd told her a bunch of times I was spending Christmas with Nik. I'd even left a note on the fridge that went, *22nd December: Ardy Going to Boston*, and included a stick draw-ing of me in a plane flying over an ocean along with my actual ticket because it was the only way I knew I wouldn't lose it. "America."

"Oh, right." A pause. "Can I come?"

"I'm going, like, right now."

"So?"

I gaped at her. "Well, you don't have any luggage or—"

"Yeah, because they don't have shops in Boston."

"I got my ticket weeks ago."

"There's still some left." She waved her phone at me. "Look, I just bought one."

"Ellery." I think, given the pitch of my voice, her name qualified as a legit exclamation. "Nik's in hospital. It's not exactly going to be the Christmas of anyone's dreams."

She shrugged. "What's the alternative? Having to spend it at Mum's with Caspian and Nathaniel playing Happy Fucking Families?"

"I thought you liked Nathaniel."

"He was only interested in me because I'm Caspian's sister." Her lip curled into its customary sneer. "Couldn't drop me fast enough when Caspian dropped him."

"It must have been hard for him when they broke up. He probably didn't want to be…reminded of everything he'd lost."

Her eyes flicked to mine briefly, their gaze too sharp. "You stuck around."

Why the fuck was I defending Nathaniel anyway? "Good point. Clearly I'm amazing and Nathaniel sucks."

"Well then. I want to spend my Christmas with people who don't suck."

This already had the potential to be a disaster. But the Ardy Friendship Code was clear: No Ellery left behind. "I guess that means we're going to Boston." I did my best to sound stern—not exactly my forte. "You've got to be nice to Nik, though."

"Why do I have to be nice to Nik?"

"Because he's got a spinal cord injury. He's in a wheelchair."

"I'm not going to be nice to someone just because they're

in a wheelchair." Ellery subjected me to her most withering stare. "That would be ableist."

I opened my mouth and then closed it again. "Okay, but you really should take something with you."

She heaved a sigh. "I guess you're right." Vanishing into her room, she emerged a minute or so later with something tucked under her arm.

"What's that?"

"Book for the plane."

"Passport?"

She patted her hoodie. "In my pocket."

"Come on, then. We're going to be late."

"Sheesh, Ardy. You are, like, the unchillest traveller. We've got ages."

"It's an hour to Stanstead and we have to check in at least two hours before we fly."

"Two hours?" Ellery looked genuinely confused. "Can't you just turn up?"

"Oh my God. You've never been on a commercial flight, have you?"

She glared.

"You little princess."

"I'm a death princess of darkness. Which you'll learn first-hand if you ever call me princess again."

Laughing, I grabbed her hand and pulled her—along with my equally rebellious wheelie—out the door. We made it to Stanstead in good time, although our flight was already listed as delayed, so that was, well, what it is.

"Okay. So," said Ellery, once we'd checked in, "what do we do for the next, like, four hours?"

"We explore the airport. Very carefully, and slowly, and thoroughly. Relishing every moment. Because there is shit all else to do."

"Seriously."

"Yep. Yep. We go into every shop. We look at every pair of designer sunglasses. Every intensive repair anti-aging pot of moisturiser. We buy a drink or a snack at every eatery."

"And then what?"

"We sit around in uncomfortable chairs feeling unspeakably depressed because we are stuck in this glass nowhere for an indefinite period."

Ellery pulled her Audrey Hepburn shades out of her hoodie and settled them on her nose. "Let's do it."

We took on that airport like Richard Burton seeking the source of the Nile, and Ellery was a surprisingly good sport about it, joining in my obsessive classification of the WH-Smith and the Sock Shop and the Sunglasses Boutique. She even managed to kill nearly twenty minutes in the Swarovski outlet by convincing the salesperson she was on the brink of buying an unspeakably heinous piece of jewellery. A manor necklace, apparently, which looked like one of those cones you put dogs in to stop them from scratching, except it was a web of black and clear Swarovski crystal pendants hanging on rose gold chains.

Between our shop visits we had smoothies from the juice bar, bad coffee from Starbucks, random glasses of champagne (which Ellery paid for) from a pretentious café, edamame from Itsu, sarnies from Pret, and sundaes from Burger King. After which we had to concede defeat—and there was still no news of our plane.

"Shit." I collapsed into one of the crappy waiting area chairs.

Ellery peered at me over her glasses. "What now?"

A glance towards the departures board confirmed we were not departing. "We're down to our last hope."

"Oh?"

"Yep." I pointed with a shaky hand towards the arcade. "Air hockey."

Ellery had never played before and was, at first, inclined to think she was too good for air hockey. Nobody, trapped at an airport, is too good for air hockey.

And within about two minutes, Ellery's sunglasses were off, her hoodie was tied around her waist, and she was making up for lack of experience with sheer, balls out viciousness. It was like the puck had personally wronged her or something, the way she was slamming the poor thing off the sides, into my fingers, and—far too consistently—into the goal. I guess insane competitiveness ran in the Hart family. Although to the best of my remembrance, Caspian had never yelled "Mother-fucking-fucker" during Carcassonne.

Anyway. Air hockey did its job too well and we almost missed our flight—dashing through the gate at so much the last possible second that my arse nearly stayed in the UK. At which point, Ellery pecked me on the cheek, muttered, "See you, sucker," and was whisked off to first class. Well, not first class. *Premium* class. This was the kind of airline that wanted to manage your expectations.

Trying to ignore the dirty looks I was getting for being the last one to board, requiring pretty much everyone else to tuck in, stand up, or be clambered over, I found my seat and plonked myself in it. And okay, it wasn't *luxurious*, but it was…fine. I could totally spend eight and a bit hours like this. Totally. I folded out my little table and then folded it back again. No reason. Just that it was there and it was my folding table, dammit. Yep. Yep. Eight hours. No problem. Also I had my Kindle. Except I apparently hadn't remembered to charge my Kindle. And I hadn't paid extra to have a USB socket. Which meant I was going to have to depend on my unwavering mental fortitude and deep wellspring of inner resources.

Oh God. I was fucked.

The plane sat around on the runaway for another forty minutes or so but eventually trundled skywards. Boston, here we came. I tried to sleep, but as ever, when not being conscious would have been awesome, I was helplessly awake and restless.

I checked the time. Ten minutes gone. Wow, the journey was just whooshing by. And I was hyperconscious of not wanting to run out of battery before we landed—since everything I needed was on my phone. After an hour or so, or maybe five minutes, or maybe three thousand millennia, one of the cabin crew came over and told me I had to follow them. Which led to me disturbing my row all over again, and also being briefly terrified that they'd decided I was a terrorist and were going to throw me out the window.

But instead, I was led into the premium cabin, which came equipped with—praise be—reclining seats and electric sockets. I'd been upgraded. Ellery smirked at me from behind her sunglasses. Probably I should have felt bad to be once again benefiting from someone else's wealth and privilege. But fuck it, I didn't. Sold out for a slightly bigger chair and a neck pillow.

"Thanks," I said, getting settled in next to her, and accepting my free bottle of water, because they really knew how to take care of you on ShitAir.

She shrugged.

"I don't mean to be ungrateful or anything but…was this always the plan?"

"Obviously."

"Then why did you leave me stewing out there for so long?"

"Dunno. Thought it was funny."

I sighed and plugged my Kindle into my socket and my phone into Ellery's. "Of course you did."

"What's the matter?" Ellery cocooned herself more deeply in her blanket. "Can't cope flying economy? God, you're such a princess."

"You're talking to a queer boy, Ellery. I've always wanted to be a princess."

She gave a snort of laughter. "Mission accomplished then." Whereupon she levered up the arm rest, plonked her head in my lap, and closed her eyes.

Since she wasn't usually the tactile type, I couldn't tell if she was experiencing some kind of Ellery-emotion or simply trying to travel in as much comfort as possible. After a moment or two, I touched her hair very gently and, when she made a rough, contented sound at the back of her throat instead of batting me away, began to stroke. She was asleep faster than a cat on a summer afternoon. Typical. With my free hand, I snagged the book she'd brought with her—*Harriet Said*—and settled down to read.

CHAPTER 19

It was close to midnight in Boston by the time we arrived, which was disorientating because it felt like we'd already travelled all night. Regardless of time zone, it was still prime Ellery operating hours, so I left her in charge of getting us taxied out to our Holiday Inn. Last time I'd been here, Bellerose had arranged for me to stay somewhere fancy, but it had been a waste of time and money since I'd practically lived at the hospital. Applying this logic to my present arrangements, I'd booked the cheapest place I could find with a hospital discount and a free hospital shuttle service. And actually, it was fine: a generic, brick box of a building opposite a wire-fenced car park and what was clearly a dive bar, and decorated inside with aggressive blandness. Of course, I had to spontaneously upgrade my booking from standard-with-single-occupancy to standard-with-unexpected-double-occupancy, which kind of went over as well as Richard Gere trying to do that in *Pretty Woman* except for me not being a billionaire businessman and Ellery not being a prostitute. The weird thing was, she could have easily got her own room but it didn't seem to occur to her. Or for whatever reason, she chose not to. Maybe she really didn't want to be alone at Christmas.

Despite the fact it was still early in the UK, I collapsed onto the bed almost as soon as I saw it. Doing nothing and not moving for eight hours was exhausting, okay? I could feel Ellery staring at me.

"I'm going out," she announced.

I jammed my face into the pillow. "We just got in."

"Which is why I'm going out."

"Do you even know anything about Boston?"

"People live here. How hard can it be?"

"So, what, you're just going to…wander out into the night?"

She thought about it for a moment. "Yeah."

"I'm sure that's how people get murdered."

"It's America. I'll buy a gun."

"Ellery." I sat up again abruptly. "Do *not* buy a gun."

"Just a little one. I wouldn't get an assault rifle or anything."

"Actually, I read it was harder to get handguns because something something concealable something something regulations something something right to hunt shit."

"Oh, okay. I'll get an AR-15 then. Thanks, Arden."

"You better"—I glared at her—"be winding me up right now."

She grinned. "Guess you'll find out soon."

Sighing, I reflopped. "At least take my coat."

"So I can put my assault rifle in it?"

"No, because it's really fucking cold out there."

"Whatever, *Mom*."

I wagged a finger at her. "I have your best interests at heart, young lady."

"You'll never understand me." She stamped her foot. "And you're not my real mom either."

She left a few minutes later, though she did take my coat. I sent a message to Nik to let him know I'd made it and passed out not long after. It felt like no time at all had gone by before Ellery was poking me awake again.

"So"—she jumped onto the bed, still in my coat and her boots—"are you intending to see Nik, you know, the friend you specifically came here to see, or are you going to sleep forever?"

I clung to the duvet and made sad noises.

"You'll miss breakfast."

That got my attention. "Have you even been to bed yet?" I asked, staggering towards the bathroom in my purple unicorn boxers.

"Bed is boring."

"What did you do last night?"

I almost heard her shrugging. "Stuff."

"Wow, thanks." My words came out muffled around my toothbrush. "I feel I have a much better understanding of the life of the city now."

"No problem. Anytime."

"Besides, we can't see Nik 'til after four. He has physical therapy or whatever and we shouldn't interrupt."

"Oh no," Ellery drawled. "You poor thing. Whatever will you do in this unfamiliar place?"

"Go back to bed?"

"Well, since you're being so pathetic about it, I guess you can come with me."

I spat, rinsed, and stuck my head back into the room. "Gosh, are you sure?"

"What can I say"—she gave me one of her *not so much dead as long ago decomposed pan* looks—"I'm a saint."

"Will you at least tell me where we're going?"

She blinked. "No."

Where we were going, I discovered, after a shower, breakfast, a thirty-minute ride on the Boston Not-Tube, and a five-floor climb to the top of a library, was Warren Anatomical Museum. Though "museum" was a bit optimistic—since it was a room with some glass cabinets in it, all of which were full of gross stuff.

Ellery was there for, like, nearly two hours. I mostly sat in the corner. Because as far as I was concerned, once you'd seen one dislocated pelvis or deformed foetus in a jar, you'd kind of seen them all. Ellery tried to cheer me up afterwards by offering to buy me lunch, but I think she was taking the piss.

"You," I said as we headed east towards the harbour and the rehabilitation hospital where Nik was staying, "are the weirdest tourist."

This earned me my first scowl of the day. "I'm not a tourist."

"We just went to a museum. Where you enjoyed yourself."

"Shut up. I did not." She pulled her feet up to rest against the seat. "I just like stuff other people might not have seen."

We had to change lines at Haymarket, something Ellery navigated with far too much comfort for someone who had been to Boston exactly never. Honestly, I was glad she was with me. My last visit had involved a car ride to and from the airport, and a daily walk between my hotel and the hospital, my memory a blur of white corridors and long roads, and a too-flat, too-wide river that didn't look anything like the Thames. Of course, now I was seeing underground tunnels and skulls with holes through them, but what could you do?

Nik's hospital was right on the tip of a peninsula in one of the city's oldest neighbourhoods—which is to say, it was substantially younger than the crockery at your average Oxford college. The building itself was sleek and glassy, with a *we care about sustainability* look to it. Inside, it was clean and bright, and slightly corporate, which, while it wasn't cosy, was more reassuring than you might have expected. It suggested they wanted you rehabilitated and out of there—an approach I could get behind.

Nik was waiting for us in the lobby. I'd seen him over Skype a bunch of times, and I knew intellectually that he was in a wheelchair now, but it turned out my mental image of him had adjusted way less than I'd realised, and so the sight of him was a little bit jarring, like when your glasses-wearing friend suddenly gets contacts. But it only lasted a second or two. And then I was just so, so happy he was there.

"Nik." I gave an excited squeal and scampered across the floor to meet him. "Shit—what's the best way to hug you?"

"Wait until we're both sitting down." He gave a wan smile. "Because if you pull any leaning over me crap, I will punch you in the face, I swear to God."

Honestly, I was already conscious of being loomy—which was extra uncomfortable because I was used to Nik being taller than me. "Wow, is that what they're teaching you in physical therapy?"

"No. But it would definitely be therapeutic."

"Punching me?"

"It would be a principled punching, not a personal one."

I pulled a face. "I don't know if that makes it worse or better."

"This is weird." He spun away with a deft, and somehow expressive, motion. I'd never been cold-shouldered by a wheelchair before.

"You're the one threatening physical violence two seconds after I've got through the door. I'm still glad to see you, though."

"Actually, you looked traumatised."

"I'm not traumatised," I protested. "I'm just not used to you being in a wheelchair."

"Using a wheelchair."

"Pardon?"

"I'm supposed to think of it as *using a wheelchair*. On account of how it's not something that limits me. It's a tool I use to get around." He sighed. "Although I'm not sure what the difference is, given it's a tool I only use because I have to."

"Um…"

"Because I can't walk."

"Nik, I—"

"Because my spine is fucked."

"Hi," said Ellery. "I'm Ellery."

Nik turned back. "What the hell? You brought a random? To my hospital?"

She tucked her hands into her hoodie pockets. "He didn't bring me. I tagged along. My home life is so busted that between spending Christmas with my family or travelling halfway across the world to meet a grumpy stranger *using a wheelchair*, you were my best option."

There was a long silence.

"Okay." Nik let out a long, rough breath. "So I do actually feel sorry for you right now."

Ellery smirked. "Last brownie for me."

"Can we," I asked, possibly ill-advisedly, "go sit down somewhere? Because I really do want to hug you, Nik. I mean, if you want to be hugged."

"Café? It's depressingly nutritional."

"I thought you'd be into that."

"I was…I guess I am, but I keep wondering what's the point."

"What do you mean?" I narrowed my eyes at him.

"Oh, just. I went to a lot of trouble to take care of this body. I ate healthily. Went to the gym every day. And it still betrayed me."

"I think the fact you got hit by a car and are still alive is evidence of your body coming through for you. Not the opposite."

"Maybe. I don't know."

"Well." That was Ellery. "I'm going to bounce."

Nik's fingers twitched guiltily in his lap. "I'm sorry. I've been an unwelcoming dick. Arden's told me a lot about you, so it's good to finally meet up."

"Thanks, but I'm still leaving. You two need time to catch up." She scuffed her boot against the pristine floor. "I can come back another day."

"I'd like that. I'll try to be nicer."

"Don't bother. Nice is bullshit." And with that, she

stomped off, pulling up her hood against the Boston chill.

Nik and I went to the café—and it was actually pretty nice considering it was a café in a hospital. It still had that diligently clean and functional air, but the windows running all down one side kept it light and airy, with the outside world just a finger's brush away. I had one of their whole wheat pasta salad things and Nik had a coffee, which I didn't offer to carry and he didn't ask me to help with.

The tables had been carefully laid out—lots of space and the furniture itself was light, so I could easily drag my chair up next to Nik. And from that position, I was able to turn my body into his, and get my promised hug. Despite our conversation in the lobby, he squeezed me really tight.

"I'm sorry," he mumbled.

I snuffled into the side of his neck. He smelled just like he always did: soap and the freshness of summer days. "Please don't worry about it. I'd rather know when I'm doing something annoying."

"Everything annoys me." He disentangled us, but gently. "It takes all I have not to lash out on the people trying to help me."

I gazed at him, biting my lip. "Is it…really hard?"

"Not being an ungrateful git?"

"The whole…rehab thing."

"Yeah, Arden." I guess I deserved the look he was giving me. "It's really hard. It's boring and frustrating and exhausting."

"Why didn't you tell me?"

"I don't know. I guess I took it as read you didn't think I was eating fairy cakes and making balloon animals over here."

"But you always said you were fine—oh shit, I'm the worst friend ever."

One of the shrugs that had become familiar to me from Skype. "It's not your fault. I liked being able to pretend it wasn't a big deal. That I was still…you know. The same."

"Nik, you *are* the same. And I can see what good progress you're making. I mean, last time I was here, you were in a bed covered in tubes. Now you're whizzing around and—not to objectify you or anything—your arms are seriously jacked."

His mouth pulled downwards. "Don't pity-objectify me."

"Oh my God. I'm not. I wouldn't." He didn't answer, so I pressed on. "You know I've had a queer boy crush on you forever. I mean, okay, I put thoughts of my penis aside when I was legit worried you were going to die. But now you're not, I promise I'm still creepily into you."

"The first thing you saw when you looked at me was the chair."

"Only because I wasn't used to it. Now I'm perving over your muscles just like old times."

"Nobody's ever going to look at me the way they used to." His hair had got quite long in the intervening months, giving him a touch of the David Hasselhoffs, and now he pushed it impatiently out of his eyes. "And I know that's a fucking shallow thing to be obsessing over when I'm surrounded by people who've suffered strokes or brain injury or lost their actual limbs."

I shrugged. "I think you can probably obsess about whatever the hell you want."

"They've got these phrases they use here: maximum possible recovery, best quality of life attainable, optimum results for you, highest level of function. It's meant to be encouraging but it's also about managing your expectations. Making sure you know that it's different for you now. That this is how it is and how it's going to be. And you can't take anything for granted ever again."

"You can take some things for granted, though."

"I'd say walking is pretty baseline for most of us."

"Bit of a sweeping statement considering the amount of times you've watched me fall over literally nothing."

He laughed—harsher than I was used to, but it was so good to hear.

"And anyway," I continued, "walking only feels baseline because the world is set up in a way that ignores people who don't use their legs to get around."

Nik snorted. "Did you read that on Tumblr?"

"Maybe, but that doesn't mean it's not true. And the point is, just because you're moving differently now, doesn't mean you've stopped being you."

"It's not that simple. Rationally, I know I'm not my legs or my spine or the titanium inside my body. But sometimes I get so fucking claustrophobic, like I'm in prison, except what I'm stuck inside is me." He finished the last swallow of his coffee and crumpled up the environmentally friendly cup. "I don't know how to feel that way and still understand who I am."

"Oh, Nik." It wasn't much of an answer but he couldn't have been expecting one.

"Don't worry. I probably shouldn't be telling you this kind of shit."

I pouted at him. "I'm your best friend. I'm exactly who

you should be telling. Well, me and maybe professionals who can concretely help."

"I've got plenty of those." He made a dismissive gesture. "It's more that I know I'm supposed to be bearing this with grace and resilience, and clearly I'm not."

"The fact you struggle sometimes doesn't mean you're doing it wrong."

He turned to look at me, his eyes and mouth framed by lines that hadn't been there before. "I guess you always think…you'll be braver, somehow."

"You *are* brave," I protested. "You are so brave."

He didn't answer for a long time. And then all he said was, "I could probably take another hug."

I threw my arms around him and tucked myself tightly against his side, and this time he did nothing to push me away, so I stayed. So we both did, evening deepening into night beyond the horizons of the windows. Quietly we sat together, as we had at Oxford, except it was Boston we watched, gleaming on the silky waters of the harbour in shades of amber and scarlet and jade.

CHAPTER 20

The next day I was woken up by Ellery punching me urgently in the shoulder. "Come on. You're missing stuff."

"I'm missing sleep."

"But...but..." Her voice rose into something dangerously close to a whine. "Arden."

"What? This better be spectacular."

Groaning, I allowed myself to be bullied out of bed. Whereupon Ellery sprang over to the window and ripped the curtains open, revealing the dirty redbrick of the bar opposite and the wire curlicues around the car park—or parking lot, as I guess Americans would call it—all thickly sugared with...

"Snow!" I yelled.

"Yeah." Ellery offered one of her rare, non-mocking smiles.

"I can't remember the last time we actually had snow at Christmas."

"Well"—she seemed to remember herself and shrugged—"give climate change another couple of years."

"Oh, come on. You were excited too."

"No I wasn't. I just thought *you* would be."

"And you were right. Let's go out and play."

It turned out, snow didn't fuck around in this part of the world. It came down in fat, fluffy flakes and piled up in pillowy drifts by the sides of the roads, bringing fresh unfamiliarity to an already unfamiliar city. I was glad of Caspian's coat and Ilya's scarf, and relieved that Ellery's various expeditions had included a shopping trip, because she was, at last, dressed for the weather, even if her beanie had cat ears on it. Caspian would probably have killed me if she'd fallen ill on my watch.

Which was when a different, but still horribly relevant, thought hit me like a freight train.

"Ellery," I said, "your family know you're with me, don't they?"

Her eyes flicked to mine and then away again. "Probably."

"What does *probably* mean?"

"You're the one with the English degree."

"I don't mean its etymology. You did tell them, right? Please tell me you told them."

"They won't notice anyway."

Oh Jesus. My mind was already whirling with headlines: HART FAMILY SCION IN ABSCONDMENT SCANDAL; POSH BIRD BAILS WITH BROTHER'S BF; GAY JOURNALIST ABDUCTS HEIRESS. "Believe me, they'll notice."

"That's their problem."

"You have to tell them. Or"—I paused beneath an ice-crinkled awning to catch my breath and calm my racing heart—"if you won't, then I will."

She pulled her hat even further down her brow. "Do what you like. But I'm not going back."

"What? Ever?"

"Until you do."

Okay. We could work with that. My numb fingers fumbled my phone out of my pocket and I began swiping through my contacts. I'd deleted Caspian's number in a moment of remembering I had pride, and Ilya—even assuming he took my call—didn't work for Caspian anymore. That one time I'd contacted Finesilver had gone awfully. So that left…

Well, fuck me sideways with a rusty banana. Nathaniel had given me his contact details when he'd invited me for dinner. And while he was absolutely the last person I wanted to be texting, it didn't seem like I had much choice. I started *Dear Nathaniel* and then realised how weird that looked. *Hi Nathaniel*, I tried again, *this is Arden St. Ives.* Wait. How many Ardens was he likely to have in his phone? *Hi Nathaniel. This is Arden. I'm afraid yours is the only number I have. Could you please tell Caspian that Ellery has decided to spend the holiday in the US. She's safe and well, and sorry not to let you know sooner. Happy Christmas to everyone.*

I hit SEND before I could obsess over it, trying not to resent how much it probably cost me to text the UK. And in a less than a minute, despite how early it must have been over there, got back: *Season's greetings, Arden. Thank you for letting us know.*

Ellery and I weren't best pleased with each other for a little while after that, but then she took me to the Public Garden, which looked so beautiful, with the stripped bare trees and the silver glaze of ice on the pond thing, that I couldn't stay cross with her. We found some untouched snow near a parade of brass ducks in Christmas hats, and tried to make a snowman. Except it ended up looking more like a penis, so we committed to the design, and fashioned a towering, majestic snowdong, complete with scrotum, instead. After we'd unleashed it on the world via Insta, I got worried about kids seeing it, as it were, in the flesh, and went full Bastard of Bolton on our creation.

From there, we stopped for French hot chocolate at a mildly pretentious coffee shop, and strolled through the various Christmas markets, arm in arm, before looping Nikwards. This time he was up in his room, waiting by the window, shadows of the falling snow dappling his face like sunlight.

"Love what you've done with the place," drawled Ellery, taking in the nice but undeniably hospitaly furnishings.

"Thanks." Nik turned towards us. "Walks off."

We'd had plans to wander a bit in the gardens, which wound gently down towards the harbour. He'd delivered the words so aggressively, I wasn't quite sure how he was expecting me to respond. In the end, I went with a neutral-sounding "Oh."

"Can't do snow," he added. "Well, I can. But I'd need to fuck around with wheelblades and I've never used them before and...I don't know. I don't want to."

"Fine with me." Ellery pitched herself onto the crisp white sheets of Nik's bed. "It is literally freezing out there."

Nik shot me a shifty look from beneath the fall of his hair. "I'm sorry, okay?"

"Good grief, don't apologise," I told him hastily. "I'm here to be with you. I don't care what we do."

"I care. I care about not being able to do things."

Ellery rolled her eyes. "It's not about doing or not doing. It's about when and how, and if you want to figure out navigating snow with us standing right there, pointing and laughing."

"I would not point and laugh," I cried, outraged.

"No," said Ellery, "but you'd look all, like, worried and shit, which is even worse."

"She's right." Nik was smiling—his old, dimple-touched smile.

And Ellery, of course, looked unbearably smug. "I'm always right."

"Before I forget"—Nik pointed to a large box in the corner of the room—"your family had that delivered. But we're not allowed to open it until Christmas Day."

I ran over to poke at it, smell it, and peer through the gaps of the packing tape. None of which helped me discern the contexts. "Oooh. What do you think it is?"

"Well." Nik scratched his stubble thoughtfully. "I'm by no means an expert but I'd say it's a box."

I gave him a withering glare. "Har, har."

And then Ellery made an odd sound, a sort of awkward half cough. "Look," she muttered, "I kind of…picked something up for you as well. But it's not a fucking Christmas present, okay? Because I do not do Christmas. Or presents."

"So"—Nik raised a quizzical eyebrow—"it's what exactly?"

"Something else." She pulled a carrier bag out of her rucksack and tossed it into his lap. "Here. You might like these. Or not. I don't care."

Gingerly—and I couldn't blame him for that—he peeled open the plastic.

Ellery squirmed in evident discomfort. "They're these really tragic choose-your-own-adventure books from the eighties or whatever. My dad was really into them because he was a big stupid nerd and my brother, who is also a big stupid nerd, used to make me read them with him when I was sick. And since you're clearly a big stupid nerd as well, I thought you might…not hate them."

"Thank you," said Nik. "I think."

"Don't do them by yourself, because that would be beyond sad. But you could play them with Arden, maybe. If you wanted."

Nik was watching her with the *confused but okay with it* expression that signified a positive Ellery action. "What about you?"

"Why the fuck would I want to play a choose-your-own-adventure book with Arden? I've got way better things to do with my time."

"No"—his lips twitched—"would you play one with both of us?"

She got super interested in the toe of her boot. "Out of pity."

"Then it's a deal."

"Do I get a say in this?" I asked.

They both stared at me. "No."

It wasn't a real complaint. Not when Nik's eyes were bright and Ellery was blatantly trying to hide a smile. And that was how we ended up spending Christmas Eve playing *The Warlock of Firetop Mountain* in Nik's hospital room. We took turns reading, passing the book between us after every decision point, and bickering constantly about whether we should go east or west, or if it was better to sneak past or stab the goblin, and whether it was ever acceptable to beat up an old man just in case he turned out to be a wererat like the last guy.

We died a lot: first to an orc, then to a giant sandworm, then to a minotaur, then to the same orc that killed us the first time because we were pretty sure you needed the stuff you got from the orc to have any chance of winning later. And before long, Nik was mapping the whole thing on his tablet, and arguing with Ellery about whether they should do it geographically, by dungeon layout or meta-textually by connections between paragraphs in the book, with my suggestion that we could just Google a walk-through being shouted down by both of them.

This wasn't a new side to Nik—he was, and always had been, a total geek in the body of a Greek god—but Ellery, despite her initial attempts to appear disinterested, was surprisingly engaged. Though, of course, her story had made me think of Caspian too: a time before grief and shame had made him theirs, a boy with restless hands and hopeful eyes, laughing with his little sister as he led her through these paper labyrinths.

CHAPTER 21

Ellery vanished again that night. Fuck knows what she was doing and probably I should have been worried, but worrying about Ellery was like worrying about water: Yes, it had the potential to cause a lot of carnage, but it was also just kind of there. And it was only when the door of my room clicked closed behind me that I realised I'd essentially committed myself to spending Christmas Eve alone in a Holiday Inn. Which apparently hadn't occurred to me in my rush to prove what an awesome friend I was.

Of course, I had my phone and my Kindle. There was absolutely no need for me to spend the time lying on my bed, watching the drift of snowflakes against the windows, as if I was the sole survivor of a very quiet apocalypse. Except, y'know. There I was, lying on my bed, watching the drift of snowflakes against the windows, wondering when I could Skype home without it looking so desperate my family would notice.

This was…this was going to be a long night.

Then my phone rang. Unknown number. Oh my God. Oh my *God*. My heart was going like the spinner in *Inception*. It couldn't be. Could it? Could it really be Caspian?

My hands were shaking so much I nearly swiped the wrong way and hung up. "H-hello?"

"Happy Christmas, poppet."

Help. Fuck.

"I take it," murmured George, "you were hoping for someone else?"

I made a desperate attempt to pull myself together. "N-not hoping. Not exactly. I'm sorry."

"Love's such a pisser, isn't it?"

"It really is." Covering my nose with my, well, my sleeve, I indulged in a sniffle or two. "I'm glad to hear from you, though."

"Of course you are. I'm delightful."

That almost made me smile. "I didn't…I mean…you're not, um, upset? Because…because…"

"Because you're not crying in a hotel room over me?" I practically *heard* the eye roll. "I think I can live without that."

"I don't wish you were him or anything."

"Poppet, I'm far too egoistical for the thought to have even crossed my mind." Her voice softened. "The things I want from you—your body for sex and art, and your company, when you're not being put to other uses—can exist with perfect safety outside whatever you need to feel for Caspian Hart. Let's not start confusing the two."

"I'm not. Not really." I adopted a less…sobby position on the bed. Maybe I *was* getting better. Because while everything I felt for Caspian still held me in a tiger-clawed grip, the wounds seemed less…forever, somehow? Or maybe I was used to the pain. "Thank you for calling. You really are the best, um, whatever we are."

"Lovers. Friends. It's not complicated."

It wasn't. And it didn't have to be. "What are your Christmas plans?"

"Beyond talking to you, I don't have any. Which," she added firmly, "is how I prefer it. Although I may well go to Mara's on Boxing Day, and lightly threaten her husband."

That sounded…something. "Threaten him with what?"

"With myself." She gave a very knowing, very wicked chuckle. "We all know better, but there's still a part of him that fears his wife is going to spontaneously turn gay and run away with me."

"You don't actually want her to, right?"

"Fuck no. Things that may not be are infinitely beautiful. Things that are…well, they tend to be tedious."

Perhaps someday I'd feel the same about Caspian. It wasn't the worst idea in the world. "Do you come up with these things in advance?"

"No, poppet. I don't have to. I'm not Mr. Collins."

I snickered. Because you could always trust George with a bit of lit-themed shade.

"Truth time, though," she went on. "How are you really?"

"I"—I had to think about it—"I'm really not too bad. It's weird being away from my family but I'll Skype them later."

"And your friend?"

"Could…probably be better," I admitted. "I don't know. It's hard to tell. I don't know what's a normal level of frustrated, demoralised, and pissed off for someone with a spinal cord injury."

"Whatever level he wants?"

"That's fair."

"Yes. I am terribly fair. It mostly comes from indifference."

"That or caring more than you let on."

She made an appalled noise. "Don't think you're safe from punishment just because you're in another country."

"Aren't I?"

"Well," she said slowly, "that depends. How obedient do you think you can be?"

I shivered, pretty much ready to be as obedient as she told me to be. Except then I remembered a night in Oxford when I'd also felt alone, and how Caspian had given me exactly what I needed: kindness and pain and surety and safety. It was easy to be with George when I was with her. But like this, when memories were closer than bodies? I was afraid Caspian would slip between us. And I just couldn't do that to her. "Can we wait until I get home?"

"Of course we can. After all"—another of those silences that left me imagining her expression—"absence makes the arse grow fonder."

"You're the worst. But you should also know my arse is incredibly fond of you."

"Good. It's very charming and I'm looking forward to spending more time with it in the new year."

Suddenly my Christmas Eve was looking way less bleak than it had before. "I'll see you soon, okay?"

"Count on it, poppet."

* * *

Maybe my Holiday Inn Christmas Eve had fucked up my sense of perspective but Christmas Day in a hospital could have sucked way more. I mean, when you got right down to it, holidays were supposed to be about being with the people you loved—and I was. I'd managed to catch my folks in the creepy window between time zones, which meant it was Christmas for me when it wasn't for them, and the sight of our pokey living room strung with fairy lights had briefly made me homesick. But even that wasn't so bad, the warm ache of having something worth missing. Someday, I'd have someone to take back with me. Except fantasy and memory were tricksy bedfellows, and kept leading me to Caspian. That weekend we'd spent together in Kinlochbervie. What Christmas with him, and my family, might be like. The games we'd play. How we could walk hand in hand along the beach in the bright chill of Christmas morning and snuggle beneath the eaves at night. All the kisses I'd steal. The smiles I'd coax from him. The way he'd hold me, with such strength and need, it had always felt like love.

Fuck. When was I going to stop doing this?

Anyway, anyway, anyway. The café laid on a proper Christmas lunch, and the staff had done their best to decorate, so we were feeling fairly festive by the time we were heading back to Nik's room to open our presents. I knew Ellery didn't Do Christmas, but I'd got her a copy of *Rat Girl*, which she accepted with enough ill grace that I could tell she was into it. And Nik and I had a gift-exchange tradition from our student days, when we'd had more time than either money or sense, although to be honest I don't think much had changed since then. It required you to go somewhere, or be somewhere, and find a piece of tourist tat from a different place entirely. This meant Nik got a baseball cap with I ♥ TOKYO on the front, purchased from a souvenir stall in London, and I got a T-shirt with the New York Yankees logo on it that Nik had found in a bin on one of his therapeutic walks.

"Do not," Ellery warned me, "even think about wearing that here."

The box from my family turned out to mainly contain a quilt for Nik that Mum had made him. We laid it over his bed, and the room seemed instantly less antiseptic, while he had some emotions he felt obviously more comfortable sharing with the window.

"She really didn't have to do that," he muttered finally.

I smoothed down the edges of the quilt and made sure it was hanging evenly. Mum had gone for geometric patterns in shades of blue—very bold, and subtly masculine. "Yeah, it's a present for you, so definitionally she didn't."

He snuffled.

"Listen…" I flipped open the card, which had a picture of a polar bear on it:

Dear Nik, Thank you so much for taking such good care of our Arden at Oxford. You deserve a medal but we thought this would be warmer, and the Internet tells us it's very cold in Boston. Lots of love and Happy Christmas, Iris, Hazel, and Rabbie.

"You'll say thank you for me, right?" said Nik, still to the window.

I nudged gently against his shoulder. "No way. I'm going to make them think you're ungrateful so they stop liking you."

There was a card for me too. This one had a picture of a cartoon squirrel on it, and said:

Our favourite Ardy, we thought long and hard about what to get you this year, and then realised there was nothing we could give our twenty-something–making-his-way-in-the world that would be better than cold hard cash. So we've sent you some direct to your bank account. And also some socks. But these do not count as legal tender, so they are enclosed. We nearly sent pants as well but we have decided you are old enough now that it would be creepy. Which is our way of saying: Buy your own damn pants. All our love, Mum, Hazel, and Rabbie.

The socks were another Mum special: They were super soft and came in all the colours of the rainbow. I donated the dark purple pair to Ellery, in case she felt left out, and she put them on straightaway. Such was the power of Mum's socks.

And the box, which I think we were all starting to believe was actually a dimension to a pocket plane of presents, still wasn't empty. The was a stocking each for Nik and me (although I shared mine with Ellery), stuffed with the usual assortment of chocolate coins, tangerines, funny little puzzles that Rabbie had found or made, card games, seaglass, pocket books, stationery, and—of course—a Rubik's Cube for me. I groaned as Ellery unwrapped it.

"What's the matter?"

"They do this every year. The fucking bastards."

Nik tilted his head quizzically. "Give you a Rubik's Cube? Wow, yeah, your family are total monsters."

"I hate the damn things. I can't do them. I might, when I was younger, have legitimately thrown tantrums over them. But"—I grit my teeth—"I can't stop fiddling with them."

"You do know there's a trick to them, right?"

"OMG, yes. I know there's a trick to them. I have read the Internet. I have followed step-by-step instructions on YouTube. I still can't fucking do them."

"Pass it here," said Nik, already insufferable. And Ellery threw him the small, plastic bane of my life. A flurry of clicks followed. And within about thirty seconds, he smugly placed a completed Rubik's Cube on the bedside table. "Boom baby."

Ellery stared at it for a long moment. "I can't decide if that was weirdly sexy."

"You"—I glared at Nik, who was making zero attempt to pretend he wasn't laughing at me—"engineering dick."

He fluttered his lashes. "I'm saving you, Arden. Saving you from yourself."

"I'm just going to get in this box and mail myself back to England."

"Don't do that." Ellery had crept over and was peering into the depths. "There's still stuff inside."

And she was correct: Right down at the bottom, lovingly cushioned in tissue paper, was a lavish assortment of all my favourite goodies. Shortbread, tablet, some mini-Dundee cakes, Tunnock's caramel wafers, packets of Soor plooms, a bottle of Rabbie's homemade mead, and oh joy of joys, even a couple of cans of Irn-Bru. I cracked one open and took a deep draught of rusty orange fizziness.

"*Ahhhhh.*"

"You know," Nik told me, "the fact you actually like that stuff makes me genuinely doubt you're English."

I made an unseemly, if inevitable, noise. "I was raised on it. It is literally magic."

Ellery made a *let me try it* gesture. It was probably the first time I'd ever seen her look shocked. "That is…horrible."

"Yes." My eyes fluttered in Irn-Brugasmic bliss. "Yes it is."

We were quiet for a while, preoccupied with eating and drinking in that lazy Christmas afternoon way when you aren't really hungry or thirsty but it's satisfying to keep doing both anyway.

Eventually, Ellery looked up from the packet of Soor plooms she'd commandeered, and said slightly wistfully, "Your family's really nice."

"They're the best." Suddenly, I realised this wasn't the most tactful thing to be saying in front of Ellery and Nik, since they both had pretty strained home lives. "But family can be who you choose, not just the people you're stuck with."

She made a contemptuous noise. "Screw family."

"Not a traditional toast by any means." Nik had made significant inroads into the mead. "But I'll drink to it."

"Family leave you. Let you down. Fuck you up." But then Ellery paused, her lips curling into a smile. "Friends, though. Maybe they're worth something."

I hoisted up my second can of Irn-Bru, and Nik waved the mead bottle. "Friends," we chorused.

Aluminium against glass was more of a clunk than a clink. But it still counted.

* * *

Ellery's nocturnal ramblings must have finally caught up with her, because she fell asleep a few hours later, sausage-rolled in Mum's quilt. I was on the floor next to Nik, my head resting against his leg, while he absently curled my hair around his fingers—something he'd often done at Oxford while he was thinking.

"Arden," he said softly, "what am I going to do?"

I twisted so I was looking up at him. "Do?"

"Yeah after"—he made a helpless gesture—"this. When I reach my highest level of functionality."

"I thought you were going to MIT."

"That was before."

I opened my mouth. Then closed it again. Then tried anyway. "I'm not sure how to say this without it sounding bad but...what's changed? I mean, I'm aware you have a disability now, not least because"—I risked a grin and he pulled my hair in return—"you won't shut up about it, but I'm not sure why that would affect what you want to do with your life."

"I know I was in a bad mood the other day, but I wasn't lying when I said I'd changed. That this stuff changes you. I just"—he sighed—"I can't figure what still belongs to me."

"Whatever you want to, surely." He didn't reply, so I asked instead, "What would you do if you didn't stay here?"

"Go back to England, probably? My parents would take care of me if I let them. They'd probably literally come on the parquet over making their house accessible for their *differently abled* second son."

"That sounds gross."

"They are gross. It'd be nice to be closer to you again, though. Except I'd have to pretend Poppy didn't exist."

"And," I pointed out, "you want to be…some kind of boring and complicated engineer that I don't understand."

He gazed at me, new shadows in his eyes. "But what if I can't?"

"You never asked that question when you could walk."

"I didn't know what hurt was before." He slid his fingers up the nape of my neck, his touch so gentle compared to his words. "I guess I learned how to be scared. How to fail."

"To…truly want something," I heard myself say, "is to make yourself vulnerable."

"Um. Where did that come from?"

"Caspian."

He scowled. "And I'm supposed to take life advice from the guy who broke your heart?"

"Maybe if it's good life advice?" I nuzzled into his leg. "I think he's right, you know. I mean, you haven't failed— to fail you have to do something, and someone else I love said that—and I don't believe you're as scared as you think. I think you just realised how much you want to go MIT and that's freaked you out. Because when you want something, you know you can lose it, whether you get hit by cars or not."

He was quiet awhile. And then said, "The thing is, I just don't know anymore."

I turned, and folded my elbows over his knees, so I could look at him properly. Both eyes. "And that's okay. Whatever you do—whether that's staying here or coming back to England or moving to, like, Mars—you know I will always be there for you."

"Thanks." He flicked a finger lightly against my nose.

"And," I went on, "I will always love you—"

Nik, in the fashion of most tragically heterosexual men, wasn't very good at emotions. Even when he needed them. He blushed. "So gay."

"So gay," I agreed, laughing. "Although I heard there's been some new legislation, so now the straights are allowed to have feelings too."

"Sorry." He was still blushing—all the way up to his ears. "I mean, I...y'know...I"—he seemed to get something caught in his throat—"you too."

I shook my head. "How do you people function? But seriously, Nik. I love you and I believe in you and I'll support you no matter what you do. And I know you say you've changed, and probably you have, but when it comes down to the colours of your dreams, and whatever makes your heart fly, and the things that really matter, you always get to choose."

"Choose what?"

"What you take with you and what you leave behind." I let out a shaky breath. "Because that's all change is."

Nik leaned down and pressed his brow briefly to mine. "I hope you're right."

I tried to smile. I hoped so too.

CHAPTER 22

In Kinlochbervie, the days between Christmas and New Year's lumbered along like concussed camels. I actually kind of enjoyed them, getting up late, falling asleep on the sofa in the middle of the afternoon, eating Terry's Chocolate Orange for breakfast, and turkey sandwiches for dinner, watching movies we'd seen about a million times before because nobody could be bothered to change the channel, and embarking on our annual game of *Twilight Imperium*, only for it to take six hours just to set up, and another six to read the instructions, by which time we'd all forgotten why we'd ever thought it was a good idea to try and play it in the first place.

But things ended up getting pretty busy in Boston. Poppy and her boyfriend arrived the day after Boxing Day, full of apologies for not having been able to make it out any earlier. At least, Poppy was full of apologies. Colt just stood there looking strong and silent and like he was going to be the cowboy from *The Big Lebowski*, give or take twenty years. They'd also secretly, and quite spontaneously, got married—

Poppy had a piece of braided corn on her fourth finger—which meant that every gossip outlet in the world knew about it. Or were, at least, speculating rampantly. She seemed happy, though. And her husband had this honey-slow smile that he only ever gave to her, so I guess he was too.

Ellery and I departed on the thirty-first, leaving Nik to his sister, and a gaggle of his MIT friends who'd arrived for New Year's. What we'd discussed on Christmas Day hadn't come up again (though we had managed to finish *Citadel of Chaos* and *Creature of Havoc*), but when Poppy had talked about buying a place in Boston, Nik hadn't immediately shut it down—so I took that as a good sign. It was hard, of course, saying goodbye, but as I clung to him and made no attempt to be brave about it, I knew with a deep, abiding certainty he was going to be okay. Nik was golden. He always had been. And I trusted him to find his happiness—wherever it lay.

Ellery and I were subdued on the return flight. I guess we'd both had our reasons for wanting to get away for a bit, but that was the thing about getting away: At some point, you had to come back, and everything you'd left behind would still be waiting. Which, now that I thought about it, was mostly awesome in my case. I had a job I loved, and was currently kicking ass at, somewhere to live that was actually within my budget, and people who cared about me, including one I was enthusiastically sexing. And yes, there was still the Caspian thing, wedged into my soft tissue like a piece of broken tooth, but it was New Year's Eve. Wasn't that the perfect time to let go of the past, make a fresh start, blah blah, blah?

Maybe I could even listen to my own damn advice.

Choose what to take and what to leave behind, I'd told Nik. Wasn't it about time I left Caspian behind? I could hold on to the good stuff—everything he'd taught me and shown me and given me. But I also needed to let go, move on, get the fuck over him. And admittedly, I'd been telling myself that for months. But then, having him get engaged in my face and being invited to dinner with his frustratingly-more-human-than-I-wanted-to-admit boyfriend hadn't exactly made it easy. If you squinted at it funny, it was almost like Caspian was having as much trouble forgetting about me as I was forgetting about him.

Still. That was his problem. It wasn't going to be mine. And there'd be no more weird interviews, or ambiguous encounters, or double-edged comments that made me think I had a chance. I was officially done.

Tomorrow was the first day of…the next bit of my life.

* * *

Between an inevitable string of delays and terrible traffic on the M1, we didn't make it back until nearly ten o'clock at night. London was sullen and drizzly, its lights tepid smears through the greying haze, and we'd turned off the heating while we were away, so the warehouse greeted us with a belch of frigid air the moment we opened the door. Mmm. Homey.

Yanking my wheelie over the threshold, I stumbled to the sofa and slumped onto it, still in my coat and scarf. Probably I would end up sleeping in them too.

"Want to see the fireworks?" asked Ellery.

I shook my head. "I'm pretty tired."

"Oh." A pause. "Want to get fucked up?"

"I'm not sure I need help with that right now."

She vanished into her bedroom and reappeared, a plastic baggie of white powder dangling from between her fingertips. "It's good shit. Best Colombian."

"Given I genuinely can't tell anymore when people are talking about coffee and when they're talking about drugs, I don't think this is the lifestyle for me."

Ellery sat down next to me, tucking her booted feet under her. "It'll be way better than coffee."

"I've never actually"—I waved my hands unhelpfully—"used cocaine before."

"Are you sure? Because you've got the lingo down."

"Oh, shut up. And also there's the nose issue."

She gave me one of her slow, contemptuous blinks. "The nose issue?"

"Yes. The nose issue. I don't want to put things up my nose. My nose is a one-way street."

"You know that's what fundamentalists say about anal sex."

"Okay, but listen." I pulled myself into a more alert position. "I've had anal sex and it's amazing. Once, when I was little, Hazel made me laugh while I was drinking a glass of milk and it went up my nose and it was one of the most horrible things that has ever happened to me."

"But did you get high afterwards?"

"Obviously not. It just made my entire head hurt from the inside of my face."

Ellery shrugged. "That's the difference."

I was not convinced.

"Coke's an anaesthetic. The worst you'll feel is numb." She uncurled and emptied the contents of the bag onto the table, cutting the powder expertly with the edge of her Coutts of London bank card. "Anyway, it's up to you."

Urgh. Decisions. I mean, I knew impulsively experimenting with Class A drugs was a bad idea. But in that exact moment, squashed between a past I couldn't change and a future I wasn't sure I was ready for, it was hard to care.

Ellery was shaping the lines now. And I was half hypnotised by the precision of her movements, the ephemeral elegance of the paths she drew in dust upon our coffee table, wondering if I'd fallen nonconsensually into a Hollinghurst novel. "You know, it's okay," she said, "to want a break from everything being shitty all the time."

"It wouldn't be real, though."

"No feelings are real." She caught my eye a moment, one of those scalpel glances. "Or all of them are."

I didn't want to think about that. "I'm in."

Last month's issue of *Milieu* had been languishing on the arm of the sofa. Ellery grabbed it, ripped out a page, rolled it into a thin tube, and handed it to me. "Be my guest."

"Um"—my bravado had apparently evaporated like kettle steam—"what do I...do?"

"Stick it up your nose and inhale. It's not complicated."

I wasn't, in all honesty, the most physically coordinated person when I was nervous, but I took heart from the fact my body had been breathing successfully for nearly twenty-two years. And that was all this was, right? Breathing with some extra powder thrown in. Also, I'd seen *The Wolf of Wall Street*. I could do this.

Here's something they don't tell you about taking drugs: It's really undignified. Like, you have to be in a bad way already not to balk at the ways you get the stuff inside you. It made me feel super sorry for heroin addicts, I mean above and beyond the fact they were addicted to heroin. Anyway, I put the magazine up my nose, bent over the table, and y'know, inhaled. And for the record, Ellery was wrong. It did hurt—this weird brain flash like a backward sneeze, followed by the buzz of spiking adrenaline, and then this numbness spreading from my nose.

While I sat there, processing the fact I was now officially On Drugs, and making unhappy cat-with-a-furball noises, because I swear to God I could feel that shit sliding down my throat, Ellery nudged me out of the way and did the second line with a lot more finesse.

"So," she said, after a moment or two, "you want to go see the fireworks now?"

And I did. I really did.

* * *

I don't completely remember how we got to the Millennium Bridge—only that, despite the crowds and having to tumble breathlessly into bathrooms to take more coke, I was feeling good. Not the jittery, frenetic joy of ecstasy or the lazy softness of weed, but this smooth conviction of well-being that—had its duration not been so fleeting—would have been indistinguishable from any other kind of happiness. A night of perfect sleep. A truly amazing shower. The best cup of coffee imaginable. The slog back from Boston had fallen away, sloughed off like old skin, taking with it every-thing that had made me sad or worried or scared. And I had this…this *clarity* now—as if I'd finally ripped off the dirty glasses of my own doubts and insecurities and could see the world as it truly was.

Full of hope. Adventure. Possibility.

Nothing I couldn't handle.

And so beautiful, as we pushed our way forward, invinci-ble amongst the press of strangers. Ellery's hand was warm in mine as I turned my face to the horizon—to the pale moon of Big Ben's illuminated face and the rainbow hoop of the London Eye.

Ten…

Nine…

Voices all around us. The sky sinuous with shadows, like a lover's body, turning in your arms.

Five…

Four…

It didn't matter I wasn't with Caspian.

I was strong. I was whole. I was *happy*.

Two…

Happy. Happy. Happy.

One!

The chimes began to strike, rolling out over the dark wa-ters. Then came the crackle of gunpowder in the distance, and suddenly everything was colour on colour on colour. With bonus Adele.

I'd always loved fireworks. I mean, they were loud and sparkly, what wasn't there for me to be into? But my only real experience of them was Rabbie crouched in the middle of our back garden, swearing and dropping matches, and then running away frantically as a couple of rockets wheezed into the air.

This was…this was…not like that. There were fireworks that whooshed upwards from the ground, leaving long comet trails in their wake, and others that exploded into vast and lavish starbursts. Some of them spun in spirals in the centre of the Eye and some poured down from the sky like it was raining light. My soul crackled with each new explosion, shining amethyst, emerald, and jade, like the reflections in the Thames. I felt…almost transparent. But in a good way. The usual mess that lived inside me, gone. Transformed into a stream of bright moments under a fresh-born sky.

I glanced at Ellery, lit up, and wanting to share it, and she grinned back at me, her eyes full of tiny fireworks, and so blue just then. The bluest I'd ever seen them. Blue enough to break me.

And then it was slipping away—whatever I'd felt, or thought I'd felt, everything I'd learned, or thought I'd learned. And I knew it was fairy gold. Had only ever been fairy gold. And here I was, exhausted, on a bridge in the middle of London, with my still heart in ruins, and nothing to show for it but handfuls of dust.

I missed him.

I missed him so much.

And he would never be mine again.

Something flicked across Ellery's face. "Ard—"

Drowning, I kissed her.

Bare seconds before she wrenched away. "What the fuck?"

"I…I don't know…I'm sorry."

"You…why…" She stared at me. And I saw her eyes had never been his blue at all.

Remorse was a slow, sick tide rising inside me. My heart rabid in my chest. "I'm sorry. I'm so sorry."

She turned, ran, and the crowd swallowed her like a great, fleshly fish.

"Ellery. Please. I'm—"

At which point, I threw up over my shoes, the pavement, and some undeserving German tourists.

CHAPTER 23

Running. Bashing against the shoulders of strangers who recoiled when they saw me. Shouting Ellery's name. Sour, breathless sobs caught in my throat. Sweat streaming down my back, clotting in my hair. My heart thrashing like some dying thing.

It was no use.

She was long gone.

And I was falling apart. I stopped, eyes full of water, and dry-heaved stringy bile into the gutter. Then I started to cry in earnest.

What had I done?

The look on Ellery's face was scored into me with a compass point. I was never going to forget it for as long as I lived.

Or forgive myself.

Oh God, oh God, would she?

I pulled out my phone with damp, shaky hands and rang her. No answer. Tried again. Straight to, "The person you are trying to reach is not available." I knew she never bothered with messages but I left her one anyway. Well, "message" oversold its coherence. It was mainly crying.

And then I didn't really know what else to do except go home. I had to get the night bus, which some might say was punishment enough.

It wasn't, though.

Ellery wasn't at the warehouse. There was just the cold, the dark, and my abandoned wheelie. And Broderick's glassy, condemning eyes. I took a shower, because I was disgusting. I mean, physically disgusting. But I guess in pretty much all senses.

Sat under the spray, still shivering, feeling beyond wretched. Like I was coming down with the worst cold of my life.

The hot water ran out. Long before I was clean.

So I put on some pj's, wrapped myself in my duvet, and lay on the sofa, phone within reach in case Ellery called or texted or…or something, trying to sleep and wanting to die of shame.

Ellery was my friend. She'd trusted me. And in one stupid second, I'd destroyed it all.

* * *

She came home a little after dawn. Sunglasses on. Hood up.

"Ellery." I flailed out of my huddle. "Ellery, I'm sorry. I'm so sorry. I know that's not enough, but please believe me I didn't mean to—"

She strode past me. "I'm just here to get some things."

"Get some things? Are you…do you need me gone?"

"I need to be gone." Her bedroom door slammed behind her.

The world lurched as I tried to get off the sofa, and I'm sure I'd have been sick again if there'd been anything left inside me. By the time Ellery reemerged, with a rucksack slung over her shoulder, I was sweaty and trembly again, but at least upright.

"This is your place," I said. "I should be the one to move out."

The impenetrable sheen of her glasses reflected only my blotchy, messed-up face. "You don't have to move out. I'm staying with Innis for a bit."

"For how long?"

"Until I can fucking stand the sight of you."

I burst into tears. "I'm sorry. I…don't know why I…why I…"

"Sex is easy." She pushed roughly past me. "Sex is boring. You were supposed to be my friend."

"I *am* your friend," I wailed.

A pause. Her shoulders tightened. "You only ever wanted him."

"God. That's not true."

"Everyone always wants him." At last she turned, an oily, mascara-darkened tear slipping down her cheek. "He's good-looking and brilliant and knows how to be charming. He draws people in. And I'm—"

I opened my mouth to…I don't know…protest or probably just keep crying.

But she continued before I had a chance. "I'm just a fuck-up."

"You're not a fuck-up."

"Yeah, I am." She thrust her wrists towards me, with their silver scars. "Even fucked this up, remember. Acting out. Trying to get attention when the drugs weren't enough."

I brushed my fingers gently over the marks. "I've never believed that."

"You should. Because I'm a shitty person." She dragged her arm over her wet face, momentarily dislodging the sunglasses to give me a glimpse of her swollen, red-rimmed eyes. "I'm selfish and mean and I'm not...I don't know...I have no idea how to show it when I care about shit."

"I think," I said shakily, "I win the prize tonight for failing to show someone how much I care about them."

She made a sceptical noise, halfway between a snort and a sniffle. "Don't bother. I know who I am and I don't expect people to like me."

"I do like you."

"Well, you betrayed me."

I hung my head, pickling in guilt. "I know. It was a mistake, and a horrible thing to do. I don't know what happened."

"I don't fucking care."

Oh God. I needed to fix this—somehow, I needed to fix this—and my brain was porridge. Turns out the grown-ups had been right all along: Don't do drugs, kids. "Look"—I flapped about despairingly—"I'm not trying to make excuses here but I *was* a little bit off my head at the time. And yes, I was missing Caspian. But that doesn't mean how I feel about you is a lie."

No response from Ellery. Just her tight mouth and the blank stare of her sunglasses.

"I'm here for you," I told her. "Because of you. And it has

nothing to do with Caspian. Even if I never see him again, which is honestly looking increasingly likely, I'll still want to be your friend."

Her lip curled.

"I know that hasn't always been the case with other people. But I'm not like that. I'm not"—my voice rose unexpectedly—"I'm not like Nathaniel."

"I don't know, Arden." She folded her arms with stony precision. "Maybe you're exactly like Nathaniel."

I probably deserved that but it still stung. I took it, though, because my hurt wasn't important right now. "I understand why you might think that way. I've lost your trust and I've made you feel used, and I regret it so very, very deeply."

"I'm leaving now." But she didn't move, which gave me this tiny fairy spark of hope.

"Listen to me, Ellery." Yep, I was begging. Probably pathetically. But I didn't care. "You're not who you think you are. I mean, okay, you're kind of mean sometimes. Most of the time, actually. But you're not a bad person. You're weird and fun and loyal as fuck, and sometimes, when it counts, you're incredibly sweet."

"Wow." Her voice was husky with unshed tears. "You really don't know me at all."

"Yes I do," I cried. "You've been the most amazing friend to me. And I'm the world's stupidest…stupidhead to have jeopardised it. I will do anything, literally anything, for a chance to prove I deserve you."

There was a long silence.

"Please." More tears spilled from my eyes. And some even

less attractive things happened in the nose region, which I scrubbed at. "*Please.*"

"I…I…" Ellery glanced away. Swallowed. "I need some time, okay?"

I let out a long, wet breath. Obviously, in an ideal world everything would have been immediately sunshine and roses again. But this wasn't an ideal world. It was just…the world. And Ellery had already been far kinder to me—far more forgiving—than I had any right to ask for. "Okay. Thank you."

She adjusted the straps on her rucksack and headed for the door. I watched her go, trying not to feel hopelessly abandoned.

On the threshold, she paused. "Ardy?"

"Yes," I said, too quickly.

"Take care of Broderick."

"Of course I will."

She half turned, her mouth twisted into its most mocking smile. "You'd better not try to snog him or anything, though. He's sensitive."

It wasn't quite a joke. Wasn't quite a barb. But I didn't even have the dregs of a laugh in me. "I won't. I promise."

And then she was gone. The click of the shutting door made me flinch.

I don't know why but I waited for two…three…five… minutes. Just standing there. But nothing happened beyond the drip of passing time. Wobbling back to the sofa, I rolled myself up even tighter than before. The warehouse closed around me, silent as a yawn.

CHAPTER 24

I sort of slept, but it was saltwater sleep, bitter and unsatisfying. And the rest of the time I lay restless on the sofa, shivering and snuffling—feeling profoundly wretched and knowing I deserved to. To say it had been an inauspicious start to the new year was the understatement of the century. But I guess that was my fault too. You couldn't turn a symbol into something real just by wanting to. God, I was a fucking idiot. A fucking *fucking* idiot.

What was left of the night dribbled into a murky grey morning. Clearly it was going to be a long, grim day. Except then came a hammering on the front door, startling me out of my duvet. Ellery rarely bothered to carry her keys, much preferring to be let into her own house like it was the 1950s and I was her wife or something. Did this mean she'd come back? Had she forgiven me?

I ran, ignoring my protesting stomach and my aching head. Flung open the door, light blasting into my face, making my eyes water. And there—hazy as a mirage through my sheen of tears—was Caspian. In jeans and a crumpled shirt, one of his endless three-quarter-length dark wool coats thrown over the top.

Was this…was this really happening?

Every wistful fantasy I'd ever had about him was suddenly colliding in my brain. He'd broken up with Nathaniel. He'd made a terrible mistake. He wanted me back. He loved me. He wanted to marry me. He was about to kiss me.

"Arden," he said, "what the hell is this?"

He shoved something at me—a newspaper, one of the tabloids, folded open—and stalked into the warehouse. Robotically, I closed the door and followed, glancing at the pages in my hand.

It took a moment to figure out what I was looking at. But it was me. A picture of me. Not a very good picture of me. And I was kissing Ellery against a blaze of New Year's Eve fireworks.

Fuck. Oh fuck.

The image was partially covered by a circle splash containing a different photo. Also not a very good picture of me. Taken, by the looks of it, over the summer when Caspian and I had attended—very briefly—a charity art exhibition on my first return from Boston. He was holding my hand, dragging me along behind him with fierce determination, while I wore my best confused rabbit look.

HART TO HART, read the headline.

Which should probably have told me everything I needed to know. But my eyes had masochistically moved on before I could stop them: *They say you should keep it in the family. And that's certainly true for bisexual partyboy Arden St. Ives,*

22, who seems to have ditched billionaire boyfriend Caspian Hart, 29, for none other than Hart's own sister, troubled tearaway Eleanor "Ellery" Hart.

I couldn't read any more. It was too horrible.

The paper fluttered to the floor. I must have dropped it, but I was numb to my fingertips.

"It's not…" My voice was a brittle thread, close to breaking. "It's not what you think."

Caspian folded his hands in front of him, his expression unreadable. "Isn't it?"

"I'm not with your sister. I've never felt that way about her." My eyes were gritty with too many tears shed. I already knew this was hopeless. Caspian had found me—platonically—in bed with Ellery once, and it had hurt him terribly.

"I know."

My heart, which had been quietly dying in my chest, jerked with surprise. Maybe my entire life wasn't going to combust in a single day. "You do?"

"Yes." He inclined his head slightly—oddly cold for a man who was not jumping to an awful conclusion. "You told me once that you had a different relationship with Eleanor. I believed you then and I believe you still."

"Holy shit." The air whooshed out of me and I had to actually put my hands on my knees in order to catch a breath. "Thank you."

"Which means," he went on, in the same impassive tone, "you have done this to hurt me."

Well. Spoke too soon. Apparently everything was broken. "Wait. *What?*"

"I've treated you so badly." He gazed at me, with those

beautiful, empty eyes. "Anyone in your place would be justified in wanting to hurt me back."

Okay, I was done. I was jacking it all in to become a mad inventor who lived in a basement because I needed a time machine fucking stat. I'd been living in this year for less than twelve hours and I already hated it. My legs were also in a state of giving-up-on-everything and I crumpled slowly to the floor.

"It's not justified," I whispered. "It would never be justified. Whatever you did to me, I would never take it out on Ellery. She's my friend. And I've fucked it up. And I feel bad enough about myself already. And I can't cope with you being angry at me too."

He crossed the room and knelt down—no cologne today, just the achingly familiar scent of him. "I'm not angry. I understand."

I lifted my head to look at him. The gentleness in his voice was cutting me to ribbons. "Why are you here?"

"I came to ask you—no, to beg you—not to use my family to get to me." He spread his hands in a gesture that could only have been surrender. "Hurt me all you wish, go to the papers, insist on millions, tell them I'm a pervert, a deviant, a monster, I deserve it, but please…strike at me. Not Eleanor."

I was dust. Particles of nothing. I couldn't even get enough of myself together to be angry. "For fuck's sake," I said wearily. "You were there at Nathaniel's too. You heard what I said. I could never hurt you. And you could never be a monster to me."

"Then why"—for the first time he faltered, a hint of some-

thing desperate and uncertain creeping into his words—
"why did you do it?"

Because I want you so badly and it hurts so much I went temporarily insane? "Because I'd taken coke earlier and was out of my fucking mind."

His whole *I'm not angry with you, Arden* thing cracked like a carnival mask, leaving him pale with fury, and glaring at me with wolfish ferocity. "You. Did. What?"

"I. Did. Drugs."

"Why?"

Because I want you so badly and it hurts so much I went temporarily insane? "Because I'm in my early twenties and it was New Year's Eve and I was partying like someone in their early twenties on New Year's Eve."

"If you ever do that again, I'll—"

"You'll what?" I asked, with genuine curiosity.

He caught me by my pyjama top and dragged me to my feet, which took some doing because I was still wobbly, and basically deadweight. "What were you thinking?" he growled, directly into my shocked little face. "I believed you would have more sense than to jeopardise your career, your future, and your health for a transitory distraction."

"Um…I don't know how to say this in a good way, but it's pretty weird hearing this from you when Ellery has been using for years."

He closed his eyes for a moment, the crease I always wanted to stroke away with my fingers appearing between his brows. "And you don't think I've done everything in my power to stop her?"

"I…" Whatever sparks of defiance I'd conjured from the

ashes of my self-esteem fizzled out. "I'm sorry. It was stupid and I wish I hadn't and I hurt Ellery and I feel awful and now…it's in the papers and it's icky."

"I'll have the story suppressed."

"Can you do that?"

"Yes," he said simply. "It's not significant except personally. But Arden?"

I peeped up at him.

"Promise me you will never do anything like this again."

"Believe me, I've learned my lesson. I promise."

He seemed to realise he was still holding me. There was nothing sexy or romantic about it—I actually felt like a puppy that needed to be yanked out of its own poo—but he let me go abruptly, a hint of pink creeping over the crests of his cheekbones.

God. How was he so beautiful? Impossible that he had ever been just a little bit mine.

Leaving me on the sofa, safely back in my duvet, he went to make calls. I tried not to listen but the warehouse was full of echoes and kept bringing his voice back to me. I think he was talking to Finesilver and he sounded angry. I even caught the words *should have brought this to me before*, which was both vindicating and uncomfortable-making.

At last he came back to me, phone in one hand, coat over his arm. Even after all the months I'd spent with him, Casual!Caspian was still something of a rare beast to me and I'd forgotten how much I enjoyed this slightly softer side to him. It reminded me of his arms around me while we'd washed dishes in Kinlochbervie. The snuggly weekend we'd spent together after Boston. I'd never seen him in a creased shirt, though. He must have dashed out of the house like whoa.

"We believe this may be the work of Boyle," he said. "I understand he's been harassing you?"

I don't know why some part of me balked at causing trouble for Boyle, because he certainly had no compunction in causing trouble for me. "Only a little bit?"

"Finesilver will assist you in filing a restraining order."

"Oh. Okay."

"The story is, of course, out there now, but I'll ensure it doesn't spread, assuming you do nothing further to feed it."

Probably I should have done more to resist Caspian's forceful brand of problem solving and caretaking. But I'd screwed up big-time. My pride could pay the price. "I won't."

There was a pause.

"As for you"—Caspian's eyes raked over the unprepossessing splat that used to be Arden St. Ives—"you will probably be out of sorts for at least a day due to depleted dopamine stores, and may experience residual symptoms, including mood swings for at least a week or two. Try to rest, stay hydrated, eat well, and under no circumstances attempt to alleviate your condition by taking any more drugs."

I blinked at him from inside my blanket. "You know a lot about this."

"The information is commonly available."

Then it clicked. "You looked it up for Ellery, didn't you?"

"Well"—he gave a bitter-edged smile—"at least someone can benefit from it."

Another pause. Then:

"Given the context, I am not insensible of the irony, but..." Caspian was blushing again.

"But?"

He glanced away. "Would you mind terribly if I had a cigarette?"

"I thought you'd given up."

"I have. I mean, I am. I just—"

"You're a grown-up, Caspian." I gestured at the pretty, hand-painted glass ashtray that lived on the coffee table and was, as usual, full of roaches. I mean, the weed sort, not the insectoid sort. I guess with Ellery it could have gone either way. "I'd rather you didn't die of lung cancer anytime soon, but smoke if you want to."

"Thank you."

"They're not mine, by the way," I added hastily. "I live with musicians."

I curled my knees up to make room on the sofa and Caspian sat down next to me. It was all very decorous but I could just about feel the outline of his thigh against my duvet-swaddled feet. Reaching into the inside pocket of his coat, he pulled out a packet of cigarettes and a matchbook. It hurt, of course. The familiarity. The deft motions of his hands as he lit up. The almost imperceptible flicker of his eyelashes as he inhaled. The sensuality of his lips parting around a stream of smoke.

"Umm," I said. "I'm excruciatingly aware this isn't my business, but didn't you tell Nathaniel you weren't cheating?"

"This is an aberration."

"You're carrying cigarettes around with you. And that isn't the first one from the packet."

He gave me a sharp, stricken look. "I don't want him to be disappointed with me."

"I think he'd be more disappointed about you lying. I know I would."

"Arden, please. The nature of my relationship with Nathaniel is very different."

"It really must be if you can't be honest with him about who you are."

He tapped his cigarette against Ellery's ashtray. "If you recall, I wasn't honest with you either."

"You didn't tell me things. Things you probably should have. But I think…I really do think you let me see you."

"A little too much, I fear."

"Not for me."

Clearing his throat, he said, "I need to—" at the same time I blurted out, "You don't have to go."

He tucked the duvet more firmly around my feet. "You should rest."

"Why?" I flashed him the cheekiest grin I could manage. "What are you planning on doing to me if you stay?"

"What? No. I…hadn't…I wouldn't…Oh for God's sake, don't be such a monkey."

I'd forgotten how adorable a flustered Caspian could be. "To be honest, I was probably going to lie here, feeling bad about upsetting Ellery, and watching *The Last Jedi*."

I'll admit that last bit was shameless. And I wouldn't even have gone there if I'd thought there was the smallest chance Ellery would come back and find us together. I desperately wanted Caspian to stay. But not if the price was Ellery.

"You mean," asked Caspian with a kind of furtive eagerness, "the latest *Star Wars*?"

In another world, I'd have taken him to the cinema to

see it. Did billionaires even go to cinemas? Most likely they had private movie theatres. But I'd have insisted on going, and he would have indulged me, and I would have held his hand and watched his face instead of the film, and there in that soft darkness, we could have been any other couple.

I nodded. "You could join me? Keep an eye on me to make sure I'm resting."

"Well"—his voice had gone very soft—"probably you shouldn't be on your own right now. You could have adverse reactions."

I had severely adverse reactions to being without Caspian, but I kept the thought to myself. "I could. I'm sure people get fucked up by cocaine twelve hours after they've taken it all the time. Should I get my laptop?"

"I…yes. All right." And he let out a breath like he had after his cigarette.

The last time we'd watched *Star Wars*, it had been in the lap of luxury at One Hyde Park, for which I'm sure our grungy sofa and my fourteen-inch screen were a pretty poor substitute. Yet Caspian looked as rapt as ever as the yellow text began its scroll. And I bedded down next to him, with my feet as near as I dared to inveigle them.

After the almighty fuck-up I'd made of last night, to say nothing of those depleted dopamine stores Caspian had mentioned, it didn't seem right that joy was uncurling inside me like a hedgehog in spring. Although as joy went, it was kind of fickle—as if I owed Ellery a misery debt. And maybe I did. The guilt was still inside me, a witch's finger, poking me in the ribs, reminding me what a shithead I'd been to someone I loved. But someone else I loved was with me right now, and the truth was, Caspian made me happy. So very, very happy.

It felt the same, you see. Being with him. Like everything that had come between us was nothing but shreds of old dreams, and this—him and me together—was what was real. He shifted on the sofa, crossing one leg over the other, his hand drifting down to rest on top of my ankle. His fingers curled, holding me through the duvet, and I knew then, half in bliss, half in anguish, that I was as much his, as utterly his, as I had ever been.

Star Wars washed over me gently. I'd seen it before and apparently drugs beat the hell out of your body, so I let myself float, anchored by Caspian's touch and the glimpses I occasionally stole of his profile. Because, yeah, greedy as ever when it came to him, and I'd missed him. Missed the curve of his cheek and the line of his jaw. The hollows of his throat. The tiny mole at his brow. The stern set of his mouth, and its secret capacity for smiles. I'd missed *making* him smile. Making him unravel. Missed his kindness and his cruelty both. His outrageously competitive streak. His unexpected shyness.

I'd read somewhere that *The Last Jedi* was the longest *Star Wars* movie that had ever been released. Honestly, I wished it had been longer. A lot longer. But eventually Luke Skywalker and Kylo Ren had faced off on the blood-coloured soil of Crait and the credits had done their thing, and Caspian and I were alone again in the silence.

I still remembered what he'd said to me after *The Force Awakens*. "I wish my father could have seen that. But I'm so glad I got to watch it with you." I think that was the moment

I realised I'd fallen in love with him. How could I not have—with such a ridiculous, complicated, tender-hearted man?

"So," I asked, hoping once again to share his *Star Wars* wonder, "how did you find it?"

He turned to me, frowning, his eyes dark. "I don't think I cared for it very much."

"What?" My mouth dropped open and hung there, gormlessly. I just hadn't seen that coming. "Why? And if you say it had too many women in it or whatever, I swear to God I'll—"

"Of course I don't care that there were women in it. What do you take me for?"

"I…I don't know. It's something people on the Internet aren't happy about."

One of his eyebrows flicked impatiently upwards. "*Star Wars* is an adventure story about good and evil. I fail to see how the number of female characters is a pertinent metric against which to judge its success in that regard."

"Then what didn't you like about it? I mean, the pacing was a bit choppy but it seemed pretty adventure story-ey to me?"

"I didn't like that they turned Luke Skywalker into a failure and a coward."

I blinked at the passion in his voice. "I…don't think he was any of those things, was he?"

"He spent three films trying to overthrow the Empire and rebuild the Jedi order. When we meet him here, he is living alone in a cave having accomplished neither."

"Caspian"—I gave him a somewhat bewildered look—"are you, like, *cross* with Luke Skywalker because he didn't change the entire galaxy by himself?"

"If that was his original intent, he should not have stopped until he achieved it."

"You do realise," I pointed out, "that you're holding an imaginary space wizard to an impossible standard?"

He shrugged. "I just didn't enjoy seeing a character we have been led to admire reduced to a broken ruin, his honour and heroism twisted into fear and selfishness."

Oh. *Oh.* "I didn't see it that way at all. I guess, for me, heroism isn't about being perfect or untested. It's about knowing what it is to fail and suffer and make mistakes, and still doing the right thing when it counts."

"But"—Caspian's foot was twitching—"he'd wasted so much time. And let down so many people."

I pushed back the duvet and crawled out of it, kneeling next to him on the sofa instead, wanting him—for once—to hear me. "I think what Luke believed about himself, and what his friends believed about him, were very different things. He was living in a cave, as you put it, because he couldn't forgive himself. Not because he'd done something unforgivable."

Caspian turned, and in my need to reach him, maybe I'd misjudged the distance, because we were suddenly close. Very close. Close enough to feel his breath against my face when he spoke. "I know I've said this before, but I wish I could see the world as you do."

I lost myself in the paler fractals in his eyes. The faint tug and cling of his upper and lower lips between the words they shaped. The soft curls at his temples.

"You don't have to," I told him. "Just let me show you."

One of his hands came up to cup my face, the edge of my

jaw slipping into the soft cradle of his palm as if it belonged there. My eyes closed involuntarily—I wanted to look, dammit—surrendering me to the long-missed pleasure of his touch.

"Arden," he murmured. "My Arden."

"Yours."

His mouth brushed mine. Honey-sweet, electric, making the hairs on my forearms dance in giddy delight. But it was only for a second.

He gasped. Pulled back. Dismay slashed across his face like graffiti. "I…I need to go. Nathaniel…Nathaniel is…"

I don't know what I said. Probably wait or stop or please or don't. It didn't matter. He was gone.

Leaving me, of course, distraught in his wake.

Because he always did.

And I never fucking learned.

CHAPTER 25

So much for a new start for a new year. But y'know what, life went on. It's the one thing you could always rely on. Well, unless you were dead, but then you probably had bigger problems to deal with. Or no problems at all. Swings 'n' roundabouts. I was inescapably down for a couple of weeks—because of Caspian, or cocaine, or the fact I was an idiot, or maybe all of the above combined—and I missed Ellery terribly. Like Professor Wossname in *My Fair Lady*, I'd grown accustomed to, well, not her face, because she was usually facedown somewhere, but the stomp of her boots, the smell of her nail varnish, the too-easy-to-take-for-granted comfort of having someone to come home to. Nobody drank my milk or ate my cereal or carved obscene sculptures into the side of my bread. But honestly? I kind of wished they did.

I cared for Broderick, as per my promise, polishing his tusks and combing his fur. But I think he wanted Ellery to come home too. I sent her regular updates about his health and general well-being, along with photographs of his activities—like the tea party he had with some of his whale friends—which took me bloody ages to set up. But, hey, what else was I going to do with my time now that I'd utterly alienated one of my best friends?

The story of me utterly alienating one of my best friends, though that was obviously not how it got reported, stuck around but, as Caspian had promised, didn't grow. Barely a day or two day after it had hit, a fresh scandal broke—something about a minor MP apparently sending dick pics to an undercover journalist posing as a teenage girl—and that largely overwhelmed the proportion of the news cycle that thrived on salacious things happening to other people. The timing couldn't have been more ideal, which gave me pause, and some pricklings of unease, especially since Finesilver had pretty much told me this sort of thing was his job. But then, if we're trusting you to run the country, you should really know better than to send pictures of your genitals to randos. Right?

While I wasn't mad keen on having pictures of me doing an incredibly stupid and hurtful thing floating around in the public domain, the practical consequence seemed to be minimal. Unless you counted another uptick in Instagram followers and a handful of calls from companies wanting me to endorse shit, and the occasional promoter trying to make me go to their club nights. I'll admit the money—which would have been more than I made in a month at *Milieu* for a single Insta—was tempting. But given I mainly posted pictures of, like, Broderick and my shoes and the view from my office window at various times of day, I would have felt skeevy as fuck suddenly being all "Hi, I'm Arden St. Ives and I totally legitimately use Brand Name Energy Drink in my daily life! #BrandNameEnergyDrink #BrandNameEnergyDrink4Life #DefinitelyNotBeingPaidForThis." Also, no power on earth was getting me voluntarily through the doors of a straight club. Ew.

Over the next month or so, I did, however, manage to write some semi-decent pieces for *Milieu* on the principle that you might as well throw yourself into your work when everything else has gone to dogshit. And there was George, of course, probably the only good thing in my life I hadn't fucked up yet. Not that she was a thing. But the truth was, it was depressingly easy not to fuck up when your caring came with carefully created limits. Probably there was a lesson in that. Except I wasn't sure it was one I wanted to learn.

Anyway, we had fun together. Fun that involved me crying and hurting and yelling. But I was crying and hurting and yelling on my own terms. And I always got to come after. Sometimes during. Often both. I never let her spank me, though. I didn't realise it was going to be a problem until the first time her palm landed crisply on what I'd assumed were my eager upraised buttocks. Turned out, they weren't eager at all, and I'd safe-worded at light speed. Had to sit in a corner in a blanket for a bit. Crops, cats, single tails, floggers—even the cane which was right on the edge of too much ouch for me to take—all fine. But the intimacy of hand to skin, I wasn't ready for. It felt like it belonged to Caspian, and Caspian alone.

"Well, poppet," she said to me one weekend, having got off my face and dragged her dick out of my wet, gasping mouth, "would you like to see some photos?"

I peered up at her through a haze of happy sex tears. "You'll probably have to untie me first."

"Shame." She unleashed a melodramatic sigh. "You look delicious all spread-eagled and helpless and covered in come."

"The truly tragic thing here," I pointed out, my throat hoarse from its recent abuse, "is that none of it's my come."

"Tragic for you, maybe. I'm having a wonderful time." She tugged on the cascade of stars falling from the barbell through my right nipple.

I whined and wriggled—not that it did much good, considering she had me spread like a Boxing Day buffet. "You're torturing *meeee*."

"Oh no, poppet." Reaching behind her, she caught up the remote for the vibrating plug she'd tucked into me earlier. "*This* is torturing you."

She clicked. I howled. And my poor cock juddered like it was trying to achieve actual liftoff from the rest of my body.

"I…I need to come," I gasped out, rattling the cuffs that held my wrists and ankles.

George regarded me curiously. "Now why do you think that is?"

It probably had something to do with the fact she'd kept me in a state of agonised arousal for what felt like hours. But I wasn't in any mood to sass her. "Be-because I need to?"

"Yes, you've made that very clear. But"—she put a hand thoughtfully to her chin—"*why* do you need to? Do you think it might be because you're a voracious little slut?"

My face flamed with shame as sweet and neon-bright as American candy. "Maybe."

"Maybe?" she repeated. And leaned over me to lick up the precome that was dribbling like candlewax down the sides of my cock.

"Oh God. Okay. Yes. Yes. I'm a slut. Please…I can't…I need…"

Lifting her head, she tsked. "Do try to pay attention. I didn't say you were a slut. Anybody can be a slut. You, poppet, are a very special kind of slut."

I quivered, my toes curling helplessly, and my fingers clawing at nothing. At this rate, she'd talk me over the edge, though, frankly, I was damn near desperate enough to take it. Sometimes it embarrassed me that she could do this to me— that she knew me well enough for words to be as potent as whips or chains—but mostly it was good embarrassment, making me feel seen and cared for and slightly toyed with.

"I'm waiting" she purred. "Tell me what kind of slut you are."

Tossing my head against the pillow, I put up a faint show of resistance. Of course, I wasn't actually resisting. I just occasionally liked to be a little broken.

"Tell me"—her fingers dipped between my pulled-wide legs and nudged the base of the plug—"and I'll reward you."

The thing is, I also knew George. Sexually speaking at least. And part of me recognised that I should absolutely clarify the nature of this reward. Unfortunately, most of me was a roiling mass of exposed nerves and thwarted desire, frantic to get off.

"I'm a…a…voracious slut," I said. Okay, that's a lie. I yelled that shit out like I wanted to make sure everyone in Swale got the message. "And I need to come. *Please.*"

"You are, poppet. You are. Look at you, wriggling and humping the air. Such a gluttonous young fuckpuppy. You'd do just about anything for pleasure, wouldn't you?"

In my present condition? "Yes. *Yes.* What about my reward?"

"You shall have it, of course." She smiled down at me. Red lips, white teeth. Princess and monster. "Your reward is to see some very lovely photographs."

I nearly goddamn cried. "What? No…I mean…yes…just. Now?"

"No time like the present."

"But"—I'm not even going to try and describe how pathetic I sounded—"I don't like denial."

She covered me with her body, which led to some very undignified bucking and squirming on my part, and kissed me deep, and rough, and nasty. "I would never deny you, poppet. I'm delaying you."

"I don't like delay either." I kicked in my bonds—the world's most abortive tantrum.

"You *love* control, though. And"—her mouth grew gentle against mine—"you always know what you can do."

I did. But this was not even remotely approaching a safe word situation. I uttered what I hoped was a heartbreaking whimper. Even if, thinking about it, trying to make a sadist feel bad about the sadism they were inflicting on you with your full consent was probably a lost cause from the outset. "Fine. Let's go see some photos."

She let me go and helped me up, but then drew my hands behind my back and recuffed them.

I gave her my biggest eyes. "Seriously?"

"What's the matter?" Picking up her paisley silk dressing gown from where she'd thrown it earlier, she draped it over her shoulders. "You don't need your hands to look, do you?"

She had a point. A mean point.

"Don't pout, poppet. Come along." Her hand encircled my cock and gave the poor, suffering thing a little tug.

Probably I should have resisted this indignity, but my hips had other ideas, and also, the friction was just too good. It took us a while to reach the studio because I kept pausing to moan, and George kept pausing to make me moan. But once we arrived, I saw the table, where I'd had many kinky adventures, was spread with pictures.

George settled into a chair and pulled me into her lap. I went submissively enough because, frankly, my brain was needy mush. Let her ease my knees apart, exposing me in all my urgent horniness to the drift of air and her tormenting touches.

"These are some of my favourites." I think she was talking about the images but her hands were gliding up and down my inner thighs. "What do you think?"

I said *glerble*. Or thereabouts.

A sharp slap to that vulnerable and sensitive flesh managed to reach me through the lust haze. "I can't believe you're trying to sex me over photos of me."

"Photos *I* took of you." She laughed against my neck, deep and rich with joy. "I did warn you, Arden, the first time we met. I like sex and I like art, and right now, you're both."

I rocked against her knee, shamelessly taking whatever stimulation I could get, the plug shifting inside me—little shocks of sensation that were as tormenting as they were satisfying. "I can live with that."

"Good. Now let's see how pretty you are."

Pushing my heavy eyelids up, I focused on the images. Gasped. I hadn't wanted my wang, or too much of my bum, in the public domain, so the shots were suggestive rather than explicit—lots of coy angles and strategically placed shadows—but there was also no getting away from it: These were some sexy pictures.

Sexy, kinky pictures.

Sexy, kinky pictures *of me*.

Kneeling, crawling, lying in a fucked-out heap, tied up, tied down, leashed, collared, marked, suspended from the ceiling, rolling around on rumpled sheets…Probably I should have been embarrassed to have such intimate moments framed, preserved, potentially reproduced, but the more I stared at the photos, the more I realised I loved them.

I just looked so fucking happy. And it was…nice—weirdly nice, but nice—to see that side of myself. I mean, I was no model but George had found ways to flatter me: the places I was sleek and the places I was soft, the silly freckles across my nose, the glint of my nipple jewellery, the dimples at the top of my arse that were probably some of my favourite bits of me, the way my mouth in pleasure made shapes like laughing. Basically, I came across like a normal boy having a whale of a time.

There were some other pictures too—one taken the night of Ellery's birthday, another at George's window—but these had a grainer quality, the colours less vivid. I seemed… distant in them, restless, my gaze slipping past the camera, like I was Penelope in search of a horizon.

"Well?" asked George.

"They're...*amazing*." I let out a shuddery breath. "I honestly can't quite believe they're me."

"Which do you like best?"

"All of them."

She gave one of my nipples a tweak sharp enough to make me yelp. "No cheating."

"Haven't I already blown you today?"

"Yes." Her touch became a caress. "And now it's time to suck my other cock."

In spite of being sweaty and naked and wracked with denied...no, delayed...arousal, I giggled. "You're completely shameless."

"I try to be. Shame is the most self-destructive of vices."

There was something in her voice, an unusual hint of fragility, that made me nuzzle at her clumsily with my chin. "I'm crazy about what you do—with me and with your camera. These are stunning. So much beyond anything I could have imagined I can't quite wrap my head round it."

"What did you imagine?"

"I honestly don't know. I guess I thought you'd realise I wasn't all that photogenic."

"There's no such thing as photogenic. Just people who are more comfortable having their photo taken."

"I wouldn't put myself in that category."

She laughed and nipped at my ear. "Neither would I, poppet. Which is why I made sure you were sufficiently distracted that your comfort was neither here nor there."

That made sense. I'd lost track of the camera so thoroughly that I couldn't actually remember half these photos being taken. Since my hands were still out of action, I jerked my head towards one of the images. "That one...I like that one."

For her own use, ever the efficient despoiler, George preferred cuffs. But that day she'd gone for rope—rope in every colour of the rainbow, wound around me as bright as birthday bunting. I was kneeling, legs bound and spread wide, my arms—also bound—braced in front of me so I wasn't flaunting my wares to the world. Knots crisscrossed my torso, the ropes vanishing over my shoulders and into the shadows between my legs. It was one of the few times I was looking directly into the camera lens and I was grinning like I'd just spotted the loophole in a deal with the devil. Which could have been incongruous with my pose but, somehow, wasn't—as if the two were not oppositional, but connected, my triumph and my submission.

"So do I." George's fingers closed around my cock and I sighed with what was at first pure relief—though no less intense for it.

"Oh God." My hips arched involuntarily, legs falling open still further. "Don't stop. Please don't stop. Even if this is seriously fucking narcissistic."

She gave an unabashedly filthy chuckle. "There, there, poppet. This is about my narcissism, not yours."

I was rapidly losing my capacity to care what it was about. Nothing mattered except the long, smooth strokes of her hand and the giddy cockscrew of my pleasure. I'd long since lost track of the remote for the plug, but George hadn't, and the sudden burst of stimulation against my inside happy place made not coming everywhere an outright impossibility. I'd got off while bound before but there was something about the position, and having my hands trapped behind me, that made my body feel like a gun someone else had fired. I came, thrashing and shuddering, in a wild jet that George made exactly zero attempt to control for me. My orgasm-wrecked brain helpfully slo-mo'ed the experience: an arc of my own semen pattering gently down on my celluloid self.

"For my private collection," murmured George.

I collapsed against her, panting and satisfied. "You are a sick fuck."

"I've never claimed otherwise."

She put a hand under my chin, turned my face up to hers, and kissed me with a kind of lazy thoroughness—like she had no compunction in using me, but no desire to possess me. It brought me gently back to myself, to the safety of being held by someone I trusted, and the comfort of knowing everything I'd gone through had been mine to choose. George had a blanket ready and wrapped me up in it, but she left the cuffs on until I got restless. I'd found too much freedom all at once could sometimes freak me out.

I'd dozed off against her shoulder for a bit, but when I stirred again, I found her uncharacteristically serious.

"Now that you're thinking clearly," she said, "you should probably decide once and for all what you want me to do with these photos."

"You...you don't want to use them?"

That earned me a little shake. "Of course I do. But now you've seen them, I wanted to check you were still comfortable with them being public."

"Why wouldn't I be?"

"Because"—she sighed—"the world has changed since I first picked up a camera. Information is forever. You need to think that your enemies will see these, your family, every reporter who ever writes about you, every employer you ever work for."

I sat up a little straighter. "They're not porn. I'm not ashamed."

"I'm not saying you should be. I'm saying not everyone will understand." She pulled me back into her arms, breath warm against my neck. "Barthes said the photograph is always invisible. But the photographer is not. Nor the subject. You need to be certain this is something you wish to reveal about yourself."

I thought about it. Not because I needed to, but because she wanted me to. "The thing is," I said slowly, "what you saw in me when you took those photos, I'm proud to reveal."

"Oh, poppet. With talk like that, you'll turn a girl's head."

She sounded much as she always did—wryly amused at something only she understood—but then she kissed me again, and there was a sweetness in it that took me by surprise.

Afterwards, though, she just laughed. "How's that hot young blood of yours? Think you can get it up again?"

"Probably"—I waggled my eyebrows like a cartoon lecher—"given enough encouragement."

"Glad to hear it. I've a mind to break you like a wild stallion."

CHAPTER 26

The *Arden* exhibition—and even thinking that made my head swim—was a single-night affair timed to fall playfully close to Valentine's Day. When I'd heard about George's shows, I'd hoped I might attend one someday. And here I was the actual motherfucking *subject*. Holy shitballs. I told my family, of course, and they were thrilled for me, but we all agreed it was probably for the best they didn't come. It was one thing for them to be a hundred percent behind me doing exactly what I wanted to with my own body, up to and including having lots of kinky sex with it, but quite another to look at pictures of me, well, doing that. I did send a copy of the accompanying book to Nik, though. Partly because I was insanely proud. But also a little bit to mess with him.

And, of course, I wanted to tell Ellery, but she was still couch surfing her way round the band and I was still working up the courage to ask her to move back in. So I didn't think I'd have much luck with, "Hey, come and look at some fairly naked pictures of me." Before I'd kissed her, I'm sure she would have found it hilarious, but now I'd turned myself into a threat instead of her ally and I wasn't sure seventy-eight photos of Broderick were enough to make her want me in her life again.

So I ended up going to the me exhibition by myself. Which was fine, and probably fitting, and I knew George would be there when I arrived. I decided to be fashionably late, since that way I'd be able to come and go unnoticed, though I got delayed making my hair cute and ended up unfashionably late. Albeit with excellent hair.

I'd heard of the Laine Matthäus Gallery but sort of in the same way I'd heard of Cirque le Soir or Annabel's; that is, I was aware it was known to be cool, but hadn't expected ever to have reason to go, or reason to believe they'd let me through the front door if I had turned up. But the gallery turned out to be surprisingly welcoming—not of me, in particular, but in general. It sat in the middle of a parade of shops near King's Cross, sandwiched between a Super Laundry and a kebab emporium, still boasting the sooty tile façade it had possessed when it had been a bookie's. The rest was window, allowing the light from within to glaze the dark pavement with a sheen of gold and the wibbly reflection of the sign which read *Laine Matthäus Gallery* in cursive red-pink neon.

Gosh, it looked busy in there. People were even hanging about outside, some of them eating kebabs. My insides did something weird, caught between anxious squeezing and excited fluttering, that ended up feeling like my heart had just sneezed. I mean, I was glad the place wasn't empty—the last thing I wanted to be was the George Chase collection nobody cared about—but at the same time…this had all got very real, real fast, very suddenly.

But still, I had no regrets. A realisation that gave me the courage to head on in. As I got close to the door, my shoulder collided with someone coming the other way at a speed best described as antisocial.

"Ow, I'm sor—" The instinctive British apology, even though I wasn't the one who'd caused the crash, died on my lips as I recognised Nathaniel.

His head came up. And for a split second he was staring at me with naked hatred. Then—and this was honestly kind of worse—his eyes filled up with tears.

"Are you—" I started.

But he just shoved me out of the way and kept walking. I watched him go, slightly worried and deeply confused. What was he even doing here?

I wasn't going to find an answer in the street. But before I really had a chance to get my head sorted out, George had spotted me, swooped over, and was dragging me into the gallery. The next thing I knew, I had a drink in one hand, George had claimed the other, and I was at the epicentre of a conversational tsunami. Questions, compliments, and introductions were boomeranging round my head, which was initially flattering, then about equal parts flattering and overwhelming, and finally just overwhelming. So I committed to an evening of forgetting everyone's name, answering what I could, smiling a lot, and trusting George to steer me right.

It worked—not enough that I ever really got a handle on things, but just enough that I was having fun. It was a strange experience, existing as both subject and object, self and image, reflection and projection. I wouldn't want to live that way, but for an evening it made me feel mysterious and interesting, like a character in an arty movie who the protagonist would fall for but never get close to, and who'd vanish one day in Prague with a few maddeningly cryptic parting words that would live forever in cinema history. Of course, I wasn't like that at all—being about as aloof as a jam doughnut—but it was cool to pretend. And I got hit on a fair bit, which was good for my ego, even if I wasn't actually about to bonk someone just because they liked a picture of me.

The pictures in question were even more, err, *something* now they were massive and hung on cool white walls, the images given space to be their own context. It was a lot of Arden, put it that way. Though what was odd to me was that they all had little stickers on the corners of their frames. I was sure they couldn't have been left there by accident, as George had a fanatical eye for detail, but I picked at one anyway.

"Don't do that please."

I turned to find Laine Matthäus zirself standing behind me and pulled my hand back guiltily. To be honest, ze wasn't anything like I'd imagined a gallery owner would be, but since I'd assumed they were all posh rich blokes over the age of fifty, this was a good thing. Ze was a few years older than me, slight and willowy, with platinum blond hair that fell in blade-sharp locks almost to zir waist and looked absolutely bloody extraordinary against the black wrap-dress ze was wearing.

"Sorry," I said. "I just didn't know why it was there."

Ze smiled, and I was relieved it was a warm smile, not a *well, aren't you clueless* smile. "It means the piece has been sold."

"Oh. *Oh.* Someone must have really liked it, huh?"

"As well they might." Ze looked up at, well, me, as I lay draped over a sawhorse, sweaty, flushed, and smug as fuck. "It's wonderful."

I blushed, in spite of my attempt to be nonchalant and enigmatic. "Wait, does this mean *all* the photos have been bought?"

Ze nodded.

"Every single one of them?"

Another nod.

"Is that normal?"

"Well"—Laine's eyes slid back to the image—"Georgia is very talented and has very devoted admirers..."

"Is someone taking my name in vain?" That was George as she extricated herself expertly from the crowd. She was in skyscraper heels, tuxedo trousers, and a black-and-white plaid jacket with a shawl collar that fell just on the sexy side of aggressive.

"And here I thought," murmured Laine, "vanity was your specialty."

George just laughed and leaned in to kiss zir lightly on the cheek. "You really must let me shoot you one day, *meine zuckermaus.*"

"I love art. I have no desire to become it." A pause. Then slightly too late, "And I'm not your *zuckermaus.*"

"I suppose not. It's one of the few things I dislike about you."

Laine smiled serenely. "Then you should up your game. There are many things I dislike about you."

"Um," I said. "I'm finding this foe yay you've got going on

really hot and everything but could one of you maybe tell me who bought the photos?"

"Does it matter, poppet?" George slid a comforting arm round my waist. "This has been a very successful show, both critically and financially."

"Also," added Laine, "I'm afraid I'm not at liberty to disclose the identity of my clients."

I breathed. Did it matter? Even if…fuck. I was jumping to conclusions quicker than a mountain goat. "Can you at least tell me if, like, it was lots of people or…or not?"

Neither of them spoke. But their faces told me everything I needed to know.

"Arden…" George made a futile attempt to restrain me.

"Oh. My. God." I was loud enough to turn a few heads, but I wasn't in any state to care. "Where is he? Is he still here? I'm going to kill him. Actually fucking kill him."

Laine looked genuinely perplexed—not that I could entirely blame zir. I'd gone from normal to literally homicidal in under a second. "He was here a moment ago. I think he stepped out for a cigarette."

"Well, of course he did." I threw my hands into the air, nearly toppling a tray of drinks. "God fucking damn him to fucking goddamn hell."

"How about," George asked gently, "I take you home?"

It was a good plan. A sensible plan. A plan I would have been well advised to go with. "No," I roared.

And stormed off.

CHAPTER 27

I found Caspian in the propped-open doorway of the fire escape, watching the rumpled indigo of the starless London sky, cigarette between his fingers. I grabbed it, threw it to the ground, and stubbed it out with the toe of my shoe.

"Make up your fucking mind," I told him. "Like, smoke or don't smoke. But stop pretending you're not smoking when you are."

He gazed at me, cartoonishly shocked, eyes wide, mouth slightly open. "What on earth are you doing?"

"What are *you* doing?"

"Well, I was having a cigarette, which you seem to have found objectionable."

"What are you doing *here*? Why did you buy all the pictures? What the fuck is wrong with you?"

He was silent, the uncertain moonlight rendering him almost monochrome, all stark lines and shadows.

"Well?" I might actually have stamped my foot.

"Oh, I thought they were hypothetical questions." His attention flicked regretfully to the crushed remains of his cigarettes and his fingers twitched. "I'm here because I…heard about the show and was, I suppose, I was curious? I bought the pictures because I couldn't bear the thought of anyone else seeing you that way. And I don't know what's wrong with me. I wish I did."

This was a lot to process. I wasn't even sure how to begin. "You just heard about the show? How?"

"Since the incident with my sister and the tabloids, I've had a Google alert for you." Caspian contrived to look both defiant and sheepish. "It seemed prudent. But I know I shouldn't have come tonight."

"Jeez, you think?"

"Regret is futile, Arden."

"You say that a lot, but you know something? I think regret is *important*. It's how you learn to live with things instead of running from them."

Again, silence. And Caspian's profile, bleak and beautiful, and pale as bone in the gloom.

I sighed. "Okay, what was that crap about not wanting anyone to see me? You know there's a book, right? Are you going to buy all those as well? Do *not* buy all those as well."

"I wasn't intending…that is, I'm not thinking…I'm not sure I can explain it."

"Fucking try. Right the fuck now."

"I will concede, it wasn't rational. They reminded me of when we were together, and I didn't want to share that part of you with the world."

"Right." I folded my arms—since it was that or start waving them around like an enraged albatross. "And so you're just going to take a bunch of pictures of me back with you to the home, or presumably homes, you share with your fiancé and hang them up in the bedroom, are you?"

"Clearly not. I'll put them in storage."

And I lost it. Flew at him, flailing, managed to land a few not very effective blows against his chest before he caught my wrists. Then I burst into tears. Not because I was sad. But because I was just so helplessly fucking angry. "You wanker. You absolute fucking wanker."

"For God's sake." Caspian adjusted his grip, stepping back just in time to avoid my incompetent attempt to kick his shins. "What's the matter with you?"

Scalding tears were streaming down my face, making my eyes ache with pressure and my lips burn with salt. "I hate you, that's what's the matter. Those pictures are *beautiful*. I'm proud of them. And you're locking them away from everyone because even though you don't want me, you don't want anyone else to have me either."

"Of course I want you, Arden." Caspian's voice had gone very low, his words ragged things creeping reluctantly from his mouth. "I don't know how to stop wanting you.

"I don't need photographs to remember you, Arden."

My head whirled. "I…I don't want to hear this." That was a total lie, for the record. I'd been wanting to hear this for months. "It's not fair."

"I'm sorry. I'll…I'll give you the pictures. You can do whatever you like with them."

"What the fuck am I going to do with a bunch of sexy photos of myself?"

"I don't know." His grip on me slackened, but he still

didn't release me, and I still wasn't stepping away. "I'm afraid I'm not making sensible decisions right now."

"You mean because the sight of your ex-boyfriend's o-face has completely overthrown your reason?"

He gazed down at me for a long moment, my hands still trapped against his chest, his heart thundering beneath them. "You used to look at me like that."

I opened my mouth—but all that came out of it was a dry sob.

"How can you believe I'd stopped wanting you?" He drew me in closer, until we were pressed together. "How can you believe I ever could? God, Arden, the things you give me. The way you surrender to me. You've crawled for me and taken pain for me. And sometimes, I think you might have ruined me."

"And that's what you think is in those photos?" I asked shakily.

"A…shadow of it, maybe."

"You still don't fucking get it, do you?" I moved restlessly in his arms, not sure whether I wanted to struggle free, or beat myself against him until we both broke. "I'm like that in those photos because that's how I like being. But how I was with you is because I love you."

"Arden…"

Staring up at him sullenly, I sniffed back fresh tears. "You dick."

And then his fingers were gliding across my damp cheeks, holding me in place as he lowered his head and pressed his lips to mine. My mouth was sticky from my crying, and salty from my tears, and I shouldn't have let him, I know I shouldn't, but it was Caspian. The man I yearned and hurt for. Who had been so kind to me, shown me such strength and such suffering, laughed with me and believed in me, and let me see who he was. Until he couldn't bear to anymore. And here he was, my Caspian at last, confused and lost and in pain, just like I was. I melted into him, twining my arms around his neck, kissing him back—yielding and eager and desperately willing, smothering the last traces of smoke with the taste of us.

It was a shattered thing, this kiss of ours, both of us perpetually on the brink of pulling back, but never quite able to do it, falling back into each other with the inevitability of sailors caught in the depths of Charybdis. Normally I liked being helpless, found it sweet and bright, but it tugged at me now like a fishhook in my flesh. Made me worry and fret, even though the possibility of resistance barely entered my mind before it was discarded. I couldn't. I wanted him too much, and his wanting of me was its own drug.

My back hit the wall of the fire escape hard enough to grind the edges of the bricks into my spine, knocking our mouths apart. Words collided in the harsh mingling of our breaths, my "Caspian please" and his "Arden, I need," and then—terrified this would stop, that I would lose him all over again—I flung my legs around his waist and dragged him, groaning, into another kiss. It wasn't enough, though. No matter how tightly I held him, how frantically we joined our lips and entwined our tongues, it felt like we were slipping away—scrabbling against a cliff face of unappeasable desire, tearing ourselves open as we went tumbling down it.

The fabric of his suit beneath my palms gave me nothing. Barely an impression of the heat of him. So I curled my fingers through his hair, twisting sharply enough to make him growl and drag his mouth to my neck. More kisses there. Then hot, heavy bites that blossomed redly in the dark behind my eyes. I felt the sting of tears on my cheeks. And my cock ached, drenched with need.

"Fuck me," I gasped out.

The universe teetered like a spinning top, Caspian its centre. He raised his head to look at me, his face a shadow-broken patchwork of passion and pain.

I let my brow fall against his. "You want it too. Say it, Caspian. Say you want me."

"More than anything in the world."

"Then take me. Fuck me." *Love me.* "You know I'm yours."

He brushed the back of his hand against my swollen lips. "I…I'll hurt you."

"Lube in my wallet."

It wasn't what he'd meant, but it was easier for both of us to pretend it was. His hands dropped to my belt, the clack and clatter of the buckle way loud in the fire escape, and then he was…well, it started as peeling but quickly became dragging followed by out-and-out tugging until he'd got my jeans down as far as they'd go—which was just below my arse. He made a sound that might have been a laugh, if not so full of other things, and pressed his cheek to mine.

It was absurd, everything was absurd, my partially exposed legs pale and blotched green from the exit sign above us, and I might have laughed too, but I was too scared of crying. If I'd known someone was going to be trying to get me out of them, I'd have worn less tight-fitting jeans. I mean, apart from the fact I wasn't sure I owned any.

"We should," I began. Maybe about to say, *We shouldn't.* Because this was fucked up. We knew it was fucked up.

But Caspian pressed his palm tenderly to my mouth and I closed my eyes and let him take the choice from me. He kissed across my cheeks, then the tip of my nose, and I trembled with the terrible sweetness of it. And when he put his lip to my ear, the heat of his breath curled around me, licked into my corners, like Prufrock's yellow fog.

"Turn around," he told me. A low rasp that could almost have been the voice of a stranger.

Except Caspian could never be a stranger to me. Even when he feared he was a stranger to himself.

I shaped a kiss of my own, imagining my heart dissolved, flowing slick and glitter-bright into the runnels of his hand. And unwound my legs from around his waist. No sooner had my feet hit the ground than he spun me, my cheek hitting the wall, the air knocked from my lungs. Catching up my wrists, he shoved my palms flat to the bricks and splayed me out beneath his body.

God, the strength of him. And in that moment, all of it was for me. With Caspian, force had never felt like a threat. It felt like a fucking gift. Everything was a gift. The weight of him against my back. His harsh breath. The fretful pressure of his teeth in my nape. The sting of his bites and the throb of his bruises. The promise of his hard cock ground into my arse, his suit dragging roughly across my legs. I was melting not just into submission but submission to Caspian, the pleasure of it a dark tide rising inside me, as deep as despair.

Caspian's fingers slid between mine against the wall,

half trapping, half holding me. "Don't move."

He stepped away, fumbling in my pocket for my wallet. I waited, my ears catching at the crinkle of foil and the swish of fabric, the murmur of voices from inside the gallery—oh shit, what if someone else decided they randomly wanted to sneak a cheeky ciggy in the fire escape? And here I was, in a fuck-me pose against the wall, with my bits hanging out. I mean, I guess it was nothing they hadn't seen, but I wasn't quite ready to upgrade from stills to live action.

Before I could get into a real panic, though, Caspian's hand landed on the small of my back, the touch remarkably steady given how harsh his breathing sounded. I arched into the reassuring warmth of him, which I suppose counted as technically moving, but he didn't chastise me for it. Just stroked, soothing me in ways I hadn't realised I needed soothing, before he moved lower and gave my arse such a possessive little squeeze it had me up on my toes, swallowing a yip.

The thing is, Caspian wasn't as awesome at not breaking my heart and leaving me in pieces on the floor as he could have been. But I also knew, with the faith Elizabeth Barrett Browning once gave to her lost saints, he would never let me come to harm. Besides, there was no way the man who had flipped his lid at the thought of other humans looking at pictures of me was going to let them stand around watching me get fucked. And, wow, my dick was an idiot: It was already looking for ways to find Caspian's behaviour secretly endearing, when the rest of me was still quite annoyed by it. But actually...it was hot, in principle, to be *that* coveted. It was just the practice that had been severely fucked up the arse.

Much as, I hoped, I was about to be. I spread my legs a little wider and nudged up into his palm—flaunting. And suddenly a different need opened up inside me like quick-sand.

"Oh God," I heard myself whisper, "I wish you could spank me."

His muffled a groan in the back of my neck. "Arden..."

"Obviously don't. That shit's not quiet." Even if the idea of it was insanely hot.

"It's what you want, though." A taunting note had crept into Caspian's voice—a delicate edge of cruelty that made my heart stutter with fearful delight. "To be spanked in a back alley like a dirty slut."

There was such...such *affection* in the words—I might even have called it love—that I lost my head. "Yes please."

"Not tonight, my wicked one. My brave boy."

That briefly reminded me that less than two seconds ago I, too, had been aware it was a terrible idea. But I still wriggled and whined, safe in the knowledge Caspian would take care of me.

His teeth scraped my earlobe. "I don't need to spank you to own you, Arden."

And then he pulled my hips back and entered me—one long, merciless push that I felt all the way to my bones, then a pounding so gloriously brutal it seemed to make my heart shake and my pulse falter. There was enough lube that it didn't hurt, but it *nearly* hurt, and that became its own strange pleasure: a haze of rough thrusts and stretched-tight muscle, fingers digging into my hips and burning breath on my neck, and the deep, shuddering satisfaction of being so thoroughly *taken*. It was an odd and tantalising paradox, my body utterly conquered by his, and yet I was free, strong, happy, as I hadn't been for months.

Caspian was a surge of ferine power at my back, snarling and gasping as he fucked me, the sweat from his brow prickling against my neck, sharp with salt and heat. And for once, I wasn't lost in the frustration of not being able to see him. Feeling was enough, the ferocity of him, and the intensity of his desire for me, becoming, in those moments of physical unity, a kind of vulnerability.

I twisted back as best I could. "Kiss me."

It emerged neither entreaty nor demand—just the stating of a private obvious. And Caspian leaned over me, his lips finding mine in a clumsy collision, words drowned beneath our tongues, and the tears on his cheeks wetting mine. I came less than a minute later, in great wrenching spurts, like I was splattering my soul all over the wall. And Caspian not long after, with a broken sound, pressed jaggedly against my open, panting mouth.

Oh God. What had we done?

CHAPTER 28

Well, I knew what we'd done. I always had. And done it anyway. But suddenly all I could see was Nathaniel's face. The way he'd looked at me, his eyes a barbed-wire snarl of hatred and despair, as if he'd already known what was going to happen. And the reality of cooling sweat and heavy bodies and my arsehole sticky with someone else's come flattened me like a cartoon anvil. A cartoon anvil made of regret, self-loathing, and discovering I had made yet another fucking awful decision.

I turned awkwardly in Caspian's arms, my jeans catching against his trousers, and my cock knocking damply into his. He barely moved, still almost fallen over me, breathing in rasps.

"Tell me," I said, "you're breaking up with Nathaniel. As in, right the fuck now."

There was a way too long silence. Probably it was a good time to pull up my pants.

I tried again. "Caspian, I need to hear that you're not

going to stay with Nathaniel. Not after what we…after, um, that."

Again. Nothing.

"We were just *really* bad." My voice rose and cracked. "Don't make it into something even worse. Please."

At last, Caspian lifted his head from my neck and stepped back. Began putting his dick away, which was never the best part of an evening. "Believe me, Arden, I'm well aware of what I've done."

"What *we've* done. It takes two to cheat."

He was buttoning his trousers. Readjusting his jacket. Smoothing the sweat-damp curls from his temples. Whether we were in a bedroom or an alleyway, the sight of Caspian Hart putting himself back together was so familiar to me. And hurt, just the same as ever. "You can't blame yourself for this."

"I deserve to be blamed," I cried. "I was right here. Doing it. Wanting it. Fully consenting to it."

"Nevertheless, it was my weakness that allowed it to happen."

"We *both* allowed it to happen." Okay, I had to cool the fuck down. I'd done enough shouting at Caspian in a fire escape to last me a lifetime. I breathed. Tried to be reasonable. "Look, this was really wrong. There's no getting away from that. But why we did it wasn't wrong."

He was still…faffing. Squaring his cuffs. Arranging his hair. Chasing nonexistent creases. "What do you mean?"

"For fuck's sake." So much for calm. "That didn't happen because we both fancied a rough screw against a wall. It happened because…because we can't keep our hands off each other. Because we're right together. You must see that now."

He let out the softest, most defeated sigh I'd ever heard. "I've never doubted for a moment that, were I a different man, you would be everything I most desired, admired, and coveted in the world."

"I don't want you to be a different man." I lunged across the space he'd put between us and threw my arms around him. Which made him go completely rigid so, y'know, non-ideal. "I love you. Everything about you. And all the things you can't love about yourself."

He closed his eyes, and I caught a glint of light upon his lashes that might have been tears. "Oh, Arden, my Arden, I can't be with you."

"You can't be with Nathaniel."

"He's…he's my only chance."

"Only chance at what? You know he won't make you happy."

"My only chance to"—Caspian faltered, choked slightly on his own breath—"my only chance to be someone not made in the image of Lancaster Steyne."

I stared at him in actual horror. "My God, you're not. I promise you're not."

"How sweet you are." Compliments shouldn't have been allowed to sound that fucking sad. "I'd half forgotten how it feels having someone think of me as you do."

"The way I think of you is *true*. It's who you are."

Caspian was already untangling himself from my embrace, though my pathetic attempts to retain a state of tangle meant he ended up keeping one of my hands. And he seemed as reluctant to let it go as I was to be let go. "I'm not like you," he said softly. "Perhaps once I was, or could have been, but what's pure and good and beautiful in you is such a twisted thing in me."

"Nothing"—I tightened my fingers around his and squeezed for all I was worth—"we have ever done together has been even a little bit twisted."

"Because of you."

"No, Caspian. No. Because when you've fucked me, used me, and even when you've hur—"

"Must you say it?"

Apparently yes, I did. Despite the pleading note in his voice. "Even when you've hurt me, you've always made me feel so absolutely cherished. Do you think that would be the case if there was anything of Lancaster Steyne in you?"

"Your capacity to find merit in my corruption is to your credit, not to mine."

"So what?" I asked, with a bitterness I couldn't quite control. "You're just going to stay with Nathaniel even though he makes you hate yourself?"

Caspian swallowed. "He…he sees me."

"He doesn't see you." I closed my spare hand over the one Caspian already held. He was so cold, trembling in my grasp. "He only sees damage and ugliness and his own prejudices."

"I want to be with him. I want to be the man he needs. Or at the very least"—his mouth tightened, as if to seal away its sorrow—"I want to know that I can be. That I'm not at the mercy of…of what I let happen to me when I was younger."

I was about to insist that he hadn't *let* anything happen. But the last time we'd had this conversation—etched as it was, in layers of horrible, on my memory—he'd described everything that happened when he was a kid as something he *did*. As progress went, it was trench warfare slow, but it *was* progress. And if that meant that some part of him was listening to me—wanted to listen to me—why the fuck was he still with someone else?

"So instead," I snapped when I shouldn't have, "you'll be at the mercy of Nathaniel's bullshit?"

He broke the tender knot of our fingers and pulled away from me, his expression shifting abruptly from sadness to a kind of savagery. "It is my *choice*, Arden. My choice. Can't you understand?"

"I understand," I said, tossing the words at him like stones, "that you're miserable. Smoking. Lying about it. And that we just banged in an alleyway when you're supposed to be engaged to someone else. Surely you can't think that's right?"

"I will do better." I watched his anger die, exhausted by its own expression. "I...I know I can."

A profound sense of powerlessness was settling over me— a familiar one, too, because this was how it had gone when Caspian had dumped me, the love that burned so brightly and so fiercely inside me such a fragile thing in comparison to all his years of fear and pain. I knew I couldn't blame him for that, but it was hard to bear. Especially when I became its casualty too. Caught in the crossfire of his self-punishment, when all I wanted was to be with him.

"Is this really what you want?" Tears caught in my voice and rose to my eyes but I was sick of crying, fucking sick of it, and I swallowed them down. "A husband you hide from. Until you get so desperate to feel something good that you cheat on him instead? And what about me, Caspian? I thought sleeping with someone else's partner would be a line I'd never cross. Except now I have, and I know that's on me, and I just have to live with it, but what we've done here changes us both."

He folded his arms, remote as marble between the cracks of moonlight. "I've never claimed to be a good man, whatever you wanted to believe of me."

"That wasn't what I meant." I came very close to stamping my foot again, but managed to restrain myself. "I'm trying to make you see this isn't fair on anyone. I'm sure Nathaniel doesn't actually want to be the altar for your sacrifice. And I don't want to be your secret dirty fucktoy."

No response from Caspian. I couldn't even tell what he was thinking.

So I gave a shaky laugh. "I want to be your openly committed dirty fucktoy."

"We're bad for each other, Arden. Tonight proves it."

"The optics right now aren't great, I'll grant you. But that's about context, not about us." I reached out to him, pleading. "I loved being with you—the kinky sex was a nice bonus but you took care of me, helped me find myself when I was lost, and you know something, when you let me, I took care of you too. I made you happy."

"What I enjoy is not what is right for me."

"Which is why you're denying yourself anything you truly want? Anything that truly gives you peace?"

He took another step away from me. Only a few paces between us but they felt like treacle, sticky and unbreachable. "With Nathaniel, I have a chance to be someone I admire. With you, I would always be someone I despised."

It was the crack of the whip before the bite. The sound of the words before the words themselves. For a second or two, there was nothing. And then, God help me, the pain damn near stopped my heart.

"Oh, Caspian." I covered my mouth with my hands. "I…I don't know to cope with you believing that."

I guess he knew he'd pulled my guts out and scattered them over the pavement, and maybe it had been an accident, because, honestly, he kind of looked like he was about to faint.

By contrast, I was floating in a cool white calm. Like I'd gone through hurting and come out the other side and found…nothing. "I think," I heard myself say, my own voice echoing distantly in my ears, "I don't want to ever see you again."

CHAPTER 29

Well. Everything was awful again. I'd slept with another person's person, which made me pretty much scum, or rather contributed a new layer of scum to the scuminess I'd already accumulated by attempting to snog my best friend. On top of which, the first man I'd ever properly loved had told me to my face that—

Actually, I didn't even want to think about it. The memory had claws. The part of me that wasn't reduced to bloody mush could vaguely recognise that Caspian's words probably hadn't been a real reflection of his feelings. But the part of me that wasn't reduced to bloody mush was very small. And also it didn't fucking matter. He'd said those things to me. Fucked my arse, my head, and my heart in the same damn fire escape. While catastrophically determined to marry someone else.

I was so sad for him. For the fact the two people he had trusted most had made him believe so little of himself that even the possibility of happiness left him terrified. But I was angry too. Angry that he seemed to heed every voice but mine. Angry that he wouldn't trust the truth of our desires. And angry-beyond-angry that he'd taken from me the time we'd shared. All my cherished memories reduced to a mistake he'd made one summer.

Fuck him for that. Just…

Fuck. Him.

Home was still an empty warehouse. Though I did have a couple of texts, one slightly concerned one from George, which I batted away with an apology and a claim of being tired, and one from Ellery asking how Broderick was. Which actually cheered me up a bit because it was the first time she'd initiated an exchange since New Year's. I sent back that Broderick missed her and hoped she'd come back soon. And then I climbed into bed with my laptop to spend a couple of hours on Skype with Poppy and Nik, who apparently had eight gazillion properties they wanted to show me—some of which were in Cambridge, which left me briefly confused until I remembered it was the fake Boston Cambridge, not Cambridge-Cambridge.

I think I was okay company, even if some of my cheer was a little forced, what with the whole *I'm someone who cheats now* thing. Which wasn't really something I wanted to share, y'know, with people who liked me. Because they'd either stop liking me, which would suck, or they'd be on my side, even though I didn't deserve it, which would suck more. Better just to look at pictures of houses and say *ooh* in the right places. Besides, Nik seemed genuinely excited and I didn't want to ruin it with a honking great ethical failure.

I can't say it was the best night of my life, especially when I finally had to say goodbye, turn off the light, and lie alone under my duvet with nothing to do except torture myself with my brain…um, I mean, try to get to sleep. I basically had the *don't think about pink elephants* problem. In that no matter what I did, I always snapped back to the alleyway, Caspian all shadows and silver, and his voice full of ice, telling me over and over and over again: *With Nathaniel, I have a chance to be someone I admire. With you, I would always be someone I despised.* It was fast becoming an echo to all my recollections of him—carried on the shush of the waves in Kinlochbervie or woven with the pattern of his breath as he held me down and fucked me. I saw the shadow of the words in his remembered eyes. And tasted them in every kiss he'd ever given me.

So yeah. Fun stuff. There were tears. And not a ton of sleep. But I got through it. And that was kind of how it went. The days came, the nights lurked, and I got through them. And slowly, things got easier: my life without Caspian, without even the hope or the dream of Caspian. Which I had finally chosen for myself. And would, given enough time, become just my life again.

About a week or so into this brave new world that had no Caspian in't, I left work as usual only to hear someone calling my name. It wasn't the first time something like this had happened—normally it was just a certain type of journalist sniffing around for a certain type of story, though Boyle, at least, had left me alone since Caspian had stepped in. So I followed what had become my usual procedure: Put my head down, tell them "no comment."

"But you are Arden. Arden"—the stranger hesitated, tripping slightly on my name—"St. Ives?"

I quickened my steps. Tried, and failed, to stop my shoulders hunching. The fact I was sort of used to this didn't mean I liked it. "I said 'no comment.'"

"I know. I'm sorry. The thing is, I'm not a journalist. I'm…" Another pause. The same uncomfortable mix of uncertainty and eagerness in his voice. "That is. I'm Jonas. Jonas Jackson. Does that mean anything to you?"

I came to a dead stop. Clarity like a blade to my throat.

"Arden, I'm your—"

No way was I ready for him to say that to me. "I know."

Maybe I'd known from the start. There was a dull inevitability to the sense of recognition. Turning, I faced the man who'd…who'd what? Provided some of my genes. Loomed with incomprehensible menace over my childhood. Nearly destroyed my mother. And he gazed anxiously back at me with his plain brown eyes. Eyes as plain and brown as mine.

"You stay the fuck away from me," I said. Which would have been tough as all hell if I hadn't sounded so trembly.

To be fair, Jonas didn't move. Just put his hands in the air like I had him at gunpoint. I wished I *did* have him at gunpoint. "I'm not here to cause trouble. I just had to find out if it was really you."

We were on a public street. The office was less than thirty seconds away. My phone was right in my pocket. I was okay. Totally okay. Totally safe. "Well, you've found out. What now?"

"That's entirely up to you, Arden."

I should have left right then. I knew I should. But…I didn't.

And Jonas—my father, I guess—went on, "I'm not here to make excuses to you. I've made a lot of mistakes in my life. I've done a lot of bad things, and there's still more I regret."

"Wow." I settled my bag more comfortably on my shoulder. "So great you came to see me, then."

"It was selfish. Don't think I'm hiding from that either. But when I saw you in the paper last month, I knew I had to come find you. You see, of all those mistakes, all those regrets, the one that haunts me is that"—his voice wavered, then steadied—"I lost my son."

I shrugged. "Well, I did fine without you."

"You did better than fine." He smiled, a fucking dimple glimmering his cheek. "You've made a wonderful life for yourself, anyone can see that. Oxford education, interesting job, lovely girlfriend. I've no right to say it but you're…I'm proud of you."

He *did* have no right to say it. And I didn't need to hear it. I'd met him less than five minutes ago. So what did it matter if he was proud? Except…something inside me twisted with the word. A thorn buried so deeply and for so long I'd forgotten it was there finally coming loose. "Ellery's just a friend. That whole story was bullshit except"—I tipped my chin up—"the bit about me being queer as fuck."

"I've got a lot of faults," said Jonas mildly. "But I wouldn't think less of you over something like that."

Nope nope. I wasn't relieved. I wasn't relieved because I didn't care. It made no difference to me if someone whose contribution to my existence had basically been some sperm turned out to be judgey and homophobic and not proud of me at all. "Congrats on not being a bigot."

"I'm not here to pressure you, Arden." He adjusted his glasses by the corner—the gesture, habit, whatever it was, oddly disarming. And why the fuck did he have glasses anyway? Monsters weren't supposed to wear spectacles. "But I'd like to give you my number. You don't have to do anything with it."

"Then why give it to me?"

"You can call me if you ever want to. You're my son. I want to know you."

That was when I realised just how little information I actually had about…about my father. Including the fact he'd been in the same city as me and I hadn't had a clue. "Are you living in London?"

"No, I'm here for work. Leaving at the end of the week."

I let out a breath. That was good, right? He'd never been close by, and he'd be gone soon.

"I travel a lot," he went on. "I can always come back."

"What even do you do?"

"I sell library software."

Oh, come on. "Seriously?"

"It's been a long time." He gave me another of those tentative smiles. "I've changed."

"So says every dickhead who hasn't changed ever."

The smile faded. "I hope you'll give me a chance. But I'll understand if you can't."

He reached into his jacket pocket, pulled out a business card, and offered it to me. I let him hang there awkwardly for a second or two—telling myself I really was conflicted—and then took it. After all, he was right: I could lose his damn card the moment I got home if I wanted.

"And"—words came out of my mouth before I could stop them—"if I don't get in touch, you won't come looking for me?"

"Never."

"O-okay then."

I hadn't agreed to anything, really. Except I ended up feeling as if I had. Jonas gave me one last look, like he was trying to fix me in his mind, then turned and walked off. He didn't glance back. Didn't hurry or linger. It was amazing how quickly I lost track of him in the crowd. How he could have been anyone, my hand sweating around his business card. I shoved it into my wallet. Maybe I should have thrown it away. But I told myself I could do that whenever.

I tried not to think about him on the way home. Impossible not to, though. I'd had enough familial love to last me a lifetime, so it wasn't as if I'd suffered for the lack of a biological father. But I couldn't say I'd never...wondered? Wondered pretty intensely, actually, even making a fucked-up teenage attempt to find him before Hazel had brought me to my senses. It had hurt her badly, not only because she was scared for Mum, but because if anyone was my dad, it was her. It wasn't about that, though. It was about the...not knowing. As if, in not knowing the man who had been partially responsible for making me, I might not know myself. I mean, what if I was like him? How could I tell?

I had memories, of course, not good ones, of a shadow on the wall, and secrets with Mum, and the sound of her crying when she thought I couldn't hear. That long, long drive, all through the night, Mum's fingers white on the steering wheel. I remembered the unpredictability of his comings and goings. The buzz of his voice in the next room but never the words. And the hush when he was home, as if the house itself held its breath.

Mum didn't like to talk about him, and I didn't like to ask. Hazel had told me he was a sociopath. And so I'd buried my not-knowing down deep and piled the years on top of it until I'd almost forgotten it was there—my little lockbox of doubt. But now it was neither buried nor little. In fact, it was wide open and spewing questions like the self-replicating charm in the Lestrange vault at Gringotts.

Fuck. That was my dad. I'd met my dad. And it had been...not how I might have imagined. But then, that sort of thing was unimaginable anyway. He'd been so...so *ordinary*. Average-looking, with a steady gaze behind those nerdy glasses, and a nice-ish smile. Thick hair for a man of his age, which surely boded well for me in the future, flopping somewhat waywardly across his brow. He hadn't threatened me or pushed me into anything. He'd actually been fairly respectful, hadn't he? Giving me the power. Promising to stay away if that was what I wanted. I knew the thing about sociopaths was that they didn't seem like sociopaths but, well, he didn't seem like a sociopath. So why did I feel all turned upside-down and emptied out?

Anyway, even if he wasn't acting in good faith, and wanted to get to know me for sinister reasons of his own, it was hard to see what those reasons might be. He was only in town for a week. What if I did go for coffee with him? To satisfy my own curiosity, more than anything. What could he do to me? How much harm could that cause? On top of which there was another possibility to consider: He could very well have been sincere. In general, parents were supposed to care about their kids. Was it so totally outlandish that my own father could care about me? After all, I wasn't exactly anyone's dream child: short, skinny, kind of weird, average student, borderline incompetent at a lot of things, semi-regularly in the tabloids for scandalous behaviour, incredibly queer. And he'd still come looking. Still said he wanted to know me. That he was proud of me.

Obviously what he'd done to Mum had been super super *super* wrong. And he'd admitted that. I mean, I think he had—he'd said something about regrets, anyway. I couldn't quite remember. But maybe he really had changed. Was it right of me to punish him for shit he'd done when he wasn't much older than me? Or would it be betraying Mum if I didn't? Probably I should have spoken to her, but I was afraid she'd freak out. And Hazel just would tell me not to do it. To not even think about it.

And…and I wasn't ready to be told that. My father had given me the choice. So I wanted the choice to be mine.

CHAPTER 30

I met Jonas for coffee a couple of days later. I wasn't sure I would, right until I walked in through the door of Starbucks, but I also knew if I hadn't gone, I would probably have…not regretted it exactly, but questioned myself for probably my entire fucking life. So yeah. I texted him. Arranged to see him. And surprise surprise, it was *fine*. He looked the way he had before, bewildering to me in his normality, with those heavy, dark-framed glasses and the messy hair, and the big, dimply smile that came much less hesitantly now. In fact, he looked positively lit up when I came in. Which, honestly, was kind of nice.

He bought me a muffin, and a hot chocolate, and it was awkward at first because we had something that felt as though it ought to be a connection but zero actual relationship. It got easier, though. And talking to Jonas was…no chore. While I still couldn't tell if he'd meant all that stuff about getting to know me, he was doing a ridiculously good impression of wanting to. Asking me lots of questions and whatever. And while I wasn't all that forthcoming at first, it turned out that you could get used to someone being interested in you pretty fucking quickly. Especially when they were, y'know, your dad. And being interested in your kid was meant to be part of the job description, right?

I mean, don't get me wrong. We weren't hugging and crying and having Kodak moments. I wasn't going to be popping round to his place on Christmas Day anytime soon. But I guess I could maybe picture taking a call from him occasionally. Meeting like this every now and again. Was that so terrible?

"I'm really glad," said Jonas, in the lull of me talking about me in order to think about me, "that you decided to come."

"Did you think I wouldn't?"

"I wouldn't have blamed you."

"Well, don't get too comfortable." I prodded the remains of my muffin defiantly. "I can leave at any time."

"Of course you can." When I'd first met him, I'd thought his eyes were like mine, but they weren't really—there was a light to them, an intensity that wasn't quite warmth, especially when he was looking at right at you. "But I hope you won't. I'm enjoying spending time with you. Getting to hear a little bit about your life."

I wasn't ready to admit I was enjoying myself too. Besides, I wasn't, at least not exactly. He'd done nothing to worry or upset me, but I couldn't shake a lingering unsettled feeling, and I had no idea why. Maybe it was just the newness of the situation. Or the fact it ran so abruptly contrary to every story I'd ever been told, which was doing an Orwell with my brain because, surely, one of these narratives had to be wrong. Unless they were both right simultaneously and we'd always been at war with Eurasia.

"I still don't know anything about your life," I pointed out.

That got me dimples. "Oh, I'm not very interesting."

"Bore me, then."

"Well, I…I don't really know what to say. I travel for work a lot, and talk to a lot of librarians."

"Doesn't that get kind of tiring?"

"The travel or the librarians?"

"I see what you did there. Both. Either."

"Sometimes I get tired from the driving and one too many Holiday Inns. But I like meeting new people."

I could see that—he gave every impression of being incredibly approachable when he wasn't popping up out of nowhere to be all *Luke, I am your father* at you. "And you rock selling that software to librarians, huh?"

"So I've been told." He resettled his glasses. Which was one of those gestures I just couldn't quite process—it was vulnerable, somehow, offering this flash of his naked eyes. "I certainly seem to have been successful at it."

"Uhh…" Why had this suddenly got difficult? I guess I wasn't as good at talking to people as *my dad*. "And, like, it's what you want to be doing?"

Flash of a smile again. "I'm not sure anyone entertains a childhood dream of working in sales. But I've tried very hard since—I've tried very hard to build a worthwhile life for myself. I have a job, I have a house, I don't drink anymore. From where I started, that means quite a lot."

"Where you…started?"

"I wouldn't want you to think I'm looking for sympathy,

Arden. My life was in a bad place. Now it isn't."

"You mean"—I swallowed, highly aware there was an emotional viper pit directly under my feet and I was about to plunge straight into it, but utterly unable not to—"with Mum and me?"

Jonas shifted in obvious discomfort. "I don't think we think should talk about that. I don't want to keep anything from you, but I don't think it would be right."

Yes. I agreed. I very much agreed. What the fuck was wrong with me? Why had I even asked? The thing is, I didn't actually want to know. But I guess I…I…did? Mainly so I could reassure myself he wasn't still obsessed with my mum, and in talking to him now, I wasn't being the worst son in the world. "S-sorry," I mumbled. "I don't…that is…it's not my business."

"It was complicated. I was drinking too much. I behaved terribly. But"—he gave a tight little shrug—"I was young, I was messed up. Iris was the only woman I've ever loved and I was losing her."

"O-okay."

"It was a long time ago."

I nodded, relieved. "Are you seeing anyone now?"

"I have a lady in Manchester I've been on a couple of dates with. It's early days." He folded his hands around his cup of tea and took a deep sip. "What about you? There's definitely nothing with your friend from the article?"

"Definitely nothing. I mean, I've got a few casual things going on but"—I sighed—"I'm kind of just out of a thing. Well, not just out. It's been months. But it still feels *just*, if you know what I mean."

"I do, I absolutely do. Want to tell me about it?"

I'd blithered on about Caspian to everyone I knew—up to the point that I'd had to make a conscious decision to stop because I was sucking on the energy of my friends and loved ones like a ginormous parasite. So I don't know if I was just desperate to get my *whining about my ex-boyfriend* fix or I'd inadvertently turned boring people about my breakup into a habit. But there I was, telling Jonas, "He dumped me."

"I dislike him already."

That made me laugh, if slightly guiltily. "It's…complicated."

He nodded. "These things tend to be."

"He'd gone through some stuff, like some pretty horrible, fucked-up stuff, which made him feel we couldn't be together."

Jonas made a sympathetic noise.

And honestly, I'd talked about Caspian with way less encouragement. "It messes with my head because…I don't know…I'd hate it but I'd get it if he just didn't love me or want to be with me." Oh wow. Was I going to cry in Starbucks *twice*? Thankfully, I managed to keep it to messy sniffles. "But it's this other thing. Basically, what it comes down to is I lost my boyfriend for reasons beyond my control that have nothing to do with me. And that's…I know this sounds pathetic, but it's not *fair*."

"I agree. It's very difficult." Jonas let out a long, slow breath. "And I'm sorry for whatever your ex went through."

"So am I. I'm sorry for everything."

"It's not your responsibility, Arden."

I sighed. "I get that. It's still a rubbish reason to have broken up, though. Because of something someone else did."

"I can see where you're coming from." There was something about the way he was looking at me, with that steady, softly glowing gaze, which—in that moment—made me really believe him. And it was a powerful sort of rush: feeling not just nebulously sympathised with but fully understood. "I know," he said, "how painful it is to be forced to live with someone else's decisions, particularly when those decisions affect you directly but you're prevented from participating in them."

"Yes." I bobbed my head as eagerly as a cartoon dog. "That's it exactly. One minute there was an us, and we were working through things, and the next there wasn't and we weren't, and I didn't even get a say."

"The thing is"—Jonas broke off with a sweet, almost sheepish look—"well, I'm not the person to be giving you advice about relationships, but in my experience, when people are reacting to things within themselves, all you can do is let them."

He was right, of course, and I hadn't needed him to tell me that. But I guess it helped hearing it out loud. "It kind of feels like there's me, and there's what he went through, but that's the only thing that counts. Except now it sounds as if I think it's a competition."

"It doesn't sound that way to me."

"I honestly don't. I just wish I could be as real to him as his pain."

"I expect this will come across as a platitude"—Jonas stirred the dregs of his tea—"but time can make a huge difference when it comes to things like this."

Considering what had happened at the Laine Matthäus Gallery, or more particularly in its fire escape, I was sceptical. "It hasn't so far."

"It's been months. Try years. There will be a point when things are better. For both of you."

"Really?"

He put a hand to his heart. "I promise."

We talked about other things after that—or I did, anyway. Simple stuff like work, friends, books I liked, my time at university, both of us edging carefully round the past. He did ask me a couple of times if I remembered anything—the weekend we'd all spent on the Cornish coast or the time he'd read me *The Iron Man*—but I was too young. Nothing but blanks. Except for a disconnected sense-memory of the widest, bluest sky, which I kept to myself.

It was only when Starbucks started trying to close around us that I noticed how late it had got. Hastily, we packed up and made for the street. Paused on the pavement in the halo of greeny-gold light that spilled out with us.

"So," I said, swinging my bag onto my shoulder in what I hoped was a nonchalant manner, and accidentally whacked a passerby. "That was a thing we did."

Jonas resettled his glasses. "I would like to do it again. If you would."

Did I? Well, why not? It had gone fine. Nothing terrible had happened. I mean, I still wasn't ready to roll out a welcome mat to my life, but he wasn't asking for that. And probably it was better to have a dad whose existence you were vaguely aware of instead of a dad who was lurking in the shadows like a spider under the sofa. "Maybe. Sure. Yeah."

"I'll be back down south in about six to eight months."

"Six to eight months?"

"I can text you. I've got your number."

"Okay."

"And obviously"—a glimmer of a dimple—"I'm here 'til the end of the week."

"Any plans?"

"I've got some people to see. What about you?"

"Work, nothing major." I toed at the pavement. "If you're not busy…since it's going to be a while…we could probably meet up again before you leave."

He got that glowy look. "I can do Friday?"

"Yeah, okay. Same Starbucks, same pack-drill?"

"I'll see you then."

To be honest, I wasn't entirely sure why I'd suggested it. Only that it had felt right at the time. And, afterwards, I wished I hadn't—despite the fact I had no concrete reason for being uncomfortable. He'd behaved exactly the way you'd want your abusive absentee father to behave if he'd appeared out of nowhere, claiming to want to be part of your life. Besides, I didn't *have* to meet Jonas again if I didn't want to. Although cancelling or standing him up would have been shitty. Especially since he hadn't done anything wrong.

Well. Anything wrong to me.

CHAPTER 31

Friday fucking sucked. Not in a dramatic, interesting way. My hair wouldn't get its act together. The Circle line was subject to "minor delays across the service," which meant everything was stuck. I knocked my Diet Coke over in my drawer. Accidentally hit DO NOT SAVE CHANGES after editing an entire article on the twenty-seven best pedicures in London. And REPLY ALL in a moment of mental abstraction. Not disastrously. But it still made me look inept in front of two hundred people, one of whom was my boss. Go me. And then, of course, I ran into further "minor delays" on the way to meet my dad. Leaving me to charge into Starbucks grumpy and sweaty, with stupid hair, and there was Jonas waiting for me at the same table we'd had last time, with a muffin, and a hot chocolate that had clearly gone cold. Which made me feel extra bad for wanting to ditch him.

"Sorry, sorry, sorry." I wove elegantly through the tables towards him. Okay, that's a lie. I stood on a lady's coat and tripped over a chair leg. But anyway, I made it, flung my jacket down, and dumped my shoulder bag. "And I'm absolutely busting for a wee."

Jonas smiled. No dimples, though. "I'm just glad you're here."

"I'll be right back, okay?"

"Yes"—his eyes flicked away, then back again—"of course."

I dove into the loo and, y'know. Then washed my hands and came running back. And Jonas wasn't there. Honestly, I just thought he'd gone to get another drink. Or also to the toilet. But I couldn't see him in the queue. And if he had gone to the bathroom, it was getting to the point where he'd been gone so long I was worried for his gastric health. So I did a quick circuit just in case…well, I have no idea. In case we'd managed to miss each other. Peered out of the window on the off-chance he'd stepped out onto the street to take a call or have a ciggie. He wasn't anywhere.

"Um. Excuse me. Sorry." I shuffled back to the woman whose coat I'd trashed earlier. "But did you see a man? I mean, not just any man. A specific man. Dark jacket, floppy hair, glasses?"

There's pretty much nothing more painful to the English temperament than having to talk to strangers. But it does mean that, when we do, the other party is aware it's fucking serious.

The woman looked gently anxious—possibly on my behalf, or more likely her own on account of the whole *talking to a stranger* situation that was happening to her. "I don't think so…oh, wait. Maybe. I think he left."

He left? Because I was late? Because I'd needed a wee? Or because of an emergency of his own? Was he okay? Had he had some kind of freak-out? Or decided that I wasn't what he was looking for in a person he had given sperm to create? It made no sense. He'd given every impression of liking me. Asked questions about my life. Listened when I talked. Told me he was proud of me. Even today, he'd said he was glad I'd come—although running the scene backwards and forwards through the dusty DVD player of my mind's eye—he had seemed a bit on edge. I'd assumed it was because he'd thought he'd been dumped by his kid. But I barely knew the man. It could have been anything.

Fuck it. I was going to phone him.

Grabbing bag and jacket and muffin—waste not, want not—I headed out. After all, people who make calls in Starbucks are the devil's spawn. Shit, where was my phone. Bag? Jeans? Left jacket pocket? Right jacket pocket? Bag again. Front of bag? Lining of bag? Lining of jacket? Some other obscure part of bag? What. What. What the fuck? It had to be somewhere. I'd definitely had it on the Tube, because I'd been playing Alphabear. Was it in Starbucks? On the table? Under the table? Had the lady whose coat I'd stood on seen it? Apparently not. Had someone handed it in? Nope. Fucking hell, had someone nicked my phone? So bloody typical after I'd blithely refused to fork out an extra fiver a month to have it insured.

I lost my grip on the muffin and it smashed into squidgy chocolate shrapnel on the pavement. Of course someone had stolen my phone. Jonas had stolen my phone. Right now, he was probably in some dodgy shop in Soho getting it unlocked so he could find out where Mum was. Because my dad was an abusive sociopath who was obsessed with her. And I was an idiot beyond reckoning.

Oh God. Oh God. Oh fucking God. I'd just ruined the lives of the people I loved most in the world.

* * *

Half an hour later, I was bursting out of a taxi at Hart & Associates. And yes, I know. Fucking pathetic. Immediately running to the guy I'd told I never wanted to see again the second something went wrong.

But God. Fuck my pride. This was my family. My *family*. And I didn't know what else to do.

Unfortunately, the other thing I didn't know how to do was get into the building. It was outside office hours, so the front was locked up tight, the atrium just a blur of marble and shadow on the other side of glass. I'd have had more luck against a wall of briars and a century-long curse. Caspian was probably still working—if I stood on the far side of the pavement and tilted my head so far back it felt like my spine was about to snap, I even thought, or maybe it was wishful thinking, I could see a light up there. But how could I reach him?

When we'd been dating, I'd had access to an app that worked as a code for Caspian's personal lift, which linked the underground car park directly to his office or his penthouse. Probably my privileges had been revoked by now, though. And, oh wait, Jonas had stolen my fucking phone.

Fuck's sake, Arden, think. *Think.*

The way I saw it, I had two options. Sit on the pavement and cry. Or keep running around in a wild panic. I opted for Option B (with a little bit of Option A thrown in for good measure). For all I knew, there'd be a security guard in the car park. And maybe I could convince them to take me to Caspian. Or I could trigger some kind of alarm by…like…attacking the lift and pressing all the buttons. Or cameras…there could be cameras. And I could wave at them until someone noticed me or write *Help me Caspian* in Lamborghinis on the floor or…or…

Fuck. Fuck. Fuck.

I'd always been whooshed in and out of the car park by chauffeurs, so I hadn't really noticed how ridiculously enormous it was. It took me about five minutes just to run down the entrance ramp, my breath rattling in my throat, and my bag bashing me on the arse with every step. The security gates I dodged round and wriggled under, and I'm pretty sure I did, in fact, trip the security system, a series of cameras whirring round to catch my image with dystopian efficiency. Not that I cared. Being arrested wouldn't have been great. But it would get Caspian's attention, right?

I mean, assuming I didn't just have a heart attack and die on the concrete floor. God, I hadn't had a stitch this bad since having to do PE at school. In the end I had to stop, put my hands on my knees, and wheeze, perilously close to throwing up from sheer terror and exertion. My jacket was tight under my arms, sealing me in my own sweat like a thermos flask. Also: running and crying. Don't recommend it. It's soggy in all the ways. I wiped my nose on my sleeve, because it was that or choke. Then resettled my bag of the damned against my shoulder and forced myself into a shambling canter.

Far in the distance, between the cold gleam of expensive

cars, I at last caught sight of the lift, shimmery as a mirage—
a boring grey mirage—through my teary eyes. I pushed forward, hair in my face, legs replaced by noodles that were on
fire, and collapsed against the door, panting, and banging on
it in what would—under other circumstances—have been a
hilariously futile fashion.

Then came the clatter of shoes against concrete and I
twisted round to see a couple of security guards bearing
down on me.

"I…I need to see Caspian Hart," I said, plastering myself
over the lift door like it was my child and elephants were
stampeding towards us.

Both the guards had a burly professional look to them.
"I'm sure you do, sir. But this is private property and so you'll
have to come along with us."

"No, but…it's…my name's Arden St. Ives. I used to date
Caspian. It's an emergency."

"This way, please." They advanced. And while I could tell
they weren't actively trying to be threatening, there was
something purposeful about the way they came forward that
made me feel very small suddenly.

"Yes, okay." I peeled myself off the lift because I was pretty
sure if I didn't they'd drag me away from it. "But if I go with
you, will you…will you tell him? Will you tell him I was
here?"

They exchanged looks, and one of them said, "Of course
sir," in the voice of a "sure Jan" gif.

And I made a helpless whimpery noise because I could
recognise defeat when it was dressed in hi-visibility jackets
and about to escort me off the premises. My mind tilted like

the *Titanic* going down. Right now, they clearly thought I was just some messed-up, possibly very unwell person who had wandered in. But if I made a run for it, that was more serious, right? Then they might *have* to inform Caspian. Except that would mean being chased, and taken down, by people who were trained in chasing and taking down. This wasn't America, and they weren't armed, so I was sure they wouldn't hurt me, like, much. But I was still scared. Too scared to risk it.

I must have looked incredibly pitiful, because the bigger of the guards actually offered me a tissue when I trudged over. Then his colleague took a firm grip on my upper arm and the two of them began escorting me towards the exit.

That was when the lift doors swooshed open. And I heard Nathaniel's voice, obviously annoyed, going "Oh, what is it now?" at the same time Caspian said, more bewildered than anything, "Arden?"

I twisted frantically between my captors, tears of pure relief flooding my eyes. "Caspian, I've fucked up. I've fucked everything up. And I don't know what to do."

"Mr. Hart, do you know this"—Tissue seemed at a loss for a moment before settling on—"person. We caught him trespassing."

"I wasn't trespassing," I cried. "I was trying to find you."

"Thank you. I'll take it from here." Caspian nodded to his security team and then turned to me. "What's happened, Arden? What's wrong?"

I opened my mouth to explain—to throw myself verbally, or literally, on my knees if that was what it took. But then Nathaniel slipped his arm through Caspian's and said, "My prince, we're going to be late."

"Not now." Caspian didn't even look at him.

"This is just another of his ploys. Can't you see that?"

I scrubbed at my eyes with the back of my hand. "It's not a ploy. I wouldn't be here unless I had to be. Please... please...will you help me?"

"Always, my Arden." Caspian had closed the distance between us in two of his long, world-conquering strides. "Anything within my power is yours."

I didn't know if it was the shock catching up with me or the after-effects of my desperate run across a car park or just...too much fear and its abrupt abatement, but the edges of the world went wibbly and I wibbled with them. Everything was sliding away from me. Except Caspian, who caught me the moment before I fell. The familiar scent of his cologne washed over me, and his arms came round me, and the promise of safety within his strength was so real to me— and I needed it so badly—that I started to cry yet again.

"I can't believe you're falling for this," snarled Nathaniel.

Caspian was already heading for the lift. "This is important."

"And I'm not?"

"We can go to a concert another night."

"Can we?" Nathaniel's shoes clicked against the concrete as he followed us. "It's taken weeks for you to have time for this one."

"You know I'll reimburse you for the ticket."

"You know that's not the point."

One of those sighs from Caspian I used to dread. "The point is that Arden has a problem that must be resolved. I shall resolve it and you shall cease distracting me."

Nathaniel actually gasped. "Caspian, I'm your fiancé, not your secretary. You do not talk to me like that."

I think them were what you'd call fightin' words. Or they would have been if Nathaniel hadn't sounded terribly hurt. Even Caspian paused. "I'm sorry," he said more gently, "but I've made my decision. Go to the concert."

"I don't want to go to the concert. Not on my own. I"— Nathaniel lifted one of his hands, almost imploringly, and then dropped it again—"wanted to go with you."

"I'm afraid that's no longer an option."

Nathaniel's lashes fluttered fretfully. "Well, what am I supposed to do now?"

"I can have the car take you home."

"Oh, don't bother. I'll take a cab."

"As you prefer."

And then we were in the lift, the doors closing on the grey expanse of the car park and the flickering charcoal sketch of Nathaniel's shadow as he walked away.

CHAPTER 32

Caspian took me straight up to his penthouse. It was exactly as I remembered, too much space and cold light, and this sense of emptiness that had nothing to do with the furnishings. I guess I'd expected Nathaniel to have had more impact—his home was so lovely I couldn't imagine him being any more comfortable here than I was. Anyway, I didn't have enough emotional bandwidth to think about that right now. Or even what had happened between them in the car park. Which was kind of my fault. But sorry, Nathaniel, my guilt was needed elsewhere. Join the fucking queue.

Part of me didn't want to uncling, but when Caspian lowered me onto one of the sofas, I forced myself to let go of him. It was pathetic to be seeking comfort after what I'd done. Honestly, I wasn't sure if I deserved to be comforted ever again. By anyone.

"Can I get you a glass of water?" he asked. "Something to eat?"

"No. I have to…" I started trembling and couldn't stop.

Had no idea how to put into words the magnitude of what had happened. So I just blurted out, "It's my dad."

Caspian's brows pulled tight. But his only other reaction was to tell me, "A moment please," before he vanished and came back, a handful of seconds later, with a blanket.

Once he'd wrapped me up in it, he went down on his knees beside me, something that always unhinged my world a little bit. "Tell me everything. From the beginning."

So I did. Starting with Jonas turning up at my work because of that godawful article. It wasn't a long story but it felt like it took forever to relate, maybe because it contained so much of my selfishness and stupidity. By the time I was done, my mouth was dry and my voice was hoarse, and I could hardly look at him. Terrified that his face might reflect back at me the condemnation I thought it should.

He took my hand, which was somehow cold and wet at the same time, and frankly very gross, and brought it to his lips. Kissed my fingers with the same archaic courtesy he'd sometimes shown me when we were dating—only this time his maiden fair had pretty much wandered into the dragon's mouth going "tirra lirra" because I was a fucking idiot.

"We'll find him," he said. "I won't let him hurt your family."

"But…but what if you can't? What if he does? What if he—"

"Arden. You have seen only a fraction of the resources I can bring to bear if needed. Very few men are beyond my power. Your father is most certainly not."

"I know, but—"

"Enough." His voice was soft, and yet still full of an unassailable intent. "Will you trust me?"

He'd asked me that once before. In a very different context. And the answer was the same as it had always been. "Yes."

"Then believe the situation will be taken care of." He rose, controlled as ever, to his feet.

Okay, that sounded great. And also a bit *Will no one rid me of this turbulent priest?* I swallowed. "By...taken care of...you don't mean in a murdery way, right?"

He looked startled. "I hadn't planned on it. Although it could be arranged if it became necessary. Or if you—"

"No. No. Please don't."

"If you weren't clearly distraught"—he gave me the faintest of smiles—"I'd be a little concerned at how casually you assumed I'd resort to assassination."

Okay, yeah. When he put it like that. "Sorry, my head is fucked."

"I know, sweetheart." He reached out and very lightly touched the mad multidirectional medley that was my hair. "I'm going to make some calls. And you try to rest."

I wrinkled my nose. "Like that's going to happen."

"I said try. I have no conviction of your success under the circumstances, but if you can, it will help."

"Okay."

I did, actually, sort of rest? If you could call it that. It was more of a nonconsensual unconsciousness that crept over me from time to time, though I never roused from it feeling refreshed. The hours were long and slow and crappy, and my body couldn't seem to figure out whether it was too hot or too cold and, sometimes, contrived to be both at once, which was pretty special. Caspian was mostly in another room—I could hear the clicking of him typing, and the low murmur of his voice occasionally—but he checked on me fairly regularly. Sent me to have a shower. Brought me tea.

"I know you aren't particularly fond of it," he said, putting the cup down next to me, "but I understand it's generally considered a consoling drink."

"I don't want to be consoled. I feel terrible and I should feel terrible."

"You should not. This isn't your fault."

I gaped at him. "Of course it is. I should never have trusted him."

"Then the fault lies with your father for being unworthy of your trust."

"I *knew* what he was like," I protested. "So I should have known he was using me."

"Perhaps. But there is no weakness in putting your faith in people, especially when they're people who should, by rights, protect and care for you."

I covered my face with my hands. "I don't know what I was thinking."

"It doesn't matter. He manipulated you."

"I'm so stupid." Tears began to drip between my fingers. "So fucking stupid. Letting myself believe that I'd mean anything to him."

"Arden, please. You…" Caspian paused, sounding oddly helpless. "You can't let yourself think this way."

"He never wanted me in the first place because I took away Mum's attention…which I'm not supposed to know but I overheard Hazel and Rabbie talking...so I should have realised he didn't want me now." I drew in a wet and shuddery breath. "I mean, why would he? Look at me. I'm pathetic and I'm stupid and I'm weak and I'm selfish and I make bad decisions and I fuck everything up. But I guess I just really...*hoped* he might—"

"Enough of this." Caspian pulled me into his arms and held me, while I sobbed and sobbed and sobbed. "Jonas is a despicable man and you are precious."

I was too far gone to even make a Gollum joke. If anything, the nice things he was saying just made everything hurt even more. "Don't. I used to love how well you thought of me. But right now, I belong in a fucking dustbin."

"You do not." He gave me a little shake. "And if you keep talking like this, I really will have him assassinated."

I yelped. "Don't joke about it."

"I'm not. I hate that he has made you doubt your worth."

"He didn't." I sat up again, drying my face as best I could. "I did. Caspian, I put my family in danger because I was just so fucking desperate to let someone make me feel special."

He closed his fingers tightly around my wrist, the band on his fourth finger gleaming with a kind of sickly sheen. "No. You made a mistake. That is all. And your family isn't in danger. I won't let anything happen to them. I promise."

"I thought promises were for children."

"You told me they were for—" Caspian stopped abruptly. *Lovers.*

"Can I have that tea now?" I asked. As much for my sake as for his.

Obviously relieved, he handed me the cup.

And I stared into the murky grey-brown liquid, somewhat dismayed. "Um. What's this?"

"Tea?"

"Are you sure?" I touched a finger to the surface, momentarily dispersing the oily film that had gathered there. "Because it looks dreadful. What did you do to it?"

A flush was creeping over his cheeks. "I don't know. I followed a WikiHow."

"You followed a…Have you really never made tea before?"

"Well, as you know, I prefer coffee and"—he gave me one of his more abashed smiles—"other people bring it to me."

God. I shouldn't have been capable of finding him adorable right now. But I did. Just a little bit. And then felt immediately guilty for thinking about Caspian instead of my family. Sick with self-recrimination, I took a heedless gulp of tea.

Caspian was watching me anxiously. "It's horrible, isn't it?"

"Uh…yeah. Really horrible."

He took the cup back, seemed to be considering trying it himself, but then just put it down on the table again.

"Look," I said. "Can you tell me what you're doing? I…kind of need to know what's going on. Do I need to call my mum? What if he—"

"There's nothing he can do that is not within my power to preempt. In the worst-case scenario, he's already on his way to Kinlochbervie, but he will have missed his opportunity to fly, so he will either need to drive overnight, catch the sleeper, or wait for the morning flight. I, on the hand, have a private jet, which has already departed. There will be people discreetly watching your family's home within two hours."

I made a wavery distressed noise I couldn't quite keep in.

"I know you won't thank me for pointing out that worrying will sap your spirit to no purpose."

"Except for the bit where you pointed it out anyway."

His lips twitched, but his expression quickly grew serious again "Sometimes it does us good to hear things even if we can't acknowledge or believe them."

"I…" Drawing my knees up to my chest, I curled my arms miserably around them. "I'm just having a hard time thinking about anything that isn't what a shitty person I am. Which, now that I say it aloud, is still all about me. Oh my God. Am I a sociopath? Am I a sociopath like he is?"

"Arden," said Caspian, very gently. "Of course you're not."

I turned my head to look at him. "H-how can you be so sure?"

"Sociopaths don't care whether they're sociopaths."

"That seems too easy."

"I've seen very many very clever people waste fortunes by failing to recognise when the easy answer was also the correct answer." His eyes held mine, nothing but the softest blues tonight and silver spirals as bright as tinsel. "Arden, you need to forgive yourself for this."

For once, I was the first to look away—hiding my face against my thighs. "No I don't. I really don't."

"It's the nature of such people to make us doubt ourselves. To make us bear the responsibility for their cruelty. How you feel now is just another of his manipulations."

"You don't understand," I cried. "He said all this stuff about how he didn't want to let Mum go and I couldn't help thinking about how I didn't want to let you go, and all this other stuff about how hard it was living with someone else's decisions when they hurt you. And I know he's bad and he was bad to Mum, but when he was talking, it felt like it was the same. And maybe it felt the same because it is the same and I'm—"

"Stop." He caught my hands, which were plucking restlessly at my jeans. "Please stop. He was clearly leading you to draw those comparisons so that you'd believe his pursuit of your mother was justified."

I stared at him, trying not to hate myself and failing hard. "And what about my pursuit of you?"

"That is categorically different."

"How?" I asked, more than slightly pathetically.

"So many ways. Some of which I'm embarrassed to enumerate." He closed his eyes for a moment and then went on. "Firstly, I've repeatedly taken actions that have brought you back in my life. Your mother has done everything she can to keep Jonas out of hers. Secondly, your mother ran away from your father because she was afraid of him. I ran away from you because I was afraid of myself. And finally, you've never…you've never…"

I nearly said *Never what?* but then I noticed how still he'd gone.

"You've never tried to diminish me," he went on softly, "or control me or make me into what you think I should be."

Getting a handle on my emotions was like sifting through stale vomit in order to figure out what I ate last night. My heart was a big ugly splash, all half-chewed bits of shame and guilt and fear. Though worst of all was the hurt. Oh, what the fuck was wrong me? That I could know exactly what sort of person Jonas was, and still be hurt by it. "I…I wish I could believe you but I can't tell if I just want to let myself off the hook."

"Please"—Caspian was crouched on the floor again, his hands covering mine—"believe me. You're the best person I know. I can't bear to see you like this."

He still sounded oddly shaken. I glanced down at him, and it was always strange—having Caspian Hart at my feet. I'm sure under any other circumstances I would have been absolutely exultant. "I'm sorry. I've dumped a lot of shit on you tonight."

"I don't care about that. I would do anything for you."

"I'm…I'm not who you think I am. This should have shown you that."

"You're exactly who I think you are." His fingers tightened painfully on mine, his voice caught somewhere between fierce and imploring. "Your father can't change that."

I gave a shaky not-quite-laugh and uncurled because peering at Caspian over my knees was getting weird. "I don't know what I did to make you so sure I'm so…whatever you think I am."

"You didn't have to do anything." He leaned forward and rested his cheek against my legs. "You only had to be."

"Oh, Caspian…" I didn't know what else to say. In truth, I wasn't anywhere near as close to accepting what had happened as he wanted me to be, but I'd already dragged enough of the people I loved into the maelstrom of my fuck-up. He was trying so damn hard to console me. The least I could do was let him. "Thank you."

"Are you sure," he asked, with just enough lightness that I was pretty sure he was joking, "you won't let me have him killed?"

"I thought you said you didn't want to."

"I've changed my mind."

"No murder. Zero murder. Murder count: nil." Tentatively, I extricated one of my hands from his and petted the soft curls at his brow. I half expected him to pull away but he didn't, just pressed into me. "I should never have mentioned it."

"You were hurt and I was unable to prevent it. That is intolerable to me."

"It's not your job to protect me from my own stupidity."

"But"—his eyes flicked to mine—"I do want to protect you."

"Well, you can't, because that's not how things work. And you shouldn't, because I need to live my own life, and yours is…yours is with someone else."

There was a long silence. And then, so softly I almost missed it, "I…yes."

"Though fuck knows," I admitted, "what I would have done without you tonight. I'm honestly so fucking gratef—"

He silenced me with a gesture. "I don't need your gratitude. Compared to what you've given me, this is nothing. Everything is nothing."

"I don't understand. I've always thought what I gave or tried to give you couldn't have meant very much, considering…I mean…considering how easily you threw it away."

"You must never think that." He sat back on his heels,

hands folded loosely in his lap, eyes steady on mine. "You gave me happiness, Arden, beyond anything I thought possible for someone like me. You made me believe, for a few infinitely treasured months, that I could be free."

I wanted to tell him he could have that again. All it would take was a word. A look. But it wasn't the time—for me or for him. So instead I said, "I hope someday you feel that way again."

And I meant it too. I really did.

CHAPTER 33

We'd sort of run out of stuff to say, though not in a bad way. There was something peaceful in the quiet, an impulse towards togetherness as powerful on its own as the impulses that had led us to misbehaving in a fire escape not so very long ago. I thought Caspian might go off to do billionaire things, or whatever he was doing in the other room, but he didn't. He just sat beside me on the sofa and let me rest my head against his arm, while my thoughts turned as helplessly as windmill sails in a gale. Until I found it: a hard, cold crystal of fury at the centre of tumult. And while I was all too familiar with the false comfort of getting angry instead of being sad, this was different. It didn't feel like strength. It felt like a splinter I needed to pull out.

"When you find him," I said. "I want to be there."

Caspian's whole body tensed. "I don't think that's a good idea."

"It's not your call." This was ... well, not a bluff exactly. But I was overplaying my hand because I couldn't force Caspian to tell me where Jonas was, and how can I put this, he wasn't the least high-handed person I'd ever met. A trait I found attractive in certain contexts, and very much the opposite in others, although I also had to accept it came with the territory of being a billionaire.

So basically, I was braced for a row. And then Caspian sighed, his brows pulling tight. "I wish you wouldn't. I don't like the thought of him being anywhere near you."

"I'm not all that keen on being near him either. But I have to know…I have to know it's over. That he's not coming for us."

"And," he murmured, "you can't believe me if I tell you those things are true?"

"It's not that I don't trust you, Caspian. I trust you more than anyone in the world. But"—I drew in a deep, surprisingly steady breath—"I think I should do this. I started it, after all. I should finish it."

"You didn't start it. The way he is has nothing to do with you."

"Well, I'm still involved."

His frown deepened. "If you insist on going, then I suppose you must go."

I opened my mouth. Then closed it. Then opened it again. But nothing came out.

"Now what's the matter?" he asked.

"I guess I'm surprised. I thought you'd forbid it."

"I would dearly love to forbid it." He turned to face me, the faintest hint of a smile softening the sternness of his mouth. "But would you let me?"

I shook my head. "No chance."

"Well then. I see no benefit in continuing to expend effort in pursuit of a futile cause."

"You don't have to worry about me," I told him, my fingers finding of their own accord the line between his brows and stroking it to smoothness. "I'll be okay."

"My concerns are my…concern."

"Except"—I grinned at him—"I'm telling you right now that you're expending effort for a futile cause."

He laughed, sounding almost more startled than amused, as if he'd forgotten he *could* laugh. "You little monkey. Though if I am to allow this, there will be conditions."

"Oh, so it's *allow this* now?"

"Don't push your luck, Arden. You already know I think it's inadvisable."

"Sorry." I gave him my best meek look. "What are the conditions?"

"You will be sensible and quiet and allow Finesilver do his job to the specifications I have provided for him. You will stop taking the blame for what has happened. And until there is something to be done, you will take care of yourself."

The words, which were delivered in his firmest tone, coiled around me as sweetly as chains, and I couldn't repress a contented shudder at them. "Take care of myself?"

"Yes. Eat properly, drink sufficiently, try to sleep."

"I'm…I'm not sure I can face food right now."

"The others, then."

I somehow started talking to my feet. "It feels all kinds of wrong to be having a nice time when my dad is going after my mum."

"I'm not suggesting you have a nice time. I'm insisting you stop engaging in unproductive acts of penance."

"Okay." Swallowing, I held out my hand to him. "I guess you have a deal, Mr. Hart."

We shook, his grip a little tighter than it needed to be. Not in a dickhead businessman way, but like he didn't want to let me go. "Please…if you don't mind…don't call me Mr. Hart. It takes me to a place I cannot visit with equanimity."

"I'm sorry. I don't mean to. It just happens sometimes, because you used to like it."

"I still like it. But I shouldn't."

I gave him a final squeeze before pulling my fingers free. "We shouldn't."

"Indeed. We…" He faltered unexpectedly. Cleared this throat. "*We* shouldn't."

"So, um," I asked, "what now?"

"There's nothing further to be done tonight. I can call for a car, if you want to go home."

Not hugely, in all honesty. Just the thought of being alone was terrifying, but I'd pretty much blown all my Caspian Credit already. And besides, I was supposed to be living my own life, wasn't I? "Okay. And thank you."

"Or if you would be more comfortable, you can stay here."

"I can?" I peeped at him hopefully, if guiltily. "Would that be…okay?"

"Why would it not be? Though, be warned, it's very late and I intend to put you straight to bed."

I nearly asked, *Will you tuck me in?* But I remembered just in time I was trying to be a less terrible person. "What about Nathaniel?"

"He prefers to sleep at his house."

"No. I mean, if I was Nathaniel, I would not want someone who felt towards you the way I do spending the night."

His eyes widened. "You've had a very traumatic experience, and have come to me for help. Surely you don't think I'm going to take advantage of you?"

"What if *I* take advantage of *you*?"

That brought a touch of pink to his cheeks. "Are you going to?"

I gave the matter due consideration. It seemed only fair. "Probably not. I'm not exactly oozing with sexiness right now."

"In which case, Nathaniel has nothing to object to."

Somehow I managed not to literally facepalm. "I'm not sure it works like that, Caspian."

"Go to bed. I do actually need to call him."

Who would've thought being summarily ordered about could be something you'd miss? But I did. Well, being summarily ordered about by Caspian anyway. If I'd been into that sort of thing in general, I could have joined the army.

His bedroom hadn't changed either—it was still this chill, bed-containing bubble that seemed to float Philip K. Dick style above the overturned jewellery box of the city. I breached the sanctity of the glass-smooth duvet and pulled it up to my chin, feeling about as weird as I had the last time I'd slept over at Caspian's. Which, hey, looking on the bright side: At least I didn't feel *more* weird. It was the lack of intimacy, I think, that gave me the willies—not so much the fact that neither I nor Nathaniel had managed to leave even the slightest trace of ourselves here, but the complete absence of

Caspian too. Even the sheets were starkly fresh and scentless. Combined with the expensive cloudiness of the mattress, it made me feel like I was nowhere.

Pushing back the covers, I leaned over the edge of the bed and peered underneath, and was so relieved to see the battered box full of sci-fi and fantasy books that used to belong to Caspian's father was still there. It was probably the most Caspian thing in the whole place. Definitely the most human. I couldn't bear to think what it might have meant if he'd packed them away. And besides, I loved the image of him, amidst all this stark design and silence, curled up with some cheesy adventure novel from the eighties. In an ideal world, I would have been snuggled up next to him, of course. But if I couldn't be, I needed to be able to picture him happy.

"What are you doing?"

Oh shit. That was Caspian. Addressing himself politely to my arse, which was right up in the air. I flipped proper-way-up as gracefully as I could, which was to say not very. "Um, nothing. I mean, just...looking. Around. How was Nathaniel?"

"Not inclined to answer his phone."

"I'm sorry."

"Don't be. It's rather childish of him."

I was really not in the mood to defend Nathaniel. But I tried anyway. "He's hurt."

"You needed me."

"I did, so I'm not going to argue with you about it. But he should be your priority, Caspian."

"My priorities are determined by objective standards of urgency, not by sentiment. There will be other concerts. You would not have come to find me were it not truly important."

"That's"—my brain fiddled with that idea like it was a Rubik's Cube it couldn't solve—"really cold and really nice at the same time."

Caspian gave me one of his smallest smiles. "Thank you. I just came to check you were comfortable. Is there anything else you require?"

"No, I'm good, I think. But where will you sleep?"

"I have some work to finish. And the sofa is perfectly comfortable."

I retucked myself in the duvet. "I guess having made a big fuss about Nathaniel's feelings, it would be epically hypocritical to suggest you come in with me?"

"I wouldn't go quite as far as hypocritical," he said. "But it would certainly be inconsistent."

"I won't jump your bones."

"We both know there are intimacies beyond sex. And for me, sharing a bed is one of them."

Probably the thing to do was leave it at that. But I was me, and I couldn't. I just couldn't. "You never did tell me why you hated it so much."

"Oh, Arden, I didn't hate it. I…far from hated it." His gaze slid past me to the window and the gleaming sky beyond. "I have trouble with the sense of…with the sense of…physical vulnerability. Of course, rationally, I know you would never…never…" And then he fell silent with the force of Wile E. Coyote crashing into a concrete wall.

"It's okay," I said quickly. "I get it."

He gave me this awful look, half-defiant, half-stricken. "I don't like feeling helpless."

"I shouldn't have asked."

"I should have told you." I was going to protest, but then he turned away and, from behind his own hand, muttered, "But I don't know how to speak of…of any of it."

I tried to beam my tangle of adoring-him-hurting-for-him-desperately-wanting-to-help-him feelings at his back. "It's impossibly difficult."

"I…Lately I…" He bowed his head. "I have come to wonder who I am protecting with my silence. If it is truly myself."

"Please," I burst out. "I don't want to be alone tonight. And I don't want you to be either. Stay with me. At least for a little bit."

Slowly, he faced me again, so much despair in him, and so much longing in his eyes. "Of course I will."

"Really? I mean…really?"

"Until you sleep."

I nodded, breathlessly. "Okay. Yes. Anything. Thank you."

We were almost painfully decorous about it. Me, under the sheets, in an unsexy ball, and Caspian sitting on top of them, having shed only jacket and tie, his back against the headboard and his long legs crossed at the ankles. We didn't touch—although I could feel the shape of him and, faintly or perhaps it was my imagination, the heat of him. I couldn't help sneaking little glances at his face. His profile offered nothing but its beauty: those fine masculine symmetries, pure as marble.

"This is, um, all right, right?" I said. "You're, like, not bored."

"Go to sleep."

I was trying. I really was. But the moment I closed my eyes, Jonas was waiting, like some smiling, bespectacled bogeyman. I flipped onto my back. Then my side. Then my other side. My back again. My front.

Caspian made a low, exasperated noise. "Arden…"

"I'm sorry. I'm sorry. I promise I'm not I'm doing it deliberately. I'm just having trouble dropping off."

"Lying still would probably help."

"It's my brain that won't lie still."

"Well"—he cast a strange, sweet look at me—"what do you normally do when you feel restless?"

The words echoed inside me, silvery as wind chimes, but way less annoying. "Oh, you know. The usual things. Read a book. Get myself off." I gave an uncertain laugh. "Which would so not be appropriate right now."

"I can leave the room."

"OMG, Caspian. No. I'm not wanking in your bed."

"I wouldn't mind. And the sheets are changed daily."

I whacked him in the leg. "Not the point. It would be weird, and I wouldn't enjoy it."

"Then…I suppose you'll have to fall back on a book."

"Look." I propped myself up on an elbow. "It's not that I don't appreciate the *Arden has a problem that must be resolved and I shall resolve it* approach you're taking to me getting a healthy amount of rest, but it's not going work. I'm scared and I'm anxious, and I really don't have the concentration to read."

"What if I read to you?"

I was so surprised, I thought I was having legit delusions. "W-what?"

"If it's something you would enjoy." Caspian drew up a knee, folding his hands across it self-consciously. "When I was young, and couldn't sleep, my father would often read to me. I remember finding it quite soothing."

"My mum used to read to me, too. It was the loveliest. But I guess it's the sort of thing you probably have to grow out of."

The shadow of a smile tugged at the corners of Caspian's lips. "Dad was very fond of quoting C. S. Lewis on that subject: 'When I became a man I put away childish things, including the fear of childishness and the desire to be very grown up.'"

"I keep thinking I would like to be grown up," I admitted. "I mean, maybe not *very* grown up. But grown up enough not to leave the laundry until I have literally run out of clothes."

He blinked. "That is not a problem I've encountered."

"Because you're a grown-up."

"No, because I have a housekeeper."

That made me laugh—a proper, unsullied, unhesitating laugh. And God, it felt good. The closest I'd come to normal this whole fucked-up week. "That's definitely cheating. But childish or not, I'd love it if you read to me. Something nice, mind. I don't think I can cope with intergalactic wars or quantum universes."

"I'm sure I can find something suitable." Caspian did not lean over the side of the bed the way I did because he had a sense of personal dignity (though he also had an amazing arse, so in some respects it was shame) and, instead, knelt down on the floor to retrieve the box.

"Will you do voices?" I asked as he sifted carefully through his father's books.

He glanced up at me. "I'm not sure that's within my abilities."

"Will you try?"

"You may very well come to regret that, but if you insist." Regaining his feet, with his usual poise, he held out a book—a red hardback with a picture of a hilltop castle in a circle on the front. "How do you feel about *The Princess Bride*?"

I actually gasped. "Caspian, I love love love *The Princess Bride*. But I had no idea it was a book."

"It's somewhat more involved than the film. Though still rather charming."

"Rather charming? I am losing my shit here." I was so excited I was practically bouncing. "I can't believe you're going to read me *The Princess Bride*. That's so much better than Columbo."

"Better than what?"

I huffed out an impatient sigh. "The granddad in the movie—he's the guy who played Columbo."

A blank look from Caspian.

"The detective in the brown raincoat. You know"—I held up a finger—"'just one more thing.'"

Still nothing.

"Never mind."

Caspian settled himself back on the bed—and this time it seemed the most natural thing in the world for me to creep into the nook beneath his arm and for him to draw me in tight against his side. "It's a little different in the book," he said. "It's a father reading the story to his son because he remembers his father reading it to him. Which"—he frowned—"in retrospect, makes it a poor choice, given tonight's events. I'm so sorry. Shall we try something else?

"What? No. Just because I have a shitty father doesn't mean I can't cope with fictional dads."

"I'm relieved. It was my intent to comfort you, not distress you. But I've never been particularly talented in this area."

"Oh, Caspian." I was so completely, perfectly, blissfully cosy that his name staggered, half-slurred, out of my mouth. "You've always been perfect for me."

At which point, he fell awkwardly silent, looking down at me, the book apparently forgotten in his hands. "Arden, I…"

"Are you all right?"

"I think so. I just…you…" He made a shaky sound, almost but not quite a laugh. "I don't know how to start."

"How did your dad start?"

There was a long silence. And then Caspian smiled—a smile I'd never seen before, private and sad and hopeful. "He would say, 'Are you sitting comfortably? Then I shall begin.'"

I nuzzled into him. "For the record, I am very comfortable."

"Then—" His voice caught and steadied. "I shall begin. *This is my favourite book in all the world, though I have never read it.*"

I'd always loved Caspian's voice—its perfectly polished vowels and sharp consonants, the richness of its deepest registers. And now it poured over me as abundantly as Biblical wine, telling me tales of fathers and sons, and lovers and princesses, and pirates and giants, and love and revenge, and friendship and honour, and all the very best things that a story could be about. I got to hear the quickening of his breath when he was excited, and the way he would occasionally stumble or skip a line when he was anxious, and the gentleness that would unspool through the words when he was moved. It made it impossible for me to feel anything but cared for. Anything but safe. And every time Caspian said, "As you wish," it was like he was saying it to me. Of course, by tomorrow morning the enchantment would pass and it would be just a line in a book.

But tonight. Tonight it was mine.

And we were each other's again.

CHAPTER 34

Arden...Arden..."

"*Mrrgggf.*" I dragged the pillow over my face. "Five more minutes, Mum."

Caspian cleared this throat. "Arden, we've found Jonas."

I sat up so abruptly I nearly clashed heads with Caspian, who was leaning over me. "When? How? What time is it? Where am I? What's happening?"

"It's early afternoon and you're in my apartment," he said, gently pushing the hair out of my eyes. "Your father has checked into a Travelodge near Leeds—we traced him by his credit card and the GPS on your phone."

I flailed wildly. "Early afternoon? Oh God. How? I need to go."

"You needed to sleep. We know where Jonas is now and where he will be. We have time."

"Okay, but...but..."

"We have time," Caspian repeated, in a voice that permitted no dissention. "You will shower, dress, and eat, and Finesilver will pick you up in an hour."

I heaved a put-upon sigh. "Yes, Mr. Ha—Caspian."

"*And* as we discussed yesterday, you will not interfere in anything that happens."

"That's sounding murdery again."

"Don't tempt me." His lips thinned on what was clearly an escaping smile. "But no, it is simply that you are emotionally involved in this matter, and I find emotion incompatible with business."

It was one of those *would have agreed to anything* type of situations again, but I wasn't actually looking to splooge my feelings everywhere. I just wanted to be sure that fucker wasn't coming anywhere near my family ever again. "I'll be good. I promise."

"Just"—Caspian twined his fingers briefly with mine—"try not to let him hurt you more than he has already."

I brought his hand to my lips and kissed it. "I promise."

And an or so hour later, with my stomach still not sure how it felt about having food in it, and my nerves ragged but holding, I was in Finesilver's car, heading north. When I'd climbed in, he'd given me one of his too-nice smiles—which I knew meant he definitely didn't want me there.

"I'm really sorry," I said, cringing. "I don't want to make your job more difficult, but I really need to be there for this."

His eyes flicked briefly to me and then back to the road. "There's no need to apologise. My job and its complexities are my problem, and Mr. Hart compensates me more than proportionally."

"Yeah, but your weekend and shit."

Another smile. "If I cared about my weekends, I wouldn't have gone into law."

The truth was, Alexander Finesilver kind of scared me. Not in the way that Bellerose—Ilya—used to, with his chilly and impenetrable perfection, but because of his carefully cultivated humanness. He seemed so nice, so normal: this slender, unobtrusive, dark-haired young man with eyes like Elizabeth Bennett. Very much the opposite of the stereotype of the sharkish lawyer, which is exactly what made me wary. Here was someone who wanted to be underestimated, perhaps even disregarded. On top of the fact he worked for Caspian, who would not have put his trust in someone any less talented, dedicated, and ruthless than he was himself.

Aaaaaand I was going to be stuck in a car with him for nearly four hours. Fun times. I squirmed in my seat. "All the same, thank you and, like...yeah, thank you."

"You don't have to thank me either."

Okay, I was too fucked in the head for this. "Jesus, I'm just being polite. You know, as people are to each other."

"I'm sorry." He laughed as easily as he smiled. "I'm not thanked very often. I will admit, my personal preference would incline strongly towards your absence. But since Mr. Hart does not agree, and I work for Mr. Hart, here you are. I'm not going to waste energy resenting it."

I could see why Caspian liked him. They both valued a brand of emotional efficiency that was pretty much beyond me. "Well, Caspian's personal preference *also* inclined strongly towards my absence. So you really do have cause to be pissed at me."

"On the contrary, Mr. St. Ives." Finesilver's eyes glittered with sudden interest. "Given you've just revealed your capacity to influence my employer, even against his own better judgement, it doesn't seem as though being pissed at you would be at all to my benefit."

I squeaked. "I'm not Anne Fucking Boleyn, you know."

"I'm sure Anne Boleyn didn't think she was Anne Boleyn."

There was a long silence.

"Are you trying to tell me," I said slowly, "that Caspian's going to cut my head off at some point?"

"I'm sure he won't." A pause. "It's the sort of thing that's terribly difficult to mount a defense against in court."

"You are not helping."

Finesilver laughed, though it sounded different this time. Harsher and realer and, strangely enough, *nicer*. "I said I wouldn't resent you. That doesn't mean I can't amuse myself a little at your expense."

"Is that wise, though?" I fluttered my lashes. "Seeing as how I have the ear of the king and all that. I could have you sent to the tower."

"You could. But then when *you* are sent to the tower, what will you do for a lawyer?"

"You..." I said, surrendering at least semi-gracefully. "You are basically Littlefinger, aren't you?"

"Dear me, I hope not. He made terrible decisions."

We tooled along quietly for a while longer, threading between traffic jams on our way out of London. I was still nervous around Finesilver, but frankly, I had way bigger things to worry about. Y'know, like Jonas. Who had my phone. And was breaking his journey in Leeds on his way to fuck up my family. Bastard.

"As it's rather a long way," remarked Finesilver, "would you mind if I put on an audiobook?"

I…had not been expecting that. "Gosh no. Of course not. Be my guest."

A moment or two later, a nice English voice filled the car: *Just because the man looked like Milton's ruined archangel and chose to appear in the hall like the Demon King through a trap-door it didn't necessarily mean that I had to smell Sulphur.*

My mind reeled with surprise and curiosity. I hadn't really given any thought to what Finesilver might to do in his spare time, but if you'd asked me to put forward some ideas, *listening to Gothic novels* wouldn't have featured.

"Sorry…can I…"

He paused the narration. "Yes?"

"What's the book, please? If you don't mind?"

"It's *Nine Coaches Waiting* by"—his voice had lost some of its usual evenness—"Mary Stewart."

"*Ohhh.* I'd thought it might be du Maurier."

"Mr. St. Ives, are you laughing at me?"

I blinked. "Not at all. I might have grinned a bit, imagining Ellery's reaction if she knew what you were into."

"Don't tell her please."

He seemed genuinely flustered. Which—and yes, yes, I was a bad person—I kind of enjoyed. "She'd like you way more if I did."

"I don't want her to like me. I want her to behave in a legally responsible fashion."

"You do realise"—and now I made no attempt to hide my smirk—"that if she liked you, she probably would."

His fingers danced against the steering wheel. "Sadly, the

acquisition of Miss Hart's good opinion lies beyond my power."

"Have you tried?"

He didn't answer.

"I mean, really tried."

"I work for her brother," he said softly. "Miss Hart's opinion of me should not be relevant."

Before I could point out that it was clearly relevant to him, he turned the book back on, and the volume up, so further conversation was impossible.

But that was fine. We'd hit the motorway, and would be on it for hours, so I was more than happy to sink into the problems faced by lonely governesses in crumbling mansions. It was a welcome break from my own, which were blackening the horizon like pollution. God, I'd made nothing but appalling decisions since the beginning of the year. Here's hoping confronting Jonas wasn't another one.

CHAPTER 35

The Leeds Morley Travelodge was…I guess you could charitably call it quaint? A cream-painted lump of a building, with a set of twin gables that looked like squirrel ears poking out the top. We parked round the back and headed inside.

"So," I said, scurrying to keep up with Finesilver's uncompromising pace, "do you think Raoul was involved in the murder attempts?"

But the only answer I got was, "Wait here a moment, please."

Mindful of what I'd agreed with Caspian, I tucked myself obediently into a corner next to the entrance while Finesilver approached the front desk. I was too far away to hear what he said, and his manner throughout was as mild as ever, but in less than a minute the receptionist was handing over a keycard. Finesilver thanked him politely, beckoned me over, and we made our way to the next floor in silence.

Well, apart from my heart, which was going like a snare drum at a metal concert.

About halfway down a white-painted, blue-carpeted hallway we came to a door. Just your basic, ordinary Travelodge door. Finesilver gave me a look that seemed to say, *Are you ready*, and I wasn't in the slightest but I nodded anyway.

He knocked. Didn't wait for an answer. Just ran the card through the reader and went in. I followed—standard Travelodge room, sparse, clean, more blue carpet, more white walls, inoffensive abstract on the wall—and there was Jonas with his suitcase open on the bed. For a moment, a sliver of a second, he didn't react at all. Like when a MacBook crashes and the little beach ball spins and spins. And then he looked startled.

"Arden?" He nudged his glasses further up his nose. "What are you doing here?"

And I know I'd promised Caspian I wasn't going to get involved. But the words "You took my phone, motherfucker" burst out of my mouth before I could stop them.

His eyes widened. "Oh my gosh, you're right, I did. You see, there was an emergency at work—"

"A library software emergency."

"We do get them, believe it or not. Universities depend on their libraries, and their libraries depend on us. Anyway"—one of his dimples glimmered and then vanished—"I'm so sorry I had to rush off without saying goodbye. I was going to call you and explain, but I must have picked up your phone by accident as I was leaving."

I'd been talking to him for less than a minute and already

my head was a Catherine wheel. "Just. Give. It. Fucking. Back. Right the fuck now."

"Well, why on earth would I want to keep it?" A bewildered expression flittered across his face like a wounded gazelle. Then he dipped into his case, plucked my phone from its depths, and held it out to me.

I snatched it. Swiped to wake it up. It was undeniably my phone. Nothing had changed on the home screen. But it felt different. Turned over. Opened up. Delicately combed through. *Urgh.*

"So you took it by accident," I said. "Then accidentally got it unlocked. And accidentally went through all my stuff."

Jonas shrugged, endearingly sheepish. "That's some interesting pornography you've got on there."

"Oh, fuck you."

"Arden, come on. Of course I had to get it unlocked. How else was I supposed to get it back to you? I couldn't ring you because I had your phone and I didn't know how else to get in touch."

"What, you couldn't post it to the work address you already knew on account of having randomly turned up at it in order to see me?"

"I should have thought of that, shouldn't I?" His hand went to his hair, fluffing it up even further. "Look, I can see you're upset because I left without telling you, and I'm sorry I took your phone by mistake, but I was going to contact you as soon I could. Although I'm not sure why any of this makes it okay for you to, well, I suppose I might say *stalk* me across the country and break into my hotel room."

My mouth dropped open. I was about to protest that I

hadn't stalked him, just come to get my phone back, when Finesilver cut smoothly over me. "Mr. Jackson, before we go further, I would advise you against mischaracterizing the circumstances of this conversation. My associate and I are here with the full knowledge and permission of the management, and should you be so foolish as to claim otherwise in a public setting, you would be opening yourself to a suit for slander."

"Slander? I don't understand. Who are you?" Jonas's eyes darted to Finesilver and then back to me. "Arden, what's this about?"

"You will address me," returned Finesilver, his tone as sheer and blank as glass, "not my associate. As for who I am, I represent a wealthy and influential client who wishes to ensure that your future behaviour remains within certain parameters."

Jonas sat shakily on the edge of the bed. "My...my behaviour? I'm just a salesman. I've done nothing wrong."

Oh my God. He was so completely full of lies. It made me furious. With a side salad of even more furious because, based on actions alone, it was hard to tell the difference between someone completely full of lies and someone terribly upset because you'd got your billionaire ex-boyfriend to send his scariest lawyer after them. And I hated that there was even a lemon rind of a question in my mind.

"What you have done or not done is not my concern." Finesilver remained standing, though his slightness meant it didn't come across as a power move, his hands folded neatly in front of him. "I'm here to execute my client's wishes, and my client wishes the following: that you sign these divorce papers immediately and that you undertake to have no further contact of any kind with Mr. Arden St. Ives, Ms. Iris Jackson née St. Ives, or any persons associated with either of them, signing these additional documents to that effect."

"I'm still not quite sure what's happening but"—and here Jonas's voice steadied, as though he was drawing courage from confusion—"but I do know I have rights. You can't come in here and threaten me."

"I have made no threats, Mr. Jackson. I am simply telling you what my client requires."

"Your client? You mean Caspian Hart." Jonas's gaze settled on me again and there was something…I don't know… unsettling in his eyes, a kind of slick gleam like oil on water. "I thought you broke up with him."

"I remind you," murmured Finesilver, "to address me, not my associate."

"I find it sort of funny"—one of Jonas's fingers stroked idly at the edge of his jaw—"that Caspian Hart is so interested in me all of a sudden. Because I actually know quite a lot about him, isn't that right, Arden?"

I basically exploded. "You fucking…fucking…I can't believe I trusted—"

Finesilver's fingers closed tightly around my elbow. "Once again, address me, not my associate. Whatever you think you know, I highly recommend against saying anything you will regret later."

"I'm not sure," said Jonas with the monkish mildness that made me want to punch him in the face forever, "it's my regrets we have to worry about here."

Okay, this was bad. And it was my fault it was bad. I'd spilled my guts to Jonas over my breakup with Caspian, except I couldn't remember exactly what I'd told him. I hadn't mentioned Caspian by name, I knew that—though it was scant fucking comfort when the fact we'd been a thing was all over the Internet. With photos. And I definitely hadn't gone into details, at least not about anything that wasn't my own stupid feelings, but Jonas could probably have joined the dots. He was way too good at that—especially if the dots were vulnerabilities and he got to join them with a knife.

Oh fuck. If Caspian's past got out...I had no idea what that might mean. He'd hate it, obviously. But how much would it damage him? He'd barely come to terms with it for himself. I couldn't imagine anything worse than seeing it splashed across the papers. Thrown about on social media like the latest fucking meme. Was this the deal, then? No matter what, someone I loved got hurt? All because I'd been weak and stupid enough to let Jonas Jackson stick his dirty fingers in my life.

I glanced at Finesilver. Maybe he didn't know what Jonas was hinting at or maybe he did and had balls of whatever Wolverine's claws are made of, but either way his poise hadn't faltered. For all his self-effacing mannerisms, there was something in the way he held himself that reminded me of an untipped fencing foil.

"If you sincerely believe," Finesilver said, "that you have correctly identified my client, who, I should stress, I am not at liberty to name, and should you further truly believe that you are more capable of harming their interests than they are of harming yours, then we have little more to discuss. I cannot, after all, legally prevent you from telling whatever it is you think you know to whoever it is you think will listen."

Jonas put his palms on the bed behind him and leaned back, almost insolently. "Then I guess we're done here."

"On that matter, certainly. Now, as to the papers—"

"I'm not signing any papers. And Caspian Hart can't make me."

"For the record, I will remind you that I have never stated that I work for Caspian Hart. But"—Finesilver inclined his head, very slightly—"you are correct, my client has no power to dictate your actions. Just as you have no power to, for example, dictate whether my client purchases a controlling share in your employer. Which, I am at liberty to inform you, they have, in fact, done."

A brief but scratchy pause. Nails on a blackboard inside a silence. "I thought you weren't making any threats."

"I'm not. I'm simply outlining the choices that certain parties are free to make. You are free to go about your business as you always have and my client is free to purchase the freeholds of certain buildings in Carlisle, acquire certain portfolios of debts from certain creditors, and do with those commodities as he or she sees fit. Which, again, my client has already done. Meaning he or she is also free to call in those debts and evict any persons living in houses on that freehold should he or she wish."

"So you're saying…" Jonas was speaking very slowly, the words heavy in his mouth somehow. "Unless I do what you want, I'm going to lose my job, my home, and my savings."

Finesilver's eyes widened fractionally with the faintest hint of indignation. "I'm suggesting no such thing. We're just making conversation while you decide how you wish to proceed in this matter."

Another of those nasty silences. And then Jonas started to cry, the tears rolling under the frames of his glasses in this procession of orderly woe. It was hard to watch because it was always hard to watch someone in distress, and a guilty feeling squirmed wormishly inside me. But I also couldn't help noticing the way he did nothing to hide his face or wipe his eyes—as if the moisture falling from them in fat, round droplets didn't quite belong to him.

"I don't understand," he wept, "why this is happening. I don't know what I've done. All I wanted was to find my son and—"

"Sign the papers, Mr. Jackson." Finesilver delivered the words with a trace of impatience—his first since we'd entered the room—although it could have been as much performance as my father's tears.

Jonas turned to me, taking off his glasses to reveal his naked eyes, red and wet and hurt. "Arden, please. I don't know what you've been told about me but you're making a mistake. I've been searching for you since you were taken from me. I've done nothing but try to know you. And look what you're doing to me."

"You used me." It came out as a wild howl, full of anger and pain and this helpless exasperation that he hadn't stopped fucking with me for a single second I'd spent in his company. "You're still trying to use me. You—"

Finesilver squeezed my elbow even harder, maybe hitting some kind of pressure point, because it sent a bolt of clicky lightning all the way to my shoulder. "Shall I inform my client that you do not, in fact, intend to comply with their requests."

Jonas sat. Stared at us. Said nothing. Tears still falling, easy as April showers. And then, at last, "Give me the papers."

Finesilver pulled an envelope from an interior pocket along with a pen and handed both to my father. Who made a brief show of scrutinizing everything carefully before turning to the final page so violently it almost tore the staple out. Resting against the edge of his suitcase, he jabbed the pen against the dotted line. His hand trembled.

"She's my wife." There was a note in Jonas's voice I'd never heard before. I think it was something he thought was truth, and it was terrifying. "I can't let you take her from me."

Something cold was slithering round my heart. Squeezing so tight I couldn't breathe.

But Finesilver only lifted one shoulder in the suggestion of a shrug. "Once again, the choice is entirely yours. Although I would remind you also that placing any person in immediate fear for their safety, even your wife and even in the absence of physical contact, fits the definition of common assault. So should you be so reckless as to risk the civil suit my client will bring against you for breach of contract in the event of your going back on these agreements, do be assured that Ms. St. Ives would have my client's full support in any criminal case she wished to bring against you. And while law enforcement sometimes lack the resources to pursue such matters as diligently as they might, my client suffers no such restriction."

"What the fuck is this?" snarled Jonas, anger breaking through him like some horrible fish from the deepest, squoogliest oceans. "I love her. I've never laid a hand on her."

He sounded so sincere that, for a disgusting, treacherous heartbeat, I almost forgot I'd seen him do it.

"I'm merely providing information." Finesilver's voice brought me back to the moment. "Sign the papers."

Jonas signed. He was breathing hard and the rasp of the pen against the paper was too loud, almost human-sounding, like it was scraping over skin. But at the same time, it was all super anticlimactic: a few seconds of ink. It didn't seem enough to change a world.

Without a word, my father passed the documents back to Finesilver, and he tucked them back into his jacket. "Thank you, Mr. Jackson. You've made the correct choice. My client will, of course, be monitoring the situation in order to ensure you continue to make correct choices."

Jonas stared at us. Still said nothing. The tears had gone and so had the rage. But behind his eyes I could see the shadows of seething things.

"Goodbye, Mr. Jackson."

A nudge from Finesilver got me moving, jerky as rundown clockwork. I didn't look back.

CHAPTER 36

I made it to the car before I turned into squidge, sweating and trembling in the front seat. Finesilver pulled a bottle of water from the footwell and passed it to me.

"Sorry," I said, when I could get the words out. "That was…that was…"

He gave me a look which I chose to interpret as genuinely sympathetic. "Please don't worry. I understand how charged such situations can be."

"I…I talked when I wasn't supposed to."

"I was not, in all honesty, expecting otherwise."

I took another gulp of water. "You were amazing."

"Thank you."

"No, but…like. That was like proper superhero lawyer shit."

"At the risk of repeating that most obvious of clichés, I was just doing my job."

"For which"—I mustered a soggy smile—"you are more than proportionally compensated."

He laughed. "Exactly."

My body seemed to be calming down again—though I was still a bit floaty and wobbly—and I took the opportunity to poke at my feelings. I found gratitude for Caspian and Finesilver, but not much else. Surely I should have been elated. At the very least relieved. Instead, there was just this fading hum, like a tuning fork going past the edge of hearing.

"Do you think…" I asked. "I mean, he's not…he won't try anything, will he?"

"No."

"How can you be sure?"

"I've dealt with far more dangerous and far more unpredictable people than Jonas Jackson." Finesilver smiled, not his usual smile, urbane and careful, but a predator's smile, full of teeth and relish. "Always successfully. If he knows what's good for him, he'll go away quietly. If he does not know what's good for him, he'll go away noisily. There are no other options."

"Yeah, it's"—I squirmed anxiously—"the noisy I could do without. I mean, what if he does try to come for Mum? What if he does go to the papers?"

"If he approaches your mother, he'll be intercepted minutes after he arrives in Scotland, and then he will suffer all of the terrible consequences with which I most certainly did not threaten him. If he goes to the papers, the story—like so many others—will never see the light of day."

I gave a stagey shudder, half in play, half in earnest. "I hope I never piss you off."

"On the contrary, it's crossing my clients that should concern you."

Hopefully I was way too irrelevant for that. "What happens now?"

"I need your mother's signature on these papers. But otherwise my part in this is done."

Oh God. Mum. It was like everything inside me, blood, bones, organs, my fucking mitochondria, *lurched* with the shame of what I'd done, and nearly done, to her. How the fuck was I going to tell her? I mean, she'd forgive me. Of course she would. She was Mum. But, somehow knowing that just made it worse. It briefly occurred to me that I could run away to France and become an itinerant baguette seller.

"I'll take them." I forced out the words in a garbled rush. "If you don't mind dropping me off at the train station."

Another one of those looks I couldn't quite read—a touch of warmth beneath that refined façade. "I don't mind at all. But I can also accompany you, if you'd prefer."

My mouth was dry as Mars. "I think…I think it should be me."

"Whatever you think, Mr. St Ives. The divorce is largely a formality at this stage but it may afford your mother some peace of mind. Assuming, that is, she wishes to divorce your father."

"Why wouldn't she?"

Finesilver suddenly got very interested in the steering column. "Abusive relationships are complicated. When you've had your power systematically stripped from you, it's no easy thing to claim it back."

I thought of Mum, with her quilts and her baking and her books, the way she spoke with her eyes, and how full of laughter they were these days, her hand slipped into Hazel's as they walked hand in hand along the treasure-strewn tidelines of Kinlochbervie's beaches. "I think she'll want to."

There was the briefest of pauses. Then Finesilver nodded. "I'll take you to the station."

He called up Google Maps and got us on the road again. I stared out the window, at the rough northern skies and unfamiliar streets, with their huddles of suburban homes, washed the dirty orange of Skittles by the streetlamps. Dread was as heavy as an unwanted coat, pressing me down into the seat. Though I fucking well deserved to feel it.

"So," said Finesilver, making a frankly tragic attempt to sound casual. "What kind of Gothic novels does Miss Hart prefer?"

I had no idea if he genuinely wanted to know or was just trying to distract me. But either way, I was very willing to talk. And Finesilver, though he maintained an air of studied indifference, seemed more than willing to listen—though it was hard to imagine what use he was going to get out of knowing Ellery was a fan of *The Monk* and *Melmoth the Wanderer*. It wasn't the sort of thing you could slip into casual conversation. But then again, it was funny to imagine him trying—standing there, with his neatly folded hands and his stiletto poise, wanting Ellery to behave in a legally responsible manner and also tell her he really liked du Maurier too.

Anyway, in fifty minutes I was at the station, and half an hour after that I was on the train, headed north. I emailed work to tell them I'd had a family emergency—which was actually true, even though I'd been the one to cause the emergency—and wouldn't be able to make it for a couple of days, and I booked myself a room in a cheapish hostel near Edinburgh Waverly, since there wouldn't be another train to Inverness until the next morning.

It was weird to be able to do that—my problem-resolving skills were obviously nothing compared to Caspian's, and having to wait for a train counted as a pretty much minor problem, but I'd still managed to resolve it. Time was, I wouldn't have been able to, at least not without scrounging money from my family. Having a job, even a job that didn't pay all that well, could really change your perspective on things. And in spite of feeling broadly terrible about everything, I couldn't help feeling a tiny bit good about this. The knowledge that I could occasionally help myself. That I could, with careful saving, buy a plane ticket to Boston. Afford to get a room when I needed one. It was reassuring and liberating and probably the closest I'd ever got to grown up. And grown up in a real way. Not a desperate pretense of it or a nebulous sense I was failing to be, or do, what I was supposed to. And all it took was a tiny piece of control, dropped like the keys to Bluebeard's castle into my hand.

This small triumph of adulting aside, I can't say it was an awesome journey. True, the last two times I'd made it, I'd been in a state of dire heartbreak, but this time I was making it because I'd almost destroyed the one place I knew I could always go in a state of dire heartbreak. And that was way worse.

One bad sleep, four hours on a train, and a juddery

bus journey later, I was on Bervie Road—a twist of grey through a world of brown, raw hills and brittle, scrub grass skeletons, and a sky the colour of stale tears. I always forgot how bleak this place could get in winter. Or maybe I stopped noticing because it never felt bleak. It was reading by the fire. And board games after midnight. And all the hot chocolate you could drink. It was the end of the fucking world, and it had been nothing but good to me. How could I have been so careless, so selfish and ungrateful, as to jeopardise it?

Pulling out my phone, I texted Hazel. Asked her to make some excuse and come to meet me. Then flipped up my collar, turned my face into the teeth of the wind, and set one foot in front of the other, making with steady steps for home.

I saw Hazel's hair first—a spark of purple against the steel horizon—and then the rest of her, coat billowing Byronically behind her as she strode towards me between the ice-crisp fields. I was incredibly glad to see her. And terrified at the same time. And it was really hard to keep walking, like I was slowly turning to stone, legs first.

"Ardy?" Hazel called out, the moment she was within earshot. "Are you all right? That was a pretty worrying text you sent. You're not pregnant, are you?"

I tried to laugh but my mouth was broken.

Her own grin faded. "Okay, what's wrong?"

Oh God, I was going to be sick. "I've…I've done something horrendously fucked up."

"Well"—her mouth tightened into a resolute line—"you tell me what's happened and we'll figure out how to get it sorted."

There was something profoundly terrible just then in being trusted. And trusted absolutely. It was like I'd been given this precious thing, and I hadn't even noticed it was mine, and then I'd woken up one day and stood on it. "It's not…I don't…I don't need help. I just don't know how to say…how to say it."

"Listen." She'd gone a bit pale. "There's nothing you could say we couldn't deal with. And there's nothing you could do you couldn't come back from."

The part of me that was just a snake-eating-its-own-tail of guilt wasn't sure that was true. But Hazel had never lied to me. Never evaded. Never held anything back. "Can we sit down? Even though it's freezing?"

Hazel nodded and we stepped off the road, crunching over the fields to some exposed scarp, where we plonked ourselves. While Hazel was digging her rainbow mittens out of her pockets and putting them on, I stared blankly at the landscape—the frost-limned grass fading into the flat silver sheen of the loch and the sky.

Come on. I could do this. I *had* to do this. I sucked in a lungful of air so cold it scraped my throat raw. "The thing is, my dad found me and—"

"Oh my God." Hazel exploded off the rock. "That shameless bastard. I'm going to kill him."

"We went for coffee, okay?"

She spun back round. "Wait. You what?"

"He said he wanted to get to know me—I mean obviously he didn't—but I fell for it." The words, which I'd been worried wouldn't come at all, came stampeding out like panicked wildebeests. "And he fucked with my head and nicked my phone and he was coming after Mum. But he's not anymore and there's some divorce papers she can sign if she wants to and I know I did a really bad and stupid thing and Mum needs to know but I can't bear the thought of it."

There was the longest silence. And believe me, nowhere could do silence as deeply and purely as Kinlochbervie in the middle of winter.

"Hazel…" I said in the smallest voice. "Please don't—"

Except I couldn't finish. I didn't know what I was trying to say. Please don't hate me as much as I hate myself right now?

She ran her fingers through her hair. "Fucking hell, Arden. I'm not sure whether to shake you or hug you."

"I'd rather you hugged me."

"Of course I'm going to bloody well hug you."

She held out her arms and I launched into them, not quite crying but probably only because I was all teared out. "I'm sorry. I'm so, so sorry."

"I know you are, love. I know."

Eventually, I was all right to be let go of again. I sat back down, wiping my nose classily with my sleeve. "I get that I fucked up. Like *really* fucked up."

"Honestly"—she jammed her hands into her pockets—"I don't quite understand what I'm feeling just at the moment."

That sounded bad. That sounded super bad. I tried to say something but I only managed a horrified gulp.

"I mean, when you were little and I'd tell you *don't run into the plate glass door* or *wait until the bus has gone by before you cross the road* or *let Rabbie lift the pan of boiling water from the stove*, you listened to me. Admittedly, not all the time, but enough that you didn't die. And now part of me is wondering...didn't you see the door, didn't you believe the bus was coming, did you think the water wasn't hot? Did I not make you understand?"

Oh no. No. No. No. "It's not your fault," I cried. "It was me. All me."

At this, her shoulders went back. "Well, that's not true either, is it? That man is a manipulative son of a prick, and there's no getting away from it. I just wish you'd..."

"Listened," I finished for her.

"Yes." She gathered the wings of her coat and dropped into place beside me. "And no. Because then you wouldn't be you, and that would be even worse."

"Are you sure? Being less of an idiot sounds like an improvement to me."

"You weren't an idiot. You just weren't a cynic. And despite my best efforts, we didn't raise a cynic." She nudged her shoulder against mine. "There's such a lot of your mum in you, Ardy."

"Well, we did both get taken in by the same person."

"That's enough of that." Hazel could go from cosy to death glare faster than anyone I knew, especially on Mum's behalf. "I can tell you want to self-flagellate about this, but leave Iris out of it. You'd been warned. She hadn't."

I wilted. "I'm sorry. I didn't mean it like that. I'm just so scared, thinking I could have brought him here. After everything Mum's already gone through."

"We've been prepared for him. For a long time." She let out a rough breath that misted in the chill like a dragon's. "But we hoped he'd never find her. Or you."

"I could have handled it a gazillion times better when he did."

She was quiet for a while. "You did the wrong thing, but I don't blame you for doing it."

"I blame me."

"Blame him. He deserves it. You don't. Mind you"—she was on her feet again, all five foot one of her primed for a fight—"if he comes anywhere near us again, I'm going full *Fried Green Tomatoes* on his arse."

And there went another of my loved ones threatening murder with too much conviction for my comfort. "He won't." It should have been such a triumphant declaration. But I just sounded tired. "When I realised what I'd done, I went to Caspian and he got his lawyer on the case. And it was horrible and ugly and scary, but…yeah. Caspian's a very powerful man and there's nothing Dad can do about it."

Hazel let out a low whistle, snatched away almost immediately by the wind. "That's…that's one hell of a happening."

"Tell me about it. Like…there are ways rich people can fuck you up that it never occurred to me you could fuck a person up. Which is, y'know, really socially problematic, but right now I'm just glad it's over."

"You didn't have to do this alone, Ardy."

"I don't mean this in the macho *High Noon* way but"—I wiped my nose again, because the cold and the threat of tears weren't bringing out the best in it—"I kind of did. And it was mostly Caspian anyway."

"I thought you and Mr. Billionaire were over."

"We are, but"—I tried to smile except it felt the same as sadness—"I knew he'd still help me."

She spread her mittens in a gesture of bewildered pragmatism. "Useful friend to have, that one."

"Yes, but I don't want to use him. I wouldn't have gone to him for anything less important."

"I've got to admit," she said with a grim look, "I'm not wildly thrilled about strangers being up in our business either. But when it comes to Jonas, fuck my pride."

"That was my thinking too."

"I've got to say, I don't quite know what to make of this."

I hung my head.

"I'm angry, a little bit in your direction, but mostly at him. And I'm sorry he hurt you. But"—and here she fixed me with a look I couldn't flinch from—"I'm also really proud of you."

I actually boggled at her. "Omigod, *why*?"

"Because you made a mistake, and you did your best to make it right."

"I wouldn't have had to make it right if I hadn't—"

"Don't be daft, Ardy. You can't expect to live a life you're happy to look back on and not fuck it up occasionally. It's not the fucking up that counts. It's what you do after."

My fingers were probably about to turn blue and drop off, so I jammed my hands between my knees to warm them. "Even if you were warned and should have known better?"

She gave me something like her usual grin. "Even then."

I...had no idea what to say. I did feel sort of better in some ways. Kinlochbervie always helped, through some combination of being literally remote, and also the place where I knew I'd always be welcome. Always be safe. Always be loved. Despite my best efforts to blow it up. But then I remembered what I was up here to do and everything was immediately terrible again.

"How am I going to tell Mum?" I whispered.

Hazel pulled a loose thread from her mittens with her teeth. "Not going to sugarcoat it for you, it's going to be rough."

I whimpered.

"But we'll do it together."

"She...she'll be okay, right?"

That made her snort. "Don't be such a drama queen. Of course she will."

She held out a hand and, when I took it, pulled me to my feet. We made our way back to the road, heading for Old-shoremore through the last shreds of the afternoon light.

"Hazel," I said, a few minutes later.

"Yes?"

"You know...you know I didn't do it, didn't let him get to me, I mean, because I was looking for...looking for something I didn't think I had?"

A slight tilt of her head in my direction. "Then why did you?"

"Well, partly because, as you've pointed out, he's a manip-ulative motherfucker. But mainly because I thought know-ing who he was might help me know more about who I am."

"Did it?"

"No." A gust of wind came howling round the hillside, al-most knocking me into Hazel. I grit my teeth against the icy blast of it, but it rushed through me all the same, sweep-ing clean the corners of me, and unfurling my clenchedup little heart like a flag. "He's nobody to me. I'm Mum's. And…yours and Rabbie's."

"Damn straight, kid."

Hazel's nose had gone pink, but maybe it was the cold. Then she slipped her arm through mine and we walked the rest of the way in silence, the crooked chimney of our cottage just visible against the darkening skyline—that ever-familiar finger beckoning us home.

CHAPTER 37

As ever, Hazel was right: Telling Mum was rough. But we got through it. To be honest, she probably handled it best of all of us. Rabbie was worried, which meant he started pacing, and the cottage wasn't built to handle someone as big as Rabbie pacing, and Hazel was angry—though not at anyone present—and ended up breaking a plate in the general commotion, and I sat on the sofa, being incoherent and crying a lot. And it was while all this was going on that Mum signed the divorce papers. Later, though, we sat on the bed under the eaves, wrapped in one of her quilts, and Mum held me like she hadn't needed to since I was little. We stayed up way too late, whispering to each other in the half-made-up language neither of us could remember inventing, and Hazel just closed the door quietly behind us, and didn't even scold us for not getting enough sleep. And the next day—after slightly subdued pancakes—Rabbie drove me all the way to Edinburgh, so that nearly wrecking my family didn't take too many days from my job.

I got back to London by early afternoon, in a better state than when I'd left, but still possessed of a strong desire to pitch myself face-first into bed and not move for a good long time. First, though, I dropped the signed papers off at Gisbourne, Finesilver & King, then shambled back onto the Tube and off it again at Bank, arriving at Caspian's building when it was actually open for once. I still had to get the receptionist to phone his executive assistant before they let me into the lift, but it was better than having to run through car parks and take on security guards.

Caspian, of course, was in meetings, which I'd been expecting. I asked if I could wait, braving subtle discouragement from The Woman Who Was Not Bellerose, and was directed to a sofa. I probably looked terribly out of place, sitting there in clothes that hadn't been much to write home about before I'd travelled twelve thousand miles in them, while workers and visitors alike passed to and fro in exquisitely cut suits.

An hour or so later, I was allowed into Caspian's office. He was in dark blue, stark and unalleviated but for the glimmer of a white shirt at collar and cuffs. It was a look that emphasised the remoter aspects of his beauty—his icy eyes, the graven symmetry of his face—and made me feel especially bedraggled.

"Arden." He stepped swiftly from behind the desk and came towards me. "Are you all right?"

"Yes. Everything's been taken care of."

"I'm glad."

He was smiling down at me and I found myself smiling back, hopelessly dizzy on the sudden softness of his mouth, the familiar scent of his cologne, the way the generosity of his lashes gentled his eyes. "I came to say thank you. And also sorry."

"You owe me neither apologies nor gratitude."

"Well, you're getting both. You saved my family."

And there it was—that sweep of pink across his cheeks. "You know, I thought only of you."

"Then"—I held his gaze as steadily as I could—"thank you. For thinking of me."

"I'm always thinking of you, my Arden."

Oh God. Time to be brave. I fucking hated being brave. "That's where the apology comes in."

He tilted his head curiously. "How so?"

"Because"—*urgggh*—"because when you broke up with me, I didn't take it very well."

"I treated you badly. I don't think there could be any expectation of you responding positively to that."

"You didn't treat me badly. We just had, I guess, noncompatible ideas about whether we should be together."

He gave a strange, soft laugh. "That sounds almost like something I would say."

"I learned a lot from you."

"Don't. I can't imagine I could have taught you anything good."

"You taught me *only* good things, Caspian. And the way I felt about you, I've never felt about anyone. So when it didn't work out between us, I didn't know what to do."

"I"—he glanced away, biting his lip—"I cannot say I have been wholly satisfied with my own behaviour. But I cannot wholly regret it either."

I put my fingers lightly to the edge of his jaw and turned his face back to mine. "I don't regret a single moment I've spent with you. But I do regret that I haven't respected your choices."

"I know you don't understand them."

"I don't. And I one hundred gazillion percent don't agree with them. But…" It seemed like a good moment to breathe, so I did, wishing it sounded less desperate and gulpy. "That doesn't mean you don't get to make them. And that's why I'm sorry, Caspian. For getting in the way of what you believe will make you happy."

His hand came up, as if he was going to touch me, but dropped again almost immediately—though not before I'd seen how it trembled.

"I want you to be happy," I told him. "You deserve to be happy. And so I hope you can understand why…why I can't see you again."

The colour fled his face. "I'm not sure I do understand."

"I love you. I can't pretend not to. But I *can* move on from it—only not when we keep falling back into each other's lives. You're with Nathaniel now. I need to accept that. And so do you."

"Must it be," he asked, in a voice barely above a whisper, "an either/or?"

"For now? For me? Yes."

"I…I…don't want it to be."

"I can't, Caspian."

"Please…" He drew in a deep, shuddering breath and then we were utterly entangled, my arms around him, his around me, our bodies finding their fit as naturally as one breath following the next, his face pressed against the curve of my neck. "Please don't leave me. I can't bear the thought of being without you."

Oh no. My heart. My already-broken heart. "But what happens if I stay? What are we? What about Nathaniel?"

"I don't know, I don't know." He drew me in more tightly still, the clutch of his fingers hard enough to leave bruises. "I'm sorry, I don't know."

I did my best to soothe him, light touches and long strokes, the soft pressure of my palms against his back, as though I held a wild animal. "I know you don't. And that's the problem."

"I…I'm lost, Arden. I'm so lost." He shuddered against me, helpless despite his physical strength. "I haven't felt this way since my father died."

"It's not too late. You can still choose me."

He lifted his head and stared at me, his eyes a wasteland of sorrow. "I wish I could."

It took everything I had not to argue. Not to insist (beg) that he could, as I had so many (too many) times before. "I understand. But I have to go."

No answer. Just a convulsive movement, too ambiguous to be either resistance or acquiescence.

"It doesn't have to be forever. I mean, I'm not waiting for you or some creepy *Madding Crowd* shit like that." I managed a vague impression of a laugh. "Maybe when you're a smug married and I'm over you, we can be friends or something. Just…not right now."

His hold on me had loosened, so I was able to pull back. It was only a couple of steps but it felt like a long, long journey. Caspian straightened, repositioned the knot of his tie, the cool grey light from the floor-to-ceiling windows turning him into his own shadow.

"Then go," he said. "Before I can't let you."

I'm sure, once upon a time, walking away from Caspian Hart would have been the hardest thing I'd ever done. Now it definitely wasn't, but it still hurt like fuck. I took it almost gladly, though, because the pain was swift and clean, and I knew I could take it.

I'd chosen it, after all. And that made it mine.

As much mine as my love.

I was weepy and exhausted by the time I made it to the warehouse, but in an okayish *welp, these are the reactions that I'm having* sort of way. Nothing sleep and time wouldn't help. Halfway to the ladder to my mezzanine, I tripped over Ellery's second-favourite boots—which had been left in the middle of the floor—and fell flat on my face.

Normally, this would not have improved my day. But the fact they were there after nearly two bootless, Elleryless months, and that she'd obviously wanted me to find them, albeit probably not nose-first, filled my battered spirit with genuine joy. She'd been here. She'd come back. Reaching for my phone, I intended to text her something funny and charming and not too desperate about Broderick, but ended up just sending: *I miss you. Please come home.* And to my surprise, a few minutes later I got back: *okay. soon.* Which was more than I could have hoped for.

I had a lot to think about as I crawled gratefully into bed. Like the fact my life had been a long string of fuck-ups recently, including but not limited to cheating with my engaged ex-boyfriend, coming perilously close to losing my best friend, and nearly destroying my family. It wasn't a time I was going to look back on with pride, but now that I was through the worst of it—please, God, let me be through the worst of it—I was starting to understand that sometimes shit just happened, and sometimes the shit was your fault, but all you could really do was deal with it and live with it and try to own it.

Though, of course, the dealing and living and owning got way easier if you had people around. People who would stick by you and forgive you and help you when you needed it. And I knew I had that—would always have that—no matter how much it felt like my sky was falling down around me. I wanted it for Caspian too, even it meant he found it with Nathaniel, and not with me.

It wasn't the ending I'd imagined for us. Not the one I'd dreamed of and yearned for and nearly lost myself trying to bring about. But it was what we had. It was still our story. And that would be enough for me.

CHAPTER 38

Right then. Dealing. Living. Owning. Not always easy, but it kept me focused, kept me moving forward. Work helped. George helped. Updates from Nik and Poppy's place in Boston helped. Ellery still wasn't back full-time, but her boots were often on the floor, and my bread and cereal kept disappearing, which I took as a good sign. As much as I missed her, I certainly had no intention of pressuring her. Check me out: all mature and shit. And thankfully, despite my brain dwelling pretty obsessively on worst-case scenarios for a couple of days, there wasn't a peep from Jonas.

Things were quiet, which was what I needed. Without Ellery for them to happen around, the warehouse stopped being a party space and became more of a *me in a blanket reading Georgette Heyer on the sofa and eating Galaxy* space. Which meant that, when there came a knock on the door one evening, it took me genuinely by surprise—especially because it was too late for an Amazon delivery and I hadn't ordered takeaway. Probably it was Ellery, returning home in royal state, carrying neither keys nor money, and so I eagerly uncurled and went to let her in.

Except it wasn't Ellery. It was Lancaster Steyne.

"Arden." He stepped past me before I had the presence of mind to slam the door on his feet, face, or any other physical protuberances he might have possessed. "I think it's time we had a talk, don't you?"

Since I wasn't sure what else to do, I followed him inside. "What could we possibly have to talk about?"

"Why"—he offered me a mocking smile—"Caspian Hart, of course."

This was...this was not happening. Apart from the bit where it definitely was. Lancaster Steyne was in the warehouse. Right now. With me. And I know I'd got my judgmental on recently about other people getting murdery, but there was part of me that quite seriously wanted to go for a knife. I mean, no jury would blame me, right? Or would they—because Lancaster Steyne was a rich, sophisticated, well-regarded pillar of his community, and I was a tiny queer in a purple unicorn onesie who had recently been in the papers for kissing siblings.

At which point Steyne broke into my bloody reverie with the remark "I would love some tea. Earl Grey if you have it."

And I was so completely out of it that I actually went to make him some.

"No milk," he added. "I really can't abide people who put milk in Earl Grey."

Under normal circumstances, I might have agreed with

him, though I'd have gone with "don't get" rather than "can't abide." As it was, I hastily splashed some into the cup. "Oops. Sorry. Too late."

He gave a deep, rich chuckle. "And I suppose were I to request bread and butter, you would give me cake."

Oh no. He wasn't getting around me with a cute literary reference. "You're lucky you're not getting a face full of boiling water."

"Dear me. Such hostility." He sounded entirely unconcerned. Which was annoying.

I brought him his tea and he made me stand there with it while he took his coat off—a velvet-collared Chesterfield that I hated myself for slightly admiring. Underneath he was in a dark grey suit, as crisp and well fitted as any of Caspian's, though a touch more dandyish, with the French cuffs, and the jewelled cufflinks, and the opulent purple silk of his tie. He looked like a man who knew how to live well, and that thought made my skin want to slough off my bones.

He picked up *These Old Shades*, glanced at it with mild amusement, and then put it carefully aside so there was room for him on the sofa. He sat like Caspian, one leg draped elegantly over the other, but with none of Caspian's restlessness. Steyne's was a bear trap poise: unyielding and cold and designed to leave you bleeding.

I handed him his fucking tea. "What do you want?"

"What I have always wanted: Caspian's happiness."

My mind flipped about like a fish on a hook. "Is that why you raped him?"

"Raped him?" Steyne repeated, with a blink of what

seemed to be genuine bemusement. "What a nonsensical notion."

"He was fourteen."

He fixed me with those rust-flecked silver eyes of his. "I must say I'm disappointed, Arden. Your views are so terribly parochial."

"There's nothing parochial in thinking it's wrong to fuck kids."

At which pointed he smiled at me. He goddamn *smiled*. "Nonetheless, I do enjoy your spirit."

"Yeah, well." I folded my arms. "I don't enjoy you at all."

"That will change in time. We have much to offer each other."

"You have nothing I want."

"You know"—he took a sip of what I hoped was dreadful tea—"that isn't true."

I was having an *if looks could kill* moment except, sadly, my glares weren't up to the task. "If you mean Caspian, he isn't yours to give. And he's with Nathaniel now."

"Do you really think I would allow that pompous little puritan to keep something I've put so much effort into creating?"

"You didn't create him. You abused him."

"I don't believe that distinction is as meaningful as you think it is." He put down the tea and leaned forward on the sofa, hands clasped lightly over his knee. "Now, listen very carefully. Nathaniel Priest paid me a visit a few days ago, quite distraught and utterly convinced that Caspian was falling back into, how can I put this, *old habits*."

It took me a moment to make sense of this. Okay, I

needed way more than a moment. "I have, like, a million questions already but let's start with: Why the fuck would he go to the guy who raped his fiancé?"

"It's true Nathaniel and I have never seen eye-to-eye, but he did seem rather desperate, and nobody knows Caspian as I do."

"You must have fucking loved that."

"I'll admit"—Steyne offered a self-satisfied smile—"to a certain *schadenfreude*. Nathaniel is, after all, both odious and tedious, a particularly unpleasant combination. Although on this occasion, I almost pitied him. He lives in so small a world."

"Is this going somewhere?" I asked.

"It will be"—Steyne's voice had acquired a sharper edge—"when you stop interrupting. The point is, Nathaniel was behaving erratically. So much so that I was concerned he might do something rash."

I did not like the way this was going. And for someone who complained about being interrupted, Steyne wasn't exactly forthcoming with information. "Rash how?"

"Well…" The bastard paused for a long moment that I rode out through gritted teeth. "He somehow got it into his head that Caspian could never be free of me, or of you, until he could be made to see how deeply his needs could hurt people."

"Yeah, well, Nathaniel's been saying that for years."

"I think, in this instance, he's decided that actions will speak louder than words."

Okay, now I was officially panicking. "What the fuck does that mean?"

"It means"—another infuriating pause—"that he intends to show Caspian the other side of his desires by subjecting him to the kinds of punishments he has taken such pleasure in inflicting on others." Pause. "In public." Pause. "At a sex party." Pause. "Tonight."

The nebulous dread that had been pooling in my stomach since Lancaster had invited himself into my house coalesced instantly into a monster of pure dismay. I tried to say something useful but all that happened was frantic noise.

"I believe," continued Steyne placidly, "Nathaniel thought it would be best to conduct the demonstration on neutral ground. Apparently, he has objections to the room I built for Caspian."

I stared at him—my face probably contorted into a series of horrified cartoon circles. "This is…what even is this? It's a terrible plan."

"Oh, I agree." Steyne smoothed the edge of one perfectly manicured nail. "I expect Caspian will be rather damaged by the experience."

Which was when everything snapped into place. "It was *your* idea, wasn't it? You lost him, so you decided to break him. To get his own fiancé to break him."

"It doesn't matter where the notion came from. What matters is what happens to Caspian afterwards." He stopped contemplating his fingers and returned his attention to me, his gaze oddly—disturbingly—intent. "Neither of them will be able to forgive themselves, which will render it impossible for them to stay together. Which means he will need you. He will need us both."

"Look," I said, ignoring the *Darth Vader, rule the galaxy as abuser and accomplice* shit, "if Nathaniel's really going to do this, you have to stop it."

He just smiled. "You seem confused, Arden. Am I Caspian's abuser or his savior?"

"Right now"—I made a wild gesture—"I don't give a fuck. Just tell me where they are."

"Think about it a moment." Another of those too-hungry looks. "We both care for Caspian, we both have his interests at heart. We could do him so much good if we worked together."

Nope nope nope nope nope. With extra nope. And a nope salad on the side. "After we deliberately let something awful happen to him."

Steyne shrugged. "I wish it weren't necessary, but sometimes Caspian needs to be reminded who is he and who he belongs to. It's time for him to come home."

"And it's time for you to get the fuck out of mine." I was yelling. Possibly waving my arms about. "You're a fucking monster, I'm never helping you, and I'm through listening to you."

"That is a pity." He rose languidly from the sofa. "You know"—why wasn't he reaching for his coat, he should have been reaching for his coat—"I would have been perfectly willing to share him, if you were." Steyne wasn't as tall as Caspian but he was still tall enough to be intimidating, broad across the shoulders and strongly built in a *two plates of foie gras from heavy* kind of way. "I even"—he took a few steps forward—"think I might rather have enjoyed it. But now, alas, you have become a problem."

Okay, so I'd seen this movie. I mean, maybe I was overreacting, but fuck it, I wasn't taking the chance. I had my mobile out of my pocket and had hit 99 when Lancaster's hand closed around my wrist. He gave it what felt like a practiced twist—pain shooting up my forearm until my fingers opened and my phone clunked to the floor.

"The difficulty I'm having here," he murmured, "is that I will not allow Caspian to believe that there is anything in his life that I cannot touch. Even you."

"Are...you fucking serious?" It seemed, in those few seconds, a lot easier to disbelieve. Because the alternative involved being fucking terrified. "Let me go."

The thing is—and under normal circumstances this would have been a massive positive—I had very little experience of being threatened, either physically or verbally. So while Steyne seemed way too at ease with both, I had no idea what to do. I tried to pull away, which didn't work because he had my arm at such a nasty angle, and then to...I don't know...strike at him with my free hand, anything to make him release me, but he just caught my wrist again.

And everything after that was a mess. Disjointed stock motion. Of kicking out at him. Of being dragged, lifted, spun. The sofa knocking me breathless. And his body covering mine until there was nothing but him. His heat all over me like tar. His eyes a dirty metal gleam. The pinpricks of sweat on his upper lip, bright as broken diamonds. I could hear myself screaming in the distance. From some other place I'd lived once, where I'd danced and painted my toenails and worn a scarf the colour of the rainbow. Not this world. Where there was only a man. And the weight of him holding me down. And the smell of his skin in my mouth.

Then. New sounds, half-drowned in his breath. A door. Footsteps. And Ellery saying, "Hello, Uncle Lancaster." And me, blank with fright, an animal hiding in my own flesh, still frantically trying to get free of him. "Get off me get the fuck off me."

Steyne rose—apparently in no fucking rush—adjusting his disarranged suit, and smoothing his hair back into place. "Ellery, my dear. How lovely to see you."

And the worst of it was, it sounded like he meant it. When she must have known what she'd interrupted. Wait. Surely she didn't think I was up for this?

"He…he…" I gasped. But I was blood and breath and fear. Couldn't get words out.

And Ellery cut over me anyway. "I know, right? Guess we should hug or something."

At this point, I was just glad Steyne was moving away from me. I wanted to run—even if it was only to flee into the bathroom and lock the door—but I couldn't move. I felt…shattered, literally shattered. Just pieces of myself I had no idea how to reassemble.

While Ellery, who was not a fan of hugging at the best of times, was stepping voluntarily into Lancaster Steyne's out-stretched arms. Whatever happened next, I couldn't see. But I heard it: a grisly crunch of cartilage, followed by a low cry, and a curse, from Steyne.

He reared back, hands clasped over his nose, blood gush-ing from between his fingers and dripping onto the floor. "That," he said, in a slightly burbly voice, "was uncalled for."

"Yeah?" Ellery rubbed her brow, which was also slightly bloodstained—though, thankfully, none of it hers. "I think it was very fucking called for. And if you ever come near my family again, including Arden, I'll kill you myself."

"You'll learn in time, my child, not to make threats you have no capacity to carry out."

Very slowly, she grinned—this crooked, gleeful grin, somewhere between the Cheshire Cat and the Joker. "I'm a poor little rich girl with a history of drug abuse and mental illness, and I've got one of the best lawyers in London. Not even I know what I'm capable of. And you"—her eyes raked contemptuously over him—"you haven't got a fucking clue."

"Well, aren't you something." Steyne had liberated his pocket square and was now holding it against his face. Of course, it didn't stop him talking. I'm not sure anything would. "You almost make me wish I had a better appreciation for the fairer sex."

Ellery rolled her eyes. "Whatever."

That earned her a cold look—well, as cold as could be managed when your face had gone all Phantom of the Opera. And then he was stepping past her. Leaving.

I let out a choked breath. The relief so intense it felt like nausea. Which was when a thought crawled out of the wreckage. Lurched through my brain and out of my mouth. "Tell me where Caspian is."

Probably I was begging. I didn't care.

Steyne paused, glancing back at me, eyes the colour of dust and pewter. "I don't think so, Arden."

The moment the door closed behind him, Ellery sped across the room towards me. "Are you okay?"

"No. I mean. Yes. I mean. I don't know." My heart rate

quintupled out of nowhere. "He tried to…I think he was really going to."

Ellery kicked the sofa, which seemed unfair because none of this was its fault. "Fuck. *Fuck*. What was he even doing here?"

"He came to—" I dropped my head into my hands. Not wanting to repeat any of it. Even to Ellery. "Oh God."

"It's okay. You don't have to talk."

I pulled my knees up and wrapped my arms around them. I wanted a shower. And never to touch my own skin again. I could still feel him. Still *smell* him. Like he was sewn up inside me. Along with the awareness that, to a man like him, I was nothing.

"What should I do?" Ellery dropped into a crouch, peering up at me anxiously. "Do you need to go to hospital?"

"No, he didn't…didn't…really hurt me." Just bruised me. Overpowered me. Scared the crap out of me.

"I could call Finesilver. The police. You could…we could…I saw what he was doing."

Surely there was a case here. I had evidence on my wrists. A witness. But the idea of it—the noise of it—turned my stomach afresh. My business would become everyone's business. To be pored over and picked at and spun into a whole new story. *You like sex, don't you, Mr. St. Ives. You like rough sex. You've had a lot of sexual partners, haven't you, Mr. St. Ives. And you prefer rich, older men, is that not the case?* God. I couldn't. I just couldn't. Even if I won, I'd have lost. It would be a black hole of scandal and exposure, not just for me, but for everyone I loved, and of everything that made them vulnerable.

I wouldn't let that happen. Even if my only weapon was silence, and some would call it defeat.

"No," I said. "I'm okay."

Ellery scowled. "He assaulted you."

"Yeah, he did. But I get to choose how I deal with that. And"—I uncurled and didn't break—"I need to help Caspian."

"What's wrong with him? I mean, apart from the obvious."

"Steyne said Nathaniel was going to make him understand the wrongness of his desires by experiencing them from the other side."

Ellery's face went through several permutations of *what the fuck*.

"I know," I said. "Nathaniel's probably convinced himself he's helping and Caspian would have agreed to it as some kind of penance."

"Penance for what?"

"Everything. For his father's death. For Lancaster's abuse. For letting you believe he doesn't care about you. For not being the man Nathaniel wants him to be. For what he likes to do in bed. For loving me."

There was a long silence.

Then Ellery pushed herself to her feet, her hands tangling in her hair. "No. No no no. This…isn't how it's supposed to be. He's the perfect one. The one who never gets hurt. The one who does everything right and takes whatever he wants and never cares who he leaves behind. *I'm* the fuck-up."

I watched her—helpless, hovering on the verge of this mad and terrible laughter. And then, suddenly, *she* was laughing, mascara-blackened tears streaking down her cheeks.

"Gah." Spinning around, she threw herself down next to me on the sofa in a flurry of fishnets and lace. "This is so typical of him. He even had to be better than me at being fucked up."

"It's not a competition," I pointed out.

"You're an only child." She tucked her legs up under her, growing serious again. "But you know, Lancaster could just be playing mind games. He's probably figured out he won't get Caspian back without you."

"If it turns out they're having a quiet night in with a cross-word, worst thing that happens is I make a complete fool of myself. Again. As usual. I can live with that. I can't live with…the alternative. Except"—I shuddered, abruptly re-membering Steyne, the helplessness he had forced on me— "I don't know how to stop it."

Ellery's hand against my arm brought me back to the warehouse, to my friend, to the home where I would, one day, be able to feel safe again. "What did he tell you?"

"Not enough—he knew exactly what he was doing." Clos-ing my eyes, I waded through the cascade of images, Steyne's hands wrapped around my wrists, and the pull of his jacket across his shoulders, and the slick red sensuality of his mouth and the dirty silver of his eyes, and tried to remember. "A sex party. Tonight. That's it. That's all."

"Well…" Ellery pursed her lips. "That's not a ton to go on, but we can narrow it down a bit."

"Can we?"

"Hell yeah. Nathaniel's a total prude, so he's not going to want to go to your basic sleazy kink club, is he? Which means it'll be some Chelsea set, masks and rose gold cock rings, and invite-only bollocks."

Thank God for Ellery. I should have been able to figure that out for myself, but my brain was half wee timorous beastie, convinced it was about to get attacked again, and half rampaging dragon, which just wanted to roar at things and set them on fire until I could be sure Caspian was safe.

"Okay," I said, "but how the hell do I get into something like that?"

She shrugged. Which, from anyone else, would have seemed dismissive. But from Ellery, at that moment, seemed genuinely regretful. "Sorry. So not my scene."

Nor mine. But knowing people who could get me into scenes that weren't my scene was literally my whole job.

CHAPTER 39

Of course, there was no guarantee George would answer her phone—not because she would screen me, but because if there was a fancy sex party happening somewhere, she was probably already at it. Which was all intensely nerve-wracking because I didn't have a backup plan. Thankfully she picked up.

"Tell me," came her familiar drawl, "this is a booty call."

"Um. It's a *please for the love of God help me* call?"

I couldn't see her, but I felt her manner change. "What's the matter?"

Somehow I babbled out the story—at least the parts of it that didn't involve Lancaster Steyne trying to rape me.

"I'm not sure I understood a word of that," said George, when I was done. "But I think you're telling me you want to go a sex party? To save Caspian Hart? From some ill-advised impact play?"

"I guess?"

A pause. "You do live in interesting times, poppet."

"Is there a thing, though? Tonight. Like Steyne said."

"Give me a moment—I vaguely recall an invitation sliding into my in-box."

I gave her a moment. Though every second of it was excruciating.

"There's a kinky masquerade in Kensington. Arranged by the sort of people who think they're terribly decadent but are, in practice, terribly boring."

That sounded…promising? Better than nothing, at any rate. "Can you get us in? Are you on the guest list?"

"Of course I'm on the guest list. I can't believe you're even asking." She gave a discontented growl. "Though under normal circumstances I wouldn't dignify such a pissant little debauch with my presence."

"But you'll still"—my voice wavered—"still take me, won't you?"

"Oh, Arden. Of course I will. It's black tie, so get ready, and I'll be there as quick as I can."

She hung up. And I turned back to Ellery. "Okay, we've got another problem."

She paused, halfway through unlacing her boots. "What now?"

"Do you know where I can get a tux at…whatever o'clock it is on a Friday night?"

"Sure. There's the twenty-four/seven formalwear supermarket just down the road."

I stared at her. "Ellery, I'm too freaked out to navigate sarcasm effectively right now. There's a dress code for the party. And I'm scared they won't let me in if I don't look right."

"Wear a suit or whatever. They probably won't care."

"Probably isn't good enough."

"For fuck's sake, it might not even be the same party."

I pressed my hands over my mouth to stop whatever screamy noises wanted to get out and flap around the room like frenzied bats.

"Shit. Fuck." Ellery's boots hit the floor with a clatter of buckles. "I'm sorry. I'm sorry."

Still. I had to be still. Inside and out. Because the twitch of a capillary could trigger some chain reaction that would end with me exploding in a burst of nuclear fire.

"Hey." Ellery's fingers brushed over mine—the touch as light as Ariadne's thread, drawing Theseus through the labyrinth. "It's okay. It's going to be okay."

"N-nothing feels okay. What if he's not there?"

Her gaze held mine, her eyes steady and almost hypnotic, full of greens that had no counterpart in Caspian's. "He will be."

"What if I'm too late? What if he won't listen? What if Nathaniel—"

"Stop it, Arden."

The sudden sharpness of her voice took me by surprise. And sliced right through my rapidly unspooling thoughts.

"I just mean," she went on awkwardly "you've got this. My brother's a dick. And also a wreck. But if anyone can help him get his shit together, it's you."

I leaned into her, rubbing the edge of my brow against her cheek—which was probably a fucking weird thing to do, but it felt comforting and I wasn't totally ready for hugs. "Thank you. And for…coming back and forgiving me. And for saving me from Stey—"

"Don't." Ellery squirmed as if I was a great-aunt in a Victorian's children's story. "You're being embarrassing."

"I just want you to know that you're the most amazing friend."

"Yeah, okay. Can you shut up about it now?"

"And I love you."

"Gross."

I laughed, surprising myself, the edges of the world losing some of their jaggedness. Impossibilities that had loomed large seconds ago shrinking like shadows until I could breathe…think…hope. "But I'm afraid I need to ask you one last thing."

Her brows creased warily. "What is it?"

"Do you have a frock I can borrow?"

This wasn't, as it might have seemed, a desperation gambit. Though Ellery's personal style tended towards an aggressive absence of fucks, the red dress she'd worn for her birthday was spectacular—and I couldn't believe it had been chosen by anyone but her. In fact, I'd long suspected there was more to Ellery than met the eye when it came to fashion, a notion proven correct when she asked, "Cocktail or evening?"

"Whatever will get me through the door."

"Leave it to me, Cinderella." Ellery practically bounced off the sofa. "You *shall* go to the crappy sex party."

And then she vanished into her room, leaving me to…fuck. Cope with the shock of being alone. Which I hadn't expected to be a shock. But in the silence, Lancaster Steyne could have been anywhere. Stepping through every doorway. Out of every corner.

Except he wasn't. He wasn't. He was gone. And unlikely to come back. And when this was over, I was going to make sure I got all the therapy. Because he didn't get to fuck me up. And I was a part of Caspian's world that would never belong to him.

I showered, since I didn't want to go to a party or, indeed, exist any longer smelling of sexual assault. With George due imminently, I didn't have long. But I could have stayed in there forever, losing Lancaster Steyne in the steam, and the ceaseless rush of water down my skin. When I got out, and had towelled off and teased my hair into something resembling attractive, I found Ellery waiting for me, her arms full of silk.

She smirked at me. "Try this."

The dress was a floor-length sheath, as achingly simple as Cruella de Vil's famous mink coat, although, thankfully, much less cruel. If it had been white, it would have been virginal, but it was silver, as bright and supple as mercury, subtly gleaming with its own wicked lustre. It slithered down me like new skin, the cling of the fabric at once revealing and concealing, turning my body into a mystery, sleekly androgynous and draped in starlight.

"Hot," said Ellery, settling a cape of dark grey ostrich feathers over my shoulders—which I was glad for because the gown was made of basically nothing and held up by the strappiest of strappy straps.

"Well"—a smile crept tentatively over my mouth—"whatever else happens tonight, at least I'm fabulous."

"Glass slippers not included, I'm afraid. There's no way you'll fit my shoes."

"Shit."

Hoiking the frock out of my way, I scrambled up the ladder to my room in search of suitable footwear. Of which I owned…let me see…at my last count, taking into account the current rate of inflation…zero. Why the fuck wasn't I a drag queen?

A horn honked outside. George.

Some rescue attempt this was going to be if I turned up too late because I didn't have any shoes. Well, fuck it. I dragged on my rainbow glittery Docs, laced them up hastily, and managed to get down from the mezzanine without ripping my dress or breaking my neck.

"How do I look?" I asked, pausing self-consciously in front of Ellery.

She surveyed me from head to combat-booted toes. "Perfect."

And that was all the encouragement I needed. Holding my cloak tightly around me, I plunged into the night, where George—looking very formidably gorgeous in a tuxedo and all the fixings, with a white scarf around her neck—was waiting for me in the Jag. She gave a low whistle as I tumbled into the front seat.

"Are you sure you wouldn't rather save me, poppet?"

I yanked the seat belt into place. "What do you need saving from?"

"I'm sure I could think of something."

I was spared from having to come up with a pithy reply because she put the car into gear and we roared into motion. Apart from an attempt to say thank you, which she dismissed, I was pretty quiet for the ride, my thoughts opaque even to myself. It was a relief that they pulled only intermittently to Steyne, though I could have done without them going there at all.

Probably I should have been putting together a kind of...I don't know...action plan. But how could I prepare for something I could barely imagine? Or if I did imagine, made my heart want to curl up and die. What was Nathaniel thinking? And what had possessed him to go to Steyne? Of all people. Knowing what he had done to Caspian. Surely he must have recognised that it was a betrayal of the deepest order. An act of cruelty, pure and simple—like the one he intended to inflict tonight.

Yet Nathaniel wasn't cruel. At least, not the way Steyne was. Not the way my father was. I wanted so much to hate him. To blame him. And part of me was definitely furious with him. But the problem was, I could see this too clearly for what it was—not an act of intentional destruction, but one of desperation. I'd been too wrapped up in my own hurt to notice before. Thought him possessive, insecure, self-righteous, and uptight, and hadn't understood he was breaking too. The interview. The dinner. The art gallery. The car park. He'd been nothing but an obstacle to me. A mistake someone else was making. But all this time he'd been afraid.

And so utterly alone.

Losing the man he loved in ways he couldn't hope to understand.

CHAPTER 40

George had masks in the glove box—plain back for her and, by pure chance, silver filigree for me.

"You do realise," said George very softly, "he might not thank you for this?"

"I know."

"People can only really help themselves."

"Then"—I stared at my Docs, glittering cheerfully from beneath the hem of the gown—"I'm going to help him do that."

She laughed. "I've never had much patience for people like Hart. Self-loathing is such a masturbatory vice. But I'm starting to think he might have something a little special, after all."

"What's that?"

Leaning over the gear stick, she kissed me—the gesture oddly chaste. "You, poppet. Now let's go, or there'll be no oysters left, and then I'll be obliged to fuck someone just to pass the time."

We left the car and crunched up a gravel drive to what I was sufficiently spoiled by high living to consider a generic Kensington mansion. A word from George to one of the solid-looking gentlemen waiting by the pillar-flanked front door and we were inside.

"Um." I took a skittish step closer to her. "Why is everyone staring at us?"

She helped me out of my cloak and draped it over her arm, a gesture I very much appreciated, since it was *some of us are getting naked soon* hot in there. "Because I'm me and you're delectable."

I glanced around somewhat wildly—it was all soft light and scarlet gauze, and the gleam of skin on marble floors, with the smell of roses working really hard to disguise the smell of disinfectant. Guests, in various states of dress and undress, streamed endlessly across the entrance hall, and up and down the wings of the staircase, masks and outfits blurring into each other like a trying-too-hard carousel until I lost track of what I was seeing.

Oh no. "How the fuck am I going to find Caspian in this?"

"Well"—George drew my arm firmly through hers—"I recommend we start by looking."

She was right, but it already felt like an impossible task, and the gathering was just diverse enough that two men together wasn't, on its own, identifying. We passed between interchangeable rooms and between interchangeable bodies, and sometimes I thought I recognised him, in the curl of someone's hair or the set of their back, but it was always a stranger, the idea that I could ever have thought they were him rendered crushingly absurd the moment they turned around. Everyone kept moving—shifting, drifting, joining—caught in some ceaseless, incomprehensible dance. And everywhere was the same, a gaudy labyrinth of chaises and cushions, red on red on red, like a too-eager mouth. I mean, I'm sure it was a perfectly okay party if you were into that kind of thing. But it came at me with all the chill of a Hogarth painting. Leaving me half-sick with the smell and the heat, the hiss of silk and the rasp of breath, the shadows of sex writhing on the walls, and the fear I wouldn't find Caspian.

And then I did…or I thought I did. Pulling free from George, I ran, slipping on marble and getting tangled in velvet, pushing my way through guests suddenly as unreal to me as mannequins, chasing a glimpse of probably fucking nothing. A butterfly of wishful thinking. On the stairwell, a glimmer of gold hair. Nathaniel? At the far end of a corridor, a backward glance—blue eyes imprisoned behind a dark mask.

And gone.

Fuck. *Fuck.* I searched. Rushed, frantic, from room to room. Ground floor. First floor. Same again.

Nothing. Nowhere. Vanished. Imagined?

Finally, I crashed headlong into George. "They were…I saw them…I did…but…I don't know…"

She gently wiped the sweat from my nose. "They must have gone into one of the private rooms. Wait here. Remember to breathe. I'm going to have a word with the hostess."

I nodded. Waited. Didn't do so great with the breathing. The passing minutes wrapped around me like the coils of a boa constrictor.

"The red room." George appeared in front of me, pressing a key—such an ordinary key—into my hand. "Second door on the left."

I gaped at her. "How did you—"

"Intense personal charisma and promises I don't intend to keep. Now go. And if you need me…" She paused, evidently reflecting on the fact we'd had to leave our phones behind. "Yell really loudly?"

"What if you need me?"

She gave one of her wickedest laughs. "Poppet, I never need anyone. In fact, I'm fully intending to collect the most attractive people I can find and take them home with me. I don't fuck in places like this. Takes all the fun out of it."

"Um…have a nice time?"

"If nothing else, it'll reunite me with my personal electronics—meaning I'm easier to contact if something goes wrong after I've left. Or for that matter, if you'd like to join us."

I gabbled my thanks and fled, key folded so tightly in my hand that the teeth bit into my palm. Found the door. Didn't dare stop. Didn't dare think. Just unlocked it and burst inside.

The seconds stretched out like treacle.

I saw red hangings. A four-poster bed with red sheets. Walls hung with whips, chains, floggers, crops. Nathaniel, arm raised. And Caspian, my Caspian, hands cuffed to a metal grid, eyes closed, back bare.

And then I was moving. And time seemed to remember itself, racing to catch up, as if the world had buffered and overcompensated.

I think I shouted "Don't."

But only because words were a habit. The truest instinct, the deepest, was to cover Caspian's body with mine.

His skin was soaked with sweat. Alive with minute tremors.

Something cut the air. Then cut me. A cane strike, landing with a pistol-sharp crack, across my naked shoulder blade. It was an ugly pain—hot and jagged, like rusted metal—and I made an ugly sound.

I heard Nathaniel give a choking gasp behind me. "What the—"

"Arden?" Caspian's voice was as raw as my scream had been. "Oh God, what have you done?"

Pain-made moisture was slipping slowly from the corners of my eyes. And I could feel a few drops of something viscous sliding down my spine. Blood? The yellow stuff that sits on top of blood? "What have *you* done?"

Suddenly he went wild beneath me, rattling the cuffs against the grid with such force that I thought he was either going to lift it off the wall or break his wrists. "Get these off. Get them off me. Get them the fuck off me."

I'd never heard him sound that way before—he'd been angry, yes, even afraid sometimes, but this was a kind of animal panic. The bewildered fury of a tiger thrashing in a hunter's trap. I pulled away, wanting to spare him the added burden of my weight, and the pain radiating from my shoulder erupted into a frenzy, nearly sending me to my knees.

"It's all right," I told him, wrapping a hand around the honeycomb of the grid to keep me upright. "I've got you. Hold still."

But I'm not sure he was capable of it, fighting against his bonds, and fighting me right alongside them. I fumbled with the buckles, light-headed, my fingers weak and trembly and useless.

I tried again, close to tears for real this time. "Please. I can't—You have to...you have to let me."

"Caspian"—that was Nathaniel, sounding exactly as shocked as he deserved to sound—"please, I—"

I half turned. "Just...shut up. You've done enough."

To my surprise, Caspian stilled, breathing heavily, hands clenching and unclenching in the cuffs. Which, after a few more seconds of incompetent tugging, allowed me to release him. His wrists were torn up, rubbed bloody and already bruising, but he didn't seem to even notice. Just grabbed me and spun me round, the stinging intensity of his gaze upon my back enough to make me whimper as if he'd touched me. "You're hurt."

"I'm okay."

Pushing me behind him, he strode across the room to where Nathaniel was standing and ripped the cane from his hand. "What the fuck was that?"

"I..." Nathaniel cringed, his face ashen and sweat-speckled. "I don't know. I didn't mean—I'm sorry."

Caspian snapped the cane over his knee and flung the pieces of it aside. "You know I consider negligence far worse than malice."

"It happened so fast."

"Then you should have been faster. And these excuses do not reflect well on you."

Oh, for fuck's sake. Surging forward, I grabbed at Caspian's arm. "For fuck's sake. That's enough. It was clearly an accident. And anyway, he didn't do anything to me he wasn't going to do to you."

"I had submitted myself to it." Caspian glanced down at me, his eyes losing some of their icy ferocity. "You had not."

It was so not the right time, but I couldn't help myself: I laughed. Well, it was that or cry. "I've never submitted to anything in my life. I've chosen. Just like I chose to take that blow for you."

A moment of silence, and then Caspian asked, very softly, "Why would you do that?"

The easiest answer was *because I love you*. But while that was part of it, the truth was more complex. "Because this isn't what you want and it isn't what Nathaniel wants and it diminishes what I want. On top of which, it isn't going to fix anything. Honestly, I don't know what either of you were thinking."

"Nathaniel thought it would help me control my nature better. And"—the tight little line appeared between Caspian's brows—"the attempt was the least I owed him."

At that, I turned a death glare on Nathaniel. "What, so, like aversion therapy? Except for kink instead of queerness?"

"No. God. No. I would...I would never—" He went, if possible, even paler. And for a second or two, I thought he might actually throw up. But then he just wobbled over to the bed and sat down, dropping his head into his hands.

When he looked up again, his cheeks were wet, and he turned his gaze pleadingly on Caspian. "You...you wouldn't touch me. You said you were too afraid of hurting me. I thought if you could forgive me for doing this to you, you could believe in my forgiveness also."

"For the last fucking time," I yelled, "nobody needs any fucking forgiveness. This stuff's just sex. It doesn't need to be diagnosed or explained or justified."

Nathaniel glanced my way. "You know it's not that simple for Caspian."

"Because of Lancaster Steyne?" Probably I shouldn't have spoken quite so bluntly, because I felt Caspian shudder. But for my own sake, I wasn't letting that entitled abusive prick become my personal Voldemort.

"For God's sake," Nathaniel snapped, "have a little compassion."

I blinked. I had moments of feeling sorry for him, but the man's capacity for self-righteousness was truly impressive. "Compassion? You just literally hit me. As part of some sick plan to fix your sex life."

"Please stop this." Caspian stepped between us, as if he could physically prevent us from wanting to bicker each other to death. "I know you would dearly love to believe differently, Arden, but Nathaniel's right. I…" He faltered, then pressed on. "I've never been able to trust that my desires are my own. If I've always had them, if they are indeed, for better or worse, a part of me. Or if they're…they're Lancaster's…and by indulging them I am only surrendering to him."

"Oh, Caspian." Unthinking, I reached for him, cupping his face gently between my hands and drawing it down to mine. "It doesn't matter where your desires came from. They aren't his because you aren't him, and you'll never be him.

And he can't control or keep you or hurt you anymore."

"But," he whispered, "what if I don't want to be like this?"

The streak of pain across my shoulder had, somehow, become deeply focusing. A talisman that steadied my heart and unknotted my tongue and let me find the words I'd been searching for since that dreadful night at One Hyde Park when Caspian had told me his truths and broken my heart rather than face them.

"I can't tell you how to feel about Steyne," I said, "and I'm not here to fix you, but the way I see it, the things that happen to us shape who we are. And so when some of those things are terrible, or wrong, you have to wrap your head round the idea that accepting yourself isn't the same as accepting what was done to you." I went up on my toes, pressing into him, my mouth so close to his that speech felt like kissing. "And if you really want to change, you can. You have that power and no one can take it from you. But for whatever it's worth, I don't think you need to."

"Arden. My Arden." He closed his eyes and lowered his head, touching his brow to mine. "Please…teach me to believe you."

Then came a choked-off sound. Nathaniel, smothering a sob into his hand. "I don't understand. I've done everything right. I've tried to help you. I've let you do…these things to me. Why don't you love me?"

Caspian broke away from me, his gaze seeking Nathaniel's. "I do love you."

"Not the way you love him." Impatiently, Nathaniel brushed the back of his wrist across his eyes. "I'm not blind, Caspian, and I'm not stupid either. I know you're still smoking. And I know you're still sleeping with Arden."

Oh fuck. Fuck. No matter what I thought of Nathaniel, I wouldn't have wished that knowledge on him.

"I am giving up smoking," said Caspian gently, "but have lapsed occasionally and have kept it from you because I cannot abide your disappointment. And Arden and I had a single encounter, which neither of us intended, and we both knew to be unfair to you."

"Do you think I care about what's fair?" Nathaniel's voice rose—I got the sense he thought he was angry, but all I heard was hurt. "I care you want him in ways you don't want me. That you show him parts of yourself that you won't show me. That you're with him in ways you're not with me."

A few graceless steps and Caspian was on his knees by the bed. "I've tried, Nathaniel, I've tried for years to be the man you wish I could be."

"That's the thing I can't bear." Nathaniel lifted a hand, as if he meant to touch Caspian's hair, but then let it fall again. "When you're with him, you *are*."

"I only wish that were true. I let you down. I've betrayed you both. And I'm not worthy of either of you."

"Was it really so important to you?" Again, an aborted motion from Nathaniel. "The whips and the chains and the pain and the humiliation?"

Caspian's shoulders hunched, and he pressed his forehead to the side of Nathaniel's thigh. "I don't know…I'm sorry…I don't know…"

Okay. I couldn't take another word of this.

"Look." I might have misjudged my volume, because they both turned towards me—taking the imperative a bit more literally than I'd intended. "I could give a big speech about how I see this stuff differently—how it doesn't humiliate me and the pain gets me off—but I'm not. Because, one, I don't care what you think, Nathaniel—"

He opened his mouth, probably about to protest or rebuke me.

But I steamed right on. "And two, I'm not going to let you make my whole relationship with Caspian about sex. He gave me confidence when I needed it and courage when I was scared, he made me feel special when I thought I was nobody, and believed in me when I couldn't believe in myself. And when *you*"—I made a gesture in Nathaniel's direction— "drag it all back to your hang-ups about kink and *you*"— a flail at Caspian—"keep making it about what you think you're worthy of, you shit all over the most important thing that's ever happened to me."

Silence, as thick as the velvet and roses of this awful fucking place. And Caspian, half-turned towards me again, something shocked and wondering on his face, his eyes searching mine for truths I was only too glad to yield.

"So," said Nathaniel, with sharp-edged composure. "That's it, then? After all we've been through, after everything I've done for you and endured for you, you're choosing him."

Caspian froze, his whole body pulling so rigid I half expected his spine to crack. "What do you mean?"

"Well"—Nathaniel shrugged—"it's what you want, isn't it? What Lancaster taught you to want."

"What? No." Caspian shook his head frantically, the same wild terror I'd seen in him while he'd been cuffed clawing its way through his skin like some alien parasite. "I don't—I didn't. Arden, please, you have to see…I can't do this. I can't be with you. I'll only hurt you."

Time was, this would have freaked me out. I mean, it still wasn't great—but it didn't scare me anymore. Not for my own sake, anyway. I wasn't the bastion of calm I would have been in some ideal world, but—mouth dry and heart fluttery—I slowly sank to my knees in front of Caspian. "It's okay," I whispered. "It's okay. There's only one choice you have to make today and I'm so sorry I haven't helped you make it before."

His breath rasped. And he was shaking again—tiny vibrations that made me want so badly to hold him as tightly and surely as he'd often held me.

"You see," I went on. "I've been looking at this wrong the whole time. I always thought it was between Nathaniel and me. But it's not."

"I…I don't understand."

"It doesn't matter if you choose him or me or neither of us. It only matters that you do what makes you happy and that you understand you deserve to *be* happy. You've spent so long punishing yourself for something someone else did to you. Questioning everything you want and denying everything you need. But"—I actually clasped my hands, uncaring of how ridiculous I probably looked—"I'm begging you, Caspian, you've suffered enough. Choose peace. Choose freedom. Choose you."

A pause and then, with painful uncertainty, the words practically dragging their tails behind them, "How can you want to be with me? After everything I've done. Now you know what I am."

"I've always known what you are—you're kind and funny and sexy and a little bit overprotective." I gave him a nervy half smile. "But, y'know, I can live with that."

"Arden, I'm not. I'm…weak and I'm ugly, and I'm"—his voice cracked like black ice—"so ashamed."

I shook my head, a few of the tears I hadn't even noticed I was shedding clotting on my lashes. "Those are things you feel—and it's okay to feel them, even if it's hard—but they don't define you and they're not what I see when I look at you."

"Most of the time," he admitted raggedly, "I don't think I can be anything else."

"You've been something else to me."

"That was *because* of you. You gave me hope for myself in ways I never thought possible."

"I'm not magic. I was just there. The person you were when we were together was someone you chose to be. Someone you always have been. Someone I fell in love with."

"But"—his eyes were locked on mine, pleading, even as his mouth offered nothing but resistance—"I kept the worst of myself from you."

"What happened to you isn't the worst of you." Impulsively I reached for his hand and he let me take it, his fingers folding tightly around mine. "I could spend a lot of time talking about your bad qualities, like how arrogant you are, and how controlling and high-handed you can be, but none of that has anything to do with being an abuse survivor. And yes, I'd have understood you better, and probably been a better boyfriend, if you'd told me earlier, but you always get to decide how and when your story gets told."

He twisted away from me, though not before I'd seen the anguish on his face. "It's a story that broke me long ago."

"It hasn't broken you. It's just hurt you and made you feel weak. But that doesn't mean hurt is all you'll ever be and it doesn't mean you can never be strong."

A pause. So deep and airless I could barely breathe. Then Caspian threw up an arm to shield his face and began, almost silently, to weep. "Don't," he gasped, "don't look at me."

"Oh, Caspian," said Nathaniel, in this small, lost voice. "Caspian."

I thought about telling him to shut up again, but I didn't have the heart. This wasn't actually his fault, and he was as damaged by it as any of us. I inched a teeny bit closer to Caspian—hoping he'd feel me there, ready for him when he was ready for me. "Look…we'll do whatever you need. It's okay to cry, and you can trust me on this because I cry all the fucking time. But you don't have to do it alone."

Nothing but uncertain breath, and the softest of inarticulate sounds from Caspian.

"Especially," I added, "when you're with two people who love you."

"I *never* cry." Something that, from anyone else, might have been a sniff. "I…I don't know what to do."

"You let it happen. And you let us comfort you."

Another sound, this one perilously close to surrender. And then, at last, Caspian Hart came clumsily—warily—into my arms. I enfolded him and drew him close, his sobs muffled in my skin and his body so awkward against mine, as if it had never learned to be held. My eyes, staring at nothing across the haze of red in that godawful room, unexpectedly found Nathaniel. He opened his mouth, then closed it again, looking so helplessly human that I felt bad for all the times I'd resented him.

I made the smallest of motions, and he slipped gratefully off the bed and joined us on the floor. Resting his brow against Caspian's shoulder, he began to cry again, and I reached out with my spare hand to bring him in.

"This," muttered Caspian, sometime later, "is mortifying."

"It's okay." I petted clumsily at his hair. "It's just, like, emotion water from your eyes. Give yourself that."

"I hate it."

He did not, however, seem to be capable right then of stopping. So I offered reassuring nonsense and Nathaniel stroked him gently, and Caspian shuddered in our arms, managing even to cry with more dignity than I ever managed—mostly rough breath and the occasional muffled sound. It was probably a messed-up comparison, but it reminded me, a little bit, of when he came. Which was something else he'd been uncomfortable with me witnessing. And then I got incredibly sad for him, realising that he feared expressing joy and sorrow alike, and had denied himself the solace of both for such a long time.

"I'm sorry," he said finally, his voice steady again. "I don't know what—I'm sorry."

"You've got nothing to apologise for."

"Nothing at all," echoed Nathaniel, sitting back on his heels, giving us space with a humility that almost surprised me.

Then I felt the prickle of Caspian's eyelashes against my skin as he lifted his head. And opened my eyes slowly to find him gazing at me through tear-heavy lashes. "Arden?"

"Yes?"

"Did you"—he hesitated and then pressed on—"did you mean it?"

"Mean what?"

"Any of what you said."

"I meant it all." I swallowed, abruptly aware of the enormity of everything I was telling him. "And I know, given what you've gone through, how hard it must be for you to believe it. But if you can't…when you can't…please, at the very least, believe in who you are to me."

"Caspian. I…" That was Nathaniel, who was still kneeling a short distance from us, his eyes so dull and his expression so frighteningly blank it was like he'd been replaced by a Madame Tussauds model. "I'm sorry. I'm…more than sorry. I've only ever wanted to help you, but I…I haven't, have I? I don't know what I've done. I always thought I loved you…I think I still do…but I…God. Have I been part of this? Have I done this to you?"

"I tried to be the man you needed." As Caspian spoke, one of his hands found mine, and held it hard enough to hurt—not that I minded. "I thought it would fix me."

Nathaniel swallowed. "So did I. But I was wrong. I…I've done everything wrong. Made everything worse when you trusted me to make it better. And I don't know how to make that right. Maybe I'm not supposed to. Maybe I was never supposed to."

"You never had a chance," Caspian told him. "I was so afraid that you would think me weak, I convinced us both I was a monster."

"I shouldn't have let you. But I wanted too much to be your hero. I know it's too late for me to tell you this, but you're a good man and a loving one. I thought I was saving you but all I did was make you doubt yourself. And I'm sorry. I'm so sorry."

"So am I." Caspian moved slightly away from me—and the part of me that was, and had always been, desperate for him wanted to cling. But I also knew it would be wrong right then. "I've had a lot to work through these past six months, and I shouldn't have used you to do that."

"Perhaps"—Nathaniel's lips twisted into a hopeless half smile—"we should spare each other the recitation of our failures. We have so many of them between us. You know I love you, and I know—I think I've known for a long time—that you shouldn't be with me. I hope you find your happiness, Caspian, whatever it looks like for you."

A cool gleam as he pressed his engagement ring into Caspian's hand. And then Nathaniel rose and slipped from the room, closing the door behind him with a soft click.

CHAPTER 41

Nathaniel was gone. And in the silence he left behind, I became acutely aware of all the things I'd been semi-ignoring: the redness of the room, the kinky shit hanging from the walls, the fact Caspian was shirtless in my arms, the mess of his wrists, and the hot throbbing in my shoulder.

"I, um"—I cleared my throat—"I don't really know what to do now. But I stand by all that stuff I said earlier."

Caspian stirred, tilting his head back so he could look at me, the corners of his mouth curling upwards slightly. "What stuff in particular? You said quite a lot of, ah, stuff."

"About, y'know, choices. And how you don't have to make them right now. I mean, I guess Nathaniel's already made one for you. But you shouldn't be with me just because he's gone. You need to do what's right for you."

He drew in a harsh breath. And then, with the defiance of someone throwing themselves off the highest diving board, half expecting to belly flop, "I want to be with you. On this point at least, Nathaniel's correct, it's what I've always wanted."

God. I was perilously close to having my very own fairy-tale moment, but I still didn't know if I was Cinderella at the ball, about to unravel into rags, or my prince had finally got his act together. "And you have no idea how much I've needed to hear you say that."

"You may have noticed I have a tendency to second-guess my desires. I've been afraid of them for so long that I find it almost impossible to accept that what I want might be what I should have."

"And," I asked, caught somewhere between excitement and anxiety, "you think you should have me?"

A sound, too raw and self-conscious to really be a laugh. "In all honesty, no. Every piece of my soul is telling me that I am a poor prospect, a wreck of a human being, who does not deserve you and will likely only cause you harm. But"—and here some glimmer of a Caspian from happier times struggled to the surface—"despite the lack of a PowerPoint, you have presented a very strong case that I should, instead, listen to you. And believe you when you tell me that none of this really matters."

"So what *does* matter?"

"That I'm desperately in love with you. And that, against all reason, you appear to…"

I stared at him, wide-eyed and absurdly, frantically, heart-soaringly hopeful. "Say it. I need to hear you say it."

"You appear to…" He stumbled, a hand coming up to half conceal his mouth. "Arden, I'm not sure I can."

No way was I letting this go. "I…"

"…you…you…love me too?"

"There." I beamed, feeling like my whole face had turned as shiny as a lightbulb. "Was that so difficult?"

He shuddered. "It was excruciating."

"Then maybe you should tell me every day."

"I think, perhaps"—pink blossomed across his cheeks—"I would rather hear it from you."

"Mr. Hart, is this your way of saying you want some sort of sentimental declaration?"

His arms tightened around me with such force I lost my balance completely and we ended up sprawled out together on the plush burgundy carpet. I was mostly on top but I managed to brace myself on my knee and an elbow before I crashed down on top of him. Except then he flipped me, turning me onto my back before I'd so much as caught my breath. The impact awoke a fresh sting from my shoulder, but I went gladly, regardless, the pain lost in the eager heat and the sweetest sense of lassitude spreading through my body in response to the dominance of his. Physical control seemed to come so naturally to him sometimes. I only wished he could learn to be as ease with it as I was. To trust himself as I trusted him.

"I thought I'd never hear that again," he said.

"Don't people call you Mr. Hart every day?"

"Not the way you do."

I fluttered my lashes at him, unable to resist asking, "What way is that?"

"As if…as if you want me to do very bad things to you."

"Well, I do want you to do very bad things to me." I gently stroked the flush that was still fading from his cheeks. "But only when you want to do them too."

He closed his fingers around my wrist, but it was only to pull my hand down to his lips so he could kiss it. "You should probably know, I'm, well, I'm terrified, Arden."

"Of being together?"

He nodded.

"If it's any consolation," I admitted, "I'm not exactly unbricking it either. Obviously, I would never want you to stay with me if you didn't want to, but I'm not sure my heart could take a second round of being dumped to feed your demons."

"It's such an inadequate thing to say, but I'm truly sorry for everything I put you through."

"And trying to marry Nathaniel to punish yourself for being happy with me was pretty shitty too."

He winced. "I know."

"I'm not trying to make you feel bad." I slipped my spare hand behind his neck and drew his face down to mine, so I could kiss the line between his brows. "You don't need any help with that. I just...I'm scared too. You're sure about this? About me? About us?"

"Oh, my Arden," he murmured. "It's the one certainty I have right now."

There'd always been something profoundly comforting to me about Caspian's certainties. And they'd never steered me wrong before. "Really?"

"Yes. But I also don't want to lie to you. I seem to be quite spectacularly fucked up."

"Well"—I gave him a mischievous look—"at least you're still spectacular. And you're not fucked up, you just have some shit going on."

He rolled onto his side next to me and tucked his head against my shoulder, like he was playing at being just a little tame. "Tonight...these last months...they've clarified and disordered my life in equal measure. I thought I knew myself, but perhaps I never have. Which, in some ways, is almost a relief. I'd rather see myself as you see me, than as Nathaniel did, or Lancaster did, or as I did for so many years." He paused and I felt the tension creeping through him before he spoke again. "Unfortunately, I suspect it will take me time, probably a long time to get there. And the honourable thing to do would be to let you go while I worked through everything I have to work through."

"Wait a minute." I did not like the way this was going. "This sounds like a breaking-up speech, and we haven't even officially got back together yet."

"Nothing of the sort. I never said I was going to *be* honourable. In fact, I was about to announce my intention to be quite otherwise."

I could breathe again. "Okay. Good."

"You told me to choose me, and choosing me means choosing you. I will do this with or without you, but"—he captured my hand again, turning the full intensity of his eyes upon me—"I am better and stronger and happier with you at my side."

I blinked against a veritable tidal wave of tears.

"Oh God. Arden." Caspian shot into a sitting position. "What did I say? What's wrong?"

"N-nothing's wrong. Everything's...the rightest it's ever been. Of course I'll be by your side. For as long as you want me there."

"I should warn you, that could be a long time."

Scrambling upright, I hurled myself into Caspian's lap, flinging my limbs around him with all the dignity of an overly devoted spider monkey. Apart from a startled "oof," he took it well.

"Then you'll have me for a long time," I said. "Me and a really exceptional, queer-friendly, kink-friendly therapist."

He arched a brow wryly. "You're bringing other parties into our relationship already?"

"The therapist is nonnegotiable. We can't do this alone."

For a moment or two, he offered no response and I started to freak out a little bit. But then he smiled. "As you wish."

Ack. Help. Melting. And all it took was a smile and a *Princess Bride* reference. I was midway through a flurry of kisses when I remembered there were still things to be mature and sensible about. Reluctantly I pulled back. Then changed my mind and gave him another kiss. Before finally getting myself together.

"There's more," I told him. Which would have sounded a lot more dignified if I hadn't still been breathless.

He gazed at me steadily, the stern set of his lips still softened by his smile, and my kisses. "Anything."

"Okay. It's…" I was kind of out of my lane here, but fuck it, for all I knew, the whole road was mine—"I need you to sort things out with Ellery."

"She hates me, Arden. She'll reject any overture I make."

"She doesn't hate you. But yeah, she'll probably reject whatever you do. At least the first…fifty…sixty times you try."

Caspian's worry line was back. "And you still want me to do it?"

"I can't make you. But I think you owe her the attempt. The attempts. I mean, this shit's complicated and can't be fixed overnight. But she shouldn't have to live believing she's worthless to you."

"You're right. Of course you're right."

"And"—apparently I wasn't done—"you should offer Bellerose his job back. At, like, twice the salary."

"Twice the salary?" Caspian looked genuinely startled. "You do realise that would make him one of my highest paid employees."

"I don't care. You can afford it. Besides, you suspended him for asking a perfectly reasonable question about your well-being."

"I admit, that was unworthy of me."

"Anyway, I don't think he'll take it. At least, I think he shouldn't take it. He cared for you way more than you ever acknowledged or valued, and it wasn't good for him."

"On the contrary," said Caspian, with a depth of regret that eased a knot I hadn't realised had been stuck inside me, "I valued it deeply. But I also questioned it, as I questioned everything touched by Lancaster."

I shivered, remembering all too vividly Steyne's hands on me, marking every place they'd landed like paint splatter. Maybe someday I'd tell Caspian what had happened, but right now, it felt too much like giving Lancaster Steyne what he wanted. "He's not the centre of the fucking universe. Sometimes it only matters what things are, not where they came from."

"I'll try to contact Bellerose tomorrow." Leaning in, Caspian kissed the tip of my nose, that tiny flicker of warmth enough to render Steyne as insubstantial as dust. "Now, is there anything else I can give you, my Arden? It's a little early for my hand in marriage. And you already have my kingdom at your feet. My heart for yours."

I could feel the heat creeping up my neck, making me blush like a schoolboy at his first prom. Caspian had once told me he wasn't romantic. It was something else he'd got beyond wrong. "I...I...guess a ride home would be nice."

"Of course." He stood, taking me with him, that heedless, effortless strength of his making me feel protected and over-whelmed and cherished all at once..."The warehouse?"

"Or..." Old worries—worries from another lifetime—dug their way zombie-like from shallow graves and made me awkward. "Or your place?"

"Certainly." Now it was Caspian's turn to hesitate. "I wonder, though, have you forgotten the...I believe you called it a sentimental declaration that I asked for?"

Ohhhhhhh. I had to fight incredibly hard against the goofy smile that tried to shape my lips. "I thought *you'd* forgotten."

"I haven't."

"You might have to remind me."

He gave me an outraged look. "You just indicated that you remembered."

"Who? Me?"

That made him actually growl—though there was laughter in it too. "You are a monstrous little minx."

"Punish me later."

"I...I..."

"When you're ready."

The panicky flutter of his pulse slowed again. "You should be careful. It would not be to your benefit were I to keep tally."

"Fuck yes it would." I squirmed naughtily against him "*Please* keep tally."

His lips covered mine, half kiss, half groan—and quite a lot of teeth. "God, I missed you. I missed you so much."

"D-don't forget your sentimental declaration," I said, when I had breath and wherewithal for speech.

He was silent for a long moment, just looking at me, his mouth still red from mine, and his eyes glittering with the promise of power. "Tell me you love me, Arden."

Okay, not so much asking then, as commanding.

But while my soul knew its equal, my heart knew its master. Even when the master didn't fully know himself.

And so, with happiness breaking inside me, like light through a prism splintering endlessly into rainbows, I obeyed.

CHAPTER 42

Caspian pulled his shirt back on and draped his tuxedo jacket carefully over my shoulders, which, of course, I loved. And then, heedless of masks and hand in hand, we fled the red room, through the dim corridors and down the gilt-encrusted staircase of the house, and tumbled into Caspian's car. He murmured something to the driver and we were off—swallowed into welcome obscurity by London's ceaseless traffic. I didn't want to let go of Caspian, still not quite believing we were actually here, together, hoping for the same future, but I kind of had to. Partly because my nose was itchy and I needed to scratch it, but also because I wasn't sure if George had managed to assemble her orgy and escape yet. I texted her to let her know that I was okay, going home with Caspian, and would she mind terribly taking care of my feathery cloak? She replied a couple of seconds later with "Your wings are always safe with me, poppet."

Then I tucked my hand back into Caspian's, leaned my

head against his shoulder, and…I don't know. Basked? In the heat of his skin and the scent of his cologne and the strength of his body next to mine. And in the perfect nothingness of the moment. Two men in a car. Going home. The simplest and most precious thing in the world to me right then. Closing my eyes, I tried to hold on to it—to that sense of peace—but the events of the evening kept fragmenting around me, vivid and unreal at the same, as if I was staring into a kaleidoscope of my own life.

Fuck, I was crying.

And despite my best efforts, there was apparently no concealing it from Caspian. "Arden, what's wrong?"

"I'm sorry. Nothing. Just…feelings. I'm having a lot of them right now."

"Bad feelings?"

"No, I'm happy. So happy it's messing me up. Like this has to be a mistake. Or maybe I'm dreaming. Or eight gazillion Hugo Weavings are about to show up because I'm in the Matrix."

"Dear me." He cast me a rather quizzical look. "You must be in a bad way, because that's a reference so dated even I get it."

I giggled in a hiccoughy way. "Oh, shut up."

"Come here." He pulled me back into his lap, helping me curl up as small as I could possibly be within the circle of his arms. "I promise you, this is real, and I'm not going anywhere. Even if I have to fight Hugo Weaving for you."

"Do you know kung fu?"

"Let's say I do."

I thought about it. "I really like Hugo Weaving. If he wanted me that badly, it would present quite the dilemma."

"He's not remotely suitable for you. He's straight, for one thing, and he must be nearly sixty."

"So? I bet he'd let me call him Daddy."

Caspian was frowning so ferociously that his brows had become cartoon slashes—turning him into the world's most handsome emoji. "Are you seriously telling me you would leave me for Hugo Weaving?"

"Are you seriously telling me"—I gazed up at him, my tears lost to incredulity—"you're jealous?"

He had the self-awareness to blush. "No. Yes. That is, I've only just got you back. I'm not ready to countenance losing you to anyone."

"I guess I'll stay with you, then." I heaved a heavy sigh. "Hugo's going to be so bummed."

"Well, he'll have to endure it."

I was quiet a moment, snuggled into Caspian. "For the record, I'm not up for doing any countenancing either."

"You won't have to you. I'm yours, my Arden."

"I like the sound of that," I whispered. Tilting my head up, I brushed my fingers lightly across his mouth. "M-my Caspian."

I felt his lips shape several unuttered words before he said, "What you did for me tonight was extraordinarily kind and extraordinarily brave. It's no wonder you're exhausted and overwhelmed, and a little fragile."

"You were brave too. It would have been a lot easier for you not to listen."

"Once, it would have been." He kissed my temple. "As you learned to your cost. I wish I could have reacted better when you first tried to help me."

"And I wish I could have done a better job of, well, helping."

"How can you say that? You've always thought better of me than I've ever been able to think of myself."

"How about," I suggested "you don't go from blaming yourself for what happened to you to blaming yourself for not instantly getting over it."

"But I put you through so much. Nathaniel too. All because—"

"Stop." Turning, I kissed him into silence. "What's done is done and this was always going to be hard. You told me I expect too much too quickly and you were right. It was super not okay of me to just assume that you'd trade your worldview for mine overnight. And then I made it all about Nathaniel instead of about you, and, honestly, I've fucked this up so many ways it's amazing I made any kind of difference."

"You did, Arden, you did. It's just I was terrified of what it might mean if you were right. And so I ran to Nathaniel to prove you wrong. But you weren't. And I couldn't go back, and couldn't go on, and then…then you came to save me again."

"And this time"—I gave him a trembly smile—"you let me."

"Well, I felt that recent events had systemically demonstrated every alternative strategy nonviable."

I wouldn't have imagined it was possible to miss Caspian's

emotionally challenged billionaire nerdspeak. But I had. I so had. "Yeah, current research indicates that Arden-centric strategies are twenty-three percent more productive than a placebo under laboratory conditions."

"Are you laughing at me?"

"I'm loving you."

He made a soft sound, a little pained, almost needy, and hid his face in my hair. "I still don't know how to respond to that."

"*I love you too* is traditional."

"And I do, but I worry it could too easily sound perfunctory when it's an echo."

"For the record, I think you're going to have to tell me you love me a whole lot more before it becomes perfunctory."

"I will, I will." Another, slightly fretful press of his lips. "I know I shouldn't think this way but even the possibility that you could...that you could..."

I glowered at him. "Say it."

"You've become quite demanding in my absence."

"Actually," I pointed out sheepishly, "I've always been demanding."

He laughed. "So you have, my dearest tyrant."

"Not...not in bad way, right?" The idea of becoming *Nathaniel II: Nathaniel Strikes Back* was horrifying.

"In the best possible way."

"I would never want anything from you that you didn't want to give."

"I know that. Believe me, Arden"—his voice had fallen into its deepest register, the one I usually associated with deliciously rough sex, but now it promised tenderness too, and just as effectively—"I've longed for this, and all it entails, as you have. I just never believed I could have it."

"You can."

"I trust you. Which I hope, in time, will help me trust myself."

"You'll get there." I nuzzled him. "I mean, come on. You're Caspian Hart. You consider no endeavour complete until you have not merely succeeded in it, but mastered it utterly."

"Thank you," he said, with a rueful look, "for reminding me how completely absurd I am capable of sounding."

"Okay, it's a little bit absurd. But also sexy. And true. There's nothing you can't do when you decide you're going to do it. Why should this be any different?"

It was cheerleading in the guise of a rhetorical question— and I would have totally let him get away with not answering. But he did. "I suppose because I've never really felt that I belonged to me."

"Well, you do."

"Yes. And"—he gave me one of his shyest, sweetest smiles—"a little bit to you."

"Damn straight. Well…maybe not straight. I've never done anything straight in my life. But you should know"— I wagged a finger at him—"I intend to take the best possible care of what's mine."

That earned an eyebrow twitch. "Oh?"

"Yes. You taught me such a lot, Caspian—about life and confidence and figuring stuff out and not being afraid to fuck shit up. But you also taught me how to make someone feel cherished and looked after and loved, even without the words."

"I also made you feel confused and rejected and devalued."

"Yeah, those times were rough." I shrugged. "But I think on some level I knew it wasn't what you meant to do—so it never stuck. Whereas the good always did."

His mouth pulled tight, his eyes almost grey in the flickering lights of the city. "Don't make excuses for me."

"I'll make excuses for you if I want to, dammit. But that's not what I'm doing here." With a tap of my finger to his jaw, I reclaimed his gaze. "I'm not trying to deny that you've hurt me. But I get to decide how much it matters."

A moment of struggle and he was back with me, the tension fading from his body and the shadows from his features. I didn't know what kind of internal battle he'd just fought, except that he *had* fought it. Fought it and won it. When a handful of months ago he wouldn't even have tried.

"Anyway," I said, claiming the spoils of victory, "what were we talking about before?"

"What were we—oh. I thought you'd forgotten."

"Nope."

He made a soft sound of resignation. "I think I was trying to tell you that the truth of your love abashes me. And I'm not sure how I will ever be worthy of it. "

"Love isn't earned, Caspian. It's given."

He slid a hand beneath my chin to angle my face to his, and kissed me—rough, and slightly desperate, his mouth open over mine, hot breath and the scrape of burgeoning stubble. "Then you are a gift beyond reckoning. How do...how do I show you that?"

"I've got to say you're...you're doing a pretty good job

already." My breath caught and I had to take a moment to catch up to myself. Apparently *kissed half out of my mind* was a way I could sound. "But," I went on, with an attempt at sensible, "what do you normally do when someone gives you a gift?"

Caspian made a dismissive gesture. "I'm a billionaire. People seldom feel the need to buy me things."

"That's rubbish. You must know the general principle, though?"

He thought about it for far too long, his brow creasing and his eyes a little frantic, like he was living one of those nightmares where you find yourself in an exam you haven't revised for. "You say thank you?"

"Exactly." I grinned at him. "Shall we try it?"

"T-try? How? What are you—"

"I love you, Caspian."

"Oh." He let out a shaky breath, followed by an almost inaudible "Thank you."

"You're welcome." I claimed his hand and was about to kiss it, when the dull shine of metal on his fourth finger made me recoil. "Um. I don't mean to throw a wobbly or anything, but you're still wearing your…Nathaniel's…"

Caspian gave a sharp gasp. "I'm so sorry."

"Take it off, please. Like, right now."

He was tugging, but the ring had caught on the joint. "Can you help me?"

I didn't want to touch it, but I also didn't want him casually wearing the symbol of his commitment to another man, and between us we were able to slide it free. I'd had to disembark Caspian's lap as we struggled, which left us sitting side by side again, the shadow of a ring between us like this was fucking Mordor. Caspian reached into his pocket and pulled out the platinum band that Nathaniel had given him earlier.

"Say what you like about him"—it came out slightly more grumpily than I'd intended—"but the man had good taste."

Caspian said nothing. Just stared at the twin circles resting on his palm.

"Can you return them?" I asked. "Is that a thing you can do?"

With the decisive swiftness of a paper cut, he pressed the button that lowered the tinted window next to him, and tossed both rings into the night. It was impossible, of course, over the thrum of the engine, but I almost thought I heard them chink as they bounced away to roll into the gutter or catch in a pavement crack or line the nest of an unexpectedly glamorous pigeon.

I blinked. "Wow. That was…"

"I'm sorry." He gave a little cough. "I may have overreacted. But I didn't want to ever have to think about them again."

"Perk of being incredibly fucking rich, I guess."

He held out his newly naked hand, and after the slightest of hesitations, I took it. "Are you angry with me?"

"N-no. I'm trying to balance my middle-class dismay that you just, like, *threw away* however many thousands and thousands of pounds' worth of jewellery with…being glad you did it."

"Perks of dating someone incredibly fucking rich."

That made me laugh. "You are a bit of a *get out of guilt free* card."

"I should hope so." His fingers pressed between mine, nothing but skin on skin. "Because I intend to spoil you quite terribly, and won't have you feeling guilty about it."

I was about to explain that I didn't need spoiling, only him, when the car drew to a slightly unexpected halt. Caspian climbed out first, and came round to help me out, which wasn't remotely necessary—me and Meghan Markle totally having car door–related manoeuvres sewn up—but what the hell. Besides, I was in a floor-length frock and would likely have nose-dived into the pavement without Caspian's supporting arm. And so with surprising grace for, well, me, I succeeded in exiting the vehicle.

And found myself in a wholly unfamiliar part of London.

CHAPTER 43

Are you kidnapping me?" I asked. "Because if you are…
that's hot."

He reached for my hand again. And, wow, I was adapting
to touchy-feely Caspian incredibly fast. Almost as if remote,
wary, locked-away Caspian was a piece of a dream I was
already beginning to forget. I gave his fingers an anxious
squeeze before I got all Zhuangzi and the butterfly, and
started wondering if this was the dream.

Caspian returned my squeeze. "Is it still kidnapping if the
subject is enthusiastically consenting?"

"Don't ruin this for me." I paused, glancing up and
down the empty street, with its rows of painted, bow-
windowed houses and the cheerfully graffiti-muralled off-
licence right next door to a hipster bakery. It looked very
much like my kind of place. Not at all like Caspian's.
"Where exactly are we?"

"Notting Hill."

I gave a little skip. "Oh, I keep meaning to come here. Go

to Portobello Market, and The Gate, and nose into all the weird little shops, and post endless Instas of myself eating biscotti and reading Sartre in quirky cafés."

"That's"—Caspian seemed to be struggling not to smile—"quite a specific vision."

"Yeah. And I don't even like Sartre."

"I see."

"Or biscotti."

He turned into me, stifling an amused sound in my hair. I hoped someday he would learn to laugh freely, but until then, or even if he never did, all his secrets would be safe with me. As cherished as his kisses. "Why haven't you? Visited I mean."

"I don't know," I admitted. "Somehow never got round to it. That's one of the most awkward things about living in London: All this exciting stuff happening nearby, and you still end up eating Twiglets in your pyjamas and watching an illegal stream of *Drag Race*. Well. If you're me. Probably you reshape the world's economy."

"Not every day. In any case," he went on vaguely, "perhaps in the future you will have occasion to spend more time here."

"Yeah, I could spill orange juice on Julia Roberts."

"Pardon?"

"God, you're hopeless. I love you."

He made flustered motions. "Shall we walk?"

"Sure. Though since you normally get a chauffeur to take you to the bathroom, I'm beginning to think you've been infected by alien brain parasites. You haven't been infected by alien brain parasites, have you?"

"Not that I'm aware of." He thought about it for a moment. "Although I suppose that's what I'd say if I *had* been infected by alien brain parasites. They would want to protect themselves."

I bit my lip, assessing the situation. "It doesn't seem as if they're the threatening kind of alien parasites. I mean, it's not like they've mind-controlled the prime minister or the pope or someone."

"Excuse me, I'm very rich and quite powerful."

"Yeah, but all they're trying to make you do is hook up with a cute boy."

"It's true." He gave a somewhat self-conscious shrug. "They're much less concerned with wealth and worldly ambition than they used to be. Apparently their priorities have shifted towards, I suppose, being in love and being happy."

Our attempt to walk wherever Caspian thought we should walk was not going well. We'd made it all of a hundred yards. And now I made us stop, so we could kiss, and kiss, and kiss forever in the tangle of moonlight and streetlight on a softly sleeping street in Notting Hill.

"I'm going to make sure you have the most satisfied alien brain parasites in the universe," I promised, when we finally broke apart.

A fruit machine spin of expressions whirled across Caspian's face before he finally settled on solemn to the point of ridiculous. "Thank you. We are, indeed, blessed."

"I'm a keeper."

"And I will keep you as long as you wish you to be kept. Although"—another of those adorable rueful looks—"I had not intended to keep you standing around in the cold."

"Where are we going?"

"Somewhere I could not take the car."

I was still so unaccustomed to questioning Caspian that it took me a second or two to realise he hadn't actually given me an answer. But I didn't mind. It was close to midnight, maybe even a little after it, which meant that we'd slipped into the magical space between days, when the teeth of the past were blunted and the future a starbright road. I wasn't looking for miracles—I knew change was the shyest of friends and powerful things weren't easily defeated—but we had time and I had hope. And the same faith I'd always had, in Caspian's strength and goodness.

We turned, passing beneath a sneaky little archway tucked between two houses and leading onto a cobbled street. I'd heard of London's half-secret Mews—the lanes that ran behind the grand terraces, once intended to serve as stables and servants quarters, now adapted into modern homes—but I'd never actually been to any of them. My loss again, because, even illuminated only by the glow from their own windows, the houses were lovely. Every single one of them was unique: Some were painted, others were redbrick, some had square balconies, others round, though most had retained the oversized barn doors from their horse-centric days, even if the styles varied, and nearly all were festooned with climbing vines, flower pots, and window boxes. Yet they all fit together perfectly, united in their difference and their charm.

"Oh, Caspian." I clutched happily at his hand. "This is the best place ever."

We had stopped outside a pale blue building, its doors and windows picked out in a darker shade, and the wintertime skeleton of a wisteria vine curling up the side. And Caspian seemed suddenly ill at ease. "I'm glad you like it."

"I love it. But are you okay?"

"I think so. That is—Arden?"

I couldn't totally control an instinctive flutter of anxiety. "Yes?"

"This"—he gestured not entirely helpfully—"is the first house my father bought in London. Would you…would you let me show it to you?"

"This one? This one right here? The completely perfect blue one?" By the time my brain caught up with my mouth, it was a bit late to rein things in. But I tried anyway. "I mean, only if you want to."

"I want to. Very much."

And then, while I bounced about beside him like an overexcited yo-yo, Caspian unlocked the door and led me inside.

CHAPTER 44

I've made sure the property is cleaned and maintained," he muttered. "Though, of course, nobody has stayed here for many years."

The place did have a slightly wistful feel—of unused space and vacant rooms, though I was relieved to see it had been decorated quite differently to Caspian's other apartments. The ground floor was an open-plan kitchen/dining room: the kitchen, with a sort of modern rustic flavour, all granite surfaces and buttercup-yellow cabinets, and the dining room almost entirely dominated by one of those picnic-style tables where everyone smooshes onto benches. It was a little lifeless, and couldn't have competed with Nathaniel's domestic paradise, but there was something inviting there nonetheless. The promise of sunlight streaming through the big windows at the front. Friends piled around the table. Two lovers discovering they were terrible cooks in the kitchen.

Flicking on the lights as he went was Caspian's only concession to acting as a tour guide. The rest of the time he was silent and restless, tapping his foot and twitching his fingers as I looked around. The next floor consisted of a living room, hung with framed movie posters for old science fiction films, and a gloriously squashy-looking sectional that someone appeared to have purchased for comfort rather than aesthetics. A door led to what was probably a guest room, with its own en suite bathroom, and a further flight of stairs—this one with a bookcase built into the wall beside it, albeit a bookcase currently devoid of books—took us to the master bedroom.

It was a really good space, and came with not only its own mini-terrace but an incredibly fancy bathroom, all pale brown marble and one of those walk-in showers that are so big they need to give you somewhere to sit down while you're in them, but the lack of habitation had hit it hardest. Reduced it simply to a room with a bed and a cleaned-out closet. It made me kind of sad. Rationally, I knew it was just bricks and mortar and a wisteria plant, but it felt like a house with a missing heart.

"What do you think?"

It had been so long since Caspian had said anything that I actually jumped. "Of the house? It's beautiful. But it's a shame it's empty."

"My father loved it very much." Caspian crossed to the window and stood looking out at the shadowy terrace, with its unoccupied flower pots. "He left it to me. Probably I should have sold it. But...I couldn't."

"Because it connected you?"

He nodded. "It's a terrible paradox. I couldn't bear to lose this part of him, but I couldn't bear to come here either.

Sometimes I tell myself if he knew what I'd become, he'd be ashamed of me. And sometimes"—his hand curled into a fist and he rested it lightly against the glass—"sometimes I am unforgivably angry at him. Because if he hadn't died—if he hadn't left us—none of it would have happened."

I followed him to the window and tugged at him until he turned. "No one could ever be ashamed of you," I told him, "especially not someone who loved you. And feelings are messy bastards—they're not always what we'd like them to be, but that doesn't mean we're wrong to have them."

He sighed. "I don't like being angry with Dad. Besides which, he's dead, so it's a futile exercise."

"I'm not sure emotions are supposed to be outcome-focused."

"That"—his mouth softened into a smile—"is one of their many design flaws."

I took Caspian's hands in mine and pressed them gently back to the glass as I leaned up to kiss him. There was no force behind the gesture but it was more controlling than I would usually have dared. To my surprise, he permitted it, and I wondered if he, too, was remembering that very first time—when we had collided in his office, a storm of confused passion and irresistible need, both of us seeking surrenders we didn't yet know how to give. Tonight, though, I was as gentle as the moonlight, and Caspian showed no fear of my freedom.

"I'm glad you brought me here," I whispered, drawing back before my touch became challenging.

"I thought"—he paused, frowning, seemingly caught in his own words—"perhaps, one day, when you're ready, when we're both ready, if you liked the house, although of course you may not, and I have no expectation that you will, or even if you did that you might wish, that you might consent, to live in it with me. Together."

For a moment, I was too stunned to react. Then I jumped up and down, squealing. "You want to live with me?"

"At some point in the future."

"You want to live with me *in this house*."

"I want to live with you wherever would make you happiest." He gazed at me, searchingly. "Did I misjudge? You're welcome to stay at the penthouse with me. Or we could move back to One Hyde Park. Or I could buy you a mansion, or an island, or a windmill, or a yacht or—"

I put my fingers to his lips. "Stop. I'll admit I'm slightly tempted by the windmill, but this is perfect."

"You can have a windmill as well. But Arden, are you sure?"

"Caspian, are *you* sure? You're the third-richest man in the UK and you're going to stay in a converted stable with me?"

"The only part of that sentence that has any meaning for me is *with you*."

I did my best to look severe, even though I knew I was grinning like a monkey with a banana. "You'll have to help with the washing up."

"You may recall, I have extensive skills in that area."

"And it won't…it won't make you feel bad," I asked. "Because of your dad?"

"Maybe sometimes. But mostly"—he offered me an unexpectedly winsome smile—"it feels…right, somehow."

"Oh. *Oh.*" Overcome, I hurled myself at him again and we

hugged for a long time, Caspian's arms tight around me, and his heartbeat steady beneath my cheek.

"Are you all right?"

"Yes. Very. I just always knew we could be like this. Or"—I peeped up at him—"hoped we could."

"I should have trusted you."

"Eh." I shrugged, the happiness of this moment already infinitely realer to me than all the sadnesses that had preceded it. "We got here in the end. That's what counts."

Gently he untangled me. "It's getting late. I should take you home."

"Can we stay? Just for tonight? If it won't freak you out."

"It won't, but…I don't know how comfortable we'll be."

I glanced around the room—at the bed with its faceless covers and the faded patches on the carpet where other things had stood once. "This is going to be our home someday. I guess I'd like to get a head start."

"You don't mind that it will take some work?"

"Our relationship?"

"Well, that too. But"—he touched his nose to mine—"I meant the house."

Oops. "I think it's mostly fine. I mean, it's going to need more bookshelves if I'm going to live here, and maybe we could put your father's posters in the spare room, not that I don't love *War of the Worlds*."

"I want it to be a place for us. Not a shrine to him."

"You'll help, though, won't you? I've never actually been responsible for a house before."

"Neither have I. Truthfully," he admitted, "I usually hire someone to take care of it for me."

I pressed a hand to my brow in shock. "No. Really? I would never have guessed."

"Shush." He lowered his eyes, blushing faintly—though a smile seemed to tremble at the corners of his mouth.

I turned and walked the dimensions of the room before returning to the bed and kicking off my Docs. "Do you think we could we get a four-poster in here?"

"I'm not sure."

"I mean, not a full one with a canopy and velvet curtains. I don't want to feel like I'm Henry Tudor. But something with, y'know—posts. I'm very interested in the whole posts concepts."

Caspian came up behind me and slipped his tuxedo jacket from my shoulders, the sudden exposure of my back to his gaze and touch enough to turn my skin into an electric storm of longing.

"We can have one made to fit," he said. "Although I don't quite understand this obsession with posts."

"God, Caspian. Isn't it every boy's dream? To sleep in a four-poster bed like a princess. And, y'know—actually, never mind."

"What is it?"

"I was just going make a silly kinky sex reference. It doesn't matter."

His lips brushed over my shoulders, like maybe he was chasing my freckles. "Please don't hold yourself back from me. I may not be quite ready to do everything I want to do with you, but that doesn't mean I won't enjoy hearing about it."

"Well, you could, like, tie me to the corners and stuff?"

Caspian made a sound like he'd choked on air.

"I mean," I went on, "since the house isn't big enough for a sex dungeon, we're going to have make do."

There was a long silence.

Then, with a kind of studied blandness, "Do you want one?"

"Nope. The whole world can be our sex dungeon." I smirked at him over my shoulder. "You can cuff me to the kitchen table. And spank me on the sofa. And put me on my knees in the shower. And, oh"—another idea occurred to me—"can we have fairy lights? I love fairy lights."

"Yes, my Arden. We can have all of it." Caspian was laughing and suddenly the whole room felt different. Warmer and brighter, its corners softer, its shadows less dense.

His arms slid round my waist and he pulled me back against him and I yelped because I'd forgotten—evidently we'd both forgotten—about my shoulder, the cotton of Caspian's shirt suddenly as rough as a goddamn Brillo Pad.

"I'm so sorry." He stepped away immediately. "That was thoughtless of me."

"Don't worry. I'm mostly fine. I think."

I twisted, trying to see, and then Caspian stilled me. "Let me look." His fingers brushed lightly across my spine—close enough to the wound that I made an anxious whimpery noise, but not close enough to actually cause me pain. "There's a little blood and some bruising. I should clean this for you."

He disappeared into the bathroom and was at my side again in seconds, damp handkerchief in hand. "I wish I had some antiseptic, though I don't think you're in any danger of infection."

His touch was ridiculously careful, but still made me hiss through my teeth and curl my toes into the carpet. "Goodie."

"I hate," Caspian growled, "that he hurt you."

"Well, I hate that you were going to let him hurt *you*. So I guess we're even?"

"Perhaps I should take you to a doctor." His palm landed, half-reassuring, half-possessive, against the small of my back "I'm worried this could leave a permanent mark."

"I hope it does," I said, surprising myself by how fiercely I meant it. "That way you'll always be able to see the difference between something like this and what we do together."

"I should learn to bear my own scars."

"You have enough. I'm proud to bear this one for you."

"Arden…" He seemed to lose his words again, pressing a kiss to my shoulder instead. Even though he was nowhere near the place Nathaniel had struck me, the heat from his mouth and the heat from the cut flowed together, rushing in a red-gold river all the way down to my cock.

CHAPTER 45

I arched and moaned—far too loudly in the silence of that sleeping house.

"I've been meaning to tell you," murmured Caspian, "that you look stunning tonight."

"I'm afraid it's"—my breath hitched as his lips landed against the nape of my neck—"it's not my frock."

"Then I'll have to take you shopping."

"Oh God. Would you really?"

The zip rasped as Caspian slowly drew it down. "Yes. We'll go to Bahnhofstrasse and the Avenue Montaigne, Fifth Avenue, Ginza…"

"Rodeo Drive?" I suggested, lost in my *Pretty Woman* moment.

"Anywhere. Everywhere." His fingers traced the straps of my dress all the way across my back—such a strange sensation, silk and skin together—until he was inching them down my arms. "I'll lay the world at your feet."

"You're the only world I've ever wanted. But I have to

admit"—I squirmed helplessly as the gown began to slip from my body, making me feel incredibly exposed even though I was still almost fully clothed—"the shopping does sound fun."

"It's not an either/or. I intend for your life to be nothing but *and*."

"You're going to spoil me."

"Yes. I am."

One final twitch and the dress landed on the floor in a puddle of silver and stardust, leaving me naked. Well, except for my nipple jewellery—a silver bar with multicoloured leaves dangling from it, and a simple pink glitter barbell—and the rainbow flower unicorn boxer briefs it had seemed a good idea to put on earlier. Not that they lasted long. Caspian hooked his thumbs under the waistband and peeled them off me, before spinning me round again to face him.

His scrutiny was, to say the least, *intense*—his gaze sweeping over me as if he wanted to claim me by the power of looking alone. It was actually a bit of a struggle, at first, to let him see me: my pretty-ish, ordinary-ish, flaw-speckled self. My knobbly knees. The chipped polish on my toenails. My skinny hips and the touch of softness at my tummy because I liked gelato way more than I liked the gym.

"My beautiful Arden," he said. "My love. My treasure. My perfect boy."

I wanted to tell him he'd made a mistake. That I was nobody special. But then I remembered: Caspian had never lied to me. And I was all those things to him. "Yes," I gasped. "Please touch me. Show me I'm yours."

"Your back?"

"Can take it."

Once upon a time, he would probably have insisted otherwise. But tonight he just lowered me onto the bed—which, I won't lie, made my shoulder scream bloody murder, but it was a price I was more than willing to pay to be able to watch him. Especially when he came crawling over me like some great predator, eyes ablaze with hunger and tenderness, and a purity of need he had always tried to hide from me.

Since we were only just beginning to rediscover our boundaries, I lifted my arms above my head and curled my fingers round the slats of the headboard. It was voluntary vulnerability, but…yikes. I'd forgotten how deep such choices could take you. Especially when you felt about someone the way I felt about Caspian—as if there was no corner of me I wouldn't yield up to his pleasure. For his taking.

At the gesture—at the offering of myself—Caspian gave this helpless groan. And fell on me like a wild beast, his hands everywhere, stroking and caressing, marking me not with cruelty, though, honestly, I would have been okay with that too, but with love. There was very little finesse to it, especially from a man who knew my body well enough to bend me to his will with ease, just a raw desire to touch me—to feel me writhe and shake and come alive beneath his palms.

"I missed you," he whispered. "I missed you. I missed you."

"I missed you too. So much. But I'm here now. And I'll never leave you again." Wait. That was a *terrible* thing to say. "I mean, unless we grow apart or our lives are no longer compatible or one of us falls in love with someone else or something."

"I know what you meant." Smiling, he kissed me, his mouth sweet with the promise of laughter.

My fingers were starting to ache—nothing I couldn't endure, but it reminded me of other, older hurts. "Caspian, it's okay if you can't, but I'd love to see you. Will you take your clothes off for me?"

He drew in a sharp breath.

"I honestly don't mind if you—"

"Of course I will."

Climbing to his feet, he began to strip. At best, it was efficient. At worst, self-conscious.

"I get that, for you, your body isn't a source of joy," I said, "but it is for me. I guess I just wanted to tell you that—so you understand what it means when you choose to share it."

"I wish I could give you everything." He joined me again on the bed, this impossible paragon of masculine beauty, who was more mine than he had ever been his own. And looked so heartbreakingly uncertain, right now, despite the fact I was stretched out like a spatchcock and drooling precome onto my own stomach.

"What do you mean?"

"You...you know what I mean."

I guess I did. I'd hinted to Caspian once before that I might enjoy it if we flipped sometimes, and he'd made it pretty clear he wasn't up for that, but I didn't think he'd remembered. Let alone been dwelling on it enough that he believed it was a problem for me. "Oh, Caspian, that's not everything. That's nothing."

"It's something to me." He covered my body with his and I tucked my knees against his flanks, offering him some small shelter. "It feels like failure that I…that I *can't*."

"It's okay to be into some things and not others. For all you know, this could have always been your preference."

"But what if he…"

"Maybe he did. Maybe he didn't. Who you are now is all that matters. And I love you, and I want you—this you, the one who's offered me his heart, and a life, and a home. Not some hypothetical you who could have existed if things had been different."

Caspian ducked his head, a deep shudder running through him. "I want…I want you to touch me."

Part of me was running around in circles, setting off streamers, and shouting *yes please*. But there was no way I was fucking this up by taking it too far. "How? Command me. I'll do anything for you."

"Touch me, Arden." His head came up again, jaw set, eyes glittering wolfishly. "As you did that night at One Hyde Park."

"You were really okay with that?"

"I'm not sure. It was one of the hardest things I've ever done. But I think about it all the time. Your hands. The way you looked at me."

"I realise now how much trust it took. And"—*eeep*, I was getting weepy—"I loved it too."

Before I could kill our boners with my emotions, I released the headboard and nudged Caspian onto his side, wriggling out from under him so I could mirror his pose. There was something unexpectedly innocent about it, lying there with our faces level, my knees tucked against his thighs—and I couldn't resist inching across the pillow to nudge the tip of my nose against his. It drew a laugh from him, which meant he didn't even flinch when my palm settled over his flank, my thumb stroking lightly over the groove of his V-cut.

Emboldened, I let my fingers wander. Over the ridges of his abdomen, and through the crisp dark hair on his chest, and up and down his throat, feeling the prickle of his stubble, and the shifting of his skin as he swallowed. I tracked his responses in the pattern of his breath, the occasional flutter of his lashes, learning in the tiniest of increments how to please him. How to show him he was beautiful. And worshipped. And safe.

When I finally wrapped my hand around him, there was as much shock as enjoyment in his gasp and I paused, until the buck of his hips drove his cock deep into the channel of my fist. And then the sound he made was all desire— as rich and sweet as chocolate. I can't say I didn't spare a thought for my lavish collection of luxury lubes, but there was something unexpectedly special, too, in the simplicity of hand to skin. The shape of Caspian's body matched to mine. His eyes so close I could have counted the silver fractals in his irises. And his soft moans landing on my lips like kisses.

And then he was touching me too, enfolding me in the warmth of his grasp, and I behaved with great dignity about it. Definitely no wild squirming or hysterical feet kicking or losing-my-mind whimpering.

"If...if you do that..." I said, gulping down air. "I'll get distracted and it won't be—as good."

Caspian treated me...subjected me...to a gloriously long

stroke, slow and tight, and excruciating, and exquisite, like he was in Ollivanders and my dick was his perfect wand. "On the contrary, I think it will be better."

I tried. I really did. But in less than a minute I was wrecked, my mind in splinters, and my rhythm all to pieces, and my mouth opening and closing on a series of high-pitched needy noises that were probably embarrassing but who gave a fuck? Not me. I was having way too much fun, although I was less wanking Caspian off now, than clinging desperately onto his cock as pleasure tossed me about with the force of driftwood on choppy seas.

"Oh, fuck...Caspian..." I curled my free hand over his forearm. "I don't think—I can't...I'm going..."

He gaze held mine, even through the tumults of passion—his love as naked as our bodies, alongside that twist of cruelty that I'd always found so thrilling. "Do it. Lose control."

I thrashed, caught on the fishhook of my need to please him. "I...I..."

"For me, my Arden."

And I came in a rush of pure surrender. Learning only when I resurfaced from the deep moon-grey haze of it that Caspian had been with me all along, spilling himself into my hand, as I had into his. It meant we were damp and sticky as we rolled into each other's arms but I licked up most of it, while Caspian blushed, and I'm not sure we'd have cared anyway. We just wanted to be close.

I stuck my nose into Caspian's neck and inhaled. "I love how we smell together."

"You're depraved."

"Yep yep." I kissed him and settled into a more conventional position in the crook of his arm. "This shouldn't be news."

He smiled. "It's not. And I shall endeavour to live up to your depravity."

"If we spent the rest of our lives doing what we did tonight, I wouldn't feel I was missing out."

"Nor would I, but"—his hand swooped down my spine and over the curve of my arse—"that doesn't mean I'm not willing to try other things."

I bounced myself into his palm. "I'm looking forward to it."

"It may take…time. Another journey, I'm afraid."

"Everything's a journey. But what a fucking amazing one to have ahead of us, don't you think?"

"Yes," he said softly. "A fucking amazing journey."

And Caspian hardly ever swore—I guess because he was all refined and sophisticated and shit—so it was how I knew he meant it. How I knew, as I let myself drift blissfully towards sleep, that, somehow, against all the odds, we really were going to make it.

CHAPTER 46

Caspian woke me...I wasn't sure...later. Though not as later as I'd have liked, because the room was still dark and I was still knackered.

"Arden," he said. "I'm...I'm sorry."

Okay. Now I was really fucking awake. "What's wrong?"

"Nothing. Just that"—he shifted restlessly and I suddenly realised this kind of anxious heat was pouring off him—"I don't think I can stay."

"In the bed. Right? Tell me you mean in the bed."

His shadow made a startled motion in the gloom. "Oh God. Yes, the bed."

"Jesus *fuck*." I slammed my head against the pillow. "You scared the crap out of me, you hopeless bastard."

"I'm sorry. I'm sorry." He covered his face with his hands. "I didn't know what to do. I didn't want you to wake alone."

Breathing. Yep. Check. Still working. "I appreciate that. It was totally the right impulse. Totally wrong delivery."

"I thought it might be different."

"Oh, Caspian." I flailed out a hand as…I guess…an option for him, and was surprised when he took it, though his own was slightly clammy. "You've been saying all along it takes time for things to be different."

"Then I suppose I hoped. I hoped I could do this for you."

I sighed, embarrassed for my past self. "Look, I know I used to lose my shit over it, but that was only because I didn't understand why you couldn't be with me."

"I want to be with you more than anything."

"I know." I smiled, hoping he would see it. "You're in love with me, remember?"

"And that's worth waking up in an empty bed?"

"It's not even in question." I gave his fingers a squeeze. "So what if you can't spend the night with me. It's enough that you wish you could."

A rustle of covers and Caspian's lips landed on my brow. "Thank you. Now go back to sleep. We'll be together in the morning."

"Hey now," I protested. "Who said anything about going back to sleep?"

"It's six a.m."

"Let's get up together."

"Arden…"

"Don't *Arden* me. You're not my mum. You don't get to say when I get up and go to bed."

He released my hand, putting his own to his brow. "This is ridiculous."

"Well, I'm not going to do it every time. Mostly, I'll want you to kiss me sweetly and slide out discreetly. Maybe bring me breakfast later. Because I'm fucking grumpy first thing."

"I'm aware," he said, rather dryly.

I pulled a Gothic heroine pose. "Oh my God, are you sure you can stay with me? How can you possibly love someone who is so moody in the mornings? What if I'm *always* moody in the mornings?"

"Well"—Caspian's voice became very grave indeed—"being moody in the mornings doesn't have to define you. And even if it never changes, we'll find a way through it together."

I laughed and he kissed me and so the two became tangled—which messed up both, but it didn't matter.

"Did you say there was a roof terrace?" I asked.

"Yes, it's…on the roof."

"Good to know. Can we see it?"

I could feel Caspian's bewilderment, but he agreed regardless. We made an odd party, groping our way up there in the semidarkness, me in my frock, and Caspian in a half-buttoned evening shirt and black trousers, both of us barefoot, and carrying the duvet I'd insisted we bring. It was lighter outside, dawn already beginning to push at the edges of the sky, ripples of pink spreading across the grey-blue clouds like raspberry sauce over an ice cream sundae.

As with the bedroom, the terrace had been maintained but not cared for: a collection of empty plant pots and one of those rattan sofas beneath a protective cover, which we peeled away. The sofa itself was surprisingly cosy once we got settled, although I was glad for the duvet because my dress wasn't exactly suitable for winter days. It was a while before Caspian felt cuddly but the fresh air and open space seemed to do him good. And eventually, he moved up behind me and drew me into his arms.

"We can go inside again," he said. "If you want."

I snuggled into him and made sure my feet were properly wrapped up. "Why don't we stay? We can watch the sun rise."

"As long as you aren't cold."

"I'm perfect. And maybe, afterwards, you can take me to a café for breakfast."

"Shouldn't we get changed first?"

I thought about it for a moment. "No."

"Then"—he tweaked my hair out of my eyes for me and folded the duvet even more tightly around me—"that's what we'll do."

We didn't speak much after that. Just sat together, watching the world shed its nighttime colours for new ones. The house was only three stories high, so, in all honesty, the view was mainly of other people's roof gardens. But I liked the higgledy-piggledy press of the surrounding buildings, with their chimneys and their sloping eaves, the crumbling forests of television aerials and satellite dishes, and we had our own piece of steadily brightening sky.

It was kind of weird to think I'd spent so long dreaming about the end of my story with Caspian: the airport chase and the promise of forever and the kiss in the rain as the orchestra soared and the credits rolled. And yet here we were. The same people we'd always been. Exactly where we were supposed to be.

All that time, waiting like a fool for an ending.

When what I'd really wanted—what we'd both needed—was a beginning.

About the Author

Alexis Hall is the billionaire CEO of a financial services company that he does not understand in the slightest.

To learn more, visit:
  quicunquevult.com
  Twitter @quicunquevult
  Facebook.com/quicunquevult

CPSIA information can be obtained
at www.ICGtesting.com
Printed in the USA
LVHW090543060919
630107LV00001B/2/P